PRIESTESS

AYCRISHI SODALITY

BOOK ONE

PHIL AERIX

Cover by Joolz & Jarling

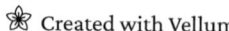 Created with Vellum

CHAPTER
ONE

Awareness came back to me like a golf ball thrown against a brick wall. It felt like I'd been run over by a fully loaded garbage truck. I groaned and opened my eyes to pure blackness. *Frigging hell. I've gone blind.*

I tried to remind the fearful part of my mind that I was in a cave, and if my headlamp had shattered, then I would be in total blackness. There is no dark like a cave when your headlamp goes out. I would be fine. I just had to take out my spare and check myself for injuries.

Honestly, I was lucky not to be dead, between the rockfall and my rope breaking.

That's when I realized I was cold. Not *don't have enough clothing on in a chilly cave* kind of cold. No. It was more a *my bare skin is in contact with cold stone* kind of thing. To reinforce the perception of my addled mind, I ran a hand down my body.

Yep. I was buck naked. Not a damn stitch of clothing on at all.

How the hell did all my clothes fall off?

Like an idiot, I swung my head back and forth looking for someone hiding nearby, someone responsible for undressing me. Of course, the only thing filling my vision was unending darkness, but I hoped a hot woman was the perpetrator and not some fat, sweaty guy named Chuck.

I shivered—more than the cold stone on my naked ass cheeks could account for.

There was only one thing I could do: gauge my surroundings by feel and hopefully find my gear. Or at least my clothing.

I levered myself to my feet and moaned as the huge bruise that was my body rebelled. In the dark, I swayed a little bit at first, a combination of light-headedness and the utter lack of light. Once my head stopped swimming, I shuffled my bare feet on the floor, feeling for any holes or cracks that might swallow me. I was out of it, but I wasn't a complete idiot.

My big toe crunched into what had to be a basketball-sized stone protruding from the floor. So yes, I *was* a complete idiot.

"Mother*fuck*er! Goddamn son of a bitch!"

I cursed, as colorfully as I was able, for much longer than was probably warranted. But damn, my toe felt like it was broken.

After my heart rate came down and I'd run out of curse words, it took me a handful of minutes to make a careful circuit of the area I was in. The good news was that I found no gaping holes to send me straight to the center of the Earth. The bad news was that I was in a roughly square—or maybe sloppily circular—room not more than eight feet across, with a ceiling low enough that at one point, my short hair scraped it.

Another happy discovery was a thick wooden slab

blocking what was undoubtedly a doorway in one wall. No knob or latch anywhere on it.

Great, so I was a prisoner of some kind.

A window at just below my head height was cut into the door. Of course, it had metal bars on it, but at least air flowed through it. Dank, putrid, fetid air, but air all the same.

I let loose with a few more curses for good measure and sat back down on the cold stone. There wasn't a bed, bucket, or even straw on the ground. Only cold. Hard. Stone.

"Hello?"

I nearly jumped out of my skin.

"Hello?" I echoed, almost hoping I didn't get an answer. How fast does insanity and hearing voices kick in if you're concussed and confused in the dark?

"Who's there?" It was a pleasant voice, and female. My mind spun off into several different directions. In some, the voice's owner was super hot to match its sound. And others...reminded me that most of the women I'd ever seen working sex hotlines were water buffalos who'd been trained to speak in a sexy voice. Don't ask how I know this.

"I'm Adam. Adam Townsend. Who are you?"

"My name is Ysduil Fennis. I'm...uh...pleased to meet you?"

Her voice inflected upward at the end, making it a question.

I barked a short, derisive laugh. "Charmed, I'm sure. Sorry, but I'm a bit out of it. I don't know where I am, or why I'm here. Did you put me in here?"

My new best and only friend was silent for a moment. Then she answered, "You're in the dungeon of the Aycrishi Sodality, though I'm not sure exactly where. I did not put you in here. I myself am a prisoner. They drugged me when they brought me in, so it is not clear to me where in the world we are. I am sorry."

"Dungeon? Like in the bowels of a castle? No, never mind, don't answer that. How did I get here? Why am I here? How long are they going to keep me locked up? Where are my damn clothes?"

Silence again.

I took a breath and exhaled. "I'm sorry, Ysduil. I'm not blaming you. I'm confused. I was doing a blind descent in a cave and there was a rockfall. The anchors or the rope itself was damaged and I think I got a concussion and fell. Not necessarily in that order. I thought I was dead. This isn't heaven, is it? Or the other place?"

"I'm sorry, Adam Townsend, I did not understand most of what you said. I do know that you arrived a few hours ago. The guards brought you in and put you in the cell. I heard them talking to each other, saying someone found you at the edge of the old sunken ruins nearby. You were unconscious already, so they scooped you up and brought you here."

I ran my fingers through my hair. Surprisingly, I only felt tenderness in one area, where the rock had struck my helmet. What I wouldn't do for some light to see if I had other injuries. For a guy who had fallen a hundred feet or whatever it was, I felt shockingly uninjured, though.

"Maybe I can talk to a guard and speak to someone higher up. I'm not a criminal and I don't know how I got here. I'm sure I'll be able to clear it up. If this was only for trespassing on the site of some ruins, I should be out in no time."

Silence.

"Ysduil?"

"I don't think you will be set loose, Adam Townsend."

"Just Adam is fine. May I call you Ysduil?"

"You may. It is my name, Adam."

"So, why won't they let me go? I didn't do anything."

"Where did you come from, Adam?"

"Well, I live in California, but I was caving in Tennessee, north of Monterey. I'm assuming we're still in Tennessee, right?"

"I have not heard those names before. I cannot tell you where we are, as I explained."

I blinked several times, trying to figure out what she meant. And remembered blinking doesn't do a thing when you're in total darkness.

"I'm confused," I said. "Maybe we should start at the beginning. Where—"

Light exploded a few feet from me, encompassing everything and half-blinding me. I threw my hands over my eyes and squinted to see the window in my door illuminated. I could barely see another door across the hall, surrounded by stone. As I looked out—hand in front of my face to shade my eyes—my sight gradually adjusted enough to make out two figures moving around.

They both wore dark clothes that had the look of a uniform. Sturdy pants, a heavy shirt or jacket, and what appeared to be padded leather armor on top. They rattled what sounded like a tin tray and the way it scraped, I imagined it sliding across the floor. Whoever locked me up was really into the whole medieval thing. I mean, *really* into it.

One of the men turned and I saw his face.

Now, let me be honest. What I saw made me want to scream like a little girl. In fact, I almost did so. If it weren't for the woman with the phone-sex voice nearby, I definitely would have. As it was, I bit down on it so fast I only emitted a squeak, no more manly than the scream but hopefully not loud enough to be heard by Ysduil.

The guy looking at me was a fucking orc.

Green skin, pointed ears, small tusks coming up from the bottom of his mouth. The ugly son of a bitch could have been in a big-budget monster movie. He tilted his head at me, like *I* was the one who was strange.

The other guard turned as well and I flinched again. He was some kind of half-man, half-monster, like a wolfman or something, but more piggish. Without looking at me, he bent down and fiddled with my door. A smaller hatch at the bottom slid open and a tray scraped across the stone floor into my cell. The little door closed and the two...monsters turned and walked away, taking the light with them. Soon, it was utterly dark again.

I sat for a few minutes, trying to reconcile what I'd seen. I was in a dungeon. Run by monsters. Being fed God knew what. And I was naked.

What the fuck?

TWO

T he illumination receded down the stone hallway. The clomping of the guards' feet faded with the light until there was neither sight nor sound to give me any more clues about my situation.

I didn't move for a while—I don't know how long. Memories bounced around in my mind as I tried to make some kind of sense of it all. I thought back to the last hours I remembered before waking up in this icy hell...

Twin balls of light had passed by my head with a muffled whoosh and the whine of road friction. Darkness had swallowed them quickly and blackness filled my vision once again.

I sighed. "How far is this place, anyway?"

Colin Gammon laughed from the front seat of his Chevy Silverado. "Dude. Relax. Why are you so impatient?"

I grumbled incoherently, knowing better than to say what I was thinking.

Greg Tollier swiveled around in the front passenger seat to look at me. "Don't worry, Adam. It's not far. It just seems like it because we were on the road before the butt crack of dawn. While we wait, why don't you tell us what's going on. We didn't get to talk much last night."

I knew this was coming sooner or later. "I was pretty wiped. The red eye tore me up, and we went to visit Colin's parents, and by the time I was able to slow down, I crashed."

"No problem, man. So what's up? You sprung this trip on us pretty quick. It's easy to see you're out of it. More than being tired would account for."

I ran my fingers through my brown hair. I'd gotten it cut really short the week before. I liked it. Easy to deal with. Just towel dry and I was ready to go out my door.

"Come on, man," I said. "I don't really want to talk about it. I came here to forget everything else and have fun with my childhood friends. Don't go and get all adult on me."

Colin looked at me in the rearview mirror and rolled his eyes. "You're stuck here with us, so go ahead and unload. It obviously has something to do with Amy, or she'd be with you now."

"Assholes," I said. "Fine, she broke off the engagement like six months ago."

"Whaaaat?" The truck swerved as Colin turned to look at me.

"Pay attention to the drive, man. I don't want to end up in a ditch or wrapped around a tree."

He adjusted the rearview mirror to watch me. I could tell he wanted to press me about it. I appreciated that he didn't, even if his mouth was trembling for want of opening.

"It's just been rough," I said. "My motivation has taken a hit. My ambition and drive was always the thing she liked most about me." I wanted to slam a fist into the window, but I took a breath to calm down. "She left me for some damn dropout who lives in his mom's house. I don't even think he has a job. What the fuck, man?"

"Shit," Greg said. "That's brutal."

"Yeah. Anyway, I don't feel much like moving mountains nowadays. They're bitching at me at the refinery, wanting me to move up. But what's the use in working hard when life's gonna kick you in the nuts anyway?"

My two closest childhood friends sat silently for a moment. Another car whooshed by on the other side of Highway 84.

Greg broke the silence. "You know, I read this story once about something that happened in the Revolutionary War. One of the big British ships, the *HMS Augusta*, ran aground on the Delaware River. It took a lot of damage and fires sprang up. Just little ones. One of them eventually reached the powder magazine and the whole thing exploded. The boom was heard thirty miles away and the blast broke windows in Philadelphia."

I shook my head. "Greg. That's all very interesting, but what the fuck does it have to do with what we're talking about?"

"Well, it's like the proverbial spark that can set the whole world on fire. Or, you know, a big-ass ship."

I looked from him to the back of Colin's head, to the rearview mirror to see my other friend holding back a smile.

"I think he means that if it only takes a spark to cause an explosion," Colin said, "even seemingly insignificant effort can make really big things happen."

I took another deep breath and exhaled loudly. "This conversation is finished. We will speak of this no more. If you can't come up with something better, keep your mouths shut. Both of you. Don't make me regret flying all the way to Tennessee from California."

We rode silently for a while, only the sound of the tires softly whirring across the asphalt and the air rush to keep us company. After we finally pulled off the highway and made our way to a turnout off some nameless dirt road, I hopped out of the truck and stretched. Colin went around to open the bed of the truck and cleared his throat.

"So...I heard you talking last night after you went into the spare room to sleep. What was that about?"

The sun hadn't come up yet. I appreciated the darkness as my face got hot.

"Uh, I got a call. If my phone hadn't been in my pocket, it probably wouldn't have even woken me up."

Greg laughed. "Yeah, you were beat."

"Who called you?" Colin pressed.

I slid my pack onto the tailgate and fiddled with it. I considered refusing to answer, but then decided I might as well come clean. "Trisha Meyer."

"Trisha Meyer?" Greg said. "Trish from school? That Trisha Meyer?"

"Yep."

Colin darted a look at me, then his eyes shot back to his pack as he wrestled it out of the truck bed. "Ah, about that. I saw her a couple of days ago getting coffee. Your name came up and I told her you were going to be in town and I...I kind of gave her your number. Sorry."

I released my nervous energy with a laugh. "It's all good. It was nice to hear from her. We're going to meet up tonight after we get back, maybe get something to eat."

Greg put a hand up and I automatically high-fived it.

"She looks exactly the same," Colin said. He waggled his

eyebrows, barely visible in the low light. To be honest, it looked creepy. Freaked me out a little bit.

"Dude," I said. "I left the state when I was sixteen. You're saying she looks like a sixteen-year-old?" Of course, even at sixteen, Trisha Meyer had been the stuff of dreams. I had the hardest crush on her but never did anything about it.

"No, I mean she looks like she did when we graduated. She's always been hot and continues to be hot."

"If she's so good, why haven't either of you gone for it?"

"I'm about ready to pop the question to Shiree," Greg said. "She's my only girl."

Colin shrugged, the gesture doing double duty to settle the pack on his shoulders. "I thought about it a few times, but now that I have Tanya, it's not an option. I like Trish, but I don't think we'd work anyway. Come on, let's get started. It's going to be a hike."

The sky was lightening, but it was still dark around us. Perfect timing for our trek. I clicked on my headlamp as we headed down a barely discernible trail.

"You sure you know where you're going?" I asked fifteen minutes later.

"Pretty much. When you told me what you wanted to do, I asked a guy I know in the local grotto. He said he and a couple of buddies found a new cave. It's not on any of the lists and doesn't even have a name yet. They checked it out once, but it's bigger than a single trip could cover. They didn't map much of it. Virgin cave, man."

I bounced on my toes to resettle my pack and adjusted the straps. "It better be worth the schlep. If I have to carry this heavy-ass pack much longer, I'm going to expect gold veins and diamonds in the cave walls."

Greg laughed. "Same old Adam. You always did overpack. Did you bring a monster rope like you always used to?"

I flipped my headlamp off because it was finally light enough to see. "I brought a two-hundred-footer. Better to have too much than not enough. Colin said there's some vertical."

"Two hundred feet. Don't tell me, eleven millimeter?"

"Shut up. Beefier ropes are better. Stronger, easier to climb. Just better."

Greg slapped my pack. "Good to know you haven't changed that much."

If he only knew. I didn't feel like the same guy who used to go caving with my two buddies. It was one of the reasons I flew all the way out here and had Colin set up a place for us to go exploring. Maybe it would bring me closer to that other guy, the one who gave a shit about...well, anything.

"Here it is," Colin said after we'd left the trail and bush-whacked through some undergrowth. A little piece of pink flagging tape was tied to a tree next to a nondescript gash in the hill before us. "The entrance is a squeeze, but it opens up once we get through. Will our resident expert worm take the lead?"

Greg nodded. "Yeah, yeah. I'll go first."

I ran my eyes across the area. It didn't look much different than what we'd been walking through. Trees, a few open grassy areas, some small hills. It was a trip to think about how many caves there were in the area, or that anyone found this one.

I watched my two buddies getting ready to enter the small cave opening. Greg was thinner than Colin and me. Not skinny, by any means, but not quite as bulky. His hair was short, like always. None of the high-maintenance afro, crazy fade, clean bald, or cornrow styles for him, just a neat cut that made him look like the kind of guy you'd want your daughter to bring home. He'd mostly taken over running his father's kung fu school in Bowling Green and was in fantastic shape.

I'd trained with his father when I was younger, though it had been years since I'd done any martial arts. My flexibility wasn't as good now as it was back then, but I'd added a few pounds of muscle, while Greg looked like he always had and could probably tie himself into knots. That would definitely help him crawl through tight spaces.

Colin looked like the stereotypical Southern good old boy. Dirty blond hair, bulky build, and the manners to go with them. It was always "yes, ma'am" and "yes, sir" when he spoke to others. By looking at him, you wouldn't know that he was a systems analyst for a large tech company.

I was in fair shape myself—through no effort of my own the last half year—and had a California tan, brown hair, and a hurried aura about me that even I recognized. I'd been thinking it would be good to move back to Tennessee. Somewhere less chaotic. Maybe sometime soon. A slower life would definitely be nice.

Greg donned his helmet with headlamp strapped on, overalls, knee pads, and elbow pads, and then pushed his pack into the hole. "I'll see you inside, fellas."

He fist-bumped Colin and me and lay down to wriggle into the crack that was only maybe a foot and a half high and a few feet wide.

"According to my friend," Colin said, "it stays horizontal, only slanting down a little bit. It opens up after a few hundred feet. There aren't any significant side passages, so you won't end up going somewhere you don't want to."

Greg flashed a thumbs up back over his shoulder, then

entered the darkness. In less than a minute, his boots disappeared like he'd never been there.

I went next, pushing my pack and my rope bag ahead of me. It was tight, but I'd been in more restrictive caves. Sooner than I realized, my rope bag dropped and I frantically grabbed at it.

"It's fine," Greg's voice sounded all around me. "Let it go. It's only about two feet to the floor."

I did as he said, then did the same with my pack. Finally, I shimmied out of the tunnel and into a larger area. Colin joined us a few minutes later and we swept our headlamps over our surroundings.

THREE

"They checked out that passage over to the right," Colin said, moving the beam of his headlamp. "There's also another one they didn't get to, right...there." His light shone on a gash in the wall to his left. "Then there's the vertical. They didn't do anything with that. He said their lights wouldn't reach bottom and they didn't want to do a blind descent."

The cavern we were in had a twisted, narrow diamond shape. A decent percentage of the floor was flattish, but we still had to be careful. One little trip caused by a projecting piece of stone could make you go down hard or even tip over into a crack, crevice, or hole. I scuffed my helmet a couple of times moving around. The ceiling wasn't uniform at all, with stalactites of different sizes protruding down toward us.

I stepped over to a hole in the floor toward the end of the cavern. My headlight showed it widening quite a bit beneath us, from a roughly circular hole about three feet in diameter to something much larger and more irregular. The walls were uneven, most of the surface covered with flow-stone that looked like smooth radiator fins.

It wasn't a simple drop, but a dogleg that went down twenty or thirty feet, over ten or so, and then disappeared into blackness. I brought out my most powerful flashlight —it easily had over half a mile of throw.

"Things are gonna get bright," I called out before I clicked it on.

I got a good look at the flowstone, but the angle didn't let me see down into the main drop.

Straight out of a horror movie. I chuckled.

"Thinking about monsters?" Greg asked. He knew me too well.

"Yeah. It's damn dark down there."

"Caves are kind of like that," Colin said. "So, are you set on a blind descent, then, Mr. Longrope?"

"What a coincidence," I shot back. "That's what the ladies call me."

"Please."

I laughed again. "Yeah, let's go vertical. You know how much I love that shit."

"I do. Let's set some anchors then. You can go first."

"Of course."

After looking for any fixed anchors bolted or screwed into the rock—and not finding any—I turned toward Colin. He already knew what I was going to say and pre-empted me.

"I told you. The grotto just found this cave. They didn't do the descent and probably didn't have drills or other tools with them. We need to make our own anchors. Try to find a BFR to tie onto."

Referring to a *big fucking rock* always made my inner

twelve-year-old laugh. It felt good. I hadn't laughed nearly enough in the last few months.

I located a nice natural bridge near the hole and a pillar on the other side. I tapped them both with a heavy steel carabiner to make sure they weren't hollow and set about rigging up a bomb-proof anchor, with the rope equalized between the two. After triple and quadruple checking them, I tied a simple overhand knot at the end of the rope and fed the rope into my Petzl Stop descender.

Colin snorted. "Really? A bobbin? Real cavers use racks. Don't you know that?"

I glanced at the descender at my chest and looked back at my friend. "You're just too cheap to get any new gear. Your ancient descender was old when your grandpa used it. This thing is awesome. Stop talking now. The adults are going to do some caving."

The little argument we had in the truck was forgotten and I focused on what was arguably the most fun to be had in caving: the blind descent. I tested the descender—twice —and then removed my cowtail, which I'd clicked into some webbing set up around the natural bridge. With a final tug on the rope to make sure everything was kosher, I lowered myself down into the blackness.

Only, it wasn't black, not in the cone of my headlamp. Pulling up on the rope below me with my brake hand, I tested the weight of the coil below. That was a lot of rope. Which meant that it was very far to the bottom. If it even reached the bottom.

The rough walls of the opening spread out after I cleared the dogleg, and the diameter of the roughly circular passage more than tripled in size. At first, it was only rough rock, but soon I started to see the effects of the moisture and the dripping water I spotted on the walls. Fan-shaped flowstone, popcorn, a bunch of straws, even what looked like helictite greeted me as I lowered myself. I still couldn't see the bottom with my headlamp, but the view around me was spectacular.

"This is awesome, guys. You have got to see this."

"We will," Greg called down. "Focus on getting down safe, then we'll take our turn."

Greg always did share my attitude of being extra careful when caving. Colin was the one likely to go off half-cocked into a dangerous situation. I liked to take every safety precaution. You never knew what could happen.

I figured I'd gone down about fifty feet and there was still no bottom in sight. Though to be fair, I couldn't get a great angle past my legs. I was enjoying the ride: the soft whir of the rope sliding through the descender; the comfortable warmth of the rope slipping through my gloved hand; and the unique deadening of some sound while other, smaller sounds were amplified. *Damn, I've missed this.*

I found a huge smile stretching my face and I gave a little whoop. This day was going to be nothing short of awesome.

A couple of small flakes tinked off one of the walls. Another small piece of rock bounced off my helmet.

"Hey! Whatever you're doing, stop it. You're spraying me with rock."

Colin called back. "We're not doing anyth—oh shit!"

A series of loud cracks drowned out anything else my friends said. It was a sound I'd heard before. Something you never wanted to experience when dangling from a rope in empty space.

Rock was breaking loose from above. Not pebbles this time.

Increasingly larger pieces of stone bounced around me. One struck my shoulder. It hurt like a motherfucker, but I didn't think it did serious damage. Yet. By the sound of things, the shower of stone was just starting. I covered my face with my hand and glanced upward. A small stone bounced off my hand and I yelped. I did not like what I saw in the brief time my beam illuminated the space above me.

I did my best to swing toward the wall, figuring that if the rock was falling from the narrower part above, I would be safer off to the side. Momentum built slowly, and any minute I might be struck by a larger rock, but it was all I could think of.

A rock the size of my fist zipped by my ear. I actually heard it whiz by.

I finally got near enough to a wall to grab at a small pillar bridging a hollow space. It was slick with moisture, but I was able to hold it to keep from swinging back out into the open. I'd stay there until the rockfall passed.

If anything, the noises and the number of rocks that passed my headlamp's beam increased. Not only that, but the sizes got progressively larger, too. Was the whole damn cavern collapsing?

"Adam?" Greg shouted down. I barely heard him over the rumble of shifting stone.

"I'm here. I grabbed a wall. Waiting."

Then, something struck my rope up above me. Something really big. It peeled me off the wall like I hadn't even been holding on, whipping me out into the empty space again. Something was wrong. The rope should have snapped tight and flicked me around.

But it didn't.

Instead, I found myself freefalling into the blackness. In the few seconds I had left to live, my mind tried to figure out what was happening. Maybe whatever had struck the rope pinched it against something else and had cut through it enough so it broke with my weight.

Mercifully, a piece of rubble struck my helmet and I lost track of everything, sinking into unconsciousness that I knew would lead to my death.

CHAPTER
FOUR

I rubbed the bruise on my head. Had Colin and Greg made it out safely? The sound of a tin tray scraping softly on stone from across the hall was my sole companion. I tried to understand what had happened to me. And what I'd just seen. An orc and a pig man. Maybe I'd taken a harder knock on the head than I thought.

Accepting the noise as a cue, I located my own tray by touch in the blackness and sat next to it. It contained a hard, crusty lump—the bread I'd glimpsed in the guards' light. A bent metal cup sloshed as I moved it aside.

My hand found a mushy, tepid pile of...something. I brought my finger up to my nose and winced at the smell. It reminded me of engine grease, cat piss, and wet rocks. My first thought was to wipe it off on my clothes, before I remembered I didn't actually have any clothes.

But I was really freaking hungry. And thirsty.

"Ugh." I touched my finger to my tongue. "Great. It tastes exactly how it smells." I wasn't sure I'd be able to choke it down, but I had to try.

The water didn't help much. Neither did the fact that it

was thicker than water should be. It was cool, but so was the air in my cell. I gagged several times. So I focused on my neighbor's cat and how it tended to fall off things like the fence, cars, even its feet, and that helped me disassociate from the act of putting the foul gruel into my mouth. Its consistency reminded me of looking down into the hole of a porta-potty on the last day of the fair. Before I knew it, though, I had cleaned the tray and swallowed all the liquid. It only took four bouts of gagging to finish. I leaned against the wall, hoping to keep it down.

"Adam?"

"Yes, Ysduil."

"Are you well? The noise you made earlier...it was as if you were frightened or surprised." I was glad she concentrated on that and not on my battle with my "meal."

I let out a breath, then opened my mouth to answer. I was going to ask what those monsters were, but then it occurred to me: Ysduil might be the same kind of creature. I didn't want to insult my only companion. I closed my mouth and framed my words in my mind.

"Those...guards. We don't have people who look like that where I come from. Where are we, Ysduil?"

"As I said before, I am not sure. I—"

"I know. I mean, what planet are we on? What world?"

"Planet? I don't know this word. As for the world, it's Tenos, of course."

"Tenos? We're not on Earth?"

"I don't know that name, either. I'm sorry."

Tenos. So, I'd just...fallen into a different world, like John Carter and Mars. *Fucking caves.* I wondered if I was in my real body or just a projection of one like in the Edgar Rice Burroughs story.

"The green one, was he an orc? And what about the

other one? He looked like he was half human and half boar or something."

"Again, the word you use is unfamiliar to me. The green-colored guard was dunim and the other was shonet, though some call his type a boarkin or boar beastkin. You truly do not have beastkin or monster races where you come from?"

"No. We don't."

"And you have never heard of the Aycrishi Sodality?" she asked.

"No. What is it? Is it important?"

Ironic laughter reached through the window in my door and tickled my ears. I knew it wasn't genuine laughter, but I liked the sound of it. Was Ysduil one of those...dunim, or was she part animal, too? Pictures of snake women or twisted, ugly monsters flashed through my mind. I pushed them out. Even if she was hideous, she seemed to be decent. She sounded nice, anyway, and she was polite. Hell, just answering my questions gave her points in my book.

"The Sodality is probably the most important thing you need to know as a stranger to this world."

The woman didn't show any disbelief that I could have come from another world. Was there magic here, or advanced technology? Judging by the primitive cells and the clothing of the guards, magic was more likely. A medieval fantasy kind of vibe, not a futuristic sci-fi kind of thing. Why not? I'd been bashed on the head, survived what should have been a fatal fall, and was probably hallucinating. I wasn't about to question reality at this point. I'd just go with it.

"Will you tell me about it?" I asked.

"Of course. The Aycrishi Sodality is the most powerful institution in Tenos, though it's not very old. They have only been in power for two decades, yet they rule the entire world. It is named after the great heroine Aycrish. Do you know of her?"

"No. I'm not even sure what a sodality is. I think I may have heard it once, in my world."

"It's like a fraternity—you know this word?"

"Yes. A brotherhood."

"A sodality is a sisterhood, usually one organized for a purpose, to change something or right some wrongs."

"Okay, got it. And Aycrish?"

"Thousands of years ago, the entire world was in peril. Zyoxi the World-Render had appeared from whatever universe it called home and immediately began to destroy large swaths of Tenos. Cities, kingdoms, even natural features like mountains and lakes, all became food for the monster. It was clear that soon, Tenos would be no more.

"Though armies went against the gargantuan beast, they could not defeat it. The people mourned, knowing their time was short.

"Then the great heroine Aycrish, veteran of a thousand wars, took up her spear and her shield. For a hundred days they fought, ravaging the land nearly as much as Zyoxi had in its rampage. In the end, Aycrish, torn and bleeding, struck the killing blow. The corpse of the monster turned to stone and became the Zyoxi Range, the largest of all the mountains in Tenos. So it was that Aycrish saved the world and became the greatest of the legendary heroes. Sadly, the great heroine died shortly thereafter of her wounds. She paid the ultimate price and is the perfect picture of heroic sacrifice in the world."

The tale had the taste of mythology, an epic feel. Like the story of Gilgamesh. Interesting, but it didn't really tell me what I wanted to know. "What about this...Sodality?

They named themselves after Aycrish, right? But what are they?"

"The Sodality began with a small group of women, unhappy with the way the world was being governed. At that time, the Isameine family controlled all the various nations and kingdoms. One particularly powerful woman, charismatic and astute in politics, gathered allies, and undermined the Isameine rule. Though young, she engineered a coup that, in three fateful days, slaughtered all members of the family, ending their rule.

"This woman, Imorith Sartyne, instituted a new governing force, the Aycrishi Sodality, with herself at the head. Her official title is Paragon, referring to the supposedly heroic nature of the Sodality's work.

"At first, most people were apathetic toward the change in government, aside from a growing number of fanatics. For many, the leaders don't matter as much as their daily lives, working and eating and enjoying their families.

"But then, the true nature of the Sodality was revealed. When they had secured power completely, they instituted procreative controls. Men were rounded up and placed in camps. Those who rebelled were killed immediately. Within a decade, there were no men outside of the official Sodality camps."

Holy shit. It's every man's nightmare.

"But it got worse. All the men, from infancy and through adulthood, were trained. They call it conditioning, but in truth it is breaking the will and mind of the men to be thoughtless servants. They perform labor, act as guards or soldiers, and most importantly, give their seed to designated women upon command. The Sodality have a strict breeding structure and schedule to create superior offspring. All pregnancies must be officially approved and the children trained in Sodality-sanctioned facilities. Especially the male offspring."

My mind spun, trying to make sense of what Ysduil was telling me. "It's one huge government-run prostitution ring."

Ysduil laughed. "It is true that money changes hands occasionally, but it is nothing so simple. It is the Sodality's way of controlling the world. Originally, the system was explained as being a way to keep male despots from arising as they had in past times. They also promised that the men would be lent out to the areas from which they had come so that others could share them. This helped to prevent widespread rebellion in the beginning. As time went on, though, the Sodality got even more powerful and progressively, the men were reserved for the higher-level women in the organization and as bribes."

It wasn't hard to tie it all together. "We're in a Sodality dungeon." My stomach roiled, but not from the gruel I'd eaten. I was at the mercy of an organization that treated all men as less than human. And I was naked. That made it so much worse.

"We are. You are what is called *khresha*, an unconditioned male. There hasn't been one for nearly ten years. The Sodality was thorough in their searching and capturing of all males. Any escape attempt, if one could even overcome the conditioning, was met with immediate execution. You are very important to the Sodality."

"For execution?"

"Not necessarily, but I overheard the guards when they brought you in. Not the guards you saw—the men talk very little, and only on command. But some women said that they sent for important Sodality officials to come and take you back to be conditioned. They will no doubt get information about the place you came from as well, but the ultimate goal is as it has always been since they took power: to train you and add you to the ranks of the other *sotin*, the conditioned ones."

"So, they're going to take me to some place and brainwash me?"

"I am sure they will bathe you, yes, but perhaps not your brain."

"No. I mean they'll take me to be *conditioned*, to remove my own thoughts and will to do as I please?"

"Yes."

"How long do I have?"

"They will be here within three days."

FIVE

T hree days. That was all the time I had until whatever higher-up in the Aycrishi Sodality came to collect me and take me back to what was certainly some kind of torture for the purpose of destroying my brain and taking away all free thought.

So many thoughts bounced around in my head. Would it be some kind of magic thing that just changed me, or was it a long procession of torture? Did the conditioning include them assaulting me to "get my seed" as Ysduil called it? Once they'd broken me, would they try to go into my world to find more *sotin* for their system? It wasn't just my violation that would happen, but possibly that of other guys in my world. *Oh, shit!*

A thought distracted me. I was in a dungeon awaiting this conditioning. Was that what the prison was made for?

"Uh, Ysduil. You're not a...I mean, the reason you are in a cell...that is, you're female?"

My unseen companion laughed again. It was a pleasant sound, melodious and soothing. At this point, anything to calm me was welcome.

"Yes, I am. Did you think I was a *khresha* myself?"

"No, not really. But why are you locked up then? Are they going to take you for *training* also?"

"Oh, no. I will be executed when the officials arrive."

"Ex—executed. Like killed?"

Of all things, the woman giggled. "Yes, that's the way they do it here in Tenos. You get *executed to death*."

That laughter threw me for a loop. Was she joking? I could only think of one thing to say. "Why?"

"I am a priestess of Odona."

I waited for her to continue, but she didn't. "Uh..."

"Right. You probably don't know who that is. Odona is my goddess, the Goddess of Pleasure and Fruitfulness."

"Pleasure and fruitfulness. She's a sex goddess?"

"She is *the* sex goddess. Everything she is and everything about her and her followers is anathema to the Sodality. They hunt us. Have been since they took power."

I had no idea how to respond to that, so I sat silently for a time, letting what she said sink in. After several minutes, it was clear that if the conversation was going to continue, I would need to push it along.

"So, you didn't commit a crime or anything. They hunted you down and took you prisoner because of your religion, and now they're going to execute you?"

"That is correct."

"If they wanted you dead, why didn't they kill you instead of capture you?"

"Because then they wouldn't be able to take my life publicly as a warning for anyone who doesn't follow the Sodality's laws."

"What kind of place have I landed in?" That last part was barely a whisper. I wasn't sure if Ysduil heard me or not.

"Would you like to hear the tale of my capture? It is mildly exciting, if tragic."

I nodded, then remembered I was in complete darkness, and she was across the hall with two heavy wooden doors between us. "Sure. If you want to tell me."

"It will pass the time, for a few minutes, anyway. Okay, so I was making my way through the Jackal Moor, heading from Rivercross to a place near Sorin's Thicket, by the western edge of the Surtoran Waste, where some of my sister priestesses have a hidden safehold."

That was a lot of names of places I'd never heard of, but she was rolling now, so I kept my mouth shut and tried to keep up.

"I neared a small farm and saw a woman out in the fields working. I was tired and it was nearing sunset, so I went to speak with her to ask if I could sleep in her barn. She greeted me coolly and I contemplated leaving right then, but I saw how she toiled and offered to help her with some of her work if she wouldn't mind me sleeping in her barn for one night. She chewed on my offer and finally agreed.

"Happily, I helped to pick garlic from a small field until the sun went down, then I helped her bring what we'd picked back to the house. I wondered why there were no other workers but didn't want to be rude or overly curious, so I didn't ask her. As soon as the cloves were put away in crates for her to take them to market, she pointed toward the barn and without a word, stepped into her house and closed the door. It was strange to me, and more than a little rude, but life is difficult for people and I understood not wanting to associate too much with a stranger. I shrugged and went to the barn, where I made myself a bed in the straw and quickly went to sleep, despite smelling strongly of garlic.

"I was interrupted in the middle of the night by a small group of Sodality soldiers. I don't know where they came from, but they grabbed hold of me, then bound me, even before I was fully awake. As they dragged me away, I spotted the woman standing on her porch, watching the whole thing. She had a self-satisfied smile on her face at my misfortune. I don't know why, but she had contacted the soldiers—who must have been close by—and told them about me. Perhaps they gave her a finder's reward.

"From there, I was moved several times, but it's all fuzzy because they drugged me and kept me unconscious much of the time. It was probably easier for them. Even surprised, I broke the noses of two of them and an arm on another one. Of course, they repaid my attacks threefold with their own, but most of my bruises are healed now. Just in time for me to be killed." She chuckled.

My heart ached for this woman. She'd been betrayed and turned over to these monsters and yet she still kept her sense of humor. I would be bitter and hateful in the same situation. I was just about there now.

"That sounds horrible, Ysduil. I'm sorry that happened to you."

"Me too, but what can I do?" She lowered her voice a little, though it was pretty evident that there weren't any guards anywhere around us. "Unless my new dungeon friend wants to help me escape."

"I...I...of course," I said. Why hadn't I even thought about that yet? It should have been the first thing on my mind. I could only blame my general disorientation and the shock of seeing those monsters. That, and the ending up in a new world thing. That was kind of a biggie. "Do you have a plan?"

"Not as such," she admitted. "With only a few days, we could not dig our way out, even if we did have tools that could tunnel through stone. We will need to attack the guards."

"Attack those..." I was going to say *monsters*, but I still wasn't sure if Ysduil was human. I liked the woman and didn't want to insult her. "...those large men carrying weapons? That doesn't sound like a good idea. Besides, we're locked up. How are we supposed to attack them from within our cells?"

"I don't know. They have to let us out eventually, even if it's when the Sodality officials are here to collect us. Maybe we can escape then."

I didn't want to shit on her idea, but that didn't sound practical. Or possible. If the ones who were coming to pick us up arrived, they would have more guards or soldiers with them, right? Besides, the whole concept didn't sound like it would work. I wasn't sure how many guards were in the dungeon, but they definitely outnumbered us and were better equipped. Hell, they had *clothes*. That alone made them better equipped than we were.

Pushing against those kinds of odds wouldn't work. I'd have to try to think of something else.

"We'll keep thinking," I told Ysduil. "Maybe we can come up with something."

"Yes, I'm sure we will. Goodnight, Adam. Dream of escapes and freedom."

I snorted. "Sure. You too."

I laid my bare ass on the cold floor and put my hands under my head to cushion them. With the cold and the rough, uneven floor, there was no way I was going to get to sleep. Besides, too many things were running through my mind. No matter how long I laid there and no matter how I moved to avoid the sharpest of the projections jabbing into me, all I could do was fidget. The stone sucked the heat from my body while giving me road rash.

Inevitably, I pictured Amy. My ex-fiancée.

Amy Sheffield and I had been dating for over two years and I thought we were happy. She liked my attitude: always striving to do better. The one source of friction we'd had was when I dropped out of school, not finishing the chemistry degree I was working on. Even that passed as I moved up at work. She told me she was proud of me for my ambition, for trying to better myself and our situation. I loved how she was all about taking control of life and squeezing the best possible out of it. I proposed to her and she said yes. We would spend the rest of our lives together.

Then, just like that, she broke the engagement off eight months later.

I asked her what I'd done. None of it made sense. She said she'd found someone more perfect for her than I was. A bitch move, but he must've been some young CEO of a rapidly expanding start-up, a celebrity, or a sports phenomenon at the top of their game.

Nope.

The guy had barely finished high school, was unemployed, and lived with his parents. I reached down and extracted a pebble that had somehow wedged itself into my left butt cheek. A pain in the ass, just like the guy Amy hooked up with.

My entire worldview had spun and crashed into the ground. The guy had no ambition, no plans or goals, and didn't seem to care about improving himself. What the hell had I been doing, working myself to death to progress, trying to build a life for the two of us?

Needless to say, I took it hard. Things didn't matter anymore. I understood intellectually that it was depression pressing in on me, but knowing didn't make it any easier.

As if conspiring to crush the life out of me, things got rough at work as well. They pushed me, trying to get me to move up, stretch myself to take on new responsibilities, a new position. I wasn't interested. At the refinery, the path upward *always* required relocation. They would move me to another facility across the country, I'd gain some experience for a year or two, then they would move me again. It was just the way it worked.

I dug in my heels and refused. Things were getting tense and I had to get away, if for nothing else than to simply breathe without someone pushing me one way or another.

Colin, Greg, and I had been inseparable as children, up until the end of my freshman year in high school when my family moved to California. If anything could snap me out of my funk, it was spending time with them. We could go caving and I could forget everything on the West Coast. At least for a week or so.

All of which led me to sitting naked in a dungeon waiting to be sent to this world's equivalent of the Hanoi Hilton. And now Ysduil wanted me to exert myself, take control of the situation. Attack the guards.

Fuck all of this. I got to my feet and considered pacing, but the cell was tiny and that would probably just stress me out more. Instead, I lowered myself into pushup position and began to pump up and down, over and over. And over.

As I reached eighty repetitions, it struck me that I wasn't burned out. Not even close. That was strange because on a good day, well-rested and motivated, I could hit a hundred pushups, though the last ten or so were pure agony. It was the one consistent exercise I did.

I blew through the eighties, then the nineties, and right past one hundred. Maybe this world had lower gravity or something and I didn't actually weigh as much as I did in my world.

I ended up doing one hundred eighty-four pushups, pushing hard at the end, but not as hard as I did normally to reach a hundred. I shook my arms out, wishing I had a pullup bar to work the opposing muscles. I did two more sets, savoring the burn in my triceps, my abs, shoulders, and chest. The situation facing me was no less severe, but everything seemed a little less urgent when I had a good pump and was fatigued from solid, honest work or exercise.

After stretching a little, I did some shadow boxing to loosen up. Without shadows. Rather, it was *all* shadow. I relaxed then, taking up a cross-legged position on the cold floor, breathing in and out rhythmically.

I'd meditated a little bit back when I was a kid, training at Greg's father's kung fu school, but I'd gotten out of the habit. It seemed like a good time to take it up again. I mean, I had nothing but time. At least for a few days, until my new jailors and torturers came to pick me up.

As I settled into slow, deep breaths, the pervasive silence cradled me and caressed me in its chilly embrace.

That's when I heard the sounds.

CHAPTER

SIX

If it had been anywhere but a silent dungeon in the bowels of the earth, I might not have heard. But since I was in my own noiseless, lightless hell, I did.

The sounds started slowly, barely audible. *Friction*. Not scraping or scratching; that was too harsh. Maybe not even a rubbing sound, which still seemed too loud. This whisper could have been made by silk being dragged across the surface of a tranquil pond.

It was so faint, I wasn't certain I actually heard anything, but as I held my breath and became completely motionless, it registered again. A slow, gentle *whisk*. I shivered...in a good way.

"Mmmm," came to my ears, almost loud to my strained hearing. Still soft, but much clearer than the previous sounds.

From there, a medley of noises flitted through the window of my door, combining and flowing into a tiny symphony that told a tale.

A tale of motion. And pleasure. And lust.

Panted breaths came next. The next murmurs might be

called grunts, groans, or even moans, though none of those words matched the beauty of what was obviously building into something greater.

I almost called out, to ask Ysduil if she was all right. The reverberations in the air carried sensuality, but maybe I was reading it wrong and she was in trouble or the guards had paid her a visit.

No. If it involved guards, there would have been light and the racket of the door squealing open. Like earlier. It wasn't that.

My questions begged for a voice and I opened my mouth to ask. Then new sounds caressed me in the darkness and removed all doubt about what was happening.

"Unh. Unh. *Oooh*."

I leaned toward the door, listening even harder. My mind matched the sounds to images. Fantasies.

I thought of Trish, the woman I was supposed to have gone out with after my caving session. Her trim, firm body, wrapped in tight jeans and the type of snug T-shirts she used to wear in high school. In my mind, she worked her hands over her shirt, then up under it to caress her breasts. The pearls of her hardened nipples interrupted the otherwise smooth and perfect surface of the cloth's tension.

"Uh-huh, mmmm."

She moved her hand down, and down, and down, somehow unbuttoning her jeans with the flick of her fingers so she could jam her hand down underneath them. Her soft purring moans matched what I was hearing outside of my cell.

"Uh-uh-uh-uh."

My body reacted as you'd expect. Slowly at first, as if fighting it, I stiffened, then got harder, and harder still as I listened and played out the movie in my mind. I sat, the rest of me nearly as stiff as my member, afraid to move and make a sound that would break the spell.

I felt a little dirty about listening to someone pleasuring themselves, but that shame washed away in the pure fire of lust. Why couldn't I be with Trish right now? I started to whisper her name but held myself back. It was bad enough I was listening to my new friend doing what she was doing without making it strange for her by speaking and inter-rupting her. Especially with someone else's name.

Instead, I focused on Trish's face, her pouting lips and her eyes squinted in pleasure. Somehow, I missed her taking her pants off and now the Trish in my imagination rubbed herself with rhythmic motions, making the sounds I could hear in real life, her fingers plunging under her panties to disappear into her body. Her other hand had pulled up her top to expose both of her perfect, firm breasts and she tweaked her nipples in turn as she panted.

The panting was getting louder, as were the rubbing and wet sucking noises. I was so hard now I ached from base to tip. I imagined somehow tearing the door open to join Ysduil in her ritual of pleasure.

I tried my hardest to think of something else. The ugly green guard, that boar beastkin, anything putrid I could bring to my mind. Ysduil might be a pig-nosed orc thing with tusks and scars and warts.

For a moment, it helped. My lustful urges subsided for a few fleeting seconds, but then Ysduil panted a string of husky breaths and the image of Trisha slammed back into my mind.

"Uh-uh-uhnnnnnn."

Even if she was a monster, I'd never heard anything so fucking sexy in my life.

I had to distract myself. Pushups were out of the question—for anatomical reasons—and there was no way I was going to meditate through those noises. The Trish in my mind stopped fondling her tits just long enough to lick her lips, look me right in the eye, and crook a finger for me to join her.

I let out a breath that sounded too much like a whimper and the noises suddenly stopped. I sat, raging hard-on feeling like it was about to explode, controlling my breathing as best I could. Through four complete breath cycles the silence hung like a shroud over my darkened world.

Then the rubbing and slushing and panting resumed. I spent the rest of eternity controlling my breathing and watching as Trish was joined by Amy, Stacy from work, and a woman I'd seen on the plane on the way to Tennessee, all of them pleasuring themselves—and each other—while looking adoringly into my eyes.

"Uhn-uhn-oh-ooooooh. Augghhh!"

Sudden silence reigned again, punctuated by a few soft, short sounds that my mind interpreted as wiping and licking. Then, there was nothing but the emptiness that seemed even more devoid of life or anything worthwhile than it had before.

It was a long, long time until I got to sleep, even after my dick softened and stopped throbbing.

In what I assumed was the morning, a pair of guards preceded by the globe of light from their lamps or torches or whatever it was they were using to see, slid the trays of "food" into our cells. This time, it was the orc—dunim, according to Ysduil—man along with a woman who had a tail that looked an awful lot like a squirrel's just above an ass that was covered with a leather skirt that made up the bottom of her armor.

While the woman waited, the man performed exactly the same actions as the day before. He stepped up to the door, shone his light into the cell, scanned it—as if I had anything I could hide in there—bent over to slide the tray through the little door at the bottom, then stepped away.

The green-skinned man had the same lifeless eyes as before, but the woman looked lucid and intelligent. She wore a scowl on her face, like she thought it was beneath her to carry food for lowlifes like me and Ysduil, but I had no doubt she was able to think clearly. And for herself.

The stuff on the tray looked even more unappetizing in the light than it felt like in the dark. I hadn't gotten sick after eating the slop they fed me the day before, but the taste told me I probably should have. I was not looking forward to choking the meal down again. The positive side in facing brainwashing or execution: we had less than three days to have to eat their so-called food.

After the illumination retreated down the hallway, I sat down and slid the tray to me, preparing to force down the gruel, the crusty bread, and the tepid water with the metallic tang.

"Good morning, Adam," Ysduil said from across the hallway. "Did you sleep well and have pleasant dreams?"

My mind flashed back to the images—and sounds—of the night before. My loins stirred, but I ignored it. "I...did. Yes. For being in this place, I actually did have dreams that were...pleasant. Good morning. What about you? Sleep well? Good dreams?"

The woman sighed and a vague image of a chest in a tight T-shirt ran across my vision. "Yes, I did. Thank you for asking. Did you think of any ways to solve our problem?"

For a moment, I completely zoned out on what she meant. "Oh, the escape. No. I'm sorry, but I haven't thought of anything. I'm not used to being locked up like this. This is all new to me."

I was afraid for a moment it sounded like I meant she was the type of person to be locked up regularly, but she only laughed.

"I understand. I haven't thought of anything else, either. I still think the only way we will be free is if we surprise the guards, incapacitate them, and sneak out. It will involve some fighting, but I believe it is possible and that we could accomplish it."

I still wasn't buying into it. Besides the plan having all the earmarks of a failed endeavor, I wasn't even sure I could manage it if I was out in the open. That orc was pretty big. Like football player big. I wasn't a small guy, but to go up against that? He even had weapons. What did I have? A little bit of training when I was a kid.

As I thought about it, something else occurred to me. "Ysduil, I'm not sure if you know what gravity is—"

"I do. It is the force that makes things fall."

"Oh, good. Yeah. It also determines how much things weigh. On my world, we've taken machines and flown to other worlds, or at least the moon. The lights in the sky? Other worlds?"

"Odona has told us of other places, some like our world and others unlike it. Many can be reached through magic, but she said once that if someone could fly very high for a very long time, they might reach other worlds."

"Yes, that's what I'm talking about. Well, I did some exercises last night, pushing myself up from the ground to work my muscles and get stronger. But I was able to do a lot more than I normally can. I think maybe gravity is weaker here and I can lift more."

"Truly? That could help us in our escape. Is it only in

pushing up from the ground that you are stronger, or is your power increased in other ways?"

She had me stumped there. "I don't know. I don't have a way of seeing if I'm stronger with other things."

"That is unfortunate. If you could see me, I could teach you some of the practice forms for the fighting style I train in. They are a set of motions I perform to remain flexible, fast, and strong."

"Oh, we have those in my world, too. I actually know some forms from when I trained in kung fu—that's a type of fighting art—when I was younger. That's a good idea. I'll do those and see if anything feels different. Uh, did you do your forms last night?"

The silence was telling. It was nearly a full minute before Ysduil answered.

"No, I didn't. Why do you ask?"

Great, I was going to embarrass and alienate her. I did what any polite person would do. I backtracked for all I was worth.

"No reason. I just thought maybe you did them every day or something."

"I should. I have gotten out of practice. Perhaps I cannot be blamed for being lazy when I only have two or three days to live."

"Oh, right. Hey, that gives me an idea. What if we wait until the officials come to take us away and then we escape them while we travel?"

I could almost hear her shaking her head. "That's not practical. I've seen the guards they use to travel with prisoners, especially prisoners who are to be executed. There are usually dozens of them, all elite warriors. They transport prisoners in rolling cages, much like these cells. If we can't escape before they take us away, I don't believe we'll have any chance of avoiding our fate."

"Damn."

"Don't worry, though. We have a few days. I know we will think of something. I have faith you will not let me down, just as I will not let you down. When we gain our freedom, Adam Townsend, we will continue to be great friends."

I liked the woman. Even if Ysduil was a hideous monster, we could totally be friends—at least until I figured out how to get out of this crazy world and get back to my own. We just needed to work out a way to get out of this damn prison.

SEVEN

After the relative excitement of getting food and forcing it down, there was little else to do but stare into the darkness and think. A few times during the day, I did sets of exercises. I settled into doing pushups more than anything else after I tried to do some burpees and nearly split my skull on the low ceiling when I jumped up.

Mostly, my mind chewed over my situation. This new world—Ysduil had called it Tenos—how I'd gotten here, how I would get back home. Part of me still couldn't quite get a grasp on everything. It all seemed so unreal. Or maybe surreal.

"Ysduil?"

"Yes, Adam?"

"I noticed the guards' eyes. They're kind of blank, like they're in a trance or something. They also move mechanically, shuffling around as if they're controlled by someone else. What's the deal with them?"

"They are *sotin*, controlled ones, as are all other men besides you."

"A *khresha*," I said, remembering what she'd called me. A wild man, or at least a man who could think for himself.

"Yes. The conditioning, it has effects. Most of them are not only expected, but are favored. Their motivation is almost entirely eliminated. They are very susceptible to suggestion and are bound by commands. From those with authority, that is. You or I could not try to convince one of them to do something or give them an order they would obey. They don't think much. In fact, a man could be told to stand still in one location and he would do so until he is commanded to do something else or until he dies of thirst or starvation."

That seems counterproductive. "Doesn't that make them poor choices as soldiers, or even guards? What if the situation changes quickly? If they don't think and aren't creative, what happens when they have to fight?"

"They are trained in combat. Simple commands, like 'protect' or 'attack' shifts them into a mode they have been trained extensively for. They can fight with skill and react to their opponents, but only to a certain extent. Certain exceptional *sotin* can appear to be quite clever in combat, but they are really not thinking, just moving and reacting according to how they've been trained."

"Weird, and more than a little creepy. You said they're used as soldiers and guards, but also to do labor. You also told me they have a role in breeding?"

"I did and yes, they do. It was their primary purpose from the start."

I examined that thought in my mind, turning it over and inspecting it closely. "Uh, if they don't think and have no motivation, how do they...you know, rise to the occasion?"

Ysduil didn't answer right away and I was about to

explain what I meant, no matter how awkward, but then it seemed she figured it out.

"You speak of erections?"

I ran my fingers through my greasy, short hair and felt my face grow warm. "Yeah. I mean, sure, even without a brain, stimulation could do that, but it's pretty much required to...um, breed."

"You are correct, they cannot do so on their own. They have no interest in others in a carnal way. There is a drug, usually taken as a tea, and it produces the necessary erection. They are trained to perform simple intercourse, but from what I understand, they are usually utilized as a stationary object on which the woman completes her work."

Ugh. So, they had a Viagra tea in this world and men amounted to little more than a mechanical dildo. What a horrible place.

"Does that surprise or disappoint you, Adam?" she asked.

Fuck yeah, is what I wanted to answer—especially to the second part—but I wasn't sure that speaking out loud about loving sex was polite here, even if Ysduil was a self-proclaimed follower of a sex goddess. God knew what this world's idea of sex was. I decided to water down my answer.

"It's...surprising. But you said you were a priestess to a sex goddess. Oh, sorry, a goddess of pleasure and fruitfulness."

She gifted me with her giggle. "Yes. I don't mind if you call her a sex goddess. Indeed, that is the ultimate physical pleasure, is it not?" She had my full agreement there. "In general, you will find that people don't talk about such things in Tenos. Much of it is the Sodality's influence, but even before, it was not spoken of in polite company, from what I understand."

"But, your goddess? Your religion?"

"Oh, I didn't say I was polite company, not in the contemporary sense." She barked a laugh. "My sister priestesses and I have fascinating conversations about many varied sexual topics. It is our primary field of study and our favorite area of knowledge. Away from my sisters, though, I have learned to be more circumspect. In fact, they often tease me that I am timid in sharing knowledge I have accumulated.

"I prefer to think of it as being polite to others and not making them feel awkward. It is untoward to say things that will alienate those one speaks to out in the world. Perhaps I go too far at times. It distresses me even to tell you these things because you might think less of me."

The turn in the conversation produced the most delicious tingling in my nether regions. I wanted nothing more than to talk about sex with this woman—well, almost nothing—but I also held back for some reason. Maybe it was a shallow belief that if she turned out to be an ugly monster, it would make our conversations awkward, or maybe that old-fashioned part of me kept me from talking dirty across a hallway in a place where there could have been a dozen ears listening. I didn't fear being overheard when we talked about escape, but who was I to analyze why I felt like this? In the end, I settled for the coward's way out.

"I don't think less of you, Ysduil. It's good that you are kind and polite and it's good that you are so devoted to your beliefs. I would never judge you for that."

"Thank you," she said. "You have eased my mind that I haven't pushed you away with my strange beliefs."

Not so strange. I looked forward to finding out more about what she and her sisters thought, but not now. For now, I needed to focus on how we'd escape. If we succeeded, there would be plenty of time later to talk. If not, well, then it really didn't matter because I'd be one of those walking zombie *sotin* with no thoughts and no interest in sex or anything else.

I needed to figure out how to get out.

The silence returned, leaving us to our own thoughts. I worked the problem, pulling on every escape story I'd ever read or seen in movies and TV, scrabbling for even an outside chance to get out. What could I do, though? I was in a cell. They never let me out for anything, even to take care of necessary natural functions. I used one particular corner farthest away from where I normally stayed by the door to take care of those bodily functions. How could I possibly get through the door?

I even sat in the old, familiar cross-legged position and meditated on it, but nothing came to me. Nothing but what Ysduil had offered: attack the guards and get the key to escape. Simple enough to say, but impossible in performance. I was still thinking when the light of the guards' lamps flared from down the hallway.

It was feeding time again.

I stood and watched—with my hand in front of my face to block most of the light—as a woman guard and that male boar beastkin approached the cells. Or maybe it was a different pig dude. I couldn't tell. As the woman went to Ysduil's door, boar-face shuffled up to mine. As the other guard had done, he stepped close and robotically held his lamp up to look into my cell.

Just as he averted his eyes to bend over and dispense my food tray, I acted without really thinking it all through.

I reached through the bars and grabbed hold of the top of the man's breastplate. Then I yanked him toward the bars on the window as hard as I could.

I realized my mistake as soon as I'd acted. Whereas I was thinking I'd pull and slam the man's face into the bars, I didn't account for his height. His boiled leather breastplate thunked against the door and bars, doing no damage to him whatsoever. His face didn't even come close to striking the metal laced across the window. Damn.

The next second, the guard snatched my wrist and twisted, breaking my grip without even dropping his lamp. With the same hand, he drove his fist between the bars and struck me so powerfully in the forehead that I flew backward, slammed into the wall with my back, and fell into the spot I used as my bathroom. It was like Bruce Lee and his fucking one-inch punch. Now I knew how that bodybuilder holding the weight plate in front of his chest for Bruce in that famous video felt.

I shook my head, glad he'd hit me where he did. If he'd have hit me in the nose, my jaw, or in the eye, I'd be in worse shape. As it was, it felt like a lump was growing on my forehead.

There had been no emotion on his face, no hatred, fear, or anger in his glassy eyes. Even now, he simply bent over, slid the little door to reveal the slot for my food, and pushed the tray inside, closing the door again.

The guards left, taking their light with them. I heaved myself onto my feet to go toward the food.

"Adam?" Ysduil's voice wafted across the hall to me.

"I'm fine. I tried to attack the guard. I can see what you mean now about how they're trained to fight. He was very fast. And strong. You may be right about attacking the guards being the only way out, but damn, we're going to need a better plan. I'm definitely not trying that again."

CHAPTER
EIGHT

That night, I sat in my cell, my forehead still throbbing from the punch I'd taken. And covered in the wet and grimy coating of my filth I hadn't been able to scrape off. Ysduil's frantic panting and moaning snatched my attention once again. Mercifully, she finished her activities quickly—this time with a louder and more insistent climax than the day before. My deplorable condition didn't affect my enjoyment or frustration during another night's performance.

In the silence that followed, I tried to take my mind off what I heard and what I'd pictured as I sat there helplessly with another steel-rod hard-on. It took a while to subside, probably because I kept going over and over the images, wondering what a priestess of a sex goddess looked like as she was generating the sound effects that had me so enraptured. The mélange of features from Trish, Amy, and other women was enticing, but less personal than if I could picture the actual woman who was just on the other side of the hall.

The next day was a duplicate, minus the stupid attack

on the guard and the resulting headache. When Ysduil and I settled down to sleep, she provided another sweet serenade of sounds that would do any porn movie proud. All I could think of were two things: I really needed to get laid before my balls exploded; and we were one day closer to her execution and my lobotomization.

A couple hours after the evening meal the day after, the familiar light approached in the hallway outside my cell. I was confused, wondering if I'd lost track of time and it was morning already.

Then my mind latched onto another reason they might be coming for us outside of the normal schedule. Had we run out of time? Were the guards coming to hand us over to the ones they'd been waiting for, the ones who would escort us to our own different brands of death?

Five forms filled the hallway. The orc guy—the same one I'd seen the first day, based on the chipped tusk—and the boar beastkin who punched me were there. Another man with lighter green skin than the other dunim, but with longer and unchipped tusks protruding from his lower lip, had joined them. A woman guard I'd never seen before— some kind of dog beastkin maybe—was present, too. Last was another woman, one who wore a fancier breastplate and clothing than the others. Her light brown hair was short, barely reaching the level of her chin. It took a special kind of facial structure to make that style look good, and she had it. She also had rounded fuzzy ears and a fairly non-descript tail thicker than a cat's but not the bushiest I'd ever seen, and standing angled from its attachment point to reach more than halfway up her back. Some kind of weasel or ferret beastkin?

I stared at her for a moment, not only wondering what kind of beastkin she was, but also marveling at her attractiveness. Even in armor, it was clear she had an amazingly fit and shapely body. And her face? I'd seen a few women as pretty as her, but couldn't recall seeing one that was *more* beautiful. Who'd have ever thought I'd find a half-animal that sexy? She was even one of the bad guys on top of it.

The world was not a fair place. Neither mine nor this new one.

The woman saw me looking at her and she raised her chin slightly and smirked.

Then she barked orders to take me out first and then "that whore" after.

I didn't resist, knowing I'd probably get another fist to the face or meet the business end of one of the weapons the guards carried. That didn't mean I wasn't curious, though.

"Where are you taking us?" I asked.

The male guards continued to stare straight ahead as if I hadn't spoken at all. The dog woman glanced at the weasel and the obvious leader deigned to answer me.

"You are to be prepared for the arrival of your...escorts tomorrow morning. We will not hand you over filthy and stinking like you are."

Escorts? Less than a day away? Fuck.

The dog beastkin pushed my shoulder hard to start me moving down the hall as the boar dude opened Ysduil's cell. I tried to turn my head to see the friend I'd been talking to for several days, but the leader smacked my face hard with an open hand that felt like a two-by-four.

"Eyes front, *khresha*. Don't give me an excuse to give you bruises. Your escorts will not look twice at any injuries you have."

I almost challenged the weasel, but decided that would be a stupid move that would gain me nothing but more hits. I shuffled along, keeping my eyes ahead. Directly on the weasel woman's tight ass and the way it swayed in the snug leather pants she wore. A hole had been cut just above and her tail wagged lazily as she moved. The whole thing was mesmerizing, and more than a little arousing. I had to avert my eyes to prevent myself from displaying evidence of how much I enjoyed the view.

God, it had been way too long. Ysduil's nighttime activities hadn't helped matters. Neither did the fact that all of me was on display and walking directly behind a hot beastkin chick.

We passed through several hallways and into a room five or six times the size of my cell. A trough went through the center of it and three large basins with four buckets dominated the space. Three more men, these in simple clothing instead of armor, stood stone still along the wall. One had pointed ears and tanned skin. An elf, I guessed. The other two were short and at least three times as wide as the elf. Their arms were as big around as my legs, and they had respectable beards. Dwarves? I'd never asked Ysduil exactly what kinds of races were in Tenos.

All three of them had the glassy, vacant eyes I'd learned to associate with *sotin*. Of course they were. I was apparently the only *khresha* in the world. Ysduil had said as much.

I was also the only one present with no clothes on.

The dog woman pushed me again, this time toward the center of the room. I was getting good and tired of that bitch—and I mean that both literally and figuratively—pushing me around. One more time and I'd...

Movement from behind and to the side of me made me turn my head. My mouth dropped open as I got my first look at Ysduil.

It was obvious who she was as the only woman without a uniform on. She wore the ragged remains of some kind of thin dress or undergarment, nearly sheer enough to see detail through. It ended with an uneven and tattered hem midway up her thighs and had several strategic holes revealing her toned tummy and even a little glimpse of her softly curving breasts.

If I thought the weasel woman was hot, Ysduil was twice as much so. My eyes locked onto her nipples, barely more than shadows under the tight cloth that defined her firm and perfectly shaped breasts. Another hole revealed a slightly obscured view of the reddish hair between her legs.

What really threw me for a loop, though, was her face. Ysduil was without a doubt the most beautiful woman I'd ever seen in my life. Smooth cheeks, searching orange-red eyes with vertical pupils that sucked me into them, and lips that were firm and curved yet not too plump like a lot of the collagen-injected lips so many found attractive in my world.

She also had furry ears protruding from her reddish auburn hair. The fur color of her ears and of the fluffy tail hanging behind her were perfectly matched.

She gave me a shy smile with a mischievous glint in her eyes as she ran them over my body.

That's when I remembered that I was naked and also recognized that my thoughts had turned to her nighttime activities. Which of course, made one particular part of me grow. Quickly.

I saw in her eyes that she'd noticed even as that part started to supersize, and I averted mine in embarrassment. I mean, I was proud of what I had, but to be on display like that in front of ten people, well, it was a little much. As I looked away, I saw the weasel woman shift her eyes to my pole and a slow smile spread to her face as well.

Shit.

A bucket of cold water hit me then, a perfectly timed insult from one of the dwarves. Another slosh announced water hitting Ysduil and I couldn't resist looking. As expected, the sheer clothing had turned all but invisible, giving me an image I hadn't seen even in the best of wet T-shirt competitions. My erection warred with the frigid water being tossed over me.

The erection won.

Several painful minutes of being doused and scrubbed with a long-handled, hard-bristled brush did little to hinder the enthusiasm of my ambitious member, but then it was over and I was being shoved by that damn dog beastkin again, back toward my cell. Honestly, I had so many other things on my mind, I barely noticed it.

Ysduil was a fox. Literally. Well, figuratively too, but she actually had furry fox ears and a fox tail. How had I have ever imagined her as a monster? One thing was for sure: if our escorts didn't get here before nightfall, I wasn't sure I could endure hearing Ysduil's self-ministrations while picturing the sexy beastkin in my mind.

My cell door clanged shut, followed by the same sound across the hall, and I sat down on the cold, stone floor wondering if there was any way I could escape and take my beautiful foxy friend out of this place.

"Adam?" Ysduil's voice said a few minutes later. The suddenness of it made me jump.

"Yes?"

"I...I'm glad I got to see you, to be able to picture your face when we speak from across the darkness."

"Me, too. I am happy to meet you, once again. For the first time."

The fox woman paused. I sat rigidly, waiting for what she would say next.

"Forgive me, please, if this is awkward or inappropriate. Please tell me if it is. Do you find me pleasing to look at?"

Oh my God. How could I tell her she was all the fantasies I'd ever had rolled up into one? Even ones I hadn't but wished now I had. Better to play it cool, though still let her know she's hot. "Yes. You are beautiful, Ysduil. I haven't ever seen anyone as gorgeous as you."

"Truly?"

"Absolutely."

"Thank you." I could hear the smile in her voice. "And your...reaction, was that for me or simply the stressful situation?"

"My reaction?" Was she talking about me blushing or averting my eyes?

"The change in your...anatomy. The lengthening of—"

I rushed to speak. "Uh. Yes. That was because of you. The sight of you and thoughts..."

"That pleases me," she said. "So much of what I have learned from Odona is unclear because I have rarely seen a man so close before and never in such a situation as that. I was unsure if there could have been other reasons. Kelena is quite beautiful."

"Kelena?"

"The leader of the guards, the amustil. Oh...ah, the ferret beastkin. Do you find her pleasurable to look upon?"

This was getting so weird. "Yes, she is lovely, but she's a horrible person. You are beautiful inside and out. My reaction was for you and only you."

"Then I am happy. Even though we will be taken to horrible fates soon, you have given me joy this day. Thank you."

"Don't give up hope yet, Ysduil. Until we're both dead,

there is always a chance to get free. We'll work together and then we can talk as much as we want once we're free."

"That sounds wonderful. We'll work together. I'm glad I met you, Adam Townsend."

"I'm glad I met you, Ysduil Fennis."

After suffering through Ysduil's nightly symphony of insistent moans and heavy breathing—made all the more difficult with an image of her burned into my brain—I finally got to sleep.

A few hours later, I was awakened as light once again encroached on our dark hallway and cells.

CHAPTER
NINE

I wasn't sure what was going on at first. Was it already morning? I'd just gotten to sleep.

The light was not accompanied by the slow, shuffling steps of any of the male guards. Only small scraping noises registered in my hearing. I got up and stood, looking out my window. A sensation like a cold, wet finger ran up my spine. Maybe the ones we'd been dreading were here and the soft footfalls were highly trained warriors coming to take Ysduil away to execute her immediately.

The person holding the lamp stopped in front of my door. Shockingly, the sound of a key being inserted into the lock came next, followed by the rusty scratching of it turning in the tumbler. The door swung open, accompanied by its own creaking.

The lead guard I'd seen before—Kelena, Ysduil had called her—stepped into the room with her lamp and swung the door closed. She looked different than earlier. More casual.

She wore only a tight undershirt and the pants I'd admired before. They looked like they had been painted onto her and when she flexed her legs to move to the side, definition stood out in her toned thighs. I wasn't aware leather could stretch that tight.

I swallowed hard.

"You find me pleasing to look upon," she said in a husky voice, much more pleasant than the commanding tone she'd used earlier. It was a statement, not a question.

As such, I didn't respond.

"I saw you steal looks at me," she continued, turning so I got a good look at one of the most fantastic asses I'd ever seen, even if it was topped by a fur-covered tail. "Was your stiffening because of me?"

I wished she hadn't asked that. To be honest, it was more about seeing Ysduil, but I wasn't about to say that. Just thinking about it had me already feeling the blood rush to the parts downstairs.

"Mmmm," she said. Her big, yellow eyes reflected the light as she set the lamp down. "I knew you desired me. Do you know that the *sotin* do not become erect unless we give them stonedraught? While it is fortunate we can cause the condition when we want, there is something missing in not being able to provoke the response...naturally." She ran one of her hands across her left breast, which was straining the shirt she wore.

I sipped a breath, trying to calm my nerves. It was downright unfair to parade a body like that in front of me after the suffering Ysduil's nightly activities had caused me. I felt myself losing the battle as my member raised and grew harder.

"I have decided to grant you what you wish." She moved her other hand down to rub the leather between her legs. "You will mount me and fill me with your seed. As an added gift, perhaps I will aid you in leaving this place before the escorts come for you. Such a shame it would be for you to lose your ability to..." She squeezed her nipple and a soft moan escaped her lips. With her other hand, she gestured toward my cock, by now standing straight out at attention.

A thousand thoughts ran through my head—the one at the top of my body. The lower one contained only one thought. Granted, I couldn't focus on any one of the ideas, but still, they were there. Was there another guard waiting in the hall? Where were her armor and weapons? Would she really help me escape? Would she let Ysduil go, too? What would it feel like to smash my naked body against hers? What did she taste like?

"Uh..." I said.

She reached her arms across her belly and grabbed the edges of her shirt, pulled it up to the bottom edges of her full breasts, then stopped. Her eyes were locked onto mine, but I couldn't look away from the slow unveiling of her fantastic tits. They were slightly bigger than Ysduil's, but still firm and shapely.

A sudden pain reminded me I needed to breathe.

God, this woman was hot. Her lips—I thought of several places I wanted them—curved into a sexy smirk and she slowly lifted the shirt up, inch by inch, until her fawn areolas and nipples bounced free.

Kelena glanced down at my rock-hard dick and licked her lips. I felt a little bit of pre-cum dribble out.

"I've always wanted to..." She bent over and licked the tip of my cock, sending a violent shudder through me. She smacked her lips and ran her tongue over them. "Yes. I think I like that. I think you do, too."

Now, I wasn't a very religious guy, but at that moment, I was praying that I could figure out what to do. Should I give in and do what she wanted? I did want her...very badly. She wanted me, too. But she was a bad guy...girl. Oh, God. That phrase in my mind, *bad girl*, sent another vibration through my body.

"Here, allow me to make it easier." She undid her pants, which were secured on the side by some sort of buttons or toggles or something, then showed great strength and dexterity by pulling the leather off in a few quick motions with a sound so much like a rubber band snapping, it made me wonder if it was leather after all. She briefly turned around to put a hand on the wall to take the clothing off her feet, and I got a full view of her perfect ass, her incongruous tail, and the swollen lips of her glistening pussy.

I almost lost it right there.

I still hadn't figured out what I was going to do, but whatever it was, I needed to decide soon, because she turned back toward me with a truly, deliciously, evil look on her face.

She sidled up to me, sniffing my chest. The cool, soft touch of her nose as it glided over my skin almost sent me over the edge—again—and I barely contained myself when her tongue flicked out and licked one of my nipples.

"I'm glad we gave you a bath earlier. It will make this more pleasant."

Her hand trailed down my belly to cup my balls, then lightly trail over my throbbing member.

"Put that inside me. You know you want to, and I want you to. Imagine the pleasure, the rapture. Don't you want to enter my tunnel and feel my wet, hot pussy caressing you?"

I almost said yes, but was able to turn it into a pitiful moan. Which only increased the smile on her face.

I thought of Ysduil, which actually made me throb harder, against my wishes. She was my friend and I couldn't abandon her. If I continued in this, would Kelena let her go free, too? Would she even let *me* go free? I really wanted a release right now, in more than one way. But could I trust her? Even if I could, would this be considered a betrayal, both in terms of good and evil and also with the friendship I'd forged with the fox woman? It wasn't like we were dating or anything. We'd just met.

That last thought disappeared from my mind like all the rest when Kelena grabbed my shaft in her fist—God, she had such soft hands—and tugged on me to follow her to the wall. She put her back against the stone and thrusted her hips forward, opening her legs a bit wider. It was an awkward angle, but it would work if I squatted down a little bit.

I closed my eyes and tilted my head back, letting out a shuddering breath as she pulled me forward a little more and positioned me. The tip of my cock grazed a warm, soft, wet fold of skin, and my breath hitched.

I pulled my hips back, just a little bit. Kelena whimpered a little moan.

Then I rotated at the waist and punched her square in the jaw.

It didn't feel like anything broke, but my punch sent her into the wall and the back of her head thunked against the stone to bounce back toward me. Those yellow eyes, squinted and fixed on me only a second before, rolled up and she collapsed.

I caught the woman's exquisite body and lowered her to the floor. She felt like she hardly weighed anything, but it could have been the crazy gravity or whatever it was that made my pushups easier.

It took me a couple of minutes to slow my heartbeat. Arousal and the response to actually engaging in a fight had my heart going like a trip hammer. I half-expected another guard to slam the door open and kill me with a sword, but there was no other light in the hallway. No other sound.

The ridiculous irony of it all smashed down on me all at once and I let loose a maniacal cackle. What kind of idiot came into a cell without weapons? The weasel woman either thought more highly of her combat ability than was warranted, or she completely underestimated my own ability to withstand her feminine wiles.

My whole body quivered. It had been too close. Another half a second and I would have given in and just enjoyed myself. I exhaled a shuddering breath and pulled a fistful of my hair. Or at least as much as I could grab with it as short as it was.

"Adam?"

"Hold on, Ysduil. Give me just a moment."

The fear in her voice reminded me that I was by no means finished with...whatever it was I was in the middle of. I spared a look for the guard, sexy even crumpled on the dirty floor as she was, then bent to pick up the lamp.

She had set the keys down next to the lamp, so I snatched those up, too. After a step toward the door, I also scooped up the leather pants and the top Kelena had discarded so casually. I hurried across the hall, located the correct key after three tries, and unlocked Ysduil's cell.

The fox woman stepped out tentatively, scanning the hallway and seeing my cell door open. Then she looked down and saw that I was still erect. One of her eyebrows quirked above her lovely red-orange eyes.

"It's a long...actually, no. It's not a long story, but I'll tell you later. Come on, we need to get out of here."

"Of course."

That was it? Where was the arguing, the curiosity, the

whining? She took my promise I'd tell her about what happened later and she was going to leave it at that? I could really see myself falling in love with this woman.

"Oh," I said, holding up the clothes. "Here. You two look like you're about the same size."

"I'm fine, thank you. This—" She spun and lifted the ragged hem of the dress she wore. "—is my priestess garb. It has seen better days, but I like it better than the thought of wearing Sodality clothes."

I shrugged. If she wanted to wear clothes that left very little to the imagination, I was all for it.

"I just thought I'd offer. They're too small for me to wear." I threw them into Ysduil's cell, then closed and locked the door. I handed her the lamp and gave the same treatment to the door of my cell. Former cell. The guard leader was going to be pretty embarrassed when she was found in the morning. That reminded me...

"It's only been a few hours since we went to sleep, right?"

"Yes."

"Then it's what, very early morning, at the latest?"

"I believe so."

"We need to get out of here while it's still dark. I don't know how many guards they have, but we saw eight at a time yesterday, so there are at least that many. I'd just as soon not run into any of them."

"I agree," the fox woman said. "Follow me."

She took off at a slow jog, her fluffy fox tail bouncing up and down above a contender for the nicest ass I'd ever seen.

What a night.

CHAPTER
TEN

For all that Ysduil seemed timid and shy, even when talking to me from across the hall in darkness, now she seemed in her element, a magnificent, ravishing ninja ghosting through the hallways while I carried the lamp and tried to keep up.

She stopped so suddenly, I almost ran into her.

She leaned her face in toward mine and I could smell her unique scent. It was partly newly cleaned skin, partly some kind of musk, partly a tangy citrus, but all enticing. One of her furry ears brushed my lobe, tickling me in the most delicious way.

"Put the lamp down," she whispered. "There's light up ahead. We should sneak up there in the dark so we can surprise whoever it is."

I nodded, my eyes unfocused, and she looked at me strangely. Then, a mischievous grin formed on her lovely face and she turned back toward where we were going.

The fox woman made almost no sound as her petite bare feet slid along the stone. I made a little more noise, but with the rigid stone and me having bare feet—along with bare everything else—I doubted anyone past a few feet from me could hear our approach.

We found two guards, both men, sitting motionless at a rough wooden table. Plates with the remnants of food that looked far more appetizing than what we'd been fed littered two plates on the table next to a couple of mugs and a lamp. Both men looked small, shorter than Ysduil, but it was hard to tell with them sitting down. They were thin, with ears and tails that identified them as mouse or rat beastkin. Just how many types of creatures lived in this world?

The left ear of one of the guards twitched, but it was already too late. Ysduil had launched herself from a standstill to fly across the room. The twitcher turned his head just in time to see her deliver a picture-perfect flying side-kick to his face. He was knocked out of the chair and slammed to the hard floor.

Before the second guard could react, Ysduil turned, grabbed him by one of his flimsy little membrane-like ears, and punched him in the face repeatedly. He fell as well and my foxy friend stomped on the first guard's neck with a horrible cracking sound. She watched the second guard for a moment to see if he would get up, but he appeared to have been knocked out.

I stood with my mouth open as she jerked her head to indicate she wanted me to join her. The incongruity between the savage attacks and the absolutely adorable look she gave me spun my mind in circles. What. The. Fuck?

"H-how?" I was able to get out, feeling like a moron.

"Many of my sister priestesses train in combat. I am fairly skilled at it."

"Uh, yeah."

She ran her eyes over me. "Do you wish to take some of

their clothing?"

"Good idea. Let me check." I went first to the unconscious rat man, mainly because it freaked me out to take the clothes off a dead person, but it was pretty evident that none of the clothes they wore would fit me. They were too short, too skinny, and I wouldn't be able to get into anything they had. I did take a slender sword that was propped up against the table, however. It was barely a short sword in my hands—more like a long knife—but that was better than trying to fight unarmed. I was nowhere near as skilled as my partner.

"I was unconscious when they brought me here," she said. "You were as well, I believe. I don't know which way to go, so we'll have to discover it as we go."

I agreed and we headed off again, Ysduil in front and me bringing up the rear with our lamp.

As we searched for a way out, we came across several other guards, but never more than two at a time. Ysduil continued to impress me with her skills, but I did fight a few as well, including a particularly tough elf that moved like the wind. That one almost skewered me with his sword before Ysduil cracked his skull with a sturdy wooden bucket she found nearby.

As the frequency of guards increased, I assumed it meant we were getting close to the exit. There were even larger rooms along the corridors, most with desks or other furniture. When we finally ascended a set of stone stairs and stepped onto a wooden floor, I let out a breath.

We were almost free.

"Oh," Ysduil said. "I recognize this design. We were not just in a dungeon. The cells were situated below a fortress."

"How do you know?"

"There are fortresses scattered all over the world from a

time of great wars almost three centuries ago. Many of them share a similar design, a common floor plan. I have been in a few and this place is built similarly."

"Does that mean there's an army here?"

She tilted her head. "Likely. More importantly, there is a commander here. A high-ranking soldier in the Sodality's forces. She is probably still asleep."

I was going to ask how Ysduil knew that last part, but then I followed her eyes through a doorway into a room with an actual window. Outside, the sky was just shifting from dark purple—almost black—to plum. Daybreak.

"We should kill the commander," she said matter-of-factly. "It will plunge the fortress into confusion and it will be a grand blow to the Sodality."

I looked at the fierce fox woman and studied the faintly vulpine features in her face. Those animals were known to be clever, but also vicious. Not a creature one should corner without expecting to be attacked. Did she only appear to be like a fox, or was she actually part carnivorous animal?

I mean, I understood how she felt. These people hunted down her sisters, hunted Ysduil herself, so they could execute them publicly. Still, I had no interest in killing someone in cold blood as they slept.

"I don't think that would be wise," I said. "Who knows how many guards are around? It only takes one to sound an alarm and then we'd never get free. It's more important for us to escape than to try to single-handedly win a war or sabotage a fortress."

She blinked at me. "You...you are right. Forgive me. It is more important to flee. Perhaps there will be time later for retribution. Come, I know where a side door lies. It would not do for us to try to escape from the main door and run into a guard station. Or worse, a barracks."

I let loose with a silent, thankful breath, both for how reasonable Ysduil was and that she knew where we should go. We might actually get free after all.

As we slipped out the door and into the open air of the chilly morning, we almost ran over a soldier who had stepped out to urinate against a wall. Ysduil's reflexes were quicker than mine and she rendered the man unconscious with a blurringly fast attack consisting of—if I could guess —five or six punches one right after the other.

"How is this one's size?" she asked.

My mind interpreted the question based on the hand holding himself to aim his stream, but then I realized what she meant. His clothes might fit, though my shoulders were a good bit wider. After stripping him quickly, I squeezed into his pants—barely. They were shorter than I would have preferred, and I spent precious seconds pulling at the crotch and kicking one leg out to stretch the material that felt like a tourniquet on my jewels. Neither his tunic nor his boots fit, but I felt fortunate just to have the opportunity to run for my life without parts of me freely bouncing.

I was definitely not a fan of the swinging pendulum.

After crossing a courtyard, staying to the rapidly disappearing shadows, we found an unattended sally door. It was latched from the inside to keep people out, but it was easily opened from where we were. We stepped out into the world as the sun was about to break the horizon. The pale light of dawn, punctuated by streams of sunlight rising upward in the sparse clouds, illuminated a wild and rugged landscape ahead of us.

"Oh no," Ysduil said, her shoulders drooping. "That's the Dreadlands. I think I know where we are now. Getting completely free is going to be a lot harder than I thought."

CHAPTER
ELEVEN

"The Dreadlands?" I asked.

"Yes." She swept her arm out to indicate everything from us to the horizon. "This whole area, it's called the Dreadlands."

As far as I could see, there were no structures that way, nothing to indicate that anyone had ever set foot there. It was a mix of heavy vegetation broken by more open areas, hills or mountains in the distance to the right, and interesting rock formations half-hidden by thick trees to the left.

"That name sounds ominous," I commented.

"It's fitting. This is one of the most dangerous places on Tenos. No one in their right mind goes into the Dreadlands."

"But we have to?"

She pointed back toward the fortress behind us. "The fortress is a Sodality stronghold. On the other side, there are some towns and villages along the road, mostly with a strong Sodality presence. There's a swamp area, if I remember correctly, but even that has Sodality outposts near it. If we try to escape in any other direction than through the Dreadlands, we'll be seen quickly and they'll throw all their troops at hunting us down."

I sighed. "But won't they chase us anyway, even if we go into the Dreadlands?"

"If they see us, they might. For a little while. Once we get past the edges and reach the truly dangerous parts, I don't think they'll continue. Like I said, no one in their right mind..."

I considered what she said, but I didn't like the look of the rugged land ahead of us. I'd camped and hiked a fair amount, even caved and rock climbed, but I'd never been put in a survival situation where I had to live off the land in a dangerous area. Plus, we didn't have monsters on Earth. That was an important difference.

"What's on the other side?" I asked.

"Far to the east is Aycrish Summit, the capital city of the Sodality, but between the Dreadlands and that, there are cities and towns, most of which are filled with people whose only concern is to live their lives and not be caught up in trouble."

"Okay. Could we hide somewhere until dark and then go around the other way?" I was pretty sure I knew what her answer would be, but I thought I'd ask anyway.

"Do you think we could evade an entire army for a whole day, and then slip past all their sentries—including beastkin who have night vision—in the dark?"

"I guess not." I felt as if all the energy had been sucked out of me. "Well, if we're going to do it, we should probably get going before they spot us."

Ysduil silently started forward and I followed her. We picked our way down a slope with scraggly bushes until we got to a flatter area. Before Ysduil plunged us into the heavier vegetation ahead, consisting of higher bushes and some small trees, I had one more suggestion.

"If it's dangerous in there, how about we skirt the edge and go around the worst parts?"

Ysduil tilted her head. "We could do that, I suppose. It would increase the time it takes to get to the other side, though."

"We're not on any kind of schedule, right? As long as we get away, what's another few days if it means avoiding more dangerous places?"

"You're right. We'll do that."

She headed off to the right, in the direction of the mountains.

"What's the deal with the Dreadlands? Is it really all that bad?"

As she threaded her way through some underbrush, she nodded. "Yes. The area has always been dangerous, for at least the last thousand years. There are monster tribes that live in some areas, mostly along the edges."

"Wait, monster *tribes*?"

"Yes. They are not the wild monsters as you might think. They are the dunim, gnosta, frelst, wustol, and others. Intelligent monster races like the dunim you saw in the dungeon. In the past, there was more trade with them and the relationship between them, the elves, the humans, dwarves, and the beastkin was amiable, but that changed two decades ago."

"When the Sodality came to power?" I asked.

"Exactly. As with the rest of Tenos, the Aycrishi Sodality imposed their will on the monster tribes as well. They sent their armies into the Dreadlands, at least as far as the tribes were, and imposed their rule. Because of the previous relationship with the tribes, there was surprisingly little rebellion until the Sodality already had a foothold. They also knew where all the tribes lived, so none escaped the new reforms. Their men were taken, as they were in all other places of the world. Since then, relations with the monster tribes have been...difficult. It is more dangerous to approach even the closest of the monster villages now."

"I still don't understand how all of that could happen. How could one group take over the entire world and capture all their men like that?"

"It wasn't immediate. It took more than ten years, and that was after planning and preparing for years to build their troops. Tenos had known peace for a long time and most nations were unprepared for such an insidious attack. Part political, part military, it was an effective campaign. I believe most of it was due to the brilliance and sheer charisma of Imorith Sartyne, the Paragon. The leader of the Sodality. She and her allies convinced the largest population centers in Tenos that a new way was better than how things had been going. No longer would women be beholden to the corrupt men that ran many of the kingdoms and nations. Once a tipping point was reached, it was easy for the military to complete the conquest.

"But we were speaking of the Dreadlands and monsters. The monster tribes are but only a small part of the danger. The truly wild monsters are far more threatening than the civilized types."

"What type of monsters?"

Ysduil held a branch back and let me pass before she released it. I nodded my thanks.

"I'm not sure. The monster tribes might know more about what's in the deepest parts of the Dreadlands, but if they do, they don't share the information. Near the edges there are beasts of tooth and claw, some that can fly, and some familiar creatures that have somehow grown to extraordinary size. In my opinion, it's one of the things that's most dangerous about the Dreadlands: one never knows what they'll run into."

"Hmmm. Yeah, it's better if we stay at the edges so we don't run into the worst of them. All I have is this sword and I'm not even that good with it."

"At least we have an implement to cut things," the fox woman said with a bright smile. "Your blade will be helpful when it comes time to make camp or to obtain food. We will be traveling for several—"

A shout from behind us interrupted Ysduil and snatched my attention. We both spun toward the sound and saw half a dozen figures in Sodality armor. One of them pointed directly at us.

I clenched my fist on the hilt of the sword. "Damn. They spotted us. So much for slipping away quietly. What do we do now?"

Ysduil winked at me. "What do you think? We run."

So we ran. My beautiful companion moved effortlessly through the foliage, her tail bobbing as she sped away from where the soldiers had seen us. My bare feet didn't give me any trouble moving through the grasses and ferns for some reason. It confused me, actually. I'd always had sensitive feet.

Another thing that surprised me was that I kept up with Ysduil. I wasn't in horrible shape, but I wasn't fit in terms of running or other cardiovascular activities. Yet my breathing was regular and even despite our speed. Even my agility seemed heightened—I cleared obstacles as smoothly as a YouTube parkour streamer. Maybe it was the proverbial heightened strength people found in life-or-death situations.

It was strange.

I almost wished we'd stayed and fought. My borrowed pants were too tight, and besides restricting my movement in running and jumping, there were...other problems. After we'd outdistanced our pursuers and continued running, I pulled the cloth away from me and tried to adjust myself so the damn things wouldn't pinch so much.

Mid-adjustment, a dark flash ahead registered and I shouted, "Wait."

Ysduil slowed but didn't stop. Which threw the timing off for the man who burst into full view ahead of the fox woman. He was already swinging a sword, but her slowed pace caused his blade to pass in front of her instead of into her.

Ysduil slammed her left foot down hard to change direction. Toward her attacker. She left the ground momentarily and drove her right knee into the man's abdomen in a way that would have pleased any WWE fan. All the air left his body with a loud *oof*.

The bushes on either side of us exploded into motion and another man and a woman came at us with their own swords. Without really thinking about it, I flicked up my blade and deflected the attacker's weapon coming at me with a loud *ting*. Taking a page from Ysduil's book, I lunged forward and body-slammed my attacker before he could get his sword back around to me.

Ysduil did some kind of complex martial arts move that broke the woman's arm, twisted her around, and wrenched her head so violently her neck broke with a loud crack. By the time I slammed the pommel of my sword into the face of my downed opponent—breaking some teeth and maybe his nose, while knocking him unconscious— Ysduil had taken the sword from the woman whose neck she'd broken and run it through the first man who had attacked her.

We met eyes and then both scanned the area around us, silent except for our breathing. After half a minute without any evidence there were others around, Ysduil tossed the sword to the ground and relaxed.

"These aren't the ones we saw earlier," I said.

"No. They're not wearing the armor of the other soldiers. They wear leather coats and soft boots. Trackers or guides or the like. They do not look of a size for their clothes to be useful for you."

I nodded. Two of them looked like they were rat or mouse beastkin, while the other had ears and a tail like a dog, but all three were too small for me to use their clothes.

"Ah," my companion said, bending to pick something off the belt of one of the trackers she'd killed. She smiled as she lifted up a hatchet.

"What, that's the weapon you choose with three swords available? In fact..." I tossed my short sword down and grabbed one that was slightly longer and a bit wider. "This is closer to a real sword. That other thing is like a big knife."

Ysduil's musical laugh sounded. "No, silly. I can fight with a small axe such as this if I have to, but it is more useful to me in another way."

She scanned the area, spotted what she was looking for, and walked up to a tree. She scurried up it—flashing a completely unobstructed view of her underside as she did —and hacked at an abnormally straight branch about as tall as I was. When she swung down, she made short work of stripping off the twigs and leaves with the hatchet. A few final chops to lop off the thin, flexible end, and she dropped the hatchet to the ground.

"There," she said. "This is a proper weapon."

"A staff? Really?"

She showed me her smirk, then burst into motion, swinging the piece of wood and spinning it around her so quickly the area was filled with *whoom-whoom-whoom* as the wood cut the air. She stopped it instantly, so quickly that it quivered.

"Okay, okay. I take that back. We should probably bring the hatchet, though. If we're going to be traveling for days, we're going to want to cut wood for fires. It'll be a lot easier with that than with a sword."

"Good point."

We looked at each other, waiting. I finally bent over and picked up the weapon. "I guess I'll carry it."

She giggled and we continued on our way.

CHAPTER

TWELVE

Though we angled away from where we'd been heading, another trio of Sodality thugs found us several minutes later. Again, we responded quickly enough that we weren't injured, though part of that was our heightened alertness because of the first group. This time, my fight lasted longer because I didn't react fast enough to surprise my attacker. Though Ysduil made short work of her opponent with her new weapon, the third person—a squirrel or weasel type that reminded me of Kelena—disappeared into the brush.

"There is no point in chasing her," Ysduil said. "An amustil will easily outrun us in this type of terrain. Unfortunately, she will report that she has seen us. The others will know where we've gone and they will not give up soon."

I grunted my understanding, but I was thinking about other things.

"Ysduil, is there magic in Tenos?"

The fox woman stopped and turned toward me, head tilted. "Why do you ask?"

"It's something I've been thinking of. The way that weasel woman disappeared like it was magic reminded me. But also, it feels like I'm...enhanced. Like physically, I'm better than I was."

"You posited before that it was because of gravity."

"Yeah, but that can't be it. I mean, it could be the reason I can do more pushups, lift more, even that I can jump higher or move a little faster. But when I punched Kelena, I hit her hard. I mean, really hard. Like if I would have used my full strength, I think I might have crushed her skull. Plus, my feet are tougher, I don't get out of breath, and overall, I feel more solid and competent, through no effort or training of my own."

"Oh. To answer your question, yes and no. There has always been magic in the world. Our stories and histories tell us of ones who could use it. But a strange thing happened. Magic started waning. It has almost completely disappeared."

"Don't tell me. It started around twenty years ago."

"Yes. Odona has not told us the reason, but many of my sister priestesses have spoken of it. We believe that once the men were changed, no longer able to think or have real motivation, it affected the world. Without wizards and mages to use the magic, the balance of the world was upset. Because the world, the universe, always strives for balance, the amount of available magic for women was drastically reduced when men stopped using it.

"It has not completely disappeared, but women who used to be powerful witches and mages have lost much of their power. Were it not for beasts and monsters that utilize magic, some believe that Tenos would have suppressed magic altogether. So, yes there is—or more correctly, was—magic in the world, but now there is very little and many people in our current time have never witnessed the true use of arcane power."

"Huh," I said. That didn't necessarily prove or disprove my theory, but it was interesting. I could barely imagine real magic in the world. The existence of monsters and beastkin—both the strange and ugly ones and the hot and sexy ones like Ysduil and Kelena—was hard enough to accept, but magic? I was definitely not in Tennessee anymore.

"Come," she said, not realizing what it did to my mind, and other parts of me, when that word passed her lips. "They will be after us. We must continue."

We gradually worked our way through patches of trees, areas with heavy bushes, even a section that was a tangle of thorns and thistles, while gradually going upward. When we stopped long enough for me to pick stickers out of my pants—and my skin—I looked back toward where we'd come from.

The view was spectacular. Ysduil said the Dreadlands was a dangerous area—which I hadn't really seen yet, except for having to fight Sodality soldiers—but it was undeniably beautiful. From my vantage point, I could not only see the green of tree boughs for miles, but at the edge of all that wilderness, the fortress stood out like a dark, brooding beacon. On the other side, there was more green, but of a different hue and peppered with flashes of sunlight on water. That must have been the swamp Ysduil mentioned before. The one where the sunken ruins lay.

The place where they found me.

My heart ached that it was within sight but so far out of reach. If I could just get back to where I appeared, maybe I could go back. Back home.

"Down," Ysduil said, squatting down.

I dropped and followed her finger that was pointing down the incline. There, stringing its way through the trees, was a large group of people.

People with the dark Sodality armor and uniforms.

"Shit." I crouched behind the leaves of a large bush. "Did they see us?"

The sound of raised voices echoed from down below. I moved a branch out of my way so I could peer through the foliage without being seen. Two of the larger figures, wearing the familiar armor of the dungeon guards, pointed up at us. Well, I guess that answered my question.

Ysduil looked around us, narrowing her eyes at the sloping land above and then swinging her head to take in other possible locations for us to go. I saw right away what brought the frown to her lips. Upward, the vegetation became progressively thinner. While that was good as far as being able to move through it, it would also expose us to those following us. She looked at me with a little furrow forming on her forehead.

It was somehow incredibly sexy. I shook my head to cast the thought from my mind. *Not the time, Adam.*

"I don't think we should continue upward," she told me. "They only know our general location now, but they will be expecting us to climb further. Watching for us. If we do what they do not expect, such as going across or downward, we may be able to lose them."

"Could we make it up to the top and go down the other side before they got to us?"

She squinted up again, calculating. "Possibly, but we will be chancing that the land beyond is even more conducive to them spotting and catching us. With them above us, if we don't find cover, they may shoot arrows down at us. Not an ideal situation."

I considered it for only a moment. "You're right. Let's go where they won't expect us. Do you have a suggestion?"

Her smile lit up her pretty face. Her furry ears even twitched a bit as she did it. "I do. Follow me."

"Always," I said, but not too loudly.

"What was that?"

"I...uh. Of course. Go ahead."

An inscrutable look crossed her face and her eyes twinkled, but then she turned and headed down what looked like the remains of an animal trail that hadn't been used lately. It was only a faint path, but one that would make our travel a little easier.

We zigzagged across the face of the hill, always blocked from view of anyone below us, and then headed down again. I mourned over the time and energy we'd spent in climbing to begin with, but surprisingly, I wasn't that tired. I'd have expected my legs and lungs to be burning, but they weren't. Instead, I felt energized, like I'd had a good warmup and was ready to work out now. It was crazy.

Ysduil dove at the ground, and her sudden movement prompted me to drop likewise. She grunted as a flash of... something went by my head.

"Arrow," she whispered. "Get ready."

I crawled closer to her on my belly, my sword in my hand. Believe me, it wasn't comfortable, with my pants feeling like they were cutting off the circulation to important bits down there and twigs digging into my bare chest.

No sooner had I gotten almost to her feet—glancing up and catching an eyeful underneath the ragged hem of her dress—than she leaped up and sprinted through the bush, moving unpredictably, juking this way and that. It was impressive as hell, but when the arrows started coming, it didn't entertain me as much.

I wanted to come to my feet as well, but there was no way I could move the way she was, dodging the arrows. I did notice that the shafts only came about once every two seconds or so. It was probably only one archer.

A sound like a branch splintering against a concrete sidewalk reached me and I poked my head up. It took a second to spot Ysduil. She was spinning her staff and squared off against a woman with a sword. Near her, I saw part of a boot. Without hesitation, I took off running, one arm up to protect my face from the swishing branches.

By the time I got to her, she had slammed her staff into her attacker's hand, disarming her, then spun around, took the feet right out from under the woman, and cracked the hard wood of her weapon across her foe's head as she went down. The woman—another beastkin by the patches of fur I saw—bounced against the grass-covered ground and then came to rest.

I scanned the area while Ysduil made sure her two victims were both down for the count.

"Any more?" I asked, still looking around us.

"No. Just the two."

I stepped closer to the figure that was wearing the boot, but he was another rodent-type beastkin. Too small for me to use his clothes or his boots. Damn it.

The woman was shapely, with tight leather clothing of the style the first trackers we saw wore. Her clothes obviously wouldn't fit me, either.

"Why is it so hard for me to find clothes I can wear without cutting off my circulation?"

Ysduil gave me her sexy, mischievous smile as she ran her eyes across my torso and tightly covered crotch, then shrugged. "The larger men are used as guards, whereas the smaller make better scouts. Not only is their type more adept at such things, but they can move more easily through congested foliage."

"Yeah, yeah. Well, I'm taking his bow and arrows. I'm not a great shot, but if we're going to need to eat, it might come in handy." I thought about it while I took the weapon and slipped the quiver off the unconscious beastkin. "That reminds me. I haven't seen anything but the few pursuers we've found. No animals, no monsters, nothing. I thought you said it was dangerous in here."

"I'm not sure why we haven't seen any wildlife. At the edges, there aren't as many monsters. Maybe the beasts are wary of so many people tramping around. Do you doubt that the Dreadlands is dangerous?"

"No," I said. "If you say it is, I believe you. I was just wondering."

She clicked her tongue. "Aww, that's too bad."

"What is?"

"I was hoping you would say you are not concerned with the monsters in the Dreadlands."

"Why?"

"Because it's clear: we will not be able to skirt the edges. The soldiers already have too much of a presence. If we play it safe, they will trap us. We need to head deeper into the Dreadlands. It's the only way to keep them from following us until we make a mistake and are caught or killed."

I blew out a breath. "Fine. Thanks for trying it my way. You knew from the beginning we were going to have to go that way, huh?"

"Not knew, but suspected."

With a final look at the two newest casualties of our little cat and mouse game—no reference to the beastkin types intended—I waved the bow at her. "Lead on. I trust you. Into the lion's den."

For some reason, she barked a laugh, as if that was the funniest thing she'd heard in weeks. I was too afraid to ask her why.

CHAPTER

THIRTEEN

Once we got down to flatter land, I followed Ysduil as she headed directly away from where we had entered the edges of the Dreadlands, due east. Almost immediately, the foliage grew denser and our passage became rougher. I looked back toward where I knew the fortress and the swamp with the sunken ruins were. The branches we'd moved aside and the grasses we'd trampled had closed up. It was as if the land had swallowed us whole.

Fifteen minutes later, I stumbled. A weight pressed down on me, like gravity had doubled for a moment.

"Wow," I commented.

"What is it?"

"That feeling as we crossed whatever boundary we just passed through."

Ysduil turned to look at me. "Boundary? Feeling? What are you talking about?"

"A few steps ago. Over there." I pointed to where I'd felt the sensation. "I felt a pressure on me, like I'd crossed an invisible line. Now it feels kind of like swimming deep underwater. Or kind of like the feeling when someone is watching you. I can't really explain it."

"I felt nothing," she said.

"Oh. Maybe I'm just freaking out because we're being hunted or it could be a change in the sounds..." I realized then that the sounds *had* changed. Rather, they'd mostly stopped. No birdcalls or squeaks or cries from other animals. All I heard was quiet rustling in the brush, like rodents scurrying around. Small, normal animals, not the beastkin chasing us.

Ysduil continued to look at me skeptically, then gave me a cute little half-shrug that shifted her tight, almost see-through dress in tantalizing ways. "Perhaps. We will be leaving the edge area soon, so you may detect more movements and sounds. Remain alert. Danger may come from anywhere."

I wasn't thrilled she didn't seem to take my paranoid feelings seriously, but then again, she was more experienced in these things.

For several hours, we traversed the wilderness. We passed over thinner patches of vegetation in which I spotted grey or brown bodies scampering from bush to bush. I never did get a full view of any of the things, but they didn't bother us, so it was all good as far as I was concerned. We found two streams as well, which we used to drink our fill since we didn't have any water containers.

I realized as I lay on the bank of one of the streams, splashing water onto my face before cupping my palm to use as a cup to drink, that I hadn't seen any canteens or skins or anything similarly useful on the Sodality scouts we'd encountered.

"Why didn't those scouts have any food or water with them?" I asked.

Ysduil, kneeling next to me to splash her own face, tilted her head at me. "I don't know. Maybe because they didn't think they would go far into the forest. Our pursuers probably thought it improbable that we would go deeper into the Dreadlands without proper provisions, so they focused on the edges. That is to our benefit. Perhaps it will delay their pursuit, or even prevent them completely from following us. It's what I hoped."

"Huh. It's going to make things tougher for us, though, not having a way to carry water."

"I believe it will be fine. From what I've seen and heard of the Dreadlands, it is lush and has many water sources. Like these." She splashed water at me and I closed my eyes and put my head back to enjoy the coolness.

She laughed and got up, putting a hand out to help me to my feet. Her hand was so soft, but it was strong, too. I may have held onto it a little too long, enjoying the way it felt in mine. She squeezed my hand quickly and I took it as a nudge to release hers.

"We have maybe four or five hours of daylight left," she said as she squinted through the tree cover at the sun that was already working its way down behind us. "I've not seen any sign of the Sodality lately, which is a good thing."

"Hopefully they've given up," I said. "Better if we can focus on the dangers ahead of us rather than being trapped in between two."

Several hours later, we emerged from a heavily forested area into one with mazes of rock formations. Trees filled the areas between the stone monoliths, but the passage wasn't that difficult because of the lack of the heavy undergrowth we'd been stomping through. When the light began to dim from afternoon to evening, we found an ideal place to set up camp.

The spot was at a junction of several different stone structures that looked like they might have been worked at one point as walls. The ten-foot by fifteen-foot space gave us enough room to move around. It featured two openings to go in or out, but the rocks were eight to ten feet high and would effectively block firelight from being seen from outside the little pen.

Ysduil browsed through some of the bushes nearby and began to pick leaves and berries. She also used a sharp rock she found to dig up some roots.

"Many of these are edible," she said.

"I'm so glad you're here," I told her. "I always wanted to learn about identifying edible plants, but I never got around to it. It's probably just as well because they're probably different here than in my world."

"I can find enough that we won't starve. Gather some wood for a fire?"

"Sure. I can do that. Let's not get too far from each other, though. We haven't seen anyone chasing us for half a day, but that doesn't necessarily mean they gave up."

She smirked at me and her left ear twitched. "I won't go far."

There was plenty of wood nearby, slender and thicker branches that had fallen, even a couple of small trees that had come down. It all seemed pretty dry, so I guessed we wouldn't have a problem starting a fire even if we couldn't find any flint to use. What I would have given for some matches or a lighter...

A heavy thud and what sounded like a feminine grunt caught my attention. I dropped the wood I was gathering and ran toward Ysduil. When I rounded the rock that blocked my view, I spotted loose plants scattered all over and a large greyish-brown thing wriggling on top of what I recognized as the fox woman's legs. No, that wasn't right. *Part* of something was on top of Ysduil's legs, just a section of the larger thing poking out from the rocks.

I sprinted up to the thing, sword in one hand and the hatchet in the other and tried to make sense of what I was seeing. As the shape writhed and exposed more of itself, it finally registered. The long, tubular body was a portion of either a giant worm or a massive snake. Since I couldn't see segmentations on the body, I figured that meant it was a snake.

"Ysduil?" I shouted.

The head of the monster emerged from behind a rock, and swung around to look at me, tongue flicking out to taste the air.

Yep, a snake. A huge, fifteen-foot long and more than a foot-wide snake.

"Mmf, unhffmmmgggg," the muffled voice said.

My eyes felt big enough to pop and my heart raced like a trip hammer. Ysduil was underneath the thing, probably suffocating just from its weight. It didn't look like it had coiled around her yet, though, so at least that was good.

It took me a second to figure out how I could help without hurting my companion. I finally settled on the sword.

I flicked the blade out, teasing the creature with it. Its head followed me, jerking like it was going to strike, but it never did. I was no expert on snakes, but with the rounded head on the thing, I figured it was probably non-venomous, probably some kind of constrictor. If that even worked the same here. One thing was clear: the damn thing was huge.

Best to be cautious.

With a few feints with my sword, I lured the monster to extend its neck so the head was close enough for me to lash out at it without hitting Ysduil. It hissed when I cut into its scales, though I didn't see a lot of damage. It was getting good and pissed off, though, which may or may not have been helping Ysduil.

Her legs barely moved, which was all kinds of bad. I needed to up my game.

I danced around, jabbing at the snake and juking left and right to force it to move to keep its focus on me. I lifted my arm to slash at it again when it tired of the game and lunged at me.

The quick motion surprised me, but my reflexes were better than they'd ever been. I sidestepped, dropped my sword, and grabbed it around the head with no conscious decision to do that. I don't know why my body didn't decide to cut into it with the weapon I had, but I now had a good grip around the thing's head. The majority of its body undulated and came at me like a length of battle rope, relieving some of the weight off Ysduil.

That part was taken care of, but it was the classic parable about riding a tiger. I had a hold on it and I was relatively safe until it coiled around me, but I couldn't let go without it striking and really doing some damage to me.

"Ungh!" I spread my feet to a wider, more stable stance while squeezing its head in my arms, almost like a head-lock. I glanced around and saw my hatchet, eight or so feet away, and my sword a couple of feet away on the ground. Slowly, I shuffled my feet and inched my way toward the sword. Meanwhile, the thick snake body, as big around as my thigh, did its best to wrap around me, starting with my left leg.

I was pleased to see more of Ysduil, and even more ecstatic to see her move a little, taking deep breaths now that she could.

When I reached my sword, I swept at it with my foot, trying to bring it closer. There was still the problem of getting it into my hand, though. I hoped Ysduil would recuperate quickly enough to grab it, but that didn't look like that was happening anytime soon. I was going to have to take a chance.

Once the sword was where I wanted it, I shifted my arms to hug the massive snake head to my chest more with my left arm than my right. The beast violently swung its head to get free, but I managed to hold on. I could hold it with one arm if it wasn't trying to shake me off, but if it surged, it would tear free. Its coils moved up my leg and started to wrap my waist.

I had to be fast.

I squeezed the head even harder and moved my torso to irritate it. The technique worked; it slammed its head around, trying to break free. It almost succeeded, but I clamped on long enough that it relaxed for a moment, no doubt getting ready to try another burst of energy.

I let go with my right arm so I was holding it with my left, squatted down, and reached for my sword. The mass and pure musculature of the snake stopped my squat with my fingers an inch from the hilt.

Shit.

The monster whipped its body, seeing its chance, and the head came free from my arm. I almost fell as I overcompensated and slammed my fist hard into the ground next to the sword hilt.

"Grrraaaugh!" That fucking hurt. I forced myself to snatch the sword up, my injured hand complaining at its treatment and, without really looking, I swung the sword as hard as I could.

It slammed into the side of the thing's face as it was

striking out at me. The blade was turned a little, so I didn't give it a clean or deep cut, but I did knock it away from my face. The sword stuck for a second and was almost ripped from my hand, but I kept hold of it. Barely.

The monster hissed and swung its head back for another try. The scales kept me from cutting deeply with a slash, so I swung my arm wide, flexing my wrist while aiming the sword as best I could. This time, I was fast and accurate enough to do more damage.

The tip of the weapon punched into the snake's head behind the eye. It didn't quite go all the way through, but the thick body started convulsing. I was thankful that Ysduil wasn't under it anymore. She'd rolled away, and the snake and I had moved anyway.

I pulled my blade out and stepped back, watching it for a few seconds. When I figured I had its timing down, I lunged in again and speared the massive reptile's head with all my weight and strength behind the strike. The sword punched down through the top of its head, all the way through and into the ground. I held it there for a good half minute while the body whipped around, nearly knocking me down a couple of times.

Finally, the thing stopped moving and I realized just how long the fucking thing was. It was more than twice the length of my own body.

I looked around for any friends or family it might have brought with it, but there was no sign of any other danger.

A slight wheezing from behind me was followed by Ysduil clearing her throat.

"Ugh. Thank you for rescuing me, Adam." I turned to watch her running her eyes over the snake's body. "Please hand me your hatchet. This will make a fine meal."

CHAPTER

FOURTEEN

My knowledgeable—and durable—companion made surprisingly short work of opening up the snake—after I helped her move it well away from our campsite—and removing more meat than we'd be able to eat.

"Are you okay?" I asked.

"Yes. It dropped on me, knocking me down, and with a good portion of its body on me, it was difficult to breathe. I don't think I suffered any serious injuries. Thank you again for saving me."

I smiled at her. "You're welcome. You've already saved me several times, so I still owe you."

"You owe me nothing. I do not take account of such things."

Her tone was so serious, I was afraid I'd insulted her. Until I looked up from placing the wood for the fire. She was beaming at me, that mischievous smile wide and gorgeous. Her left ear twitched twice and I wondered what her ears felt like. *I bet they're soft.*

"Some of the plants I saw can be used as herbs as well,

so I can season the meat. Snake is not my favorite thing to eat, but it should be passable."

"You've eaten wild snake before?"

She laughed. "Of course. I travel a lot as a priestess of Odona. Even more so since the Sodality has been more intent on executing all of us. I am proficient in many survival skills."

"I believe it."

"There." She rubbed her hands together and stood. The meat was in a hollowed-out piece of wood she'd found somewhere, the herbs beneath and on top of it. "I will let the food absorb some of the flavor and we can cook it later. It will be dark in less than an hour. We can wait to light the fire until then, I think."

"Sounds good to me. Thank you for preparing that."

"Of course." Her eyes darted to mine, then to the ground, then to her hands, which she was wringing in front of her. "I have to...go and do something. I will be back shortly." She picked up her staff and moved toward one of the openings in the rocks.

"Are you going to do your...umm, nightly ritual?"

The fox woman froze, then turned around slowly. Her face was flushed. I hadn't meant to embarrass her.

"My...ritual?"

I almost said never mind, but I was going to have to ask about it sometime. It might as well be now.

"Yes. I noticed that you...uh, did something each night when we were in the cells. Is that what you're going to do?"

If anything, her cheeks reddened even more. She didn't have her ubiquitous smirk now. Her mouth twisted as she chewed her inner lip, almost like she had eaten something that didn't agree with her.

"I'm sorry. I hope I didn't embarrass you or disgust you.

I try very hard to be polite to others and to be considerate and not annoy or pester them. I tried to be subdued, but if you are mad at me, I understand. I just—"

"Whoa. Stop. Ysduil, you did not embarrass, disgust, or both—well, you might have bothered me a little bit, but in a good way. In a *very* good way." My mind replayed the sounds I'd heard each night and the little movies I imagined to go with them. I had to shake my head and strain to focus. "It seems like something you do every day. Will you tell me about it?"

She took more of her bottom lip into her teeth. She didn't look as uncomfortable now. Just super fucking sexy. She even turned one of her knees in with a shy gesture.

"You want me to tell you about my...my ritual?"

"Yes, please. Sit down. Tell me about it so I'll understand. After you do that, if you want to go somewhere else and do what you need to do, I won't stop you."

She took a flat stone that was almost the height of a chair and sat with such grace, even in her ragged remnants of her priestess garb, I could imagine her as a princess or a queen. The queen of the foxes.

"You must understand, Adam, what things are like here in Tenos with the Sodality. I don't know what it is like in your world—"

"I'll tell you all about it," I said. "Anytime you want."

"Truly?" her orange-red eyes lit up in the most adorable way. She cleared her throat. "I would like that very much. As I was saying, though, things are difficult here. The Sodality sees many things as unnecessary, even wrong. Much of what is important to me as a priestess is detestable to devout followers of the Sodality doctrine. Even those who are not as zealous as others do not appreciate my beliefs.

"I am a priestess of Odona, and to my goddess there is nothing higher than the pleasure and value of the procreative acts. Not just for the intended purpose, either. The act, the philosophy, the physiology of intimacy is sacred. As such, one of our core tenets is that we must seek physical pleasure every single day. Carnal pleasure."

She had turned her head slightly away from me and now she looked at me from the side of her eyes, as if she wanted to see my reaction, but was also afraid to look.

"That sounds awesome."

"Awesome? Is that...good?"

"Yes, actually. So good that it inspires awe, thus the term."

"Oh." She giggled. "Yes, I see it. Umm, where was I? Oh, yes. We must seek pleasure every day. In the past, that meant usually with others, most often men. Before the Sodality. Now it is with women, though for some even back then, women were preferred. Failing to secure a partner, we...ah...self-pleasure."

"You masturbate."

She dipped her head. "Yes."

"That's perfectly reasonable, and to be honest, what I figured those noises meant."

"I am sorry, Adam. I—"

"Ysduil! Please stop saying that. Don't be sorry. I think it's a fine requirement. A very good one, in fact. I'm sure it helps to reduce tension and, hell, it's just fun. It was amazing to listen to you. I loved every minute, even if it did...uh, cause some tension to build up within me. Good tension. Desire."

"Desire?" She leaned toward me, giving me an even better view of the slopes of her breasts. My pants immediately grew tighter. Somehow. "You enjoyed hearing me, even subdued as it was?"

Subdued? God, I needed to change the subject. I answered as succinctly as I could. "Yes."

"Then it does not bother you that I pleasure myself?"

"Not at all. It turns me on."

"Turns you on?"

"Yeah. Excites me. *Arouses* me."

"Mmmm." The way she said it sent jolts through my nether regions.

"Can I ask something?" I asked. "You don't have to answer, but I'm curious."

"Of course. What is it?"

"Your tenets, do they require that you...umm, finish?"

"That I complete the circle? Climax? Orgasm?"

"Yeah."

"No. That isn't required. Many women, even priestesses of Odona, do not *finish* every time, even in sex with others. I have met sisters that have been in service for many years who have *never* had an orgasm."

"Oh, that's kind of sad."

"I think so, too. As for me, I climax every single time. With partners or without. I am reckoned as being fairly skilled, from both sides of the encounter."

I was not going to drill down into that, so to speak. Well, not precisely anyway. "That's with men and women both?"

She tilted her head at me, confusion on her face. "No. I was barely three years old when the Sodality came into power. I have only ever seen a few men in my life, before I was interned in the dungeon where I met you. I have never been with a man. You are a mystery to me. I have read the books and scrolls, but have no practical experience. If I can be honest with you, Adam, you intimidate me. I am unsure how to act with you, thus my fear I might have insulted or disgusted you."

"You could never do that, Ysduil. Don't worry about that. Thank you for sharing all that with me. Now I understand better. You don't need to go away to perform your daily activity. Stay here, and I'll go around one of those big rocks so you won't have to be embarrassed by me being here when you're doing what you do."

"You do not want to hear me or watch me?"

A slight hissing moan escaped my lips. I shifted a little to try to relieve some discomfort. My dick was bent and the pressure was getting painful as it tried to swell to its full size.

"I would like nothing more, but I'll go if it makes you uncomfortable."

"I am very comfortable with my pleasuring activities. I would like you to stay and watch if you desire."

"I do desire, Ysduil. I truly do."

CHAPTER

FIFTEEN

My blood was already pumping pretty hard. Especially in the lower part of my body. If I spoke anymore, it would come out breathy and probably creepy, so I merely sat down on another rock a dozen feet away from her.

At least, I tried to sit down. The pain from my member, which was bent in half still, was too much to complete the action. Halfway down, I had to stand up again. Looking over at Ysduil, I found her watching me, so I couldn't hide what I was going to do next. I thought of turning around, but it would still be obvious.

I sighed a little bit and tried to inconspicuously nudge myself straight. It didn't quite work. I ended up having to grab hold of my cock through the tight pants and shift it to remove the bend. I exhaled in relief and met the fox woman's eyes as my cheeks burst into flames.

Her left ear twitched and her dark pink tongue flicked across her lips. She stared at my crotch for a moment and I thought for sure she would say something, but instead she prepared for the sacred ritual for her goddess.

The whole thing confused me, to be honest. I mean, she was the priestess of a sex goddess, one who required her to obtain sexual pleasure every single day. Yet she'd never made any overt moves or suggested that I help her with the chore. She came every day, and she climaxed every time she was with a woman. Did that mean she didn't like men? Ysduil admitted she'd never really been physically close to one. Before me. We'd been together for an entire day. Granted, we were running for our lives and fighting, but still, I couldn't make sense of her.

She was preparing to pleasure herself, right in front of me, but she seemed never to have thought about letting me pleasure her. Was she not attracted to me at all or was there some other problem? The look she'd just given me didn't indicate she was disinterested.

I was probably overthinking it all, especially since the super-hot fox woman was getting comfortable in front of me, settling onto her stone seat and primly rearranging her dress as if it were a pristine gown instead of a torn and dirty dress with more than half its material missing.

Enough thinking. I promised myself I was going to enjoy the show and stop analyzing.

The dress fit her so perfectly. I tried to imagine what it looked like whole. The top V of the garment framed the swells of her breasts so perfectly it was hard to take my eyes off them. In fact, torn as it was, the V was more like a squashed U, letting me see not only her cleavage, but the tops of her bust as well. It was so tight that her areolas were visible as shadowy circles, and her nipples showed clearly as bumps in the fabric. Bumps that grew before my eyes as they became more rigid. The dress hugged her slim waist like she had been born with it on, and that perfect blend of tightness continued down to the top part of her thighs, showing me every little curve.

Sitting as she was, legs slightly apart, I could barely see into the darkened area between her legs, enough to see the silhouette of her toned thighs. Not enough to actually see skin, but as she shifted, little flashes of what might have been part of her teased and tantalized me.

Ysduil slipped a hand under the dress by her shoulder and rubbed it across the very top of one breast. Then, with a delicate motion, she pushed the cloth over her shoulder, letting it go slack. Her left globe moved a fraction of an inch as the clothing holding it up disappeared, but no more than that. She repeated the action with the other side, pulling the cloth down to her taut belly and letting her breasts bounce free.

And fantastic breasts they were. Not huge, but more than enough to grab onto, they were perky and had moderate areolas of a color that made me think of expensive milk chocolate, smooth and delicious. Standing out at the centers were her swollen nipples. I licked my lips and she smiled at my response.

Her left hand raised up, her fingers running lightly over her collar bone and down the outer edge of her perky tit, then circling up the inside. For a few seconds, she orbited her nipple, gradually spiraling inward. I watched it tighten. She grabbed it between a finger and thumb and pulled gently, letting out a soft sigh that made me anything but soft.

When she licked her finger and rubbed it across and around her nipple, she tilted her head back and narrowed her eyes, a slight moan rumbling in her throat.

I had to force myself to blink. My eyes were drying out because I hadn't wanted to miss a fraction of a second of her ministrations. With her eyes still slitted, she looked over at me. I'm guessing she liked what she saw in my eyes because she moaned a little louder as she rubbed her entire hand across her chest and grabbed a handful of her flesh, kneading it and swaying her body.

Ysduil's eyes drilled into me, and a wry smile stole onto her face. It said that she knew a secret that I didn't, and that she would use that secret to share her pleasure with me.

Her legs opened a little more as she continued to work her chest. Her other hand slithered down her belly, stopping to lightly trace circles delicately near her navel. The cloth was thin enough that I could almost feel the sensation of skin against skin as she played her hand across her abdomen, inching downward.

Painfully slow, her fingers found the hem of her dress and lifted it, like a peek-a-boo show. Switching her top hand to her other breast, she used the lower to flip the cloth up to reveal her treasure.

The reddish hair was pretty neatly trimmed for having been in a dungeon cell for several days. It matched her hair, ears, and tail perfectly and looked delicious. Her hand worked down the inside of her thigh and she spread her legs a little wider, giving me a better look at her glistening slit in the evening light. I had to lick my lips again, and swallow, because my mouth had gone dry, too. She gave me another knowing look, then dropped her dress back down to cover what her hand was doing.

My dick throbbed at her teasing.

She left off playing with her tits and ran her hand down to her belly, down her thigh, and up again to pull her dress up once more as the other hand continued to creep more slowly toward her waiting pussy. When it finally reached the goal, she barely touched the outer lips, soft as a butterfly's wings, and threw her head back again with a hissing breath.

Ysduil teased herself, rubbing lightly on her lips and up to where her hooded button was, but didn't spend any time on her clit. Not yet. The heat in her half-closed eyes, her flushed cheeks, and her breathless sounds continued to build.

As she dipped the tiniest edge of her finger in between her lips and ran it up to massage the fleshy covering of her clit, her eyes rolled and a husky groan emanated from her.

Then she started the complex circles, pets, flicks, and massages on her clit. The hood retracted and I saw the nub of her pleasure, wiggling under the movements of her fingers. She looked me right in the eye as she took her lower lip into her teeth.

Ysduil breathed more heavily now. It quickened as she scrubbed more and more frantically on her clit, while the other hand caressed up and down her belly. The tempo built, as did the volume of her sounds, and she wriggled her body to maintain the perfect angle for her pleasure.

"Oh, oooh, oooooh."

She licked her lips, gasping as she did it, which only heightened my arousal. My cock hurt so much at this point, I almost put my hand down to open up the tight pants to set it free, but I was afraid if I accidentally touched it, I'd explode.

Her hips bucked as she rubbed faster and faster and then, just like that, she stopped.

I found I was holding my breath, waiting to see what would happen. I didn't have to look to know that pre-cum was dripping from the tip of my dick, seeping into my stolen pants.

After three seconds of silence and stillness, Ysduil, in a

quick, practiced movement, curled her first two fingers and made them disappear into her pussy.

It was like a starter's pistol.

"Yes. Oooh, yes. Uh-uh-uh..."

While she worked her fingers inside herself, she pressed down on the area below her belly with the other hand, like she was increasing the pressure inside her, pushing from both sides. The slight thump of her shapely ass on the stone seat mixed with the wet, slushing sound of her fingers sliding up into her glistening slit.

Every second brought a more frantic pace and the graceful curves of her body moved in a perfect balance of agility and pure, animal passion. She continued for a handful of seconds, working...working.

"Uh-uh-uh-uh-oooooh."

With a final powerful thrust of her hips, she froze again for a tiny, perfect, silent moment, in which she held her breath.

"Aaaaaaahhhh."

Ysduil's entire body relaxed and she sucked in a huge breath. Looking over at me, her forehead damp with perspiration, she brought her hand up to her face, twitched her nose to smell it, then licked her fingers.

I closed my eyes and shuddered, wanting so badly to close the few feet between us. I found myself breathing hard and, as I opened my eyes again, found her looking right into them with a wicked smile on her face.

"Did you like that?" she asked.

"God, yes. I—" I stood up, ready to go to her. Her eyes widened slightly.

A loud roar somewhere close shattered the relative silence.

What the fuck was that?

That was enough to break the spell.

Ysduil's face flashed disappointment, but she smoothed it away quickly. "We need to start a fire. Some of the denizens of the Dreadlands hunt at night. It will help keep them away."

She adjusted her dress to cover herself again and a profound sense of longing sprouted in me.

"Of course," I said, more than a little disappointed. "I've got the wood." I paused for a moment when it occurred to me what I'd said. "Uh, let me see if I can get a fire started."

I imagined slapping my dick along the side of the sword. At this point, I was pretty sure it would send out enough sparks to get a fire going.

CHAPTER
SIXTEEN

Ysduil took her staff and disappeared around one of the boulders sheltering us while I arranged the wood and the dried detritus and kindling I'd gathered. I tried sparking off my sword with several types of rocks I'd found, but finally realized I'd never start a fire that way.

As I worked, my companion came and went, sometimes bringing more wood and at others just checking in before going out to scout a little bit. It made me uncomfortable that she was out there alone, but I'd seen her fight and she was no easy prey for beast or pursuer.

Shifting to the old method of using a stick to cause friction to start a fire, I wondered about what had happened earlier. It almost seemed like Ysduil had used me to get off, some kind of mental exhibitionist fuel, but I rejected the idea immediately. She'd proven what kind of person she was, and if it weren't for whatever monster out there roaring, the look on her face moments before said she would have happily helped me to relieve my sexual tension.

Still, she did have a strange way of keeping apart and not giving me more overt signals she wanted me. For a priestess of a sex goddess, anyway. I mean, she'd given me flirty looks and seemed to enjoy gazing at me…and specifically certain parts of me. Maybe her religion specified that the man was to take the lead. I'd hesitated—I was new in this world and didn't know its customs. I didn't want to push away or insult my only friend. I definitely didn't want her to think I was trying to take advantage of her. In the exact situation in my own world, I would have made a move, but I was out of my depth here.

Did that make me a pussy? Some guys would say so. Of course, a lot of those guys would also roofie a girl, or at least get her drunk to get into her pants. Assholes.

I'd have to talk to her. If it wouldn't be ill-mannered, I would totally go for it. Then I chuckled. I'd just watched her bring herself to climax while I greedily watched every second of it. And I was afraid of making *her* uncomfortable? Ridiculous. What the hell was I doing?

"What are you thinking about?" she said, noticing my smile. I hadn't even realized she'd returned.

"Oh, just silly things. My mind is kind of wandering while I try to get this damn fire started."

She cocked her head in that adorable way she had and those sexy lips curved into her trickster smile. "I've searched around and couldn't find what made the noise. We'll need to keep the fire going and take turns standing watch so we don't get surprised in our sleep. Do you need help with anything?"

My mind went straight to what I'd observed earlier and my desire kindled again. I pushed the thought away, though. We had survival things to think about, and even if ravishing that tempting body of hers *seemed* like life or death, it really wasn't.

"No, I think I—" A little curl of smoke wafted up from the stick I'd been rotating with the strip of cloth I'd cut off the bottom of my already too-short pants. I put some of the crumbled dry leaves on the little bowl in the larger piece of wood I was using as a base, but got no flame. "Aww. Almost."

The fox woman set her staff aside and moved closer to me, kneeling down over the tools I was using to try to start the fire. The soft curve of her shoulder against my chest made me start thinking about our earlier activities all over again. She moved her hair over the other shoulder and as she got into position to help, one of her ears tickled my face.

She smelled of exertion, both perspiration and a slight hint of sex, left over from before. On top of that was a slightly musky smell, with a hint of citrus. It didn't quite match any woman I'd been with, but it was intoxicating and reminiscent of past lovers. I couldn't help but to wonder if she tasted as good as she smelled.

"Oh, sorry," she said when she realized she'd grazed me.

"No, don't be sorry. Your ears seem very soft. I don't mind at all."

"You like them?"

That left ear twitched a little bit and I reached toward it before stopping myself. "Yes. People in my world don't have furry ears. Or tails."

"Really? Are there no beastkin at all?"

"Nope, none. There are myths but none of them are based in truth."

She twisted so her orange-red eyes met mine. "Myths? Like what?"

"Well, for one, there are legends of what are called

kitsune. They are basically fox beastkin, but they're magical and powerful. Do you...uh, grow more than one tail?"

"What? Why would you ask that?"

"In the kitsune stories, the more powerful they get, the more tails they grow. If you encounter one with nine tails, you know that she—or he, I guess—is extremely powerful. I just wondered if it was the same here."

Ysduil's rolling laughter sucked all the tension from me, instantly relaxing my entire body. It also did marvelous things to her chest and twitched the muscles in her abdomen. "That's ridiculous and very humorous. No, we do not grow more than one tail. That would be inconvenient and unseemly."

I laughed along with her, feeling a bit of relief. She was perfect the way she was. More than one tail would be awkward. "Like I said, it's a myth. I've seen a lot of pictures drawn and painted of kitsune, almost all of them are beautiful and sexy women, but none of them compare to you."

The fox woman blushed slightly, bringing her fair skin closer to the shade of her hair, even in the rapidly dimming light. "Aww, thank you Adam. Would you...like to feel my ears?"

My heart rate spiked. It was strange, because it wasn't like she asked me to have sex with her or anything. I don't know why I was overreacting, but my body didn't seem to want my opinion on the matter.

"I would love to."

She turned so she faced me squarely and shook her hair back, chin lifted while she looked into my eyes. I set down my fire-starting tool and wiped my hand on my pants, then reached out tentatively to touch her left ear. The fur was as soft as I'd imagined, sort of like velvet, but with longer strands. I had felt velveteen stuffed animals that were super soft and had always loved the sensation.

This was better.

I ran my fingers up and down her ear, enjoying how it glided across my skin with hardly any friction. Down to the base, along the edges, and up to the tufted tips, I softly massaged the pliable flesh under the fur, focusing on the feeling and the sight of the fine hairs.

Ysduil shifted a little and let out an almost-silent moan. My eyes snapped to hers and found them half-lidded. Her mouth lay partly open in a look of ecstasy.

My crotch immediately twitched. Between the sensation of the fur and her response, I was ready to pick up where we'd left off earlier.

Damn it, I thought. There were monsters about and it was getting dark. I pulled my hand back. How fucking stupid would it be to dodge the Sodality and get eaten by a monster because I couldn't keep it in my pants? I tried to calculate how much time we had, but the simple fact was that we needed to get the fire started and we needed to be prepared in case the danger of the Dreadlands came knocking on our door. Grumbling inwardly, I settled for watching Ysduil's beautiful face slowly return to neutral as her eyes opened.

"They're so soft," I said, almost in a whisper.

She giggled. "You should feel obsil ears. They're so much softer than mine. But thank you. I'm glad you like them." She sighed. "Maybe we can relax sometime and you can feel them some more?"

Again, I almost caved. I was sure now that she would be open to more advances. But it was our safety I had to think about. Damn responsibility and all that came with it. "I will hold you to that."

"I certainly hope so."

"Umm, what is obsil?"

Her tinkling laughter brightened the area again. "I'm sorry. I keep forgetting you're not from this world. Obsil are another type of beastkin. They have rabbit ears and fluffy rabbit tails."

"Bunny girls?" It came out without me even thinking about it.

"How funny. I have never heard them called that, but yes, I suppose it's correct."

God, I had to see one of those. And their ears were softer than Ysduil's?

We kept our eyes locked for several more seconds, until I felt like I was going to lose control, getting lost in her gaze. I cleared my throat.

"We should probably get the fire started. If it's as dangerous as you've said, we need to stay vigilant."

A disappointed look crossed her face and she turned to focus again on the kindling. "Tomorrow, then," she whispered, almost too softly for me to hear even with us this close together.

I don't think I was meant to have picked up on it, so I silently took up my stick and the bow and began anew to try to squeeze fire from the wood.

With Ysduil's help, I finally got a little flame going. She placed some of the dried leaves, moss, and fluff while blowing softly, then added twigs, sticks, and finally the larger kindling. I almost lost my concentration when I saw her cheeks puff out and her lips purse to blow on the burgeoning flame, but aside from a few stumbles, I maintained my motions.

As I watched the flame crackling and dancing on the larger pieces of wood, I realized how long I'd been trying to start the fire. I'd done the same thing in the past, though not for nearly as long, and I'd developed blisters and had to stop to rest after only a few minutes. It was deceptively strenuous work. This time, though, I kept going and going, without the blisters and without tiring. I wasn't even breathing hard, no matter how fast or forcefully I pulled on the strap to rotate the stick. I chalked it up as another strange occurrence in the overall weirdness of this new world, and its effect on me.

I sat on the opposite side of the fire, chatting with Ysduil as we cooked some filets of snake meat. After dinner, I volunteered to take first watch so she could settle down to sleep.

"Thank you," she said. "I am a little tired. Wake me in three hours and I will take over."

"Four hours," I said, though I wasn't sure how I'd count the time without a watch or a phone. "Get some rest. We have a lot of hiking ahead of us. Hopefully without the interference of the Sodality."

"Mmmm," she mumbled as she settled onto a flat spot in the grass near the fire. "I'm not worried about them. They have probably given up. It's the Dreadlands that concerns me now. Good night, Adam. Thank you." She closed her eyes and settled in to sleep.

I didn't ask why she had thanked me. It would only have required me to recount the many things I needed to thank her for. I watched the beautiful beastkin as her chest rose and lowered in the deep breaths of slumber. I adjusted myself in my tight pants and wondered what tomorrow would hold for us. My feelings were surprisingly peaceful for being trapped in another world, in the middle of a dangerous monster-infested area.

Danger aside, my surroundings were stunning. With

the wind-sculpted rock formations, the lush trees and bushes, and the clean air, people from my world would pay good money to visit and hike through. Of course, there were the monsters, none of which we'd seen yet, though that roar wasn't a joke.

It occurred to me then that this place, the Dreadlands, was like Ysduil. So gorgeous it almost hurt, but also deadly.

CHAPTER
SEVENTEEN

After waking Ysduil for her turn at watch, I tried to get comfortable on the hard ground and, surprisingly, drifted off to sleep. I woke to the sky brightening around me. The fire was still going strong and my foxy companion sat on the same rock she'd used for her *ritual* the night before. Her eyes were on me as I groaned and stretched out the kinks in my neck and back.

"Good morning," I said. "Anything happen while I slept?"

She flashed her little smirk at me but shook her head. "Nothing came near, though I did hear sounds out farther. Something caught up to its prey and ate it early this morning."

I shivered at the thought. "Same with me. I heard a few little shuffles over the sound of the fire, but it sounded like they were from small feet. See, we survived a whole night in the Dreadlands."

"We did, though we're still only in the outskirts. I will reheat some of the meat from last night and we can eat and be on the move soon. I don't know if the soldiers still pursue us, but it is to our advantage to continue our journey quickly."

I got up and wiped the dirt and bits of crushed vegetation off my arms and torso. Then I adjusted the crotch of my short, tight pants. What I wouldn't give just to wear something that didn't crush my balls every time I moved. It might even be worth waiting for some of the larger Sodality guards, like that big orc, just so I could get his clothes.

One nice thing about having nothing was that it was easy to break camp. We ate, crushed the coals, and buried them with a mound of dirt. I didn't want to be the guy all the monsters blamed for their homes burning down.

We left the rocky terrain and entered another forested area, with bushes crowding in between the many trees. We'd only been picking our way through the crowded understory for an hour before more space opened up between shrubs and trees. My focus lapsed as the morning sun shone in my face and I drifted over a little from where Ysduil was walking.

A sharp stinging sensation broke me from my stupor. I yelped and swatted at my arm, thinking it was an insect, but what I found was something else entirely.

A thick vine had grabbed the upper part of my left arm. The sting I felt was one of the thorns that covered the plant as it broke my skin.

"Ow, ow, ouch! Son of a *bitch*!" The vine contracted, squeezing my arm and jamming more needle-like thorns into me. Worse, another one swayed and dangled from above like some kind of creepy snake wanting to hug me. It reminded me of the creature that had attacked Ysduil. The one we'd eaten the night before.

I cut at it with my sword, but it was tough as an old root and my sword couldn't get through it, at least not in one swipe. I managed to score the thing and knock it away, but another vine came up from underneath and wrapped around my calf, punching more of those damn thorns into my skin.

Ysduil leaped to my defense, batting away two other vines, but her weapon wasn't made for damaging such things. I swapped the hatchet in my unmovable hand with the sword in my right and slammed it down as hard as I could on the vine around my calf. The blade barely missed my own leg and my breath hitched when I realized what I'd almost done. The blow did sever the vine, but the part still left on my leg continued to squeeze and drive its spikes into my flesh. Dribbles of blood trickled from my wounds, but surprisingly little.

"Augh! Get it off, get it off..." I yelped. I'm not proud of my reaction, but damn, vines don't move on their own and try to eat you in my world.

With only my arm held again, I pivoted to get my legs as far away from the bundle of vegetation where the vines originated and hacked at the plant holding my arm. That one was a little thicker and tougher than the first and it took three swipes to sever it. Maybe part of the reason for that was that I didn't want to swing the hatchet hard at the expense of accuracy. I'd just as soon not end up with one arm, having to explain I chopped the limb off myself, by accident.

Ysduil continued to try to help me, slamming her staff into more vines trying to get to me. She spun the thing so fast, her limbs blurred.

I got enough distance that the vines, or whatever creature had vines for limbs, gave up on me. The woody appendages slithered back into the thick vegetation and just like that, there was no sign they'd ever been there. You know, other than two separated sections still tightening around my arm and leg.

We got well away from the site of the attack before Ysduil helped me carefully remove the vines. As we pulled them off, the thorn holes dribbled more blood, dripping down both my arm and my leg.

"I'm sorry I didn't get to you sooner, or that I didn't notice the lasher before it was too late. At least it was not a mature plant. The older ones have barbs on their thorns."

The thought of it made me nauseous. "It's not your fault. I should have followed you more closely. The sun in my eyes made me drowsy and I lost my focus. Thank you for the help. Please tell me those thorns don't have poison."

"Those thorns don't have poison." That wry smile was back. "Some mature lashers, though not this variety, I think, have poison. You would know if it did. The toxin is said to burn fiercely as it works through the bloodstream. I will find some herbs to help with infection and to stop the bleeding as we travel. They are very common, so I don't doubt I'll find them soon."

She did find some, and we also ran across a stream so I could wash some of the blood off me. I wished we had cloth to make bandages, but the bleeding wasn't that severe and the herbs she applied made it stop altogether.

We continued on after that, traversing the rough ups and downs of the terrain, fighting the vegetation—none of it moving on its own, thankfully—all the while. Judging by the way the sun had moved since we'd started off that morning, we were heading something near southeast.

I was trying to construct a general map in my mind when a crash in the undergrowth made me snap my head up to find the familiar brown and black armor of the dungeon guards and soldiers moving toward Ysduil. At the same time, from my left came the dull brown and green of the clothing we'd seen on the scouts earlier. I caught a glimpse of Ysduil spinning her staff to meet a sword swung at her by a green-skinned soldier and then I had to focus on my own situation.

Two of the scouts, one male and one female, rushed at me with their blades already in motion.

"Shit." I leaped back to get some distance and swung my sword wildly at the beastkin charging me. By pure luck, my blade hit one of theirs and bashed it away with a clang. The other missed my arm by an inch or two.

My reaction displayed zero skill gained in training with the sword when I was younger.

In my defense, I trained with a Japanese sword, a katana, and I mostly did forms. I hadn't progressed enough in Greg's dad's school to learn any kung fu weapons, so I gravitated to learning katana forms on my own. Funny thing, forms training. When a sharpened blade is coming at you, you forget everything you've ever learned. That's a pro tip.

Both of my attackers had furry ears and tails, but one tail had hair on it and the other was scaly like a rat's. For a brief second, I was transfixed on how that scaly tail darted as its owner regained his balance to come at me again. I blinked. What the hell was I doing? Daydreaming during a battle? *That's a good way to get skewered.*

With a firmer stance, I prepared to defend myself. It was actually easier than I thought. The weapons came at me slowly enough that I was able to modify my two-handed sword forms to use with my one-handed sword. I managed to parry both blows and counterattack with my own slashes. Why would they send warriors who moved so slowly?

My heart jumped when I cut into the male's chest. I mean, cut deep into it. He squealed like a...well, like a rat, and turned to flee. I was still within range, so I rammed my sword through him. Maybe it was the whole deal with my strength being higher here, but it seemed too easy to punch the blade through his armor and all the way through his body. I pulled the blade out quickly, bringing it around to block a strike from the woman.

She launched into a flurry of four strikes, each of which I was able to dodge or block, with various degrees of poise. On the last one, I pivoted as I blocked, moving her sword down so I could reach out and grab her arm, with our bodies pressed together. Though she was bigger than the rat man, she was nowhere near as large as me. Even if I had normal strength, it would be a bad matchup for her.

Once I had control of her arm, I locked it in place, pivoted on my left foot, and slammed my pommel onto the side of her head. I did my best to keep from using my whole strength, but even so, she dropped to the ground and didn't move to get back up.

It only took one look at my companion to see that she had handily taken care of the orc. Dunim. Whatever they were called on this world, he was lying on the ground much as my own opponent was. With the danger mitigated, I felt the downed woman's neck for a pulse and located one.

"I found you some clothes that may fit you," Ysduil teased while wearing her smirk and spinning her staff effortlessly.

"You always give me the best gifts," I said. I started toward her to strip the clothes from the man.

"Just wait."

Was that a promise? I stumbled and almost fell.

EIGHTEEN

The orc Ysduil had brained was the same one I'd seen first when I woke up in the dungeon. I recognized that chipped tusk. He was close to my size, enough that I could wear his pants without massive circulation problems like on my current pair. I could use his shirt and pliable leather tunic as well. I put them all on, but didn't feel right about stripping him of his undergarments.

No, that's not entirely correct. The thought of wearing the orc's underwear freaked me the fuck out. Commando would be fine.

I was also pleasantly surprised that his boots fit me. I took them and his socks, but decided to wait until I could wash the socks in a stream before putting them on. Who knows what kind of foot fungus an orc had? I didn't even want to think about what could have happened if I chose to wear his underwear. A shiver racked my body.

Ysduil's laughter brought me out of my analysis of the orc's hygiene. I looked over to find her watching me.

"There is a common herb that will help to clean those socks. It is, in fact, the same one I put on your cuts earlier.

I'll pick some more and you can use it to wash the socks so you don't have to scowl at them anymore."

I laughed. "Thank you. You know, you are probably the perfect travel partner. I can't think of anyone I would rather be trapped within a monster-infested wilderness while being chased by mindless puppets with weapons."

She rolled her eyes at me. So that was a thing in this world, too.

"You sure you don't want to take this woman's clothes? She looks like she's about the same size as you. Or even just the boots so you don't have to walk barefoot?"

She pushed out her bottom lip in a pout. "You want to cover me up?"

"God no," I said without a thought. "I just figured you might want to be protected a little more for our upcoming battles."

Her pout broke into a smile and let loose a giggle. "I know. Really, I am more comfortable this way. This staff will protect me enough, I think."

I was about to voice my agreement when I heard more crashing through the vegetation nearby. A *lot* of crashing. I knew what that meant, but Ysduil spoke my thoughts before I could.

"This is not a scouting group. One of the large groups has found us. Maybe the same one we saw from the rise."

"Lead on," I said, stooping to pick up the sword belt I'd taken off the dunim to get his clothes. It had a scabbard with a proper sized sword. I hefted it with two hands comfortably. It was a little more curved than a katana, but not overly so. I thought it would be more comfortable and effective than the one I'd been using. I strapped it on as I followed Ysduil. She raced away from the scene, angling in a more eastern direction than we'd been going before.

We were making a huge racket, and I was probably creating a trail that was easily followed, but at the moment, speed was the main thing we needed. It was hard enough juggling the bow, the boots, the hatchet, and keeping the quiver and the scabbard from slamming into me in irritating ways. I didn't have the time or the skill to move silently and without a trail.

Ysduil didn't seem to have that problem. Besides being smaller than me, she gracefully bounded through the grasses and ferns like she was a gazelle. If we weren't running for our lives, I would have taken the time to watch more closely and appreciate the view from behind.

Aww, hell. I watched her carefully anyway. Honestly, I was lucky I didn't run into a tree.

We got to a stream and she plunged into it without hesitation. She bounced with her knees high, moving upstream and around a bend. We got back onto dry land, then found another stream and did the same. Finally, we lucked upon some rockier terrain and she swung back toward the southeast again. An hour and a half after we'd fought the surprised Sodality people, we finally stopped to take a breath.

We waited for some time, watching and listening. I thought I heard voices on the breeze, but wasn't sure. Ysduil's ears twitched and I wondered if she had better hearing than me, like most animals did. I mean, were those adorable fuzzy ears just for show, or did they heighten her senses?

Our pace slowed as we continued. It always seemed that she knew where she was going, even if I couldn't tell one direction from another without watching where the sun was for an hour or more and then estimating the direction we headed.

The next stream we found had some of the herb Ysduil had told me about scattered on the bank. She turned the socks inside out, crushed the leaves on them and rubbed in the thick, yellowish sap, then rubbed the cloth just like we did with stain remover on my world. After a few minutes, she washed them thoroughly in the water, turned them right side out, and handed them to me.

"You can wear them now or you can let them dry first, but they're cleaner than anything else we have at present. Including us."

I chuckled. She was right about that. I'd been covered from head to toe in mud while caving in the past, but I had never felt so grimy as I did at that moment. Part of it may have been that I was wearing the orc's clothes. Just the thought made me itch. Did orcs have fleas?

I jumped all the way into the stream as we crossed and since I was already wet, I went ahead and put the socks and boots on when we climbed up onto dry ground. They fit acceptably. It felt good to have a layer between the sensitive skin of my feet and the ground. I hoped they wouldn't wear blisters on me.

It seemed we were in the clear from our pursuers. At least for the moment. I finally started to breathe easier, when a swirl of shadow from the side lunged at me.

I turned my head just in time to see a huge hairy body and too many legs emerging out of a tunnel. It was still halfway in, with two of its legs pushing up a big clod of dirt that was an off-white color underneath.

For the second time in a few hours, reflexes I didn't know I had kicked in and I leaped to the side. The hurtling giant spider barely missed me. Hissing and clicking, it turned to face me and I finally got a good look at it.

I'd seen close-up pictures of spiders and other insects

on the internet, just like everyone. I looked at them, recognized how creepy and otherworldly they looked, and then went on with my life. That's not the feeling I had when I stared into the many, *many* eyes of this spider, and noticed the clicking, moving sabre-type things on the front of its face.

For the first time in my life, I felt like I might shit myself.

When it lurched forward, faster than anything the size of a passenger car should be able to, I thought of turning and running. I realized, a fraction of a second after the thought shot through my mind, that it could easily run me down.

I needed to stand and fight.

I fought to pull my sword free, but my training in quickly drawing a weapon was a long time ago. I was never going to get the weapon out in time.

Crack, crack, crack.

The huge arachnid hopped and rotated in midair to face the source of the noise. It lurched to one side before I realized what had happened. Ysduil stood, facing the thing down, her staff still moving. Had she actually hit the damn thing?

I didn't waste the distraction she provided, finally pulling my sword free of the scabbard and slashing at one of the monster's legs. It hissed again, and hunched down like it was ready to pounce.

My sword bit into it again, on a different leg. Even with my improved strength, there was no way I was going to cut through those limbs with one swing. They looked flimsy compared to its body, but they were still almost as big around as my own legs.

"Run," I said, hoping we could do that without being

trapped and eaten. If we stayed and fought, one or both of us would die. One bite and the venom would probably end us in an instant. I absently wondered if all spiders had poison.

Ysduil, to her credit, hesitated for a moment to make sure I wasn't trying to sacrifice myself. Even in the full rush of battle energy, I felt my face flush. I hadn't even considered doing that. I guess I just wasn't the hero type. I'd rather run alongside her to escape than to be eaten to let her go free. Like any sane person.

The spider lunged at her as she got ready to leave and she slammed her staff into its face several times in succession. The way she wielded the thing, it spent half its time so blurred I couldn't even tell where it was.

For good measure, I cut at its legs again, drawing its attention, and then I took off like a shot after Ysduil.

We played a game of run-stop-attack-run for the next several minutes. The spike-like hairs on the thing's legs cut like a dull knife. It was enough to scratch or part skin, but in the most painful of ways. I found that out as its scurrying appendages rubbed against me when it got too close. Luckily, the clothing I wore blocked most of the damage, but since the leather tunic was sleeveless, the contact did a number on my arms. Ysduil didn't get any damage that I saw, but whether that was because she was more agile than I was or because when I saw the monster get close I attacked it to get its attention, I don't know.

Across the shrub-dotted landscape, between trees, and even over or through small streams, the spider chased us. None of the damage we inflicted was serious enough to keep it from continuing. I was just happy it didn't seem to have any friends around.

Finally, as we crossed yet another stream, possibly large

enough to be called a river, the monster slowed and stopped. Its multifarious eyes glared hatred at us as we climbed the bank on the other side.

"It's not going to keep following us?" I panted. "Is it afraid of the water?"

Ysduil leaned on her staff, breathing hard. "No. I think maybe it's afraid of something else."

"Great."

CHAPTER

NINETEEN

"Okay, I believe you." My eyes darted around, searching our surroundings for any other dangers. "This place is definitely dangerous. Even without the Sodality chasing us."

Ysduil's tinkling laugh went through me, soothing some of the tension in my body. "We're barely past the edge of the safer area. There are much scarier things ahead of us, I think."

"Yeah. Like whatever frightens that huge spider enough that it won't come into this area."

"Yes. Like that." She leaned on her staff to pull herself up. "We should put more distance between us and...everything back there."

I wanted to lie down and take a nap, but I knew she was right. We needed to lose our pursuers once and for all and I wouldn't mind getting as far as possible from that spider. Those hairy legs...and so many eyes. A shiver ran through me, from my lower back to the top of my head.

We waited until the next water source we came across to wash and treat the wounds we'd received. The wounds *I* received. Ysduil got a few scratches, but none of them bled. Thankfully, even mine were relatively minor. I was accumulating a nice collection of minor injuries. All in all, we were pretty lucky considering the thing that had tried to kill us. If those fangs or the sharp pincer things on its face had gotten to us...yikes.

As we walked—she turned us so we were traveling due east again, as near as I could tell—we chatted softly. I was half-distracted, watching and listening for signs of danger, but it was still pleasant listening to her voice.

"It is my hope that we can avoid most of the danger, but it would be foolish to think we will not be required to engage in combat," she said. Her tone was so calm and clinical. Just the thought of more monsters made me nervous. If I'd had a gun, I might feel a bit better, but I was no medieval warrior. Unlike my companion.

"How, exactly, did you learn to fight so well?" I asked.

The foxgirl shot me a shy look and colored slightly. "It wasn't always like this. Before the Sodality, the priestesses of Odona were more respected. Some of our tenets were perhaps a little uncomfortable for some people, but overall we were seen as an important part of society. Some of my sisters have herb lore that can aid women in their pregnancies, as well as for general health. Others are skilled with people and act as advisors in matters of marriage and relationship. Back then, there no need for training in combat.

"True, there were some sisters that did dedicate themselves to such pursuits. Primarily, the fighting arts started as a way for the sisters to exercise and maintain their body shape and fitness. The skills developed into an efficient system of combat. There are stories of some priestesses who hired themselves out as guards or even soldiers. Those were few, however.

"When the Sodality changed the world, and especially when they began to look at us more and more with hatred and fear, the Grand Priestess decided that all would learn at least rudimentary skills in fighting. The world was becoming dangerous for us and if we didn't protect ourselves, no one else would.

"Though required, some sisters only put in a minimum of effort, focusing more on other facets of our worship. While I love everything about my worship of the goddess, I find the martial movements to be...enjoyable. At times, I have neared climax during a particularly rigorous workout."

She gave a little gasp and put her hand to her mouth. "I am sorry, Adam. I don't mean to embarrass you or make you feel uncomfortable."

I could only shake my head and laugh. "Ysduil, I've told you before, it doesn't embarrass me. I don't know why you would think it does."

"Many do become uncomfortable with the subject of sexual activities."

"I'm definitely not one of them. Where I come from, people talk about sex all the time. It's one of the biggest parts of our society."

"Truly? Even the men?"

My laughter grew. "Especially the men."

She threw me a suspicious look. "That is difficult to believe. A big part of my worship is compassion for others. While I would happily talk about all of the subjects that are taboo to many, I try to keep my zeal from alienating others. Some of my sisters do not see it that way. They say that if someone doesn't want to hear what they say or see what they do, then they can go elsewhere. I want all people to be joyous and feel pleasure. For some, though, pleasure is sitting silently and not being exposed to the wonders of the goddess. If someone feels thus, it is good for them."

I took a really good look at my foxy companion. "You are a special kind of person, Ysduil. Even with the persecution you've suffered, you're still compassionate and considerate of other people and their beliefs and feelings. I'm glad I met you in that dungeon."

The gregarious woman averted her eyes. Was she so unused to people complimenting her? What a shame.

"I'm sorry we couldn't go to search the ruins," she said.

I blinked repeatedly at her, trying to keep up with the change in the conversation. "Uh, that's okay."

"You must want to go to your home. All you have found here is danger and mistreatment."

"No, that's not all. I've found you." I paused, feeling like I was getting sappy. "I would like to see if I can find my way home, but it's more important that we help each other and get you to...wherever it is you want to go. Someplace safe."

"I want to reconnect with my sisters. I have no plans beyond that. Perhaps once we have found them, we can help you find a way to return to your home. You must miss it terribly. All the familiar things, people you care for..."

I shrugged my shoulders. "It's not that great, really. Lately, it's been even less so. I don't have many people there that I care for. A few friends, my parents. No one really special. I mean, my parents are special, but you know what I mean."

"You...don't have a mate. A wife or lovers?" She kicked at a plant as she passed it. "A *khresha* in this world could have any number of wives or lovers. For those who are not so devout in the Sodality's teachings."

"Nope. No wives, no lovers, no mates. Just a couple of good friends and my family. There are more men than women where I live, and I'm nothing special."

My eyes scanned the sky, unfocused. I almost ran into Ysduil as she stopped to look at me with her mouth open. "I have not known you for more than a few days, but it is easy to see that you're special. I think you are mistaken."

I rubbed the back of my neck. "Thank you." Dredging up as much wisdom as I could, I left it at that.

She looked deeply into my eyes and held it for half a minute. It was uncomfortable, like she was reading my soul. Looking closely at those gorgeous eyes, slightly luminescent as reflected sunlight revealed the swirls of deeper red in them, made me forget to breathe.

Her neutral expression suddenly shifted into her wry smile and she scoffed. "Not special. Indeed."

Then she turned and continued walking, leaving me to deal with the aftereffects of our eye contact. I sucked in a shaky breath and followed.

As the sun was three quarters of the way through the sky, we chanced upon a pond and decided to take a break. Ysduil dug up some more roots, found some wild vegetables, and set them out on a flat rock near a river. Relaxing by the water, we ate.

With as much as we'd already done that day, I should've been more tired. But other than the nagging cuts, scratches, and bruises, I felt pretty good.

"I'm surprised we haven't seen any other monsters." I regretted saying it as the words came out of my mouth. I didn't want to jinx us.

"Nighttime is more dangerous, I think," she said. "At least on the outskirts. I know little about what the heart of the Dreadlands is like." She angled her head to look up at the sun. "We will need to think about hunting for more meat in a few hours, and about finding suitable shelter. It will be more important than it was last night."

"I'll keep an eye out as we go." We'd seen animals as we moved through the trees. Mostly the smaller kinds, but a few larger shapes I didn't recognize as well. "How are you with a bow?"

"I have trained a little with the weapon. I have a fair aim."

"Do you want to use this one?" I held up the bow I'd been carrying since I took it from the Sodality scout. "I can carry it, no problem, but I didn't spend a lot of time with archery and even what little skill I had is rusty."

"Rusty? Covered with red scale?"

"Ah. No. It's just a saying in my world. It means my movements aren't fluid. Rough, like a rusty hinge on a door?"

"Oh. Rusty." She chuckled. "I like that saying, the imagery. I can see in my mind a door opening and can hear the creaking and grinding. I understand." She clapped her hands. Her enthusiasm made me smile.

"We've got some good ones in my world. I'll be sure to tell them to you, when they come to mind."

"How exciting." Her left ear twitched, and her tail jerked. Her joy was infectious. "As you suggested, though, I would appreciate you carrying the bow so my hands are free to use my staff if necessary."

"No problem. You're the better fighter anyway. Taking the time to drop the bow and draw my sword won't be nearly as important as you being able to defend right away with your staff."

Less than an hour later, as we trod through a large depression filled with trees, we heard the sound. The racket brought to mind someone cutting at a stone with a cheap sword. The clangs and shrieks of metal on stone made me cringe. Like a shovel on rock.

"Let's go around this way," Ysduil whispered. "Whatever it is sounds occupied. Better we go wide and not allow it to see us."

Intellectually, I knew she was right. But my curiosity got the better of me.

"I'm going to sneak a peek. I just want to see what it is in case we come upon it later."

She frowned in the most adorable way but didn't argue. Maybe I was taking advantage of her politeness, but all I wanted was a quick look. I might have done exactly what she said if it was any other sound, but it would drive me crazy trying to imagine what caused the noise if we avoided it completely.

I handed the bow and quiver of arrows to her and commando crawled over to the ridge of a depression. Toward the bottom of the hollow, the noises—though muffled by the trees and other vegetation—got louder. It sounded like combat, but not like steel on steel. The mystery tugged at me, needing to be solved. I couldn't have turned back at that point even if I'd wanted to.

Finally, I reached the area from which the racket was coming. I slowly moved a pair of branches out of my way and looked out into a clearing. What I saw there made me wonder if I should have left well enough alone.

CHAPTER

TWENTY

Between the leaves and branches, I scanned the area of the small clearing. The ground was uneven—kind of wavy—and carpeted with grass and low bushes. The trees at the edges dangled leafy branches a few feet into the space, but there were probably thirty or more feet of visibility.

In that clear space, a large group of figures were gathered, all focused on something else standing on a large rock.

As far as I could tell, the monsters were some kind of insect. Their bodies were segmented like ants, but not quite so exaggerated. I chuckled inwardly when I pictured the old timey pictures of curvy women with really big hips and thighs, really big chests and torsos, and extremely small waists. Not quite like an ant, which seemed like they could easily fall apart, but still...unnatural.

Of course, insects that were close to five feet tall shouted *unnatural* anyway. Their dirty grey skin looked thick, but not like exoskeletons. I was betting a weapon could penetrate them. With difficulty. In fact, as the thought crossed my mind, a sword slashed through one of the monsters, splitting its skin cleanly so that a viscous yellowish liquid flowed out.

It was hard to keep my eyes on the insects, to be honest, as strange as they and their antennaed heads were, simply because of the other figure on top of the rock, currently slashing at them with a sword.

A very striking individual. No pun intended.

She was female, unless males of her species grew a magnificent pair of breasts. They were barely held in by a boiled leather breastplate. Black hair in a topknot with the end free and flowing with her movements, she was a picture of grace and skill with the flashing blade. I would have bet on her to win any day, if it weren't for the sheer number of the monsters attacking her. More than twenty gathered around and though they seemed weaponless, they did have wicked claws that I had no doubt could tear skin easily.

All of that was interesting, fascinating even, but it wasn't all. The woman's determined face was surprisingly beautiful, especially considering that she appeared to be an orc. Her skin was a smooth, creamy green, nearly the same tint as the dunim I'd seen—and interacted closely with—from the dungeon. The one whose clothes I now wore. She didn't have the unsightly tusks coming up from the bottom of her mouth, not that I could see, but I had no doubt I was looking at the female version of the dunim race.

She was...captivating.

I found a hand clamped around my arm and realized I had started to move toward the battle. I gave Ysduil a look of confusion, then shifted my eyes to her hand.

"Come, let's go," she whispered. "This is not our battle. Dunim are very aggressive and violent, and if we interfere, she will no doubt attack us as well."

I couldn't believe what I was hearing. Ysduil seemed to be the type of person who was kind to everyone, not the type to disparage someone's race.

"We can't just leave and not try to help," I whispered back. "Those things are going to overwhelm her. She's from one of the monster tribes, right?"

"Yes, but she would probably attack us on sight. They only like their own kind and don't mix with other races. Especially since the Sodality has treated them so poorly."

"I'm sorry, Ysduil. I can't leave an intelligent person to such a fate if I can do something about it. You don't have to help, but I'm going to. It looks like with just a little assistance, she'll be fine. She really can use that sword."

The foxgirl hissed, but released my arm. I patted her shoulder and drew my sword. One more look toward the insects, then I leaped out of my hiding spot and raced at them as quickly as I could. I hoped they couldn't hear or sense me until it was too late.

My hope didn't pan out.

Three of the closest monsters turned to see me charging and turned to address the interruption. I lifted my sword, ready to cut into the first one I got to, but I had to settle for the second one.

The first dropped to the ground, an arrow sticking out of its face. *Good old Ysduil.* Of course she was a dead shot.

My sword sliced down, bouncing off the hard shell of one insect's claws and cutting into its neighbor. As with the woman's slash earlier, my blade cut the second ant's skin and made it bleed. It also screeched in a way that made my ears ring, a whistling, shrieking sound I hoped I'd never hear again.

I circled my sword and cut into another insect, avoiding its claws and aiming for one of its tiny waists separating the segments of its body. I nearly cut all the way through, causing convulsions in both halves of the body. *Goooooaaaaaalllllll!* It was apparently a killing blow. Eventually. Its body thrashed and fell to the ground.

The orc woman's blue eyes flashed to me, then toward where I came from, no doubt finding Ysduil, but if she had any thoughts about us, she didn't reveal them. Her face, as stoic and controlled as it had been the whole time, went back to regarding the ants she methodically cut at.

The toll on the insect monsters added up until they realized it was not a good place for them to be. With a clicking whistling sound from one of the larger of the monsters, the rest turned and scuttled into the trees. The one who gave the command turned to me, somehow displaying hatred in a face that didn't move at all, then it also fled. In a handful of seconds, the only insects still in the clearing were either dead or dying. As if to emphasize that, the woman speared a figure at her feet, ending its wriggling.

Then she threw her arms in the air and shouted at where the ants had fled, like she was challenging them to return. "Zartuka!"

She turned her face to me, and those pale blue eyes drilled into mine. The intensity—and honestly, the sheer beauty of the woman—put a hitch in my breath.

Then she pivoted, pointing the sword at me while positioning herself exactly on the opposite side from Ysduil to prevent the priestess from shooting her with an arrow.

"Call off your *sotin* and I will let the two of you live," she said in a voice that seemed half growl.

"We just helped you," I said. "Show a little gratitude."

The warrior woman tilted her head like I was a rock that had sprouted legs and started dancing and singing.

"What is this? Has the Sodality learned how to train its pets to speak like a real person?"

She was still directing her voice toward Ysduil, who calmly walked out of the bushes where she'd been sniping the insects.

"Hey!" I said. "Don't talk to her. I'm trying to have a conversation here. Are you so rude that you can't answer me?"

The green woman looked even more confused. Her grip tightened on her sword and she shifted her stance, weighting her back foot like she was getting ready to attack me. She ran her eyes up and down my body. If anything, her puzzled look grew deeper, brows crinkling and eyes narrowing.

It occurred to me suddenly and I felt like slapping my forehead. "Oh. The clothes. Don't worry about what I look like. I took these from a Sodality guard we defeated. He was a...uh, he was a guard from the Sodality prison. We were being held there, waiting to be transferred to be executed and, well, trained."

Her gaze flicked from me to Ysduil. I turned just in time to see the priestess shrug her shoulders.

"Honest," I said, "we don't mean you any harm. We just wanted to help you with—" I kicked one of the bug corpses. "—these things."

"Aanem," the dunim spat.

"Come again?"

"Aanem. That's what they're called."

"Oh. Okay, so we just wanted to help with the aanem. We'll just go now. No need in swinging your sword around at us."

Her blade lowered marginally. "You are telling me you're not of the Sodality?"

"That's exactly what I'm telling you. I'm not even from this world and Ysduil here, she's a priestess of Odona. You can tell by the...dress." As I gestured at the foxgirl, I realized that what little cloth was left of the dress didn't really look like anything.

"A priestess of Odona? You were in the dungeon of the Sodality fortress?"

"I was," Ysduil said.

"They would have executed you."

"Yes. But Adam here helped me escape before they could take me to Aycrish Summit."

The dunim woman waffled for another full minute. I almost expected her to bite her bottom lip as she ruminated. Finally, she lowered her sword completely.

"I am Glasha Axecrusher. I thank you for your aid. It is true: if you meant me harm, you would not have helped. I am no prize like a priestess of the sex goddess, so there would be no need for subterfuge."

I let out a breath I'd been holding. "It's nice to meet you, Glasha. My name's Adam. Um, Axecrusher?"

"That is correct."

"How does that make sense? An axe cuts, not crushes."

"I received the name when I was young. Do you routinely disrespect the names of those you meet?"

"Oh. No. I'm sorry. I just thought...it's a nice name. Very...vicious?"

I must have jumped three feet straight up when Glasha barked out a sudden laugh so loud that a pair of birds nearby fled for their lives.

"You're funny, Adam. It is my honor to meet you, and you, Ysduil, priestess of Odona. I thank you for your aid and am in your debt. I have but one question, in two parts: what are you doing in the Dreadlands and where are you going?"

"It's simple," Ysduil said. "We escaped from the fortress to the west. We couldn't very well take the road to escape, and the other areas are infested with Sodality troops. There was only one option: to go east. As for where we're headed, it should be obvious. We want to get through the Dreadlands as quickly as possible and back into civilized lands."

Glasha eyed the priestess with a hawk's gaze. "Civilized lands?"

"Pardon me. Safer lands?"

"Ha! Much better. Do you realize how stupid it is for an outsider to try to cross the Dreadlands to get to the other side? A smarter person would have tried to go along the edges to avoid the worst of the danger."

I wiped the goo from the insects off my sword with some leaves from a nearby bush. "We tried that. The Sodality soldiers that came after us were too thick on the outskirts of the Dreadlands."

"Ah, yes. They would be. Are they still following you?"

"We don't think so. We're hoping they think we're dead and that they'll be afraid to go further to the heart of the area."

Glasha nodded. "Maybe they will, maybe they won't. They came farther into the Dreadlands when they seized the males from our tribes, but they had powerful armies with them then." She shrugged. "If they follow, they will find more than two fugitives. Stay here for a moment. Let me fetch my pack."

The dunim woman plunged into the foliage as if there had not just been two dozen monstrous insects in the area. When she disappeared, I turned to Ysduil.

"Do all orc—ah, dunim—females look like that?"

"Like what? Green? Yes." She wore her little mischievous smile again.

"Not green. I mean..." I used my hands and described an hourglass shape. "You know. Gorgeous."

"She is very good looking," the priestess said. "To answer your question, though, she is very pretty for a dunim, according to our ideals of beauty. Her lack of visible tusks would make her decidedly less so for dunim tastes, however. I think she would probably be considered plain or even below average to interested dunim, either male or female. Her face is too symmetrical and her skin too smooth and clear."

"Oh." I'd never really thought of an orc being attractive, let alone being a drop-dead gorgeous creature like this one was. The thought that she would be considered ugly by other dunim saddened me a little.

My thoughts were interrupted when that very dunim reappeared with a large pack strapped to her back.

"To repay you for your aid, I will take you to my village. You may resupply there and—more importantly—you will not be attacked on sight when you stumble through our territory. That uniform you wear, and the simple fact that you are male, would be a death sentence to you otherwise. Follow me."

CHAPTER
TWENTY-ONE

Glasha strode confidently through the vegetation as if she was walking down a sidewalk. Or a runway. I couldn't get over how startlingly beautiful the woman was. Cosplaying women covered with green paint at conventions didn't come close to luscious tones of her skin. Even the pretty ones—though they did try to uglify themselves—couldn't compare to Glasha's natural beauty. I couldn't keep my eyes off her body. How it moved, the muscle fibers flexing and twitching with every motion.

Ysduil chuckled to herself, sometimes even pushing my shoulder to tease me. I didn't want to openly gape at the dunim woman, but damn! At least my foxy companion didn't seem to mind my eyes wandering.

"It will take a day to get to my village, so we will need to make camp tonight," Glasha said over her shoulder. "It's foolish to travel at night unless you are part of a full company of huntresses."

We acknowledged her statement and continued in silence.

I was back to carrying the bow so that Ysduil could more quickly use her staff, if necessary. She wore the quiver and, depending upon what danger we came across, I could throw her the bow or I could drop it to draw my sword. With Glasha in front, I was sure we'd have time to react if something came across us. Besides, we were still not seeing much in the way of fauna.

"Don't step over there," the dunim said, pointing to the left as she swung a few feet to the right. "Only an idiot strays close to them."

The sudden statement made my head snap up and toward the place she'd indicated. I caught the slightest movement and recognized the outline of a few of the leaf-covered shapes. More lasher plants. The thought of being grabbed by one of those again dropped the temperature around me by about twenty degrees, though my face still felt warm.

Once we made it to a more open area, not quite a plain, but larger than a simple grassy meadow, Glasha slowed so we could walk next to her instead of following behind. I took one last look at the curve of her ass, only the edge of which I could see under her leather battle skirt—battle mini-skirt, actually—and moved up to her.

"How is it that you exist, *khresha*?" she asked.

"His name is Adam," Ysduil snapped.

"Ah. My apologies. Speaking with a male is...something I do not remember doing. I was very young when the Sodality...visited us and took our men. I have grown to see others treat them like pets. How is it that you exist free, Adam?"

"I'm not from this world," I told her. "I don't understand how I got here. In my world, we don't have any of this Sodality stuff. Everyone is free to do what they want." I thought about it and amended my statement. "More or

PHIL AERIX

less. The point is, there's none of this *training* that takes away someone's will. At least, not to the extent of the Sodality." I thought of all the different places in the world where people were oppressed and forced to do things or be a certain way, but decided not to talk about that. As bad as that got, it wasn't actual brainwashing like the Sodality was doing.

"Another world. That sounds like powerful magic, to travel from one world to another."

"Maybe. I don't know. I was exploring a cave with my friends and then I was here. I woke up in a dungeon cell, completely naked."

Glasha looked over to Ysduil, taking her in head to foot. "It must be a naked dungeon, judging by what you say and the look of your vinem."

"She's not *my vinem*," I snapped. I guessed that was the name for fox beastkin. Strangely, a glance at Ysduil showed her with a smile on her face, chuckling softly.

"You think it's funny that she called you mine?" I asked.

Ysduil snorted. "Naked dungeon." She laughed again.

I noticed that Glasha was smiling as well. For the first time I did see some long teeth on the bottom of her mouth, but they weren't big enough to extend beyond her lips. It finally made sense. What she'd said.

"A...joke?"

The dunim looked at Ysduil, growing more serious. "He doesn't have a sense of humor? Or is he not smart enough to grasp the concept?"

Ysduil's laughter only increased.

Luckily, our green companion turned to continue on our journey. Ysduil patted my shoulder as she followed, still chuckling. As embarrassed as I was, I had to laugh a little myself. A naked dungeon. I rolled my eyes and caught up to the women.

Glasha stopped us a little later, gesturing for us to lower ourselves to hide in the vegetation that had been gradually growing taller. She pointed and I spotted some animals ahead and to the right. She gave Ysduil a significant look and the fox woman held her hand out to me while lifting an arrow from her quiver.

I handed the bow to her and took the staff she offered to me in turn, then I crouched silently and watched her face get serious. She drew the bow smoothly, the wood creaking slightly. The animals, which looked kind of like deer, but blockier, stopped grazing and lifted their heads, ears pricked up.

The soft whisper of Ysduil releasing her breath preceded the too-loud twang of the bowstring as the shaft flew toward the herd. I lost track of it but soon located the back end of the shaft sticking out of one of the creatures, at the center of its neck.

The other beasts took off running. The one Ysduil had hit tried to take off as well, but another arrow appeared in its side. The animal stumbled, then fell to its front knees and, after a few seconds, dropped completely to the ground.

I'd never seen such a display of accuracy in person. I found Ysduil with a smile on her face and the bow held out to me. I mindlessly traded her staff for the bow as Glasha led us out to collect what I imagined would be our dinner.

"You've 'practiced a little' with the bow, you said. Those were amazing shots."

The fox woman shrugged delicately and left me shaking my head as she followed Glasha.

If anything, the dunim woman was even more efficient at dressing the kill than Ysduil had been with the snake. I thanked whatever luck it was that I had them along. I didn't know the first thing about hunting and killing food.

We made camp a few miles away, just as the sun was setting behind us. I wondered what a dunim village would be like. I was a little nervous and a little excited about getting there the next day.

Making the fire was much easier with the flint Glasha carried in her pack. She smoothly struck the it the back of a knife, showering her tinder with sparks that sprang into flames almost magically when she puffed the perfect amount of air at precisely the correct time. So unlike the epic struggle I'd had trying to make fire the day before.

She noticed me watching. "It only takes a spark," she said with a smirk that communicated there might be a joke involved. Probably at my expense. Something clicked in my mind at her words. That's exactly what Greg had said after his story about that ship blowing up. *It only takes a spark.* I missed my friends.

In no time, we had flames to warm us and cook the meat. After full darkness had fallen, we ate as we sat around our small fire.

The green woman shared her water skin with us, which we'd filled at the last stream we crossed. It was nice to be able to get a drink when we wanted instead of drinking our fill at each water source and hoping we'd find the next one.

As we ate dinner, I peppered Glasha with questions about the Dreadlands and how it was to live in a place everyone else was afraid of. She joked about how weak others were if they thought it was so dangerous in the place where her tribe resided. It was nowhere near as deadly as the inner part of the Dreadlands. Still, what she told us was interesting and helpful, considering we had to traverse the entire region to get out on the other side.

Ysduil shot me a look at one point, an expression I wasn't sure I could interpret. She rolled her eyes and stood. She seemed intent on doing whatever it was she was trying to hint to me.

"I have...something I must do," she said. "Over there." The foxgirl pointed toward the darkness nearby.

Glasha nodded and something about the serious, yet understanding look on her face made me think she interpreted Ysduil's words to mean she needed to heed the call of nature.

"Be careful," the dunim said. "The fire may keep most of the dangerous creatures away, but there may be some skulking close. Finish your business and come back to the firelight."

Ysduil raised an eyebrow at me before starting off into the dark, carrying her staff. I finally understood. She was heeding a type of nature's call, but not the one Glasha was thinking.

I prepared myself to be serenaded by the sweet, sweet sound of Ysduil performing her duty for her goddess.

Sure enough, a short time later the sound of heavy breathing reached us over the crackling of the fire. Glasha started to rise from the rock she sat on, but I put my hand on her arm and shook my head.

"It'll be fine. You can expect other noises, too. She'll be all right."

The green woman narrowed her eyes at me. She opened her mouth to speak as a stifled moan punctuated the breathing sounds. It was hard to tell in the firelight, but I believe her cheeks darkened.

"Is it...is she...are the stories true, about the priestesses?"

I wanted to laugh, but Glasha was so discomfited, I

contained myself. "You'll have to be a bit more specific than that, I'm afraid."

"There are tales of the priestesses of Odona, that they spend much of each day seeking pleasure. From physical...contact."

"Sexual pleasure," I stated.

"Yes."

"Then yes, the stories are true. At least, if they said that the priestesses must seek pleasure once per day, that is. From what Ysduil has—" A particularly rough breath and a groan that most certainly was muffled by a hand over her mouth derailed my train of thought. "From what she told me, the requirement is just one time a day, not to spend most of the day engaging in it. Still, she has to...do it. At least once a day."

Glasha's mouth formed an O, but she didn't actually say anything. The sound of Ysduil pleasuring herself continued unabated. If anything, it sounded restrained but desperate, like she'd compressed the entire episode into a shorter time and thereby made it more powerful, yet still tried to be silent out of respect for her bystanders. Listeners. Whatever.

I tried to sound casual, though in all honesty, her sounds—and the resulting images in my mind—were stealing away any calmness I had. "She is very considerate and doesn't want to insult or offend you. That's why she went over there."

Glasha stared toward where the sound was coming from, as if she could see the foxgirl in the dark. Hell, for all I knew, dunim could have good enough vision to do so.

"I...appreciate it," she said. "But I would not want her to put herself in danger to keep me from having to see her. Doing what she is doing."

I laughed. "I know. I told her the same thing last night."

Glasha's eyebrows shot up her forehead. "Oh. Did you? Have you...?"

"No. It was the same as now, or close enough. I haven't touched her, nor she me."

The dunim woman swallowed and fidgeted. Her pale blue eyes, the color merging with the reflected firelight, wouldn't meet mine.

"I'm sorry," I said. "This is a little awkward, even more so because I'm sitting here with a hot woman and talking about...what we're talking about."

"Hot?" she said. "The fire is warm, but with the chill night air, I am comfortable. Except on my face. Perhaps I will move back from the fire a little."

I snorted. "No. It's a saying in my world. I'm saying you're hot, which means you're beautiful. Arousing. Sexy. You look good enough to make my blood rush and my heart pound. Hot."

The warrior didn't seem to know what to do with that. I could see her chewing on it behind her eyes, even moving her mouth as if she were physically biting down on it. Finally, she said, "Thank you, but I know I am plain. At best."

I leaned in to look into her eyes, but she stared at her hands in front of her. Slowly, I put a finger under her chin and lifted up so she was looking at me.

"I don't know how the dunim reckon beauty, but I'm telling you, Glasha, you are beautiful. And sexy. And hot. From my point of view, you are all those things."

Her cheeks were definitely darkening now. "I...what of Ysduil? Is she not your mate? You two seem to be...compatible."

"She's not my mate. I've only known her for a few days.

She's great. I really like her, and she's hot, too, but she doesn't seem to be interested in me in that way."

"She is a priestess of Odona, of course she is interested in you in that way," Glasha said.

I thought of a response, but then noticed the sound had stopped. I replayed my memory and realized I had heard what could have been a muffled climax. I stood to go check on Ysduil, but didn't even get all the way to my feet.

"I hope I didn't bother you," Ysduil said, entering the firelight. "What are you two talking about?"

"Hot," Glasha said without hesitation. "I believe I will go to sleep now. Thank you for volunteering for the first watch, Adam. Goodnight. Goodnight, Ysduil."

With that, the dunim laid down as far from the fire as she could while still feeling warmth, turned her back on us, and settled in for the night.

Ysduil looked curiously at me, but I waved her question aside. I'd have to tell her about it later.

Once I figured out exactly what it was that happened.

CHAPTER
TWENTY-TWO

I woke up Ysduil at the appointed time, or as close as I could figure it, then laid down to get some sleep myself. Surprisingly, I wasn't all that tired despite the battle and all the hiking I'd done during the day. That lack of fatigue didn't stop me from falling right into a peaceful slumber, though.

Before I knew it, diffused light coming through the nearby trees tickled my eyelids, insisting it was time to get up. I found a warm lump next to me and blinked my eyes into focus to realize Ysduil had snuggled up against me, probably for warmth. The poor thing with her shredded dress was probably freezing.

I turned my head to find Glasha watching me.

I cleared my throat. "Good morning. Any creatures come around on your watch?"

"No. The fire and the sight of someone on watch probably kept them away. Did you see or hear anything on your watch?"

"Nope. It was pretty quiet." I started to get uncomfortable with her looking at me with her unblinking—albeit mesmerizing—eyes. Without thinking, I adjusted myself. Morning wood is a bitch. Halfway through the motion, I froze.

"I have heard stories about men. From before. Before the Sodality took them and trained them. It's said that when a man is...aroused, his parts grow and stiffen."

There didn't seem to be a question in there, but I was pretty sure the statement required a response.

"Uh, yeah. That's true. One part, anyway. There are other things that can cause the effects, too, but that's the most common cause. Often, a man will wake up like that, though." I gestured vaguely. "Stiff. And bigger."

"Hmm."

That was it. She settled her gaze on the sleeping Ysduil. Her eyes lingered on the woman for a moment before Glasha got up and searched through her pack for her water skin. I breathed a sigh of relief. I wasn't sure I was the one to be explaining these things to a woman who'd never talked to a man before. Then again, if not me, then who?

I nudged Ysduil. Several times. It seemed that my gorgeous foxgirl was not a morning person. When I finally roused her, her wide smile brightened the entire area. Soon enough, we smothered the fire and headed out.

Today was the day I'd see the dunim village.

The trip was uneventful and by mid-morning, I spotted a few plumes of smoke wafting into the air. Shortly thereafter, we were within sight of what amounted to a large clearing with primitive structures of wood and twigs. They were mostly round, with grass roofs thatched to a thickness that probably kept the rain out. If it rained in this world.

I spotted a few splotches of color that I thought might be sentries or guards as we approached, but no one stopped us. I thought about what Glasha had said about us being killed before we even got to the village if she hadn't been with us, and I was grateful I'd decided to help her with those insects. I wasn't sure what kind of reception I'd get, but at least I had one local on my side.

The few people we saw—all female and with varying shades of green skin—looked over at us with interest. At me, really. I'm sure a half-naked fox woman was not a common sight, but from what I'd been told, a man was even more rare. Some of the villagers whispered and one or two pointed at me, but that was it. Thankfully. I'd been afraid they would make the same mistake as Glasha, thinking I was a Sodality *sotin*.

Glasha led Ysduil and me to the largest of the homes. Just before we reached it, the door—basically a bundle of branches lashed together and tied to one side of the door frame—swung open and an intimidating dunim woman stepped out.

Judging her height next to Glasha, she was a little taller than I was, whereas Glasha was maybe an inch shorter than me. My dunim escort dipped her head in greeting, but it seemed to me to be a strong sign of respect, not obeisance. I didn't think that dunim went in for bowing and the like.

"Shagar Bladedancer, the leader of our tribe," Glasha said.

The woman radiated authority. I fought the urge to bow or salute her or in some other way show respect. I settled for nodding my head in greeting, trying to imitate Glasha's effortless motion.

Eyes darker than any I'd ever seen before drilled into me. They may have been a very deep brown or they could have been black, but as my eyes met them, I couldn't see any pupil at all. Shagar's face was...well, it was what I would have thought a powerful orc woman would look like.

She had the tusks I would expect, and what looked like a perpetual sneer had etched lines into her leather-like skin.

Though her black hair had streaks of grey through it, her body was fit and robust. I mean, like a twenty-something yoga and gym fanatic type of shape. I spotted a few scars on her skin. It wasn't hard since she wore what was basically a cavewoman's bikini, small scraps of leather or fur. Still, I tried to keep my eyes on hers. The last thing I needed was to be accused of checking out the tribal leader of such a warlike people.

"Glasha." The matriarch said it almost as a sigh. "Why have you brought one of the Sodality's pets to our village? Don't you know Imorith would raze the entire area in retribution for taking one of their *sotin*?"

"He is not—" Glasha started to answer, but I got impatient and spoke over her.

"I'm not a *sotin*. I'm what you call a *khresha*, I guess. I stole this uniform from one of the guards when we escaped from the Sodality dungeon."

Shagar's rough face scrunched as her eyebrows lifted. "You speak like no *sotin* I have ever heard of. It's...I have not spoken with a male in a real conversation for nearly twenty years." She glared at me for a moment, but I didn't take it as personal. It seemed like her face always looked like that. "Come. We will talk." She turned and went back into the building she'd come out of.

I traded looks with Ysduil and Glasha. The dunim woman rolled her eyes and followed the older woman. Ysduil and I followed.

Once inside, I was surprised to find it looking more civilized than I had imagined. Several chairs were spread throughout, most of them at a rough table made from a massive cross section of some type of tree.

"Sit," Shagar said. She glided to the largest of the chairs, so graceful I had to keep myself from staring.

Glasha laughed. "Shagar was named Bladedancer when she was young. Both because she is a horror with a blade and because of her grace in movement. Within combat and without."

Bladedancer, Axecrusher. The dunim tribe seemed to follow the tradition of taking names later in life to indicate their accomplishments. Like some Native American tribes. Shagar definitely looked like she could be a dancer.

After sitting, Glasha introduced us. She didn't fawn over the leader. She was respectful, but it was more like how you would treat a family member, not a political leader.

"This is Adam Townsend, a stranger to our land. Our vinem friend is Ysduil Fennis, priestess of Odona. They aided me when I was attacked by more than two dozen aanem."

Shagar's eyes locked onto Ysduil for a moment, then shifted to me. "Well met, both of you, and thank you for your aid. Glasha can find trouble in her bath water. It is her special talent."

Glasha chuckled at that. "Adam is new to our world. He knew nothing of Tenos when he woke up in the Sodality dungeon, completely without clothing."

Shagar placed her elbows on the table, steepling her fingers. "Another world. Is there no Sodality where you come from?"

"There isn't anything like what I understand you have here. We don't enslave half the population and use them as labor or breeding." A bit of my anger at their system leaked into my words, but I didn't think a little fire would put off such a warrior as Shagar.

"And is your world like many places on Tenos used to

be, with the men lording it over the woman and oppressing them?"

That was a bit harder for me to answer easily. "There *are* places where women are respected less than others, but nothing like what you're saying. Where I come from, there are women in positions of extreme authority, just like there are men. Some lead entire nations."

"No *training*?" The way she stressed the word, it was clear she was talking about the Sodality's brainwashing.

"No. We have our problems with prejudice, violence, and other crimes, but nothing like the Sodality's *training*."

"It sounds like a better place to live than here. Why, then, have you come?"

I ran my fingers through my hair. "I didn't exactly have a choice. I was exploring a cave and there was an accident. I fell, and then I woke up here, in a dungeon cell. Ysduil helped me understand where I was and we escaped. We've been running since then. We intend to cross the Dreadlands and get to the eastern side."

Shagar laughed, a rough gritty sound, like rocks shaken up in a bucket. She glanced at Glasha, who was smiling but not laughing, then at me and Ysduil. The light of understanding entered her dark eyes.

"You're serious."

"I am."

"Then let me say that it was a pleasure to have met you, Adam. Ysduil. I shall likely never gaze upon you again after you leave the village. Traveling the Dreadlands is not safe, even for great warriors. You may stay here for a time, if you like, but we have little to share."

"I appreciate it," I said. "We'll take you up on that for tonight and we'll leave in the morning. Ysduil needs to get back to her sisters and I need to try to find my way back home. I'm sorry if this is inappropriate, but if your village is having a rough time, why not go somewhere else that isn't infested by wild monsters?"

Shagar glanced at Glasha again. "You are ignorant of this world if you ask such a question. You do not know the history of my people?"

"I'm sorry. No."

"Then I will tell you. When the Sodality was first formed by Imorith Sartyne, the Paragon, my people were strong. We had no great cities; that was not our way. Our tribes, though, were respected and feared. Even then, we preferred to live in the wild places. Cities full of large populations may provide some safety, but what is the sense of an easy life?

"It was not immediate, but all too soon the Sodality set its eyes on all of the assorted tribes and communities of the world. They started with those closer to their great cities, but then once they had accomplished their goals, they went after the more remote areas.

"I remember it well, when the vast armies of the Sodality marched into the Dreadlands, devastating the landscape and killing anything in their path. They searched out each community, my tribe included, and announced clearly what they would do.

"All males were forfeit. They would take them to be trained, leaving only the females. Of course, as warriors, we did not simply go along. There were fierce battles and many lives were lost on both sides. In the end, however, we could not resist. Our numbers were vastly depleted, our men were taken, and as a punishment, we were not even afforded the opportunity to interact with our former husbands and lovers.

"The groups who cooperated willingly were granted

such privileges, to mate with the males that had been taken from them. It was according to a schedule and there were strict rules, but it happened. At first. All male children born of such activities were seized, of course, but some tried to hide the infants. Eventually, the system developed that drastically reduced such interactions, so much so that they rarely happen anymore except in special colonies to control it all.

"Without our men, and with the far lower numbers of tribe members, life became more difficult. The areas trampled by the soldiers have recovered, but our tribe, as well as many others, whether dunim or gnosta, frelst, wustol, even the zynchly, are slowly dying out. Ones such as Glasha, who were children when the Sodality came to power, are strong members of our society, but most others are of advanced age. It will only get worse. Meanwhile, the stigma of our initial rebellion has made us unwelcome in most places except here, our historical home."

As Shagar explained it all, I thought of how it must have been. Their lovers and sons were either killed or taken, only to be reduced to mindless slaves. For all I knew, the orc we'd brained to get the clothes I wore was from this very village. I found myself clenching my fists, a slow fire building in my chest.

"That's horrible," I said. "Why haven't people risen up and taken the Sodality from power?"

Shagar looked at Glasha again, a slight smile growing on her face. "I like this one. I would mate with him, were I not so old. He will produce fierce children." Her significant look at the other dunim implied that she might want to take on the task. "There were attempts at rebellion, but the Sodality armies are vast and most of the soldiers are the loved ones of those who would rebel. All attempts were squashed almost immediately. As shameful as it is, we and the other tribes are a people beaten down. Especially the intelligent monster races are thus. Some of the more populous people—humans, elves, and many beastkin—are comfortable with the Sodality and do not cause trouble. Such is the world we live in."

I wasn't about to act like a know-it-all and suggest what they should do. What did I know about living under such a system or about rebellion? Besides, what good would it do? Better to learn to live within the restraints of something we couldn't change.

"I wish I could help," I said. "Maybe when I figure out how to get back to my world, I can bring others back with me."

"You are honorable," Shagar said. "You remind me of my beloved Oguk. He was a strong warrior, with honor like a steel sword. If you survive the Dreadlands and find your way home, I would be glad to hear of it."

We talked for half an hour more, but my mind kept coming back to what this world had done to itself. It was a tragedy. Shagar finally released us to one of the buildings used for guests. Glasha, Ysduil, and I relaxed in the small hut until it was time to eat dinner, talking over how we'd try to survive the trip through the Dreadlands. By the time the sun went down and I'd eaten a meager dinner, I was ready for bed.

CHAPTER

TWENTY-THREE

"Tell us of your life," Ysduil said.

I supposed that meant I wasn't going to get to sleep at the moment. After handfuls of minutes with the three of us sitting in silence, I had kind of hoped I would be allowed to drop off into blissful slumber.

Not that I minded chatting with the two beautiful women. My mind was just tired after busily spinning all day long.

"I've told you about my world. What do you want to know?"

"No," the foxgirl said. "Not about your world. About your *life.*"

"Uh, my life?" I looked at Glasha and though she didn't say anything, her expression was expectant. Those striking pale blue eyes, set off by her creamy, green skin, fixed on me as she waited for my story. "It's not that exciting."

"Please tell us anyway. I would know what your days and nights were like in that other world."

"Okay, fine." I repositioned myself on the bed I was sitting on, leaning my back against the wall. "I grew up in a place far from where my current home is. I had good friends that I have kept from that time, but none as good where I live now. I work for a place that makes...something like the oil for lamps. Except it's made from liquid we mine from the ground. The process is almost like magic, turning it into something that burns better than oil and powers machines we can use to do work and to travel quickly."

Ysduil sat on another bed, her legs crossed beneath her. She leaned toward me, captivated. Still, I think I'd told them about as much as I could about gasoline and cars without describing our entire society. I tried to think of what to talk about next. Luckily, the two were interested enough to have questions.

"Do you have a mate there. A wife?" It was Glasha who asked.

"I...no. I had a girlfriend that I asked to become my wife and she said yes."

"You would wed a girl?" Ysduil asked.

"I mean, not a young girl. In my world, we call women who are mates *girlfriends*. She was an adult, about the same age as me."

"And she died?" the foxgirl asked innocently.

"N-no."

"Then why do you say that she *was* and not *is*?"

"It's just that...well, she agreed to be my wife, but then, before we could get married, she decided she didn't want to be my wife after all."

"She betrayed your contract to become your wife?" Glasha asked, her voice taking on a deadly edge.

The word betrayed struck me hard and I must have shown it in my face, because the dunim softened her voice.

"I'm sorry. I didn't mean to bring up painful memories."

"It's fine," I said. "She just decided that she wanted

someone else. It happens in my world. People change their mind all the time. Even after getting married."

Ysduil gasped. "Women break the solemn oath of mateship in your world? They are not punished for this?"

"Not just women. Men do, too. They're not punished. Well, not unless you can count child support, alimony, and bashing on social media." I chuckled but noticed both women with confused looks. "Sorry, forget about that." I wasn't about to try to explain social media to these women. We'd be up all night.

"So your *girlfriend* changed her mind," Glasha said. "Did you hunt down the one she chose and slaughter him, as was your right?"

I couldn't help but to laugh, confusing them both even more. "No. I just, I don't know, kind of folded in on myself. It was rough, and with other things going on in my life, I needed a break. So, I fl—uh, traveled to where my friends were. The ones I knew when I was younger. We went caving. Umm, exploring in some caves. As I've already told you, that was when I ended up here. I'm not sure how it happened. I hope they're all right. It was a bad rockfall."

Both of the women waited for me to continue, but I didn't know what else to tell them. I had to be the worst storyteller in two worlds. After a thousand years of silence, Ysduil finally spoke up.

"You have no other mates in your world?"

"Nope. I had planned on spending the rest of my life with Amy. That's her name. I wasn't really in the mood to look for another girlfriend."

"Did no other women come looking for you?" the foxgirl asked. "You are a desirable man, pleasing to look at and to interact with."

"Thank you, but no. Even if they did, I wouldn't have

been receptive. I...you know, I just don't understand what happened. The things that Amy loved about me—my ambition and my drive to improve—those were things that tied us together. The man she chose over me was a loser. He didn't even have a job or a plan for his life. He was the kind of guy she never would have looked at before. Or so I thought.

"I always thought our relationship was like a nineties romance movie. Love so strong that it could conquer anything. I just don't get it."

I jumped when something touched my hair. I'd been staring at the ceiling as I talked, zoning out, and Ysduil had sat down on the bed next to me and she was stroking my hair. Basically petting me. I looked down to meet her orange-red eyes.

"I'm sorry women in your world are disloyal and fickle. I don't know what a movie is, or why you would need ninety of them, but I'm sure you would have been a good and faithful lover."

"I...uh, thank you. I thought I was."

My thoughts were interrupted when the foxgirl leaned over and brushed her lips against mine. An explosion of sensations shot through my lips and face, and down through my body. Her lips were so soft! More than that, though, they tingled, almost like some of the magic she'd said was waning in the world was concentrated on her mouth. I reacted as should be expected.

I slipped an arm around her, pulled her firm body against me, and crushed my mouth to hers, parting her lips with my tongue to touch it to hers. She responded in kind, apparently no stranger to kissing. Sure, she was a priestess to a sex goddess, but who knew what things were different in this world?

We held our kiss for a blissful eternity, the passion building up in me from days of sexual frustration.

Until a deeper voice than Ysduil's cleared its throat and spoke.

"I'll leave you two alone."

Ysduil jumped to her feet so quickly, I found myself leaning over with my mouth open. I had to put a hand down to keep from falling.

"Oh," she said. "No. I'm so sorry, Glasha. Did I offend you or irritate you? We haven't spoken about what your views are on my...activities in conjunction with the worship of my goddess. I didn't mean to act so rudely, and after you have shown me hospitality. It's just that I felt sympathy for Adam and I acted thoughtlessly. Please, forgive me."

It took a moment for me to think with my heart beating so rapidly and...other parts of me taking some of my focus. "Yeah. Sorry."

"It's fine," the dunim woman said. "I will return to my own home and you two can continue to...talk."

Ysduil grabbed the green woman's hand and pulled her down to sit on the bed where the foxgirl had been sitting before. "No. Please, stay. We can keep talking. Maybe you can tell us about what we'll find as we leave and go east. We appreciate your help."

Glasha looked anything but comfortable, but she relented and began to explain what dangers were further into the Dreadlands. Even she didn't know what was at the heart of the dangerous area, but the information she had would no doubt be beneficial to us. I listened, half-heartedly at first, but then with more interest. It seemed our friend had traveled a fair amount.

After nearly another hour, she stopped mid-sentence and drilled into my eyes with her own. "Actually, if you would allow it, I would like to repay your aid when you helped with the aanem by going with you. I have wanted to expand the area I have explored anyway. I would accompany you all the way to the eastern edge of the Dreadlands, if you allow me."

Ysduil shrieked and wrapped Glasha in a hug. The dunim looked over at me with wide eyes, but allowed the show of affection.

"That would be wonderful," the foxgirl said. "I was sad to say goodbye to you. Now we can travel together and become even better friends. Right, Adam?"

"Yeah, it would be great. Thank you. You don't really need to repay us anymore, though. As far as I'm concerned, we're already even."

"My honor has not yet been satisfied. I thank you for the opportunity. I will do my best to lead you to the most favorable route and help keep you safe."

I smiled, but my heart wasn't in it. Sure, I liked Glasha, and she was definitely going to be useful when it came to combat, but one thing weighed on my mind.

When the hell was I going to be able to get Ysduil alone and continue what we'd started? If possible, I'd like to end at least one day in this world without blue balls.

CHAPTER
TWENTY-FOUR

Ysduil and Glasha chatted for a while and, once my body cooled and accepted there wouldn't be any more excitement, my eyes drifted closed. I didn't want to be rude, and I was interested in what the women were talking about—basically comparing notes about the places they lived and traveled—but I found myself in a twilight sleep, not quite completely under, but useless to the world.

Two or three times, as much as I can remember, there were scuffling sounds, but not enough to wake me completely. The next thing I knew, I woke with dim morning light squeezing through the spaces between the wooden poles of the walls.

I was surprised to find Glasha sleeping in the bed closest to the door, with Ysduil curled up like a cat near a fire on the bed closest to mine. Was the dunim woman so set on keeping me and Ysduil from being alone that she stayed with us instead of going to her own home?

As if my attention triggered hers, Glasha snapped her

head toward me. I watched the pupils in her pale blue eyes grow large, then contract as she focused on me.

"Good morning," I said, my voice rough from disuse.

She cleared her throat and reciprocated. "Good morning."

"Glasha stood guard over you last night," Ysduil's voice said from beside me.

"Guard? Is it so unsafe, even in the village?"

The green woman's throaty chuckle made me smile. "No, no. Not dangers from monsters. Several of my fellow villagers tried to sneak into your bed. I convinced them to go away."

I stared at Glasha's beautiful eyes. The color was so striking set against her green skin and black hair. Then what she said hit me. "Wait. What?" Women were trying to sneak into my bed and she *stopped* them?

"Many of the younger women—born in the last years before all ours were taken away—have never seen a man. They were...curious."

Ysduil laughed her merry, tinkling laugh. "But that's not all."

Glasha turned a cold glare on her, but then her mouth twisted into an evil smile. "No, that's not all. The older women, ones who have known a man, have missed the experience. They were the most insistent."

"Wow." There was nothing else I could say. Things were so bad in this world that women resorted to trying to sneak into my bed. Coming from a place where women held all the cards when it came to sex—at least for a normal guy like me—it was quite a shock.

"It's no problem," Glasha said. "We will leave shortly and then we'll only need to contend with monsters and beasts that want to attack you and eat you for food."

The dunim's mouth twitched. Mine dropped open and she couldn't maintain the façade anymore. She burst out laughing.

"Come, let's gather supplies and head out. Daylight is too precious to waste."

Glasha brought us to her house and I wondered why we hadn't just stayed there, but then I remembered she wasn't originally going to stay with us. I thanked her for running interference, though I wasn't sure if I really appreciated it. I had been wrestling with a certain...lack of attention lately.

After stuffing her own pack with more items and procuring two more for me and Ysduil, we said goodbye to Shagar and were off toward the east.

As we traveled, the terrain changed, but not as strikingly as the vegetation. Some plants that I'd become accustomed to remained, but new and different types popped up. They weren't all green, either. By late morning, I got the feeling I'd fallen into a Dr. Seuss story, fantastical shapes and colors all around me.

Fern-like fronds brushed our legs, of colors ranging from red to a deep purple like the leaves of a black plum tree. Bushes with razor-toothed leaves sprawled in some areas. Glasha told us to stay away from those lest we be cut. Some innocuous looking bushes even had hidden thorns that were closer to what I would call spikes. These last ones moved more than the wind could account for, so I was grateful for Glasha leading us and pointing out where not to step. I'd had enough of battles with plants.

It wasn't just plants, though. Very large insects scuttled around—though not quite so large and aggressive as the aanem Glasha was fighting when we found her.

"That is an ootsar," Glasha said, channeling her inner tour guide as she pointed out a long creature that looked like a stick bug. If stick bugs were the size of a baseball bat. "They're harmless, for the most part. You have to watch out when sleeping with no one to stand watch, though, as they are curious and learn about things by chewing on them. The flying ones there are zinlas." She gestured toward a trio of what looked like giant wasps in a dark green color. "They're not so bad to deal with unless a dozen or more gather and attack at once."

I watched them warily. Each was the size of a softball, and I did not like the idea of a swarm of them attacking. I'd been stung by a wasp once and it hurt enough that I didn't want one or more of these monstrosities punching holes in me.

We saw more animals, too. Some were the ordinary kind like birds, some rodents, and the occasional squirrel or badger. There were also strange variations that looked like a cross between two or three types of creatures, like a blocky, pig kind of creature that moved quickly on catlike paws. At least none of them were aggressive toward us, even if it did bother me that they didn't flee from us, either. The pig-cat glared at me so hard, I nearly walked into a tree trying to keep it in sight for fear of it attacking me when I was unaware. The women enjoyed that little trip-up.

Mid-afternoon, I heard movement ahead of us and turned to find five shapes moving through the foliage. Several game trails criss-crossed the area. We were on one, and apparently the other figures were on the other. When we got closer, the hair on the back of my neck prickled and I tightened my hand on the hilt of my sword.

They were beastkin women, but not of a type I'd seen before. Their tails were like a dog's, but kind of scraggly, and their ears were rougher than Ysduil's, the fur coarser. Their bodies were shorter than Ysduil was, but powerfully built. They moved with a certain grace, but more than anything, their movements exuded strength. Three had bows as well as blades, and two had only swords.

I watched them, examining their faces and the different colors of their ears and tails. Like Ysduil, those colors matched the hair on their heads. One could be called pretty, but the others were plainer, though that could have just been the tired looks on their faces.

Glasha raised a hand in greeting and the first woman in line did the same. The others warily joined her and, finally, Ysduil and I did likewise. Though it seemed friendly and respectful enough, I couldn't help but notice that they had not taken their eyes off me since we came into view. They had a hungry, needful look to them.

We soon passed and I swung my head to look back at them. Five tight asses swayed in snug leather pants. One of the women in the middle of the line turned and met my eyes, then gave me a sad, tired smile. I returned it and waved to her before swinging my eyes back to the front of our group, on Glasha's muscular back.

"Gnolls," Ysduil said.

"What?" I asked.

"Gnolls, also called gnosta. They are a type of dog or hyena beastkin. They are relatively few and because they are so tribal and—I hate to use the word—primitive, most classify them as monster tribes rather than beastkin. I believe they only live in the Dreadlands now."

"Yes," Glasha said. "They used to have greater numbers, but they fought the Sodality harder than many and lost the majority of their people."

"They're friendly with the dunim?" Ysduil asked.

"Not friendly, but not hostile. Most who still reside in the Dreadlands do not pursue aggression with others. It is enough to defend against wild monsters. We have no desire to engage in the wars of history. We are too few to waste lives thus."

I glanced back toward where the dog-women had gone. "Huh. We have legends of gnolls in my world, though they're not real. Funny that the name is the same. From the illustrations I've seen, though, they look more animal than those women did. These...looked like they were kind of sad."

"Most who live in the Dreadlands are," Glasha said. "It's a rough life here, especially without hope of family. Those five must have been born just before—or just after—the Sodality took the men from all the tribes in the Dreadlands. They are young."

The beaten down expressions saddened me. I knew that most of the things in life weren't negotiable, but it still weighed on me that so many were miserable. I had my own experiences of being squashed down by life, but it didn't mean I thought everyone else had it great.

I sighed, wanting to get the images out of my mind. A thought occurred to me and it seemed the perfect time to ask about it.

"So, Glasha. I noticed that Shagar's last name was Bladedancer. You said it was because of her grace with the blade and in dancing. Do all dunim take names later in life? Do they not have last names when they're born?"

"We do not use family names as some peoples do," she said. "We receive a name when we are born, but only the first name. When we do something to earn a last name, then we obtain that second name. Some gain it in childhood, others not until they are adults."

"I see. So then, your name, Axecrusher. I asked about it when we met because it doesn't make sense to me, but you didn't tell me where it came from. How did you earn it?"

One side of her mouth raised in a half-smile. "It was when I was barely an adolescent. I was sparring with another warrior and was struck by the broad side of a practice axe, one made of wood. I became...enraged. I cut viciously at my opponent with my sword, bruising her arms severely and causing her to drop her weapon. A weapon that I took, carried to a nearby anvil, and proceeded to mangle with a heavy blacksmith's sledge. Our instructor looked at the destroyed weapon, sighed at my temper, and proclaimed me Axecrusher."

Glasha's laugh was loud enough that I was pretty sure the gnolls—who were probably half a mile away by now— could hear it clearly.

CHAPTER

TWENTY-FIVE

I t surprised me that we didn't run into any of the dangers both women had promised abounded in the Dreadlands. They'd talked it up so much, I had started this leg of the journey tentatively, watching the brush constantly. Waiting to be attacked.

I mentioned it and Glasha shrugged.

"We are still near my village, and other villages. This area is the *civilized* part of the Dreadlands. It's still dangerous, but to one who lives here and knows what to look for, it isn't overly so. We haven't reached the truly hazardous parts. Tomorrow afternoon or evening, then we will have to be more careful. Take the opportunity to relax while I know what to expect. I haven't gone too far into the heart of the Dreadlands."

I didn't figure I was going to relax anytime soon—or ever—in this world. Still, her words comforted me a little bit. There was nothing like street cred to help one feel a little safer. This was Glasha's 'hood, so I'd trust her to keep us away from the worst of things.

At least until tomorrow evening.

When we stopped for the night, I gathered wood while Glasha prepared to start a fire. Ysduil excused herself and the sounds of her daily ritual—still muffled compared to when she was in the dungeon—reached me. Several times while it lasted, I glanced over at Glasha. Twice, I caught her looking toward where the sound emanated, a strange expression on her face. Curiosity? Longing? Admiration? It was something like that, definitely not annoyance or disgust like Ysduil feared. The dunim woman didn't seem to have much sexual experience, but it wasn't anathema to her, either.

We didn't bother hunting during the day, having brought a lot of food from the village. After a quick dinner, I went to sleep soon after dark, since I had the third watch. Ysduil settled against me, her back to mine for warmth, and actually fell into the rhythmic breathing of sleep before I did. She would be saddled with the dreaded middle watch, so I didn't begrudge her a little rest.

Sometime during the night, I felt Ysduil move and then get up. My cooling back where she'd been was what roused me, but I was too sleepy to move or say anything. She picked her way across the campsite and sat down next to Glasha.

"How are you?" Ysduil said.

"I'm fine. There was nothing of concern during my watch. It's a quiet night."

"Hmm." The silence stretched on for a time, though I don't know how long with me being on the edge of sleep like I was. Then Ysduil spoke again, almost startling me. "Have you...engaged in giving or receiving pleasure with another?"

On the surface, it was a simple question, but considering it was coming from the priestess of a sex goddess to a woman who seemed inexperienced in such things, it was loaded with meaning.

The volume of Glasha's voice changed and I could picture her swinging her head to look toward me. When her words came out, they were almost a whisper and I barely heard them. "I...have not."

"No? I looked admiringly on some of the members of your tribe. At least two of those I saw last night—of the number you shooed away from Adam—I would gladly take into my bed. Does saying that...disgust or offend you?"

"No. I'm not a Sodality adherent to think all pleasure is unclean. I'm simply inexperienced."

"If you haven't taken advantage of the attractive females within your tribe, then do you practice pleasuring yourself? Please forgive me if my words are rude. I only ask because...because you are very comely and the thought that you do not enjoy pleasure, either by yourself or in the care of others, would wound my heart. The goddess tells us that receiving and giving pleasure is the pinnacle of our mortal lives. I believe that is true."

I cracked one eye. Luckily, I was in a position where I could see the two women. Not in any great detail, due to the slit I was looking through and the darkness of the scene, but I could see that they looked at each other as they spoke. Not at me.

That was good, because their conversation was definitely having an effect on me. Especially after suffering through Ysduil's sound effects for so many days and having our kiss—and what may have followed—cut short.

Glasha wrung her hands, dragging her eyes away from Ysduil's. "I have trained my whole life as a warrior. Because of my appearance—"

"You are beautiful," Ysduil interrupted.

"Ah. Thank you for your kindness, but among the dunim, I am not attractive. Plain, at best." She suddenly laughed. "Adam tried to convince me that I was pleasing to look upon the other day. He said I was *hot*."

"Were you too close to the fire?"

She opened her mouth to bark her normal loud laugh, but then she whipped her head toward me and stifled her sounds, though she still chuckled. "That's what I asked. Apparently, in his world, calling a person *hot* means that they are...attractive, arousing. Sexy. He said you are hot as well. By that definition..." She trailed off and I was afraid she'd said something too softly for me to hear it.

"What?" Ysduil pushed. "What were you going to say?"

I could almost hear the blush in Glasha's voice. "By that definition, I would agree that you are hot."

Ysduil wriggled in a way that made my cock jump.

"Ooh. Thank you, Glasha. As I've already said, you are all those things as well. Truly, you have never, you know..." I barely caught the motion of Ysduil wiggling her fingers, sort of like the *come hither* motion.

Glasha tilted her head, confusion painting her face.

Ysduil giggled. "I'm sorry. I do not mean to poke fun at you, but it is the height of irony that one with your... obvious graces would never have availed yourself of playing with your...charms."

"I don't understand."

Ysduil took one of Glasha's hands and brought it to her mouth, kissing it softly. She watched Glasha's face, which had turned from confusion to surprise to contentment. Then the foxgirl licked the green palm in her hand, from the fleshy heel all the way up her fingers. She took Glasha's index finger into her mouth and the dunim sharply inhaled.

"Does that feel good?" Ysduil asked.

"I...it...that...oh, yes. I have never felt anything like that. It made me feel stirrings."

"Did you feel it here?" Ysduil brought her other hand up to Glasha's breast. The warrior had taken off her breast-plate and wore a snug undershirt. Without opening my eye wider, I couldn't tell if her nipples were erect, but I imagined they were. She gasped as Ysduil's hand cupped her firm globe.

"I..."

"Or maybe it was here," Ysduil said as she slid her hand down to Glasha's inner thigh and moved it slowly up under the leather battle skirt the dunim wore.

"Oh."

I didn't have to see the flash of white to know Ysduil was smiling hugely.

"Glasha, I would like to help you to find pleasure."

The green woman stiffened. "I don't think—"

"Shh. Don't overreact. I don't expect you to do anything, nor will I take any actions that may be too much for you right now. All I propose is that you let me show you how you can help yourself. How you can give yourself plea-sure. I can either demonstrate by showing you on my own body, or I can go slowly and show you on your body, or both. Personally, I vote for both."

"This is all new to me, Ysduil. I'm too tense about it, I think. I thank you very much, but..."

Glasha trailed off as Ysduil started to caress her own breast. She carefully peeled away the delicate cloth remaining of her dress and ran her hand along the sides of the firm swell and then around, to cup the entire thing and squeeze. She let out the most deli-cious moan. When she moved her hand to her nipple and rubbed it in little circles, Glasha's breathing quickened.

The entire time, the foxgirl was looking into Glasha's eyes. The green woman's gaze was locked on Ysduil's chest.

"Doesn't this look like fun? Do you want to try it?"

"T-try it?" Glasha asked. I wanted to chuckle that the confident warrior was so nervous. She would enter battle without a thought, but seeing Ysduil like that had her all discombobulated.

"Yes," Ysduil purred. "You can feel my breast or I can show you how to stimulate your own. You have magnificent tits, Glasha. If it weren't for going slow, I would love to take your nipples into my mouth and suck them. Maybe nibble them."

"Uh..."

Ysduil took Glasha's hand and brought it to her breast. The dunim woman tentatively rubbed her hand over the areola and stiff nipple. The foxgirl sucked in a breath.

"Mmm. Like that. More, please."

Glasha complied, trailing her hand lightly over Ysduil's chest, barely touching the skin, like Ysduil had done herself just moment before. She wasn't watching, though, and when Ysduil caressed one of the green breasts by reaching up under her shirt, Glasha moaned slightly, then immediately retreated. I could almost feel the heat of her cheeks from where I lay.

Ysduil wasn't deterred, though. "Let me show you something else, Glasha. Pay attention, because this is something you can do for yourself. You don't need anyone else to help you, if you don't want to. Of course, it is more fun to have someone else help."

The fox woman's delicate fingers slid down to Glasha's

muscular thigh, rubbing lightly and caressing her way up to the junction between her legs.

"May I?" Ysduil asked as she pulled the tiny thing Glasha wore under her skirt. If I didn't know better, I would say it was a thong or a G-string. I'd scoped out her tight ass as she walked in front of me, so I knew exactly what the undergarment looked like. At least from the back.

Glasha wriggled and I thought she might object, but Ysduil was so quick, she had the garment off and lying on the rock beside her before Glasha did anything to stop her.

Ysduil began to use her fingers deftly to stimulate the green woman's lips.

"Do you feel that?" Ysduil cooed.

"Feel...?"

"The slickness. Give me your hand, please."

Glasha's eyes were lidded and she complied immediately like she was in a trance. Ysduil guided the woman's hand down to her own crotch and rubbed the fingers across the folds.

"Do you feel how wet you are?"

"Y-yes."

"If I wasn't bound by my word to take it slow, I would lick your wetness to see how you taste. Maybe someday, when you have become more comfortable. For now, pay attention to how my fingers feel sliding across you. Imagine they are my tongue, if you wish. That's what I'm imagining."

She worked on Glasha, but with the angle and the poor lighting I couldn't see clearly. It didn't matter. My dick was so hard I could have punched it through a tree at this point.

The dunim woman wriggled and moaned and gasped.

"What is...oh! I've never felt anything like—" She

sucked in a breath so hard, the hiss probably was going to attract any giant snake within miles.

It went on for a few minutes, but Ysduil was as good as her word. She kept it brief, bringing Glasha to what was probably her first orgasm ever. A small one, granted, but even so, I was sure it was unlike anything she'd ever experienced.

When the green woman relaxed and pushed herself back to a normal sitting position, I thought the show was done.

Not so.

"Do you mind greatly if I finish myself?" Ysduil asked in a voice so husky and sexy I seriously contemplated jumping up and trying to get in on the action.

"Finish?"

"Yes. You have aroused me so much, I ache for release. If you don't mind, I would like to finish, give myself an orgasm, similar to what you just felt. I won't, though, if it bothers you." Her hands had been busy as she spoke, one clenching to squeeze her breast and the other fingering her own slit.

"I don't mind. If you don't mind me watching."

"Mmmm," Ysduil purred. "You watching makes me even hornier."

True to her word, Ysduil worked her magic on herself, even more urgently than when I'd watched her a few nights before. Glasha stared at the spectacle, unblinking, until Ysduil's final orgasmic tremors settled and the woman collapsed on the rock.

"Think about this, dear Glasha. We'll talk about it later and see if you want me to show you more. Maybe you'll let me demonstrate by making you have a real, powerful orgasm."

"R-real? Do you mean they get stronger than that?"

"Oh, yes. You think about it. About doing it yourself. Or letting me do it for you. I will eagerly await your decision."

Glasha took back her undergarment and slipped it on, lingering on the feeling as she wriggled her hips to adjust the clothing. "We'll talk about it." When the dunim passed me to lie down to sleep, she bit her bottom lip, then smiled.

CHAPTER
TWENTY-SIX

The next morning, I watched the two women as they gathered up their gear and got ready to continue our journey. Ysduil acted exactly the same as she always did, bouncy and upbeat. Glasha seemed withdrawn, like she was embarrassed.

"Will we be leaving the safety of the area you know today?" Ysduil asked.

The dunim nodded but wouldn't meet the foxgirl's eyes. "By the time we camp again tonight, we will have passed the extent of where I have traveled before. We will need to be more careful."

It was clear the green woman was going to need to reconcile the new relationship between the two, but that was their thing and had nothing to do with me. I hoped it didn't cause problems but the best thing for me to do was to act like nothing had happened.

"Do you know anything about the area deeper in?" I asked. "From talking to others or something?"

She didn't seem to have problems looking me in the eye. I appreciated it. I loved her eyes and could get lost in them if we were close and I could study them. "I do, but I'm unsure how accurate it is. We'll have to see. I'm experienced with being out away from the village. I spend most of my time away. Still, not all my skills will translate to great advantage in an area I am unfamiliar with."

"You'll be a huge help, Glasha," Ysduil said. "We trust you."

When we started off, Glasha went up ahead to find a path for us. I walked after her, like I had the day before. Ysduil lagged. When I looked back to see if anything was wrong, she jerked her head and shifted her eyes toward her left. I took it to mean she wanted me to hang back with her for a moment, though it would put us quite a distance behind our scout.

When I joined the foxgirl, her serious look turned into a mischievous one.

"How are you doing?" she asked.

I narrowed my eyes at her. "Umm, fine. Did you want me to come all the way back here to ask me that?"

"Of course not, silly. I simply thought I would start the conversation politely and ask about your welfare."

I snorted. "Okay. Then, I fare well, thank you for asking. How fare you?"

She smacked my shoulder and leaned closer. "How did you like the show last night?"

I stopped and stared at her. "W-what?"

"Don't pretend with me, Adam. I know you were awake and saw what happened. I'm a fox beastkin, remember. I have very good hearing and excellent night vision. I saw your eye slitted and heard your breathing change. I also saw—" she reached down and rubbed my crotch "—your response."

I tried to think of something to say. What did you say

when you were busted red-handed? Or blue-balled, as the case may be.

"Don't worry. I won't tell Glasha if you don't want me to. Part of the reason I did it was to let you see. I'm sorry that I made her climax. Actually, no I'm not. It was very satisfying...and arousing. I'm sorry that you couldn't be the first one to give that gift to her, though. I do believe she has never felt that kind of pleasure, either with someone else or by her own hand. I wanted you to be her first."

"You...wanted me to be her first?"

"Of course. You can still be her first penetration or her first strong orgasm. She is very...hot. Is she not?"

I chuckled weakly. I heard Glasha explain the term to Ysduil last night, but was a little surprised at the foxgirl speaking so plainly about it. "You're saying that you want me to get together with Glasha?"

"Yes. How many ways do I have to explain it? I would love to watch, if you both agree, but I think you two could give each other much pleasure."

I scratched the back of my neck, flummoxed. "Oh. I thought that maybe you and I had...could..."

Ysduil cocked her head. "We have had moments that are delicious and magical. I didn't say that she should be *your* first in this world. I will claim that privilege..." She trailed off and color came to her cheeks. "If that is something that you would want."

"I...of course...you...hold on." I took a breath so I wouldn't stumble over myself. "Let me get this straight. You're open to, uh, having pleasure with me, but you also want me to do it with Glasha, too?"

"Exactly. To be clear, I want to have sex with you, as my first male partner ever. I will test out what I have learned from books and training and will try to give you as much pleasure as possible. You, in turn will...what is the old-time term? Ah, you will fuck me until I cannot walk straight." She flashed those perfect white teeth—including the sharp canines—at me.

I blinked at her several times, processing what she'd said. "I thought you were uninterested in me, or at least shy about telling me."

"I was intimidated because I have never been with a man. Since I have come to know you, and especially since the kiss we shared, I am not afraid anymore. I want you and, if you agree, I intend to have you. Several times. Many."

"And Glasha?"

"We can share her. I would not try to keep such a body to myself. That would be selfish."

I shook my head. "This world is a strange place. I'm not used to this kind of sharing. That you don't mind if I get with other women is different for me."

"You are likely the only man any of us will have access to, so it would be unfair not to share you with others. That should be clear from what the Sodality has done."

My head swam as I thought about it. Of course, she couldn't speak for Glasha. Even if Ysduil got the dunim to enjoy sexual things, she might prefer females, but God! Despite the danger and being away from home, this world definitely had its benefits.

"Now," she continued, "all we need to do is—"

"Is everything all right?" Glasha said. She'd backtracked toward us because we continued to lag further behind as we talked.

Ysduil skipped up to where the dunim was and surprised her with a kiss on the cheek. "Sorry. We were talking and weren't paying enough attention. I'll stay up here with you and Adam can be the rear guard for a while. She wagged her tail at me, shaking that shapely ass of hers, and winked. She also tried to put her arm in Glasha's, but the blushing green woman wouldn't have it.

One thing at a time, I thought to myself. *Take it slow, Yssy.*

The two women stayed up ahead of me for most of the rest of the day. I glanced at them occasionally—they did have marvelous asses and Glasha's back was a pure, sexy etching, a work of art—but mainly kept my eyes on the surroundings. It felt more dangerous than it had, like the risk had doubled when I traversed that invisible line days before. I had a kind of sick feeling in my stomach that something was watching me. Watching and waiting.

At one point, in the afternoon, the women stopped and allowed me to catch up.

"I need to check on something," Glasha said. "Stay here until I get back."

I grabbed her arm as she started to walk toward the foliage. "Are you sure? It's dangerous out there. Shouldn't we stick together?"

She looked down at my hand on her arm. She didn't flex, but her flesh was already tight, stretched over hard muscle. I could feel striations beneath the skin. She didn't pull away or comment. Her look was more curiosity.

"I won't go too far. I can move more efficiently and quietly alone."

I let her arm go. I was a lot of things, but stealthy wasn't one of them. She was probably right: I'd bring more attention to her than she would get going alone.

"Well, be careful. Yell out if you need any help with anything."

Her smile was the kind an adult gave a child who said he'd help you fix your car. I decided to shut up.

Ysduil and I dropped our packs and I sat down to wait, bringing out the water skin Glasha had given me before we left the village. Ysduil plopped down next to me. So close that her arm was pressed against mine.

"Can I call you Yssy?" I asked. I'd already done so in my mind a few times, but I would stop if she objected to it.

She silently mouthed the word. I watched her eyes as she did as if they were the most fascinating thing in the world. They were pretty damn close to it, actually.

She giggled. "Did you make that name up just for me?"

"I, uh, yeah. It's just a shorter version of your name."

"I love it. Yes, please, call me that. I will enjoy having a special name only you will use."

"You don't have nicknames in this world?"

"Nick names. Are those names stolen from somewhere?"

I laughed. "No. I actually looked it up one time and it's from an old language and means 'an additional name.' It means names we call others that aren't their real names, though a lot of times it's a shortened version of their name. Like, if someone is named Steven, we may call him Steve."

"We don't usually change people's names. I know some women who offer shortened names for themselves and others oblige. Sometimes we'll call someone other names. Like with Glasha, some of the villagers call her the Axecrusher, but I think that's different than what you are speaking of."

"Yeah, a little bit. If you don't mind, though, then that's what I'll call you. Consider it a term of endearment."

"Awww. I will consider it a privilege for you to call me your special name." She snuggled into my shoulder and one of her ears tickled my face.

Without thinking, I reached out to run my finger along

her ear, mostly to move it out from under my nose. I loved how soft it was, but I didn't want to sneeze on her. As I rubbed it lightly, a *mmmm* rumbled from deep in her throat.

I'd almost forgotten that she liked her ears rubbed. Well, we had to wait for Glasha anyway, so I might as well make Ysduil feel good while we sat there.

She shifted her head so that my fingers hit a spot that caused her to huff a breath out. I promised myself to remember the spot and the angle I'd rubbed it. I ran my fingers along the edges of the fur on her ear and then down to the base, caressing gently where they attached to her head. The combination of the soft fur and the pliable skin felt good to me, too.

I started to heat up, especially when her breathing got deeper. I shifted to the ear on the other side of her head and rubbed that one, too. She wriggled, squirming closer to me, pressing her body to mine. I have to say, I enjoyed the feel of her. I found my breathing changing, too, and my heart sped up.

The thought occurred to me that this was like petting a cat, but no cat was ever as sexy as my foxgirl. Actually, there might be cat beastkin in this world. I'd have to ask later. Definitely not now.

As I went at it on both ears, Ysduil couldn't take it anymore. She tilted her head and moved her face to mine, lips slightly parted and her eyes lidded with pleasure. I could be clueless sometimes, but now was not one of them. I pulled her closer and our lips met. A taste of tangy citrus lingered on their pillowy softness, and the closeness of her body to mine drove me crazy.

I eased my tongue into her mouth, seeking hers. When I found it, the two warm and wet appendages danced with each other, activating sweet spots that sent sensations through my body like little jolts of electricity.

It could have been the magic in this world, could have been that she was a beastkin, or it could have been one of a hundred other things. It didn't matter. It was the type of kiss that made you think you'd be content if a boulder dropped on you and killed you because at least your last act in this life was the pinnacle of kissing.

I left one hand on her ear, rubbing it and rolling it around in my fingers, and I snaked the other hand down to run along the taut skin of her back, careful not to tear the delicate remains of her dress. Slowly caressing her skin was bringing my body to a boiling point.

"Mmmm." The vibration in her mouth when she did that doubled the pleasure of the sensations radiating up and down my torso, migrating lower with every second. My hand shot down farther and snuck under her butt to grab her ass cheek.

"Unnnh."

Making soft, sweet sounds, she reached around me. One lifted up the back of my shirt to scratch at the skin on my lower back, but the other plunged down beneath my pants to run her fingers down toward my butt crack. Surprisingly, it felt good. *Very* good.

I had to take my hand off her ear to reach down and adjust myself because my throbbing cock wanted its freedom. She felt my motion and moved her hand from my back to the front to help out.

That was it. I needed her. Right now. I was about ready to shred what was left of her dress to release her fantastic body from its constraints when something rustled in the bushes.

I stood, nearly dumping Ysduil onto the ground, and

turned to find Glasha standing there, a guilty and decidedly embarrassed look on her face.

"I—I'm sorry," the dunim said. "I'll go and leave you to—"

Ysduil reached her before I did. "Nonsense." She was panting slightly. "We're sorry. We should have been alert for danger. It...just happened. We got carried away. Forgive us?"

The smile she flashed the green woman was so perfect, so angelic, I would have forgiven her anything at that moment. Glasha visibly relaxed.

"Of course. Please forgive me for interrupting..."

"It's fine," I said. I even managed not to sound breathless when I did it. "I hope we didn't embarrass you."

Glasha blushed slightly, but shook her head.

"Good. Okay..."

"Did you find what you were looking for?" Ysduil asked.

Glasha's eyes were pointing much too close to where my super-hard dick was showing its full stature with a pronounced lump in my pants. "What? Oh, yes. I found some worm sign."

I barked a laugh.

"No. Umm, I mean, I found traces of great grey worms." Her words weren't helping me. I seemed to be coming down with a case of the giggles. *Coming* down with them. Oh, God. I was going to start laughing uncontrollably any moment. Like a twelve-year-old.

She shook her head. "I'm not making sense. There are monsters nearby. I found castings and some residue of tunnels from the grey worms. They're a very dangerous monster. They appear like an average worm, though with many teeth lining their mouths, but they are also four or five times the size of a person. They are known to swallow people whole, though they prefer to tenderize them slowly by munching them with their teeth as they slowly go down their gullet."

That stopped my humorous streak. "Are you serious?"

"Of course. I suggest we hasten from the area. Toward the southeast, where the terrain is rockier. It will hinder their movement and it will be safer for us."

"As you say," Ysduil said. She picked up her pack. "Let's go."

I nodded, but took one last look at Ysduil's sexy form, barely covered by her damaged dress, then at her ears, finally at her tail standing out above her tight ass. With a sigh, I followed Glasha toward the southeast, with a slight limp in my step.

CHAPTER

TWENTY-SEVEN

As we traveled, Ysduil gave me an apologetic look. I shrugged my shoulders and she blew me a kiss. I'd learned she wasn't intimidated by me, and she was definitely interested. I would get the benefits of her training as a sex priestess. Eventually. I could wait, I guessed. I would have to.

Still, it was a rough thing. After a short time of walking behind the two women, with my eyes constantly being drawn to someone's leg or twitching ass or a toned back, I sped up to join them. Watching them was its own pleasure, but it didn't do wonders for my aching balls.

"Yssy," I said, "maybe you can take a turn guarding the rear."

The foxgirl smiled at me and pecked me on the cheek. Then, surprisingly, she turned and gave Glasha exactly the same treatment before slowing down and taking up a position behind us. She even gracefully slipped the bow off my shoulder as she went.

"I'm really sorry about earlier. We didn't mean to embarrass you."

"It's fine," Glasha said, continuing her scanning of the area ahead of us. "It worries me not. I am not some Sodality adherent who chastises those who partake in such activities. Any embarrassment is because I am unfamiliar with... personal interactions."

"Like I said, I'm sorry it was awkward. I would never want to make you feel uncomfortable, Glasha. I hope you know that."

The dunim woman stopped and looked me in the eye. "I appreciate your sentiment. However, as a warrior, I know that discomfort is the only way one can grow. The moment was awkward, but I find the memory of it...pleasing. I am glad to have seen it. New experiences are the seeds in our lives that grow to make us better versions of ourselves. If I truly take offense at anything you do, Adam, I will tell you. I do not hide offense and plot in the darkness for recompense."

"Uh, okay. I'm glad. Yes, definitely tell me if I offend you. I would never do that purposely."

She gave me a smile, wide enough to reveal her small tusks. They were essentially the same size as Ysduil's canine teeth, but from the bottom instead of the top. And a little more curved. Both of these women were fierce and strong. Both of them were also beautiful and sexy. I thought again about this world and what I'd find as I explored more of it. If these two—and the guard woman Kelena who'd tried to get me to have sex with her—were representative of the women in the world, it was going to be very interesting indeed.

At one point during the day, a racket from ahead of us caught my attention. Glasha had already slowed us down as she scanned our surroundings. The way she laser-focused on things impressed me and excited me a little. Her body flowed gracefully through the vegetation, bringing to mind nature documentaries of big cats hunting prey. The intensity and pure determination in her movements made me feel sorry for anything she hunted.

She motioned us to join her, and Ysduil and I carefully moved up until we could see what was causing the noise. It was a battle, of sorts. Scaled figures half the size of a man fought with some giant rats.

I narrowed my eyes at the scene. The humanoid creatures, their skin a grey-green with delicate lines indicating scales rather than skin, viciously tore into the rats with small weapons. Pointed sticks, large shards of sharp rock, and crude clubs were their weapons of choice. There was an organization to it. Not quite a battle formation, but they did coordinate their attacks.

The rats fought back just as vigorously, biting and scratching at the small figures. On the ground, at least half a dozen rats and two of the little scaly creatures lay still.

Ysduil looked at me, as if expecting me to jump to the defense of the humanoids like I did with Glasha. I shook my head at her and she gave me a silent laugh, her head bobbing.

Glasha led us away, going wide around the group. This wasn't one person severely outnumbered, but a proper battle with numerous combatants. That fight for survival was no business of ours.

"Kobolds," she said after we'd gotten far enough away.

"Kobolds?" I repeated. "Really? I've heard about them. In stories. They're...kind of ugly."

The dunim's blank face made me think I might have been insensitive. Maybe the normal dunim concept of beauty thought the repugnant little creatures were actually cute. After all, most dunim thought Glasha was ugly, according to her.

Thankfully, she didn't comment on what I'd said. "Kobolds used to be one of the intelligent monster races. They lived with their tribes, much as we and the gnosta do. Several hundred years ago, a strange sickness swept through them. It attacked their brains, killing a vast number of them."

"That's horrible," I said. "It affected their brains and made them more primitive?"

"Not really. Somehow, it targeted those who were most intelligent, almost as if the sickness took pleasure in eating the intellect of those it infected. Strangely, those of a... simpler nature recovered if they contracted the disease. The thinkers did not. When the plague finally stopped, their numbers were vastly reduced and those left did not have the mental capacity to continue to run their civilization. Over the decades, they declined, eventually to what you just saw. They have all but lost their ability to converse intelligently and they have reverted to their baser nature. They are now essentially wild monsters."

"At least that can't be blamed on the Sodality," Ysduil said. "One of the few tragedies in the world that cannot."

It made me sad that an entire race of people had been brought so low. But I wondered if they weren't perhaps more content with their primitive lives than those who could think about what the Sodality was doing to oppress them.

It was all relative.

"I need to check on something," Glasha said, her forehead crinkled in concern. "I...won't be very long." She shot a glance at Ysduil, then me.

I nodded my understanding and chuckled inwardly.

That last statement might as well have been *I'll be back quickly, so don't try to have sex.*

After shifting her gaze from Glasha's back to me, Ysduil let loose with a laugh. She apparently read the same thing into Glasha's words. We sat down on the ground to wait like responsible adults instead of hormonally driven teenagers. It was hard.

True to her word, the dunim returned in a few minutes, seeming surprised to find us with our clothes on and sitting a few feet apart.

"I have confirmed it. Something is stalking us. I'm not sure exactly what, but I have my suspicions. Stay alert. I will share more with you when I am certain."

Ysduil stood and brushed off the dried leaves from her half-exposed butt and her tail. "What do you think it is?"

"I would prefer to wait. I don't want to scare you."

That didn't sound good. I got to my feet and looked around. Whatever the green woman had seen, I'd completely missed any of the signs. I wasn't thrilled about what she said, but I was glad she was with us. We continued, the forest seeming more oppressive than it had before.

It wasn't long after that two of the giant rats, like the ones we'd seen fighting the kobolds, leaped out of the foliage in front of us. I have to admit that I jumped a little bit, but to be fair, the rodents' beady eyes somehow displayed shock too, even though they were solid black. Glasha reacted before the rats, a hair before Ysduil, and before I could think well enough to even begin to draw my sword.

The dunim cut into one of the monsters, which looked a lot bigger a few feet away than they did when they were at a distance fighting other monsters. They were somewhere between the size of a rottweiler and a great dane. That didn't help them against Glasha's sword, though, or even Ysduil's staff that struck the other one a second after the green woman's attack.

Glasha followed up with a thrust, spearing the monster so quickly through the head it barely had time to screech. Ysduil, on the other hand, slammed her staff into the side of the other monster's skull so hard that she sent it flying several feet. It went limp when it landed, but Glasha speared it, too, just to be sure.

I was left holding my sword with nothing to swing it at.

"Uh, good job, girls."

The two looked at each other, then back to me, and both laughed at the same time. Like it was on command or something. Whatever. I slipped my sword back into the scabbard.

Glasha cleaned her blade on some leaves and then sheathed it. "It looks like we have something to eat for dinner."

I looked back and forth from the green woman to the rat carcasses. "Are you serious? Can we actually eat those things? I mean, they're rats. Don't they eat...shit or something?"

She gave me a look that I would have expected from Ysduil, tilted head and everything. "They are scavengers, yes, but their meat is edible. It's not very tasty, but it won't make you sick. Not too much."

An image of me in the bushes with a case of diarrhea while being attacked by our mysterious stalker made my sphincter clench .

Again with the laughter. Both of them.

Glasha went to pick the carcasses up while Ysduil patted me on the shoulder. "I will try to find some herbs as we travel so the flavor won't be as bad. You'll be fine. If it upsets your stomach, I can find herbs for that, too." She gave me a sugar-sweet smile and went to help Glasha dress the animals.

I ended up carrying one of the filthy beasts while Ysduil carried the other. Glasha, ranging ahead of us a little, needed to be unencumbered to find the path and respond if anything jumped out at us again.

We finally stopped at a place Glasha had found for us to make camp. There was even a small stream nearby, so I could wash off a little bit. I definitely didn't want to continue to smell like stinky rat fur and blood for the rest of our trip.

CHAPTER
TWENTY-EIGHT

I was pleasantly surprised by the taste of the giant rodents. After I helped Glasha process the carcasses—a messy and disgusting process—Ysduil rubbed the meat with a mixture of herbs she'd made up. It was still slightly gamey, but after a few tentative nibbles, I found it not that bad. As we took our time to eat and then to chat a little bit, it was clear that I wasn't going to have any effects from the meat. What a relief.

The watch for the night would be me first, then Ysduil, and finally Glasha. That being the case, I planned on chatting with one or both of them for as long as they wanted before they decided to go to bed. It was still early after we cooked the rest of the meat all the way through and stored it in some huge leaves Ysduil had found somewhere. The woman was a wonder. I hadn't seen any plants with such leaves as we traveled, but she'd located them and brought them back along with her herbs.

"You know, you two are fantastic," I told them. "I mean, you know how to do all this useful stuff, how to live off the land and to fight monsters and all that. There's a term for people like you in my world."

"Really?" Ysduil asked with a side-glance at Glasha. "Is it hot?"

I let out a roar of a laugh. "Oh, you're definitely hot, but though that means a lot of different things, being able to do all that stuff isn't one of them. Though, I suppose, the fact that you can do all those things does make you hotter."

The foxgirl winked at Glasha, who rolled her eyes.

"Nope, the term is badass."

"Ooh, that sounds like we're naughty and need to be spanked." As she said it, Ysduil wiggled her ass and wagged her tail.

I lost my train of thought for a moment.

"Umm...yeah, well, it's not really like that. Sometimes, when people say someone is bad, it means they're very good."

"So you're saying we have good asses?"

"You definitely do, but sadly, no, that's not what it means. It just means that you're awesome, fantastic, and very talented at fighting and stuff."

Ysduil slinked closer to me, giving me a prime view of nearly her entire left breast as it threatened to pop out of her ruined dress. "And stuff?"

"Y-yeah, you know, like what I said. Living off the land and...stuff."

She giggled. "I know what you meant. I was just teasing you. Badass. I like it. I think I like being hot better, though."

My forehead felt damp. The woman could lead me around by the nose with her teasing. I'd need to tease her back. Eventually. "You can be both. You two *are* both."

"Is this common in your world, for women to be both?"

Glasha asked. Honestly, I was surprised the laconic woman was engaging in the conversation at all.

"Absolutely not. There are some hot badasses, but you don't run into them every day. I've never met any woman that was more badass and hot than either one of you. It makes me scared a little bit. If your whole world is filled with women like you, well, it's going to take some getting used to."

"Aww, you'll be fine, Adam," Ysduil said. "Don't worry. Wait and see as we meet more people. Maybe you'll be disappointed."

"Somehow, I doubt it."

We sat silently for a time, Ysduil looking around at the two of us in turn. Finally, she stood up. "Well, I need to go do...something. I won't be too long." She met my eyes and softened hers a bit. I could have sworn that her lips moved into a moue, but it was hard to tell because I couldn't drag my gaze from those orange-red eyes. She waited for a moment, then her shoulders sloped up in a small and delicate shrug before she turned and went into the darkness.

"You should go with her," Glasha said. "Help her with her ritual."

Again the dunim surprised me. I hadn't thought she'd pick up on the subtle invitation, with her admitted lack of social skills.

"No. I wouldn't feel right about it, leaving you sitting here alone to hear...well, it wouldn't be polite. So talk to me, Glasha Axecrusher. What do you think of our Ysduil?"

A look as close to panic as I'd ever seen on Glasha's face made me wish I could take the words back.

"I—I think she's wonderful. Hot. Badass."

I grinned. I loved this woman.

"You are not what I would have thought an orc—uh, a

dunim would be like. You're kind and funny and pleasant to be around. Not to mention hot. Badass is kind of a given."

She met my smile with her own. "I'm a little strange for a dunim. Don't tell anyone."

"Your secret's safe with me. Really, though, what do you think about her and this whole"—I waved my hand—"sex goddess thing? Tell me honestly, does it really not bother you? I know you said you're not a Sodality fanatic or anything, but...I don't know, is it awkward for you? Especially when you saw us, umm, you know."

"Many things in this world are awkward. Simply talking to you is awkward. I never thought I would speak with a man in an intelligent conversation. I think you are interesting and funny—though maybe you don't always try to be—and pleasant to be around as well. That's just an example of awkward things. Awkward does not mean bad, though. I enjoy learning new things. Experiencing new things."

As if on cue, Ysduil's heavy breathing filled the air.

"She's actually trying very hard not to make noise," I said. "You should hear her when she doesn't try to suppress it. In the dungeon, I was in a cell across the hall from hers and there were times when her moaning rattled my teeth."

"Did her sounds do anything else to you?" Glasha said, her eyes narrowing slightly. They snapped open wider when she realized what she'd said. "Oh, I mean...never mind. I'm sorry. I—"

I scooted up next to her on the grassy mound she sat on. "Don't be sorry. Do you really want to know?"

The green skin on her cheeks darkened in the most adorable way. "Yes." It was very nearly a squeak.

"Then yes, it did things to me. It made me excited, increasing my breathing and my heartbeat. It made me long for...the ability to touch another person. I didn't know what she looked like then, didn't even really know for sure that she was a female like I was used to. I had no image to look at in my mind except for those from my world."

"Were you disappointed when you finally saw her?" She leaned toward me, watching my mouth, as if this was the most fascinating conversation she'd ever had.

"Oh, God no. She is everything a beautiful and sexy woman is in my world, and more. I was surprised when I saw her ears and her tail, but now, they really turn—uh, I love them."

"They are very attractive," she said. "I...noticed you were stroking her ears. The other day. Do you like that?"

I closed my eyes for a moment as the sound of Ysduil performing her ritual wafted over to me. "I do. They're so soft, and she seems to really like it when they're rubbed."

"Hmmm."

I didn't want to embarrass Glasha, but I went ahead and said it. "You should ask her if you can rub them."

"I am...unacquainted with such actions. I would not know what to do."

I picked up Glasha's hand. Her palms had calluses, but they were still surprisingly soft. "She would be more than happy to help you figure it out. She would love to teach you, if you wanted her to."

Glasha looked from her hand to my face. "I do love to learn new things."

"New things can definitely be fun."

"What were you doing when I saw you and Ysduil?"

I blinked at her. "What were we doing?"

"Yes." She closed her eyes and moved her lips. With her lips thrust out and her mouth half open, I halfway thought she was trying to do an impression of a fish, or of chewing, or even of a fish chewing something. I had to stifle a laugh.

"Oh, that." I let out a breath at dodging the bullet of explaining what we were just about to do when she saw us. "We were kissing. Don't the dunim have kissing?"

She moved her hand and I traced a finger across her palm, causing her to freeze. It took a moment for her to answer. "I don't know. Dunim do not show things publicly. Perhaps the others do, but I am more of a loner among my tribe. I have never...kissed."

I turned to square myself to her. "Do you want to?"

"I..."

"Tell you what. Let me do something and you can tell me if it makes you too uncomfortable, okay?" An image of Ysduil saying almost the same thing to her went through my mind and I felt bad for a moment, like I was taking advantage of the innocent dunim woman, but the thought went away. I wasn't doing anything but exposing her to the new experiences she'd talked about. I would be careful not to push and let her set the pace.

"Okay," she said.

"Good. Just relax and sit there."

I leaned forward and brushed my lips on hers with the lightest touch I could manage. Though the heat building up in me urged me to go faster, I resisted. Just a soft, gentle caress of lips on lips and then I leaned back to look at her.

She stared at me, her tongue touching her lips where mine had contacted her.

"That's not really a true kiss—or at least a deep one— but it's a start," I said. "What do you think?"

"It was so soft, so fleeting. Maybe it was too quick? Could you do it again?"

My mouth turned up into a smile and she looked

shocked at first, but then her lips curved upwards, too. Those soft, delicious lips.

Ysduil continued with her sounds, building to what seemed like it would be a strong orgasm, but we had another few minutes yet. My body was reacting to the symphony as well as the closer interaction with Glasha.

I leaned in again and my lips met hers. This time, I took her bottom lip between mine and applied the slightest amount of pressure. She hummed a hungry moan. Taking that as a good thing, I pushed my tongue slowly between her lips and ran it along their length, then edged it a little farther to run along her teeth. The tip of my tongue touched the sharp tusk-like teeth, and they excited me a lot more than I ever would've expected.

Then Glasha opened her mouth slightly and my tongue touched hers. Her breath hitched and I stopped all movement until she tested with her own tongue, finally running across the tip of mine. We immediately found an angle and a rhythm and entwined our tongues slowly, purposefully. I wrapped my arms around her and pulled her close and after a moment, she did the same. One hand pushed through the long section of her hair above her topknot, then tickled the pointed tip of her ear while we continued, joined at our mouths, speaking with our tongues but not using words.

When I broke the kiss, Glasha gasped, then did so again when I trailed my mouth down her neck, then back up, kissing and flicking my tongue out along the soft, taut skin there. I worked my way up to her ear and nibbled on her lobe, all the way up to the tip. She panted, throwing her head back as I ran my other hand along her muscular back. I made my way back to her lips and gave her one last, long kiss, then slowly pulled away. I was too heated up and needed a break or I would push too far.

Her eyes fluttered open and met mine. I watched her luscious lips form a smile and knew I had provided her a new, valuable experience.

"Was that too awkward?" I asked, still holding her loosely.

She worked her tongue over her lips, making me hungry for more. "It was—"

The sound of Ysduil's footsteps caused us both to jump and release each other. Glasha's eyes went wide and she got up abruptly and all but ran to the spot she'd chosen to lie down and sleep. The graceful lines of her body teased me as her back, legs, and just a little part of her fine, green ass flashed me.

"Mmmm," Ysduil said, totally oblivious. "That was a really good one. Do you want me to tell you what I imagined when I was doing it?"

I sighed, but then it hit me what she'd just said.

"Definitely. Start talking."

CHAPTER
TWENTY-NINE

I really don't know what got into me. I felt so bad about the way Glasha reacted, I was too distracted to truly take advantage of the situation with Ysduil. I didn't minimize her experience, though. The explanation was super-hot, but something inside me told me what an asshole I'd be if I did Ysduil right there a few feet from Glasha.

I needed to talk to the dunim and find out what the deal was. Was she simply embarrassed or did she suddenly realize it was all a mistake? Or was it something else? I really liked the dunim woman and I didn't want to make things awkward.

In any case, Ysduil didn't seem too put out. I mean, I'm sure she would have been more than happy to have sex right then and there. She had gotten over being intimidated by me completely, it seemed. Still, she'd already had a really good orgasm, so she could be patient. After all, she had to get up in a few hours to take her turn at watch. So, after she described the little movie that ran through her mind—with roles for both me and Glasha—and gave me a questioning look that probably excited me as much as her play-by-play, she gave me a quick kiss on the mouth and curled up with Glasha to go to sleep.

I could only shake my head. I had a few doubts before, but I was damn sure now that Ysduil was a priestess of the sex goddess. She was one big scorching chunk of sexual energy and sensuality. God help all us poor men. Actually, only me. Apparently all the other men in the world were permanently cockblocked. *Poor bastards.* Or lucky bastards, depending on the point of view.

Ysduil was cheery and lovely when I woke her up for her watch. She kissed me again—a little longer this time—and I curled up for my turn at sleep. It felt like I had only just laid down and was drifting off when a sound like Ysduil falling off the rock she'd been sitting on and a hurried "Augh!" sent all my senses into overdrive. I twisted, grabbing at the sword lying next to me and trying to see what was going on.

The foxgirl was on the ground, struggling to get to her feet. Looming above her was a puddle of blackness, darker even than the area around it.

It was shaped vaguely like a human.

I scrambled to my feet as it caught sight of me and started forward. I was glad it didn't continue to go after Ysduil, but was more than a little concerned I'd caught its attention.

My limbs didn't seem to obey my commands, like those dreams where you're running from some danger and keep tripping. Like those dreams, I felt like I was going to die. The pinpricks of red that made up the creature's eyes were locked on me and coming closer all the time.

Then, with a screamed battle cry, Glasha flew through

the air, bringing her sword down in the most beautiful display of martial competency I'd ever seen.

Her sword passed right through the monster, as did her body. She landed hard on the ground, rolled to her feet, and turned back toward her adversary.

Just in time for its arm to lash out and strike her in the chest so hard she was thrown off her feet. The huff of air as it happened left no doubt she'd had the wind knocked out of her.

I finally got to my feet and ran toward the humanoid shadow. A few slashes of my sword confirmed that if it didn't want to be hit, it couldn't be. It didn't have any problem solidifying part of its body to strike back, though.

I kept my distance and was able to block some of the thing's blows with my sword, though it batted me around quite a bit. I chanced on a useful technique where I blocked with the edge of my blade. When I did that, the monster phased its appendages so as not to be cut. Its fine control of the ability wasn't advanced enough to phase out to go through the sword but then solidify again quickly enough to strike my body right after it passed through the blade, so I considered that a minor victory.

Still, I couldn't damage it, either.

Ysduil was suddenly beside me, bashing at it with her staff, and Glasha, panting to get air into her lungs, joined us. We had to be careful not to hit each other as we attacked. We were successful at that, but overall, we weren't winning the battle.

The shadow managed to hit me in the shoulder and it felt like someone had slammed me with a baseball bat hard enough for a home run hit. The blow spun me and my sword dropped as my arm went dead.

"It's a nightwalker," Glasha yelled out. "As I expected. I

hadn't thought it would attack so soon. I'm s—" The monster landed another blow to Glasha's midsection, interrupting the dunim.

I genuinely didn't know what to do. I wasn't some great warrior and I definitely didn't know how to fight magic monsters. This thing was going to take us apart little by little. It didn't seem to breathe or get tired and even with my newfound endurance, I wasn't going to last for long.

It lunged suddenly at Ysduil and I could tell she wasn't going to be able to rebuff its attack. Glasha was tough and I was more durable than I'd ever been, but the foxgirl's main defense was her agility and speed. I wasn't sure she could take a direct hit from the monster. It punched like a heavyweight.

Not thinking clearly, I panicked and threw myself at the monster. As if I could do anything to animated shadow.

Surprisingly, I felt solid flesh when I grabbed at it.

The shock of making contact didn't only surprise *me*. The monster twisted to see what had taken hold of it, its pale red eyes radiating its hatred.

"What the f—" I started, but then found myself lying on the ground looking up toward the monster and the two women continuing the battle. At least Ysduil had created some space between them.

But still, I wondered...

Moving my aching body, I reached out and grabbed a shadowy leg and found that, once again, I had something solid in my grip.

The dull whoosh of Ysduil's staff ramming through the air ended suddenly with another sound. A very welcome one. It was the noise the staff made when it struck an opponent.

For the first time, the nightwalker made a noise. It was a screech of pain.

"Keep holding it, Adam," Glasha said, slashing at the monster. It was still fast and used its arms effectively to mitigate the blows it received, almost like a warrior with steel gauntlets would move to parry a blade, but it wasn't made of steel. Without its ability to phase out, it could be injured.

I held on for all I was worth.

So, despite being kicked hard and being dragged around by a creature with greater strength than me, my hands stayed latched onto the thing's calves. My forearms burned, but I didn't let go. I poured every bit of my focus onto just holding on, even closing my eyes. I had to trust my companions wouldn't hit me by accident.

The thumps and the whistles of weapons in the air and, more importantly, the sounds of those weapons as they landed blows on the monster, were the only things I heard above the thumping of my heart in my ears. I don't know how long I held onto the nightwalker, but when the thing suddenly fell, I was holding onto its legs in a horizontal position. I opened my eyes to find Glasha standing over our opponent, her sword driven through its head into the ground. "Zartuka!"

I was exhausted, and dizzy. My shoulder was a mess and I literally couldn't feel my fingers. "Can I let go now?"

Glasha dropped to the ground beside me, laughter bubbling up from her. "Yes, Adam. You can let go now. Well done."

I pried the claws that were my hands off the thing's legs and kicked at it to break the connection. Ysduil sat down on the other side of me, her breaths coming in gasps.

I looked to Glasha. "What the hell was that thing?"

"A nightwalker, an animate shadow. They are not too intelligent, but they have highly developed hunting instincts. They can eat the life of creatures they bring close to death, finishing the job. They are...very difficult to damage."

"No fucking kidding," I said dryly.

She continued. "The only times I've heard of them being killed, aside from magical weapons or magic spells, is when a large group of warriors strike out in concert so that its ability to become insubstantial is confused. Once it is in solid form, it can take damage and die like anything else."

Ysduil leaned over, tilting her head to look into my eyes. "The question is, why were we able to strike it at all with only three of us?"

"I don't know," Glasha said, shaking her head. "When Adam grabbed it with his hands, it seemed to lose the ability to phase out. What did you do?"

The whole thing was news to me. "I didn't do anything but just grab it."

"You used no magic on it?"

"Ysduil told me there really isn't much magic in the world right now. Even if there was, I'm no wizard. I don't know the first thing about magic. I can't even do a decent card trick."

"Hmmm," the dunim said. "A mystery. A happy one, but still. Thank you. Without that, we would perhaps be dead right now. And I apologize for not doing more to prepare for its attack. It is my failure that allowed my friends to be injured."

I rolled my shoulder carefully. It would be tender for a few days, but it didn't feel like anything was broken. "It's not your fault. If you had told us about the thing, we still probably wouldn't have been ready, and I definitely wouldn't have been able to sleep knowing what was chasing us." I turned toward the foxgirl. The shreds of her dress were dirtier than ever after rolling on the ground at least a few times. "Are you okay, Yssy?"

She smiled at the nickname. "I'm fine. I found some herbs earlier that are good for bruises and aches. Our little sores won't last more than a day or two before we're as good as new."

"Should we do something about this thing's body?" I asked. "Will scavengers come to get it? Do we need to move camp?"

Glasha winked at me for some reason. "What body?"

I scrabbled backward as the humanoid form of the nightwalker flattened and began to dissolve. In less than a minute, there was only a pool of shadow that seemed to defy the firelight, and then even that disappeared.

I whistled. "Wow. I'm not sure if I'll ever get used to this world."

"Go to sleep, you two," Glasha said, glancing up at the stars. "It's only three hours or so until dawn. I'll take my watch now as recompense for my mistakes and in thanks for your assistance in fighting the monster. We will start traveling at daybreak. I desire to get through the heart of the Dreadlands as quickly as possible."

CHAPTER
THIRTY

The sound of Glasha moving around was the first thing that registered when I woke. The sky was lightening and Ysduil was once again snuggled into my back. I extricated myself as gently as possible, trying not to wake the foxgirl. She seemed like she was really enjoying her rest, her face lit up with a smile at some dream. I'd let her sleep a little longer.

Glasha eyed me as I walked toward her and sat down on the ground near the fire.

"Good morning," I said. "Thank you for taking watch. Are you tired?"

"No. I wouldn't have slept anyway. Too many things on my mind."

"Oh? Like what?"

"Just...things."

"Glasha, did I make you uncomfortable last night? When I kissed you?"

Her face took on an introspective look, her eyes going unfocused for a moment. "It was something I had never felt. I was not uncomfortable, but neither am I comfortable with it."

Damn. I guess I messed up. "Can you explain that to me? I'm so sorry if it made you feel awkward. I didn't want to do anything to ruin how we get along. I enjoy traveling with you."

She shook her head sadly at me. "As do I. It's not that you did anything or that it was too awkward. I enjoyed it. Very much."

"Then what's the problem?"

"My people..." The dunim sighed. "We hold great value in tradition. True, many customs do not apply the way the world currently is, but still, we have rules. Etiquette."

"Uh-oh. Did I break some kind of taboo or restriction?"

"No, no. It's not that. Simply said, if one of the dunim is to carry on mating practices with a man, she must gain permission from his existing mate or wife."

I focused on her face, the way she looked down at the ground, the slumped set of her shoulders. I tried to contain myself, I really did, especially since she looked so much like she was miserable. I failed. I snorted and her head snapped up to me, anger boiling in those cool blue eyes of hers.

"You find it humorous?" she growled and for a moment, a little bit of apprehension seeped through me.

"No! I mean, yes, kind of. But not about what you said. Rather, just because of the confusion. I have no mate. I have no wife. There is no one you need to ask about 'carrying on mating activities' with me. Besides, just kissing you probably doesn't count as mating activities."

"No? Then what did we...? No, a better question is what do you mean you have no mate? You and Ysduil..."

"Ysduil is my friend, just like you are my friend. I have

kissed her, but I haven't gone any further than that. Not much further, anyway. Even if I had, she's a priestess of Odona. Performing mating activities, as you say, would hardly bond her to someone. At least, that's my understanding."

"You would be right," Ysduil said as she stretched and got to her feet. "Priestesses of my goddess have been known to marry and to bond with someone, or a few someones, for life, but engaging in pleasure with someone is not the defining factor in those relationships."

Glasha's face bounced from looking at me to looking at Ysduil. Her mouth twisted, almost like she was going to be sick. "I am so sorry, Ysduil. I didn't mean to do anything. I would have asked you, but it was all so sudden and you were busy with your ritual and—"

"Oh, Glasha. I thought I made it clear the other night. I don't expect to have you solely to myself. I told Adam I wanted him to have you first, but you were just too delicious for me to wait. If I were to be disappointed in anything, it would be that I wasn't invited last night. But I understand that for you, all of these things are new, so given a choice, I would have stepped away to allow you privacy. I want you to learn how wonderful it is to feel physical ecstasy. With me, with Adam, or with anyone else. I want you to be happy."

The dunim woman still looked a bit frazzled, but the longer she thought about what Ysduil said, the calmer she became. Finally, when she settled down, she asked meekly, "Did you really tell Adam you wanted him to have me first?"

"I did. I'm glad I could bring you to climax, your first one ever, but I feel like I was being selfish and greedy. Both of you may punish me for it if you like. Maybe tie me up and spank me?"

I barked a laugh. "Hold on there, Yssy. Why don't we

work on the normal stuff before we introduce kinks? You're going to scare poor Glasha away."

"Kinks?" the foxgirl said, scratching one of her ears.

"Oh. Uh, yeah. Things like spanking or tying you up or blindfolding you, stuff like that. And other things I won't even get into right now."

"Blindfolding? Mmmmm."

"You are absolutely incorrigible."

"That's a good thing," she said.

"Yes. Yes it is."

We wrapped up the conversation and Glasha seemed to loosen up and become more comfortable. Which was good because we still had a fair way to go through the dangerous Dreadlands and we needed her to be able to focus.

Because of the dunim's skill, we only had one close call that day. Some kind of giant crocodile thing in a lake we passed moved like it had spotted us, and I prepared to fight, but it turned out it had actually seen another animal nearby. It snatched the hapless creature up while we made a beeline for the nearest trees. For us being in what was considered the most dangerous part of the Dreadlands, I considered it a successful day.

"Something is strange," Glasha said as we set up camp that night. "The number of monsters we saw today, it doesn't make sense."

"We only saw that big reptile and a few other smaller monsters from a great distance," Ysduil said.

"Exactly. There are fewer dangers than I typically face in my safer part of the Dreadlands. Something has their attention. I can see signs that more monsters still exist, but they're not in the area right now."

"Do you think the Sodality is still trying to find us?" I asked.

Glasha shook her head. "I don't think so. Something is distracting them, though. Or luring them away. We are lucky indeed. If that luck holds for another day and a half, we may make it through to the safer areas nearer the edges. I've taken us—as far as I can tell—through the narrowest part of the Dreadlands."

That was excellent news. To try to skew the odds a bit, we were up before the sky even lightened, and we were moving again as the sun came up. We traveled the entire day, our dunim guide tirelessly plotting out our path. Again, we came to the end of the day without having been attacked by anything. What's more, we found a nice, shallow cave that nothing had taken for a den.

"How active are the gods and goddesses in this world?" I asked, having wondered about it a few times since I'd landed in this new world.

Ysduil answered immediately, of course. "Many of them interact with their worshipers, but they don't usually act directly on their behalf. There are some types of covenants or the like that keeps them from interfering too much. Why do you ask?"

"It seems weird to me that we got off so easy the last couple of days," I said. "It almost seems like someone is manipulating events to help us out."

"No, the gods and goddesses would not do that. We are simply fortunate, or have been for the last two days. I would hope it continues tomorrow, but we will see. I will be glad to get through to the safer part of the Dreadlands. It means we will be closer to where we can travel freely to find my sisters."

"Freely so far as monsters are concerned," Glasha said. "Don't forget the Sodality is still looking for you."

"Yes," Ysduil said. "We must not forget that."

Glasha glanced around the cave we'd found. It was at least fifteen feet high, but only a dozen or so feet deep, more of an alcove than a true cave. She lingered, as if inspecting the wall for cracks.

"Adam," she said. "What are your plans? This is not your world and you have spoken of finding your way back to your own place. What will you do when we cross out of the Dreadlands and into what some call the *civilized* lands?"

"That's a good question. I've been so busy trying to keep from being captured or killed, I haven't thought much about it. Right now, my main goal is to help Ysduil to get through the Dreadlands to a place where she can look for her sisters without being chased or attacked by monsters every time she turns around."

Ysduil's face softened into a sweet smile and she stepped over to me and put her head on my shoulder, tickling me with her ear. It felt...nice.

"After that, though," I said, "I need to work on getting home. I'm not really sure what to do. The logical thing would be for me to try to find those sunken ruins to see if whatever way I came here will let me go back. I'd have to travel all the way around the Dreadlands to go back there, and the fortress and Sodality soldiers are still there." I tapped my temple with my finger, thinking. "What about you, Glasha? You've escorted and guided us through the Dreadlands, but your village is on the other side of the most dangerous part. You may not be as lucky as we have so far, with the powerful monsters distracted by something. What are you going to do?"

The dunim woman shrugged. "I don't know. I can do as you describe, going all the way around and back to my village from the western side of the Dreadlands. I could even accompany you, if you would let me." She left the statement hanging. It sounded hopeful to me. "Aside from that, maybe it's time for me to see more of the world. Dunim aren't treated with the same respect as other races, but neither are we hunted or attacked. Mostly."

"That sounds lonely," Ysduil said, dropping to the cave floor and pulling on my arm to drag me down with her so we could sit side-by-side. "You could always come with me to find my sisters. I have actually heard of a dunim priestess of Odona, but I have never met her myself."

"Really?" the green woman asked. "Thank you. I will think on it. We will need to safely pass through the rest of the Dreadlands, first, of course, but I think the worst of it is behind us. I hate to say it that way because our trip has been fortuitous so far and I would not like to hex our future."

I laughed. "The sounds like superstitions we have in my world. We call it jinxing something when we make a statement like, 'Well, that wasn't as bad as I thought it would be.' Some people believe that saying such things will make something bad happen."

"Our worlds are not so very different, I think," Glasha said. "In some respects."

"People are people," Ysduil said, nestling her head into the crook of my neck.

Glasha watched the foxgirl for a moment, then looked at the area surrounding the cave. "I think I will scout the area a little bit before the darkness of night comes. I will most likely be some time. Enjoy your...uninterrupted time to...talk. Or relax in whatever way you see fit."

"Are you sure?" I asked her. "We can go with you."

"That is not necessary."

"Okay, but be careful out there. We're not out of the Dreadlands yet."

"It worries me not. I will take care. If I need your assistance, I will shout for it."

She nodded a bit too forcefully and headed out with her sword in hand.

I considered the foxgirl leaning against me and said a silent thanks to Glasha. She and I would have to have a long talk soon, one in which I could express my thanks for giving me this opportunity of uninterrupted time.

I rubbed Ysduil's ear and kissed the top of her head as her arms snaked around me and squeezed.

"We have some time," she purred. "What ever will we do with it?"

THIRTY-ONE

I had a few ideas about what to do with the time Glasha had given us.

"You're not intimidated by me anymore?"

"Uhn-uh," she hummed, her lips in that perfect shape that made me want to kiss and lick them off her face.

"You haven't done your duty to your goddess today yet?"

"Uhn-uh." This time it came out a little breathless.

"Would you like me to help you with that?"

"Mmmmm-hmmmm."

She squinched her eyes, just slightly, and pursed her lips. The subtle movements of her body caught my attention immediately, the way she moved her shoulders ever-so-slightly back, causing her breasts to rise as she breathed in to animate them even more.

I put my hands on her face, moving my own close to her while searching her eyes. They reflected the remaining sunlight so beautifully.

"God, you're gorgeous," I said, moving in to brush my lips

across hers. But she wasn't having it, instead wrapping her arms around me and pulling me in hard. She smashed her lips to mine and darted her tongue into my slightly open mouth.

Her sweet and musky scent filled my nose as the even sweeter taste of her mouth exploded across my tongue.

I responded by running my hand down her back while the other reached to her left ear. Her taste and the feel of her body was intoxicating and for a time, I thought of nothing but how good she felt in my arms.

Her dress, as fragile as it looked, felt sturdy, but I easily raised it with my hand to expose her tight ass. I'd noticed before, of course, that she wore no undergarments. All the better to catch a peek at her naughty parts as she went about her frenetic motions while we traveled. The feeling of the smooth skin started the heat building in me, even faster than her kisses had. I traced my fingers up the back of her leg, around her cheeks, and in between them, barely grazing her tail above. When I grazed her hole, her breath hitched. I could feel it in my mouth.

She leaned her head back to look at me. "Do you like the feel of my body?"

"Oh, my God, yes. Can I explore it?"

"Mmmmm. I would love that." She put her finger on my lips. "Remember, though, we won't have a lot of time, even if Glasha is giving us the gift of some."

"It could never be enough. I want to play with your body all day long."

She ground her hips against me. "We will. Not today, sadly, but we will. Promise me."

I lost my train of thought for a moment as she rubbed her body perfectly on the edge of my rapidly hardening cock. I'm not embarrassed to say I gasped a little.

"Yes, yes. I promise. I want you, Yssy. I want you so badly."

She dragged her lips over mine, so softly I held my breath so there was nothing to distract me, so I wouldn't miss any of the sensation. I felt those lips curve into a smile as she moved just enough to whisper into my ear. "Then take me."

I pulled her in for a rough, passionate kiss, my tongue wrestling hers like they were fighting for dominance. My right hand kneaded her perfect ass while my left thumbed her ear and pulled her head into me.

She moaned into my mouth and worked on getting my shirt off, twisting my torso as I sat. I was glad I'd taken the breastplate off earlier. I don't think I could have waited while she worked on the straps. One of us would have ended up cutting them.

Our kisses got more and more urgent and I hungrily tried my best to merge our bodies, though we still had clothing between us. We had to break the kiss so she could pull my shirt over my head and as soon as it was off, I plunged down to kiss the base of her neck while tugging lightly on her ear to raise her chin. I just barely caught her eyes rolling up as she threw her head back, allowing me full access to her slender, sexy neck.

I kissed her along the collarbone, flicking my tongue out to tickle the hollow of her throat. The animal noises—almost growls, but not quite—stirred the blood in my nether regions, my cock throbbing with every beat of my heart.

Tracing my tongue along her clavicle to her shoulder, I gave her a gentle little bite. Her shoulders were toned, muscular without being bulky. She giggled at my nibble, writhing and smearing her body against mine.

Then I went lower, kissing down her arm, then across to the very top of her breasts. Her humming sounds told me I was on the right track.

"Too much cloth," she said breathlessly. "Take off my dress."

I tried my best never to argue with a lady, so with one final kiss in the center of her chest, I carefully lifted her tattered dress up, revealing her amazing body, inch by tantalizing inch. Her pussy, somehow with even less reddish hair than it had when I saw her pleasuring herself several days ago, glistened with wetness, her folds plump and engorged with blood. I licked my lips, but managed to restrain myself. I had other things to do first.

Up the dress went, and though I had seen the better part of her taut stomach through the large holes in her dress, it was nothing compared to seeing her completely bare. Her navel was so perfect and the smooth skin with the hint of her muscles called to me. I couldn't withstand the temptation and leaned down to kiss her belly, lingering when her muscles twitched involuntarily.

I considered going south at this point, but I focused on my immediate mission and raised the dress a bit more, following with my tongue.

At the bottom of her breasts, I stopped and looked up at her. Her mouth was parted and her eyes glassy, waiting to see what would happen next.

"I love your body," I said, licking her up the vertical line of her ab muscles. At the top, I pulled the dress up to expose the inner swell of her breasts and had to exhale a shaky breath. I'd been wanting this woman almost from the time we'd met.

I couldn't stand going so slow any longer and pulled the dress the rest of the way up and then over her head. Seeing her completely naked, her firm breasts slowly moving up and down with her breathing, I growled low in my throat and began to kiss.

From her cleavage up and around her left areola and nipple, I kissed, licked, and gently sucked on her skin. When I took her nipple into my mouth, she sigh-moaned.

I followed with a groan myself because she had decided not to passively wait for me any longer. As I serviced her fantastic tits, she had undone my pants and thrust her hand down to grab hold of my dick.

"Do you like that?" I asked, referring to what I was doing to her nipple.

"I do," she purred. "I've never felt a real one, only those made out of glass or wood." She swirled her hand around my shaft and my breath shuddered.

"I want to lick you, to taste you down there," I told her.

"Mmmm. I want that, too. And I want to try what I have read about, taking you into my mouth and tasting your seed."

I squirmed, ramming my cock into her palm.

"But we probably don't have time," she said.

I caught myself before I whimpered. Really? She was going to leave me with blue balls again?

"Put your manhood inside me, Adam. Fuck me like you promised you would do."

Now she was talking!

Using my dick like a joystick, she guided me to sit down on a nearby rock about the height of a chair while she moved my pants down with her other hand. With them around my ankles and my bare ass on rock, it wasn't the best position I could think of, but there was no way I was going to complain at a time like this.

She backed up a couple of steps and ran her eyes over

me, making a humming, purring sound as she ogled me. Her amazing body was half shadowed with only a little light coming in. She looked like a goddess herself. Odona would be jealous, I was sure. My eyes lingered on the lines of her, the curves, and the way her whole body was shivering with her breaths.

As if by agreement, our eyes reached each other's and her devious, evil grin stole onto her face. As she swayed forward, my dick jumped in excitement. She stepped up, her feet on either side of my legs, so close that the tip of my cock bounced slightly against the trimmed ruff over her slit.

She leaned forward and kissed me, long and hard and hungrily. As she did, her wet thatch caressed me, promising the things to come. Quite literally.

I grabbed Ysduil around the waist and pulled her into me, latching my lips on her right nipple and sucking hard, then biting softly down on it. Her groan decided it for me. I wasn't waiting any longer.

"I want to be inside you," I told her.

Her only answer was that evil smile.

That, and grabbing my shaft and guiding it into the wet folds of her pussy.

I froze, wanting to feel every second, every inch going in. She must have had a similar thought because she stopped with barely a fraction of my head inside her. Slowly, painstakingly, she wiggled and moved to take more of me.

I dropped my head back, letting out a trembling breath, maintaining my will to not ram myself as far into her as I could go.

It was a monumental task.

She wasn't having an easy time of it, either. Fraction by fraction, she guided me, letting me bury my rock-hard cock into her. By the time her tight lips stretched over the bottom of my head, she was whimpering, her eyes bare slits.

I took control and grabbing her at the waist, I lifted her to pull myself almost completely out of her.

"No," she cried. "No, don't stop. What are you doing?"

I bit the center of her left breast, just beside the nipple, within the areola. "Do you like me in you?"

"Yes. Goddess, yes. Please. Put it back in."

I did as she asked, but this time, I was the one putting it in slowly and in small increments. When I got the head all the way in again, I pulled it out, but immediately started going back in.

For a time, I pumped slowly, all the while working just a little more of my dick into her. By the time I'd gotten half of my shaft wet, she was pleading with me to go all the way.

"Do it," she shouted. "Stop teasing me and fuck me. I want you all the way inside me."

I held her still for a moment as she threw herself forward, trying to take me entirely inside her. When she realized she couldn't overpower me, her breathing increased and she started to finger herself, above where I'd entered her. Then she started pinching her nipple and gyrating, breaths coming faster and faster.

I'd teased her—and myself—enough. It was time.

I let up on the hold I had on her and let her body sink toward me. She moaned as more and more of my cock entered her. I felt the tip bottom out against her soft inner wall and she gasped.

Again, I froze, holding it there. This time, though, it was for me. I needed to gather my willpower or I was going to come. I didn't want that just yet.

When I was over the hump and had control once again,

I tensed and my cock jumped while inside her. I had to close my eyes and concentrate not to explode right there and then. When I felt I'd gotten myself under control, I started to move slowly in and out.

"Yes, yes, yes," the foxgirl gasped. "More. Oh, Adam, give me more."

I fingered her ass and the hole there as I slowly—but erratically—built her excitement. I moved up to squeeze and pull on the base of her fluffy tail and she trembled while a moan erupted from deep in her throat. Once I found the angle and the rhythm she liked, I let her mostly guide our actions.

"Do what feels good to you," I told her. "I promise, whatever you like will drive me crazy, too."

Her eyes opened a little to look at me, as if in surprise, but then they squinted again as she did what I suggested.

She did an admirable job. From the urgency of her actions, she'd found a spot that really sang to her. Of course, that wasn't the only clue.

"Goddess, Adam. Yes, oh yes. Fuck me, fuck me, fuck me, fuck me. Your dick feels so good inside me."

The feel of Ysduil's body, the muscles of her tight pussy clamping down on my cock, the sight and smell of her, it all swirled together into a tsunami of sensations that threatened to make me explode. We pumped in synch as if we were born to do so and when I grabbed her ear in one hand and her tail in the other and tugged on both, it was too much.

"Oh, Adam. I'm going to...oh-oh-oh-oh." She arched her back and bucked, welding our bodies together for a single, perfect moment. Frozen, every muscle tense, she fell motionless and also soundless, holding her breath.

Then her internal muscles clamped down on me like a

delicious guillotine and I lost all control. My body jerked and my dick pumped what had to be gallons of my seed into the sexy beastkin.

Then we both released huge breaths and slumped, all the energy gone out of us.

"Oh goddess, Adam. That was...hot. Did I use that word correctly?"

I snorted, and even that exhausted me. I tilted my head and kissed her. "You did. You are amazing and hot and sooooo fucking sexy." I breathed out onto her chest and held her to me for a few more minutes, until I could move.

When she finally swung her leg over and got off me, I took her hand and kissed it.

She sighed. "Thank you for helping me do my duty for today. Without a doubt, that was the best climax I have ever had. Until the next one, of course. When we have more time..."

CHAPTER

THIRTY-TWO

A handful of minutes after Ysduil and I put our clothes on and settled near the wall of the cave, Glasha sheepishly came into view. She took in our positions and let out a breath of relief.

I sat with my legs wide and my back against the wall, with Ysduil sitting between my knees with her back pressed against my chest as I stroked her ears with long, gentle caresses. Glasha glanced down at the fully exposed juncture between the priestess's legs and raised an eyebrow.

"I'll need to borrow your knife again soon," Ysduil said, sinking back into me as I worked on her ears. "Sometimes I like to be clean shaven."

Glasha snorted.

"Did you find anything?" I asked the dunim woman.

"No. The area is...secure."

"Thank you. For everything."

She looked away, nodding.

Over the next two days, I talked with Glasha alone when I could. It was clear right away that she wasn't bothered by what Ysduil and I had done. After all, she had engineered the opportunity, for which I thanked her multiple times.

But not in the way I would have liked to.

After the first conversation, though, we didn't talk more about sex or how she felt about it all. One thing especially was on my mind.

"Are you going to let me kiss you again?"

It took a moment to answer. "Yes. I enjoyed it."

My face broke into a grin. "Good. Me too. Does it bother you that Ysduil is more affectionate to me now?"

It was a valid question. The foxgirl would often trail her hand along parts of my body as she passed, or embrace me for no reason other than it felt good. To both of us. She even kissed me often, both the chaste little pecks and the hotter, more passionate kind. It was obvious she was feeling more comfortable with me.

"No. I know she would treat me the same if she weren't afraid it would make me feel uncomfortable."

I hadn't thought about it that way. I was concerned she might be jealous that Ysduil was lavishing attention on me and it turned out she focused on me taking some of Ysduil's affection from her.

To be honest, the whole thing was surreal. I was traveling with two beautiful women, neither of whom seemed to care what I did with the other. In fact, Ysduil made it clear, and often, that she wanted me to pursue Glasha.

"How can you stand to watch her and not want to touch her and taste her?" Ysduil asked me later that day. We were walking several paces behind Glasha and Yssy had brought her mouth close to my ear to whisper. "Don't you find her irresistible?"

"Of course. As I do you. But she needs to go slow. It's all new to her. She can have all the time she needs. I can't get over you always trying to push me to get with her. You really don't mind?"

Her tongue flicked out, tickling my ear and sending a jolt down through my chest to my lower half. "Mind? I love the thought of you two pleasing each other. As long as you don't mind me wanting my turn with her, everything will be fine. Don't get selfish on me and we will be three very happy people."

I shook my head. I'd asked her enough at this point that I knew she was telling the truth. Strange, but awesome. It would probably more than make up for all the crazy creatures trying to kill me in this world.

Not that our travels were all chit chat and kabuki dances. Watching Ysduil's body, barely covered in that torn dress, wasn't nearly enough. I had to run my hand down her legs, over her stomach, across her arms and shoulders, and on her firm ass. She looked good enough to eat, but that was something I hadn't yet been able to do. Not for want of trying.

Finding a few minutes together was hard enough, so when we got them, we quickly got to business. I wanted to taste her, but she did enjoy penetration and wanted us both to come. We would get the time and circumstances to linger and enjoy each other later. I pictured it often.

We held back, too, because of Glasha. Though Ysduil believed that the dunim woman wouldn't mind if we carried on in front of her, I wasn't so sure. Until she got more used to sexual acts, I refused to let Ysduil lead me into some form of exhibitionism. No matter how much I thought I'd enjoy it in this situation.

During the daytime, when we continued to travel through the Dreadlands, it was frankly underwhelming. We passed into the edge area without dying, which is always a plus, but we never found a reason why the heart of the Dreadlands was so empty of monsters. Once we were in a relatively safer area, I supposed it didn't matter.

We saw a few other creatures. I got a glimpse of a solitary centipede, as large as an anaconda, but it didn't bother with us, continuing on with its many legs moving like a wave. Giant rats seemed ubiquitous in the Dreadlands, and Ysduil took down a couple more for us to eat. There were other sightings, but nothing attacked us. It seemed that the area we traveled through was even calmer than where Glasha's village was.

Our little group did cross paths with two other dunim. Their manner of dress was different than Glasha's, the style of their armor blockier and thicker. They carried spears and wore swords, looking fierce and deadly, much like Glasha. What they weren't was beautiful. One of them was very plain, but the other one was honestly pretty fugly.

They both waved their spears lazily toward us, their eyes shifting from Glasha to Ysduil, then locking onto me. I was used to it by now, the way the eyebrows raised, the confusion in their eyes. Especially when I smiled and waved back. The plain one actually tripped and reddened when I greeted them.

The dunim continued on their way, the flushed one darting glances at our backs after she'd regained her footing.

"Do you know them?" I asked Glasha.

She shook her head. "I know nothing of them or their tribe. They are on the other side of the Dreadlands. I'm glad to know there are other dunim still."

"Do you want to talk with them?"

"No. Perhaps in other circumstances I would, but for

now, I would like to get out of the Dreadlands as soon as possible."

Almost as if what she said was prophetic, we cleared the trees that afternoon and found ourselves in a hilly, less heavily forested area.

Ysduil clapped her hands and twirled around in circles. "We made it. We're outside of the Dreadlands. Yay!"

Glasha and I traded looks.

"Are you sure?" the dunim woman asked.

"Yes. I recognize this landscape. If I'm correct, we're in the Frelen Lowlands."

I had felt a difference in the air a little earlier, like the pressure had changed, but it hadn't been all that significant. Though the ground spread out before us had fewer trees, there appeared to be forest off some distance to our left and to the far right. North and south if we were still facing east.

I was about to ask what we would do next, but Glasha interrupted my thoughts.

"What is that?"

I turned to where she was pointing. A long column of smudged sky drew my eyes. The wind curled it slightly toward us. "Smoke?"

"Yes. Not the smoke of campfires, though. Too large, too sooty. Something big is burning." She sniffed the air. "Not a simple forest fire."

"We have to go see what it is," Ysduil said. "It may have something to do with my sisters."

I wasn't sure why she thought it was connected to the priestesses, but I was curious about it as well. "Fine. Let's go check it out, but we need to be careful. It could be anything from a massive forest fire to someone laying siege to a castle, if that's a thing here. The last thing we need is more trouble."

After two hours of trudging through the trees, the scent of smoke got stronger. It didn't smell like a forest fire, but had the sharp aroma of other materials burning as well, like trash. Or buildings. The forest got thicker before we broke out into what looked to be fields reclaimed from the trees. In the center of the farms was what was left of a fair-sized village.

No structures still stood whole. Most were collections of collapsed wood with bits of stone mixed in. Flames flickered in a few spots and a handful of the buildings smoldered.

There were also soot-covered lumps on the ground in various locations. Some were wearing clothes.

Glasha drew her sword and I followed suit. Ysduil adjusted her grip on her staff and glanced at the bow hanging across my chest as if she was debating which weapon would be more useful for the situation.

A breeze passed through and created eddies in the smoke, stoking the fires so a few flames stretched upward like they were preparing to attack us.

"Who would do this?" I asked. "Do you have bandits in this world?"

"We do," Ysduil answered.

A flash of dark blue caught my eye, off to the right. I spun toward the movement, preparing myself to be attacked. It took a moment until I spotted the color again, passing behind one of the stone chimneys of one of the larger buildings. It had to be a person, judging by its size and movement. I took three steps, building up my speed into a sprint, but Ysduil yelled at me.

"Adam, no. Stop. Don't chase."

I split my attention between where I'd seen the blue and where Ysduil was standing. Her posture was relaxed. Had she seen what I did? Had she seen *more* than I did?

"Please," she said again. "Remain still."

My instincts rebelled, but I trusted her. Besides, Glasha stood by, not seeming perturbed in the least. In fact, she sheathed her sword.

"My name is Ysduil Fennis," the foxgirl yelled out. "I am a priestess of Odona, though maybe you don't recognize my dress because of the hardships I have suffered. Please, come out. We mean you no harm."

I sheathed my sword to back up Ysduil's words, though I felt unsure about putting my weapon away.

For several minutes the three of us stood there, the smoke swirling around us and stinging my eyes. I was surprised we hadn't been attacked yet, but even so, why were we wasting our time?

Then another glimpse of the same indigo peeked around the carcass of a wagon. It was accompanied by a straight slash of yellow-brown.

"My friends' names are Glasha," Ysduil said, pointing toward the green woman, "and Adam. There's nothing to be afraid of. Do you need help?"

Half a head emerged from behind the wagon, honey-colored hair atop it, arranged in intricate braids smudged with soot.

"You can come out," Ysduil said, putting her hand out.

Timidly, tentatively, the rest of the person showed herself. It was a young blonde girl wearing a dark blue sleeveless dress with grey and black smudges on it. Though she was pretty, her amber eyes were haunted, darting around nervously. At us, at the surroundings, at the sky smeared with smoke.

She also had long furry ears coming out of her head. Rabbit ears.

My first obsil. A rabbit beastkin.

I watched her move carefully toward Ysduil. It wasn't lost on me that she stayed as far from me and Glasha as she could. I tried not to stare at her pretty ears. I wondered if she had a cotton tail as well. The ears weren't quite the same color as her hair, but almost. They were a tawny color with a few dark spots spattered on them. At least, I think she had dark spots. I supposed it could have been more ash.

Her light amber—almost yellow—eyes held not only fear, but refused to meet Ysduil's, though the foxgirl was smiling kindly at the bunny girl.

"Awww," the priestess said. "You've had a rough time of it. What is your name?"

"A-A-Amelie, priestess." Her voice shook so much, it wrenched my heart. It made me want to disappear, if only to make things a little more comfortable for the girl.

"Amelie. What a lovely name. Would you like something to drink? I have a waterskin. It may be a little warm, but it can help wash some of the smoke from your mouth."

Amelie nodded, her long ears bouncing on her head. She took the proffered skin and drank deeply out of it. Handing it back, she sighed. "Thank you, priestess."

"No, no, no. Please, call me Ysduil. Priestess is my profession, not my title. I appreciate that you speak it with respect, but we're all friends here."

Amelie nodded again, and swung her head to check to make sure Glasha and I hadn't moved. Though the ground was dirty with ash. I slowly sat down, hoping it would help to ease the girl's tension. Glasha imitated me a moment later.

Ysduil's smile grew fractionally. "Come here, Amelie. Tell me what happened."

She did as directed, stepping close to Ysduil. The foxgirl reached out slowly and pulled the bunny girl into a hug. Amelie tensed for a moment, then relaxed.

That's when the tears started.

CHAPTER
THIRTY-THREE

After Ysduil soothed the girl for a little while, Amelie finally got comfortable enough for me and Glasha to stand up and move. All of us walked out of the village to a miraculously unburned wagon near what had probably been a farmhouse. Sitting in the bed of the wagon, Amelie told us her story.

"I was out picking herbs for Hara, our Wise Woman, and the sun's warm rays made me drowsy. I fell asleep near the spring. When I woke up, it couldn't have been more than a handful of hours, but the sky was filled with smoke and I got a terrible feeling in my belly. I ran back toward town and saw what had happened.

"A large group of people were rounding up those left from the village and marching them to the south. They were too far for me to see individual faces, or even to tell what kind of beastkin they were. Or if they were monster people.

"I hid, not wanting them to see me and take me, too. Once they were all gone, I went to the village and found some people dead, but most missing. I didn't see my family's bodies, but I didn't finish looking. It was...too hard, searching through the dirty bodies, recognizing my neighbors."

She wept some more, her face covered in soot with tracks cut through them from her tears. "I fled, then came back, then fled again. So many people..."

"Now," Ysduil cooed. "It's all right, Amelie. Of course that would be traumatic to anyone. You're safe now. We'll help you search the village, if you want. Did you notice how the people were dressed? Were they one of the big bandit groups?"

Amelie sniffled. "I don't know. It seemed like they were dressed mostly alike. They were in armor and clothes of brown and black. They...they looked like his clothes." The obsil pointed a trembling finger at me, and buried her head into Ysduil's shoulder.

"Don't worry, Amelie. Adam would never hurt you."

"He's a man. They are all with the government."

"He's not with the Sodality. He took his clothes from a Sodality guard when we escaped from them. They want to hurt him, and me."

It took a while for the girl to calm down. She finally fell asleep in Ysduil's arms and the priestess laid her gently in the bed of the wagon before getting up and motioning for us to follow her a short distance away. When we were in a group a dozen paces away, she looked back at the bunny girl and then to us.

"Poor thing. The Sodality were responsible for this."

"But why?" Glasha asked. "They don't have men for the Sodality to take. Why would they attack a village, kill some of the people, then take the rest away?"

"I don't know. I hope it didn't have anything to do with us."

"How would it have anything to do with us?" I asked.

"There has been plenty of time for them to get messages from the fortress on the other side of the Dreadlands to here. Maybe they predicted we'd come out and they're searching for us."

"That doesn't make sense. We're not that important. They wouldn't destroy an entire village just to find us."

"You don't know the history of the Sodality," Glasha said. "They are brutal. When they want something, they have no problem killing to get it."

It still didn't make any sense. There had to be something else going on. I wasn't going to argue about it, though. We had other things to think about.

"We aren't going to figure it out speculating," I said. "What I want to know is what we're going to do with that girl. She's obviously desperate. We can't just leave her here to fend for herself."

"Girl?" Ysduil asked.

"Yeah, that bunny girl. Uh, the obsil girl over there."

She smacked my shoulder. "I know which person you were referring to, silly. I wondered why you call her a girl."

"Because she is. I mean, she can't be more than fifteen years old."

Glasha smirked and Ysduil got that mischievous look in her eye.

"Can't you see her body with that tight dress?" she asked me.

"Her body? What?" Sorry to say, I *had* noticed her body, but had tried my hardest not to look—or think—about it because her face looked so young. "Okay, yeah, maybe she's got an adult's shape, but I've seen young girls that were... developed like that before."

"Just tell him," Glasha said with a sigh.

Ysduil giggled. "Do you wager on your world? I will bet you she is twenty years old, possibly nineteen, but no less than that."

"You're crazy. If I had any money, I'd wager with you."

"Obsils always look much younger than they are," Glasha said, frowning at the priestess.

Ysduil had the decency to look embarrassed. She'd been trying to scam me!

"Really? Wow. Okay, I'm sorry. What are we going to do with that obsil *woman*, then?"

"We're going to help her with whatever she needs help with, of course," Ysduil said. "Don't you think that's the best thing?"

"Honestly, yes. I guess I agree."

Amelie woke a few hours later. I'd gone back into the trees to collect some wood and we started a fire near the wagon, which seemed ironic to me considering we were still close to the smoldering village. The three of us spoke softly about what we were going to do when the bunny girl stretched and climbed down to join us. The way she skirted around me to sit near Ysduil tried to tug my mouth downward, but I resisted and kept my expression as neutral as I could. But I did notice her incredible curves, now that I knew she was old enough for me to appreciate. It hadn't really occurred to me until I was collecting wood that she *had* to be nearly twenty years old, since there were no men left to procreate with in small towns like hers.

"Are you hungry?" Ysduil asked.

Amelie nodded but when she saw what we were eating —the leftover meat from our dinner the day before—her eyes dropped to the ground.

"No, don't worry, sweetie," the foxgirl told her, pulling out some vegetables from her pack. She'd gone out before it got dark and searched for herbs and edible plants. "Here. Will these do?"

Amelie nodded, her ears bouncing. "Yes. Thank you." She took dainty bites, but I could see she was working hard to restrain herself from gulping it all down.

Ysduil glanced at me over the obsil's shoulder. "How old are you, Amelie?"

"I'll be twenty years old in a couple of months. I'm old enough to be on my own..."

Ysduil's triumphant smile made me roll my eyes. Okay, so it's probably good we didn't make that bet.

"Have you ever left your village before?" Glasha asked.

The bunny girl didn't seem to have a problem with the dunim. "No. I never had a need to go anywhere else."

"What do you plan to do now?"

"I don't know." Amelie stopped eating and her eyes grew liquid. "Everything and almost everyone I knew was in the village. Sharton's Hollow was my whole world."

"That's the name of your village?" Ysduil asked. "Sharton's Hollow?"

She looked back toward the burned-out husk of the village. A few hotspots still glowed occasionally. "Yes." Her shoulders slumped, the poor thing. But then she perked up. "Oh! Auntie Nemia."

"Who?" Ysduil asked.

"Auntie Nemia. She visits me sometimes. Well, my family. She lives in Riverview. I don't think it's very far, maybe two or three days away from here. Maybe I can go there and tell her about what happened."

"Riverview. I know that name, though I have never visited. Do you know how to get there?"

"No. All I know is that it's to the southeast."

The foxgirl clapped. "Well, then, that's where we'll go. We will take you to Riverview so you can find your aunt."

Amelie's big eyes locked onto Ysduil. "Really? You would take the time to take me there? Are you heading that way?"

"Of course we would. We're heading that way now. We can't leave you to wander around. There are dangerous things out there."

For some reason, the bunny girl looked over at me. I smiled at her and nodded, but she swung her head to Glasha as soon as she saw that I noticed her looking. Glasha had the same response as I did, but Amelie returned a smile to the dunim.

"Thank you so much," she said. "It is rather scary out there. Having people to travel with will make me feel much safer."

Ysduil put her hand on Amelie's shoulder and squeezed. "Well, there we go. After a nice rest, we'll set off for Riverview."

Amelie cleared her throat softly. "Umm, could I search the village more first? I want to see if my...family is there." Her voice hitched as she said it, but though tears were making her eyes glimmer, none were shed.

"Of course, honey-bunny." The priestess pulled her into a hug. "We'll help you with that difficult task. Then, whenever you're ready, we'll head out for Riverview. Is that okay?"

Amelie hummed affirmatively while sinking into the foxgirl's embrace. She started nibbling on her food again as Ysduil held her.

We were apparently going to search through the wreckage of the village for the bodies of her family. I hoped we didn't find them, though if not, we'd have to figure out if we could do anything to get them back. Wherever they were.

We now had a direction to go, and it was the right thing to do for the poor bunny beastkin...but one thought kept nagging me.

Every step we took seemed to bring me farther away from finding my way back to my own world.

THIRTY-FOUR

S earching through the village of Sharton's Hollow, looking for the bodies of Amelie's mother and sister, went how I expected. It sucked. Not only was it a dirty, sooty task, but digging corpses from the rubble and heaps of ash was not fun on the best of days. The first two bodies I saw, half burned like so much meat left on a barbecue grill, had me running to throw up where the women hopefully couldn't see me.

The part that probably bothered me most was that after a while I started to get used to the grisly scene. And its smell.

All of the dead were bunny beastkin, as far as I could tell. Some were so burned that I couldn't see any ears. Or hair. Or facial features. At all.

By the end of our search, which was many hours long, we had not found Amelie's mother or sister. Which was good, because it meant they weren't killed during the initial attack or due to the fire and the collapsing buildings. But bad because they were likely taken by the Sodality troops.

It still didn't make any sense to me why soldiers would

swoop in, kill some people, take a bunch of prisoners, and raze a peaceful village. What was the purpose?

Amelie must have been feeling the same thing. She stood next to Ysduil in the middle of what had been the town square, a despondent look on her face. Her dress looked even more ragged than it had earlier, smeared with dark lines like sword slashes and hanging on her like a weight. Her shoulders slumped and her back bowed as if her clothing was as heavy as if it were made of lead.

"I found these," Glasha said, walking up to us. She had gone to search ahead of us, letting us know if she found any evidence of bodies so we—and mostly I mean *I*—could do the hard work and uncover them. She held a barrel in her arms, remarkably intact. "The cask had been knocked into a cistern and so was saved from the fire, I think. There were some apples in it. I also found this bread. It's a little singed on the edges, but still edible. It was sitting in a stone container."

"Oh, those are good finds," Ysduil said.

"Then there's this." Glasha scratched her head. "I don't know how it survived. It was in a hole in the ground, some charred board that I think were floorboards above it. It was wrapped in some leather and cloth."

The dunim held up a light blue garment. The cloth was thin and airy, like chiffon on Earth. It was exceptionally clean compared to literally everything else around us, including my own clothes. The only thing that came close was Ysduil herself, with her tattered priestess dress, which somehow had managed not to turn black from the ashes. In fact, now that I looked, I only saw smudges on her feet and ankles, and a few marks on her hands and arms. That and a little dot of dark grey on her left cheek.

Amelie sucked in a breath. "Oh, I recognize that dress.

Sheela Sawsin had that made for a special occasion. She hoped that one day she could wear it for a husband, maybe even during the marriage ritual itself." She dropped her head. We'd found Sheela during our search. Amelie had told us the names of everyone we found, though I didn't know how she could tell who some of the damaged bodies were.

"Maybe you can wear it in her honor?" Ysduil said. "Your current dress is in bad shape."

Amelie eyed the priestess and I was waiting for her to tell Ysduil that her dress was in worse shape, but she only let her eyes linger on the foxgirl's chest and sighed. "I suppose I could. She was about the same size and...build as me."

Ah. Under the torn dress, Amelie's chest was a lot bigger than Ysduil's. I mean *a lot* bigger. If the dress was made to fit someone with her curves, it wouldn't fit the priestess's lithe body as well.

We took turns bathing in the river before we left. I volunteered to go last so the women could all bathe together. Ysduil said she'd stay on watch with me so we could perform the chore in pairs. I was afraid—and maybe a little hopeful—that it would lead to something more than washing off, but the priestess was all business. She was probably concerned with embarrassing our newest group member.

"So, what do you think?" she asked me after Glasha and Amelie stomped over the little embankment to a shallow spot in the river.

"About what?"

She rolled her eyes at me. "About Amelie, of course."

"I feel really bad for her. I mean, at least her mother and sister weren't killed here, but they were still captured by the Sodality. It's got to be rough."

"Not that, Adam. What do you *think* of her?"

"She seems to be nice. A little quiet, maybe."

"Yeah, yeah, yeah. Most obsils are shy. But she's beautiful, right? What about that body?"

"Oh." I gave her a sidelong look. "Is everything about how pretty or sexy someone is?"

"Of course. I *am* a priestess of Odona."

I winked at her. "And an excellent practitioner of your sacred duties. To answer your question, she's pretty enough and having a body like that at almost twenty years old makes me feel a lot better than if she had been fifteen. She still looks young, though, and—"

I caught motion from the edge of my vision and turned to see Amelie leading Glasha back over the embankment. She was wearing the new powder-blue dress, and it fit like she had been born with it on.

"Oh my God!" I said.

Ysduil leaned over and pushed my chin up with her index finger. My mouth closed with a click.

Whatever I'd been saying about Amelie had gone right out of my mind. The way she filled out that dress, and how short it was...

It was an off-the-shoulder style with ruffles wrapped around the upper arms. Of course, that meant quite a bit of her chest was exposed, including at least four inches of cleavage. Even without support, her firm breasts stood up like she was a Southern California wife of some Hollywood producer. The thought of that chiffon getting wet started sent jolts skittering around inside me, to finally gather at a certain point lower down. Did no one wear a bra in this world? Did anyone need to?

The thin material layered down, the hem fluttering at the tops of her thighs. Even the breeze of her walking made it float, flashing a bit of cloth that had to be an undergarment, but if it wasn't a thong, I'd gladly eat the sword at my waist.

In a word, she was super fucking hot. Okay, three words. One word would never be able to describe her.

Her beautiful face—scrubbed clean and framed by thick braids—fit well with the rest of her: sexy and gorgeous but at the same time cute and adorable. If she was on Earth, she'd be an instant celebrity on nothing but her looks.

"Wow."

"I'll take that to mean that you agree with me," Ysduil whispered as the two beautiful women, now nice and clean, came up to us.

"Your turn," Glasha said, winking at me.

Ysduil took my hand and glided toward the river. I gladly followed. As if I had a choice with her soft, delicate hand clamped in a surprisingly strong grip on mine.

As soon as we crested the little hill and started down the other side, the foxgirl swayed her hips provocatively, knowing full well my eyes would be glued to her ass.

"See," she said, "you *do* think Amelie is hot."

"Now that I know she's old enough, I will admit it. Yes, she is very...okay, hot. Three of the hottest, sexiest women I've ever seen in my life are traveling with me. Maybe I actually died in that cave and I'm in heaven."

"I've heard of this heaven thing. A place you go when you die, right? Some place where gods reside?"

"Well, one in particular, but yeah, that's the general idea."

"You are not dead, Adam. I am willing to try many things in my service to Odona, but necrophilia is not one of them. Your warm, throbbing cock tells me that you are very alive. But maybe I need to experience it more to be sure. Hmmm. How can I do that?"

She dropped my hand and skipped to the water's edge and stepped in. Then she dropped a shoulder and gave me a smoldering look. "Are you coming? Into the river, I mean."

I pulled my boots off and made a beeline for the water.

Before anything else, I had to clean off the clothes I was wearing. I didn't wear my armor when I was wallowing in the soot, but that only meant my clothes were filthy. As I rubbed and scrubbed them, the ash floated away on the river. It was a sizeable plume.

Once Ysduil judged my clothes clean enough, she started peeling them off me. I raised an eyebrow at her.

"You have to clean your body, too. It would be silly to clean your clothes and not your body. Don't worry, though. I'm here to help."

Her hand slipped as she was *helping* me with my pants. My breath hitched when it slipped exactly enough to wrap around my dick, which sprung to attention at her touch. Okay, it was already well over halfway there.

"Uhn," I grunted.

"I'll help you clean yourself," she said. She leaned in and took my bottom lip in her teeth. "All of yourself."

I reached out and put my hands on her ass. "Aren't you going to clean your body?"

She glanced down at herself, then back up to me. I got the distinct feeling the look she gave me was meant to tell me I was an idiot.

"The water goes through the cloth easily. I can leave it on. Besides, if I strip down, you will only want to sample me. We don't have time. This is my service to you. Your job is only to enjoy it."

"Mmmm," I said. "I might be able to do that."

At this point, her kisses were enough to get me ready. The way she moved her hands under the water, touching me in places I'd been touched before, but never in that way, had me rock hard in seconds. She continued to pet and caress my shaft while she kissed me. Something about the current added to the effect, like a mini massage all over my body. It was better than a hot tub, just exactly the right amount of pressure to created tingles all over my chest, abs, and legs.

"God, you're good at that," I panted.

"You like it?"

"Of course. I like everything you've ever done to me."

"Would you like Amelie to do this to you?"

The question caught me off guard, as did the little twirl she made with her hand around my shaft. I sucked a breath in.

"You would, wouldn't you? Maybe we can ask her. I'll help convince her if you let me watch. I'll owe you a favor if you let me participate."

Oh. My. God.

"I...please, don't talk...about that when you're... ungh." I couldn't even get a sentence out while she was doing what she was doing to me. I wasn't even sure what that thing was, but God, it felt sooooo good.

"I bet she likes to have her nipples licked and sucked. Most obsil I've been with love their tits played with."

"Oh, Yssy. Please..."

"I'm curious. I'll let you have her first, but I want my turn. Maybe Glasha will want some, too. We'll have to ask her." She kissed me deep and hard. When I tried to tangle my tongue in hers, she caught it in her lips and sucked on it. She did it in waves, almost like she was trying to make my tongue throb.

She succeeded.

I couldn't take it anymore. She had me just about ready to explode, but I'd be damned if I would go there alone. Ysduil was panting as much as I was, though she was doing a great job at keeping her noises and her voice down.

I crushed her chest against mine with my left hand around her shoulders and reached down to put the tip of my hard cock into position. The cool water rushed around us, caressing my skin, adding a counterpoint to the heat building up in me as I found my target.

"I told you, this—ooooh."

"Shhhh," I hissed into Ysduil's hair as I sheathed my dick in her warmth. "It makes me happy to make you happy. Right now, I want us to come together. Is that okay?"

I didn't let her answer right away, moving my lips to hers and kissing her desperately. She hummed and moaned into my mouth, putting her arms around me and thrusting with her hips.

That was a good enough answer for me.

I cupped her tight ass, then moved my hand up to the base of her tail and squeezed it while I steadily thrust into her. We were in perfect rhythm, as if we were born to perform this task. As I played with her tail and kissed her, she pulled harder and increased the tempo with her thrusts. I was more than happy to match her motions.

It didn't take long. A few dozen thrusts and a finger dragged along her asshole, and she let out a muffled scream into my mouth. The pure bliss of being inside her, feeling her clench around me while kissing her sent me over the edge. I came like a firehose.

Our bodies shuddered together as we grunted and

PRIESTESS

moaned. I didn't see any flocks of birds frightened into winging away, so I hoped our noises didn't carry too far.

When we came down from our climax, I held her for a while, kissing her gently and nibbling on her soft, fuzzy ears.

"Mmmm," she said. "I knew if I brought up Amelie, you would fuck me."

I sighed. "Yssy, if I was on my deathbed and you brought up putrid, rotting corpses, I would want to fuck you. You. There's no need to tease me with other women to get me to play with you. You are plenty hot enough on your own."

"Oh, I wasn't just talking about you. The thought of being with that sexy obsil makes me hot, too."

"You're too much." I slapped her on the ass, but since it was underwater, it didn't really have the usual effect. Still Ysduil giggled and splashed me.

She leaned in and sniffed me. "Clean yourself off. You smell like sex."

"You smell sexy," I said. "Like tangy citrus. I love the smell and taste of you."

"You do?"

"I do."

"I guess we'll have to figure out how you can smell and taste me more in the future."

"Definitely."

She strode out of the river, shook the water out of her tail, wiggled her ass at me, then crooked a finger.

"Coming?"

I laughed and splashed at her. "I just did. Let me get dressed and we can go back to the girls."

Her expectant face made me shake a finger at her.

"Leave Amelie alone. She's had a rough time. She needs

to be consoled and feel comfortable right now. Be gentle with her."

That evil grin came back, then magically transformed into an angelic smile. "I know. I'll give her time, but as soon as she's ready, I want some of that and I want you to have some of that. The goddess teaches us that sexual pleasure is healing to the heart in difficult times."

I shook my head and got dressed. "Incorrigible."

THIRTY-FIVE

Heading southeast from what was left of Sharton's Hollow, we passed through lush forest with plenty of animals, but not a single monster. From the start, we stayed near the road, but out of sight of other travelers.

"Why are we traveling through the forest and wild areas when there's a road nearby?" Amelie asked the first time we stopped to take a break. She spoke so softly, I had to strain my ears to hear.

"There are several reasons," Ysduil said. "But there are two major ones. First, Adam and I escaped from the Sodality, killing some of their soldiers to get free. I might be able to hide among others, though someone might recognize my dress and figure out I am a priestess of Odona. There is no way Adam can hide, though. All other men are under the Sodality's control, so he would be spotted easily. It's better if we stay off the road so we're not seen by anyone who might report they've seen him.

"The other big reason is that if the Sodality is close

enough to attack your village, they probably have a presence along the road, maybe even checkpoints that would have to be passed through. Something as simple as a couple of soldiers walking the road could end up with us captured. I will be executed, Adam will be trained so he can no longer think for himself, and you and Glasha would probably be taken or killed because you're our accomplices, as far as the Sodality is concerned."

That made the bunny girl go quiet, her eyes shimmering as she bit her lower lip.

As we traveled, I watched Amelie carefully. For the most part, she stayed near Ysduil. When she wasn't close to the foxgirl, she was hanging around Glasha, like she was hiding behind her. She rarely looked in my direction and she never let herself get close to me, no matter how cramped the trail through the vegetation was. I could sense her shifting her eyes in my direction, but never actually caught her looking my way.

Two days after we'd left Amelie's ruined village, we caught sight of Riverview. It was significantly larger than Sharton's Hollow, with several dozen structures visible. In the town proper, many of the streets were cobbled, though the roads into and out of the city were hard-packed dirt.

We walked up the wide roadway, our heads swinging to and fro. There weren't many people about. It gave me a sinking feeling. Something seemed wrong.

"Do the rest of you feel like something's not right?" I asked.

"Yes," Glasha said, her hand on her sword. Her body was tense, prepared to draw her weapon in an instant.

I was more worried about hidden archers. I didn't see any. I stopped in the roadway, mentally slapping my forehead. *Of course, dumb shit*, I chided myself. *It's in the name.* Hidden *archers wouldn't be seen*. Silently cursing my stupidity, I started walking again, searching for any sign of a trap.

The road went through the middle of town and the four of us stopped to watch warily as an older woman slowly approached us. She was human and, though she had probably been pretty enough when she was younger, she merely had that kindly-old-woman appearance now.

"Can I help you?" she said, her eyes washing over us all. They stopped for several seconds when she saw me, but didn't make a big deal of whatever had tripped her up.

"I hope so," Amelie said in her quiet voice. "I'm looking for my aunt. I've never visited her here before, so I'm not sure where she lives."

"Of course, young one. What is your aunt's name?"

"Nemia. Nemia Tillis."

"Oh, yes. I know Nemia. That would make you...Amelie? From Sharton's Hollow?"

The bunny girl's eyes brightened. "Yes. That's me. Can you direct us to my aunt? I would so appreciate it."

The older woman's smile faded. "I would love to, but I can't. I mean, I could show you where her house is, but it wouldn't do you any good. She and your cousin are no longer here."

"No...longer...here?"

"I'm afraid not. Some Sodality troops came through a few days ago. When they left, they took everyone except for those of us who are older, or those who were ill. We have only a few dozen people left here."

Amelie stared at the woman, her mouth agape.

"Can you tell me why?" Ysduil said, when it was clear Amelie wasn't going to say anything. "Why all of a sudden is the Sodality taking people? They destroyed Sharton's Hollow, burned it to the ground. We believe they took most of the people from the village, too. Those they didn't kill."

The old woman tsked. "They didn't do violence here, but they took the others anyway. We don't know why. They wouldn't answer our questions." As she spoke and listened, the obsil woman kept darting looks at me.

We had to figure out what we'd do now. I supposed we could leave Amelie in the town, though there was no telling if more Sodality people would come and scoop her up if we did. We'd need to talk it over and figure out our next move.

"I'm sorry," I said, "but Amelie, do you think your aunt would mind us staying at her house tonight so we can figure out what we'll do next?"

The older woman gaped at me as if she'd just seen a dog stand on its hind legs at a podium and give a physics lecture.

"Uh..." was all the woman got out.

Ysduil rushed into the conversation. "May I have your name? My name is Ysduil Fennis. I'm a priestess of Odona."

The woman blinked, considered Ysduil for a moment, then looked back toward me. "I'm Melly. Why are you traveling with a *sotin*? Did you steal him from the Sodality?"

I realized that, once again, the armor had confused things, just as it had with Amelie. Well, the armor and the bothersome detail that I was male.

"I'm not one of those men," I said in a monotone by rote. "I'm a *khresha*. I'm not from this world."

Ysduil tried to explain more clearly. "I met Adam when we were in a Sodality dungeon. I was to be executed and he was to be taken to be trained as a *sotin*. We escaped and he took that armor from one of the Sodality guards. He was naked before that."

"Executed?" Melly repeated, then something clicked. "Oh, priestess of Odona. I can hardly recognize your dress. I have clothes you could wear..."

"Thank you, but no. I will continue to wear my damaged dress until I can find my sisters and get a suitable replacement dress. As for Adam, he is *khresha* like he says. He's probably the only man in the world who can still think and act without being directed."

"If it's not too rude to say so, I think I may have some other clothes, even armor, that would fit you. My husband was about your size. He passed before the Sodality came to power, thank the gods. I wouldn't like to have seen him being taken away and turned into a mindless puppet that way. I still have a chest of his clothes. Never could bring myself to get rid of them. Henny would be proud to contribute them to a man who has resisted the Sodality."

"That would be very generous of you," I told her. "It would be nice to get out of these. Everyone keeps thinking I'm one of the Sodality's men."

"Follow me, then. As for Nemia's house, I don't think she'd mind Amelie's friends staying there. I can show you where that is, too."

It was a short trip, but even so, we saw several more of the older women in the village, some human and a few obsil. They all watched us—especially me—as we trailed after Melly. I hoped the sight of the Sodality uniform didn't cause them too much turmoil. They'd already been through so much.

The clothing Melly had fit me rather well, as did the leather armor. It was a little better quality than the armor I'd been wearing and more comfortable, too. I raised my arms and turned in a circle in front of my companions.

"Well, what do you think?"

"Better than the other armor," Glasha said.

"You look like a hero," Ysduil added.

Amelie nodded shyly, hands clasped behind her back. It did wonderful things to the front of her dress, but I did my best to tear my eyes away from her and look toward Melly.

"Thank you so much, Melly. I wish I had money to give you for these."

"Psh. Nonsense. Paying me would rob me of the joy of giving it to you. Use it well and help to protect these women, even as they will help to protect you. With the world the way it is, you can't underestimate the value of good friends."

She led us to Amelie's aunt's house. The door was unlocked. It surprised me at first, but then I thought about the simple lives of the people here and the general safety a town would provide. They probably didn't have much trouble with crime. I checked on the way in and noticed there wasn't even a lock on the door. What would that be like, to know that you could leave your door unlocked and that you wouldn't get robbed?

"You let me know if you need anything," Melly said. "Please stop by before you leave, to say goodbye."

"We will," Ysduil answered cheerfully. "Thank you."

Once she was gone, the four of us sat down at the kitchen table. We looked at each other for a moment, but no one seemed to want to talk, so I started us off.

"What are we going to do now?"

"A better first question might be what Amelie plans on doing now," Glasha said.

"Yes," Ysduil added. "Do you want to stay here in Riverview? It seems pretty safe here."

"Unless the Sodality comes back," Glasha said.

Amelie lowered her face. "I don't know. I don't want to get taken away like all the others. Who knows what will happen to them."

"Do you have any other place to go?" I asked. "Any other relatives or friends?"

She glanced at me for just a second, then put her head down again. "No. I don't have anyone." The anguish and loneliness in her voice felt like a punch in the gut.

"Sure you do." Ysduil, put her arm around the bunny girl. "You have us."

"Can I go with you?"

Before Ysduil could answer, I said, "The Sodality is looking for us. Things will be dangerous wherever we go."

"I...I'm not afraid. Much."

I wasn't trying to talk her out of joining us, but I wanted to make sure she knew what she was getting into. "We're not even sure where we're going to go. Ysduil? Are we still going to find the other priestesses?"

"Yes, I must find my sisters to warn them that the Sodality is hunting me. They will be even more at risk than normal because I escaped their fortress and hurt their people."

"Okay. Well, there you go. We're going to go searching for the other priestesses of Odona. I'm fine with you coming along, but I don't know how Ysduil or Glasha feel."

"She can come with us," Ysduil said. "I don't know what we'll do after we find my sisters, but as far as I'm concerned, Amelie can stay with us as long as she likes."

Glasha shrugged. "Fine with me."

"Are you sure that's what you want to do, Amelie?" I asked.

For a change, the bunny girl flashed her amber eyes at

me, actually holding eye contact for almost two seconds before dropping her gaze. "Yes."

"All right," I said. "Welcome to the group. We can leave tomorrow morning and head..."

Ysduil flashed all her teeth. "Northwest."

CHAPTER

THIRTY-SIX

After our little discussion, I helped Glasha cut up some vegetables for a stew, while Amelie sat on the edge of a chair watching us. Ysduil excused herself and went into one of the rooms and closed the door.

I traded looks with Glasha and she raised one of her shoulders in a lazy shrug. I guessed Amelie was going to be inducted into what it was like to travel with the foxy priestess.

Sure enough, a few minutes later, the sound of Ysduil panting, punctuated by a few stifled moans, filtered out through the door.

I glanced over at the bunny girl, who sat still as a stone. I had to turn away and hold my breath to keep from laughing out loud. Glasha shook her head at me, since my entire body was trembling with the effort to keep the laughter inside of me. I don't think she understood.

A few times, I'd seen rabbits crossing the road as I was driving. If the headlights shone in their eyes, they'd freeze in place.

That was what Amelie was doing at the moment. For

some reason, the sounds of Ysduil's...ministrations had triggered that same playing-dead instinct in the bunny girl.

Glasha and I continued with the preparation of dinner for the several minutes it took Ysduil to finish her daily duty. After the house was silent again, Amelie started, then looked around. I averted my gaze, not sure what I'd find in those eyes.

Shortly thereafter, Ysduil came out of the room, her cheeks flushed. Amelie wrinkled her nose, sniffing before her eyes went wide. For another full minute I couldn't look at anyone or risk bursting out laughing. Bunnies had sensitive noses, apparently.

Not a word was said up until dinner was ready and we sat down to eat together. The conversation was very conservative, with topics like the weather and crops and how nice Aunt Nemia's house was.

After we cleaned up the dishes and everyone went to bed—I was awarded my own room while the three women shared the other two—I lay awake, staring at the ceiling. It had been such a whirlwind since I'd landed in this world, it was really the first chance I had to relax. Something about possibly being attacked by monsters at every given moment wasn't conducive to taking it easy. Go figure.

I padded silently to the kitchen and poured some water from a pitcher into a cup, taking a long drink. I'd been in this place for almost two weeks and in all that time, I'd done nothing to get back home. I thought, too about the future. And if what I was doing, helping Ysduil, was even the best thing to shoot for.

The fire was still struggling to burn in the fireplace, the flames weak and spindly. I sat down in front of them and allowed the heat to wash over me as I closed my eyes.

"Couldn't sleep?"

I was proud of how I didn't jump out of my skin at the sudden voice.

"Not really. It's been so long since I've been safe to sleep without thinking about being attacked, I don't think my mind knows what to do with it."

Glasha came and sat down near me, both of us cross-legged, with our knees almost touching. She had on the tight red sleeveless shirt she wore under her armor and the thong of the same color I'd caught glimpses of when her battle skirt moved enough to give me a view as she walked. The shirt was cropped, small enough that it was covered when she wore her breastplate, which left her abdomen bare. It also molded to her like a second skin. It was more of a tube top or small band of cloth, really, barely covering her nipples and areolae.

"What about you? How come you're not sound asleep?"

She reached out and I handed her my cup of water. She took a drink. "I don't know. Being in a town like this is strange for me. It's not a danger thing, just...I don't know... too much comfort."

I laughed. The hardened warrior was out of sorts because of the softness of her surroundings. I watched her pale blue eyes reflect the firelight for a while. It was comfortable, sitting her with her, even in silence. I liked it.

"What do you think about all this?" I finally asked. "Amelie joining us, going to find the priestesses, all of it?"

She shrugged and I watched the muscles jump in her right shoulder as she fiddled with the cup in her hands.

"I didn't know what to expect when I joined you. I would never have thought of finding the obsil and haring off to this place." She grinned at her pun. "Having no expectations is nice. It worries me not. There has been less combat than I thought I'd find, but we are in the soft lands, after all."

"And Amelie?"

"She's okay. I like that she doesn't always need to fill the silence with words. She's timid, but from what I understand, all her type are. Or most, anyway. I don't know what she expects to accomplish by following us. We'll need to keep her safe. I feel like she is a younger sister. I never had one. The Sodality saw to that."

"Yeah. The Sodality."

That was the kiss of death for our conversation, turning the easy, contemplative mood into something a little more irritating.

Glasha put the cup down and sighed. I reached over and took her hand. I half-expected her to pull it back, but she allowed me to hold it, her eyes locked onto mine.

"Thank you again for coming with us," I said. "We really wouldn't have made it out of the Dreadlands without you. You are an amazing warrior and a good friend." I weaved my fingers in between hers and squeezed, enjoying the feel of her skin and the way her hand fit so well into mine.

"Ysduil plans for you to mate with Amelie," she said in a serious tone.

"Yeah, she's sex-crazy. She keeps telling me how I should try to get together with Amelie. I keep telling her to leave the girl alone. She's been through a lot and doesn't need things like that to complicate her life."

Glasha stared at me, and not really in a good way. It looked more like...surprise?

"Do you know anything about obsil?" she finally asked.

"Nope. Just that they have bunny ears and a bunny tail

—though I haven't seen more than a flash of Amelie's tail yet—and that's about it."

"Hmmm. I, too, am ignorant of them, but one thing I do know. They, as a species, are very...amorous."

"Amorous?"

"Yes. Have you noticed, even though she seems frightened of you, that she positions her body in ways that call attention to her...assets?"

"All women do that. I think it's instinct."

"I do not do that," she said.

I squeezed her hand then brought it up to kiss it. "You don't need to. Every graceful movement you make is sexy."

She cocked her head at me. "Truly?"

"God, yes. I've already told you, you're so sexy it makes me ache."

"Do you mean that when you stiffen, it causes you pain?"

I chuckled. "Well, sometimes. A little bit. That's not what I'm talking about, though. I mean that I ache to hold you, to kiss you, to...be closer to you."

"Do you ache now?"

"Of course. Your beautiful face and sexy body in the firelight..."

She leaned toward me, her mouth slightly open. I met her halfway so our lips would touch. I don't know if she was a fast learner or if she'd been practicing or getting lessons from Ysduil, but it was nowhere near as clumsy as when we first kissed.

Almost in synch, we unfolded our legs and sprawled out on the floor, resting on our sides, facing each other. I put my arm around her and pulled her close to continue our kiss. Her firm breasts smashed against me through her thin, tight top.

"Have you thought about experiencing more than what we did before?" I asked breathlessly when we came up for air.

"Yes."

"And?"

"I...ache to feel more. Do more."

I pulled her lips into my smile and ran my hand up her shirt to caress the bare skin of her back. She mirrored my movements and we wriggled and wrestled for a moment.

"Your body feels as amazing as it looks," I told her.

"You like it?"

"I love it. Would it be okay to..."

I brought my hand around and cupped her breast. She hissed out a breath. I wasn't sure what that meant, so I stopped where I was.

"Do you want me to stop?"

"Uhnn. No. I enjoy that."

"Me, too."

I lifted her half-shirt up and moved my palm in swirling motions over her firm tits. When I finally got to her nipples, they were as hard as I was. I pulled her shirt over her head and watched them for a moment in the flickering firelight. So round and perfect, with narrow dark-green areolas and rigid buttons for nipples. I couldn't help myself. I had to taste them.

Her woodsy scent was even stronger as I brought my mouth to her chest and licked in circles around her left nipple. Her breaths came in raspy, uneven spikes as I took the nipple into my mouth and sucked lightly, then bit down gently. She arched her back and growled softly as I ran my hand along the muscles of her lower back, pulling her into me. The slightly sweet taste that was a shadow of what her mouth tasted like made me hungry for more of her.

I felt movement down near my crotch and was surprised to find her hand lightly rubbing the front of her panties, grazing me as well. It was hard to tell in the low light, but I thought I saw a wet spot in the red material.

I wanted to tear her thong off and taste her juices, but I promised myself I would take it slow. I sucked hard on her nipple, then let it fall out of my mouth, intending on asking her how far she wanted me to go.

Instead, I heard a door squeak open.

Glasha had her shirt back on before I could blink and by the time I heard the soft footsteps in the hallway, the dunim was sitting on the floor with the cup in her hand. She was still breathing harder than normal, but she looked perfectly natural. Especially compared to me.

I was lying on my side, the front of my pants tented out, and a sheen of perspiration on my forehead.

I scrambled to sit and managed to do so before Ysduil sat down next to me and leaned her head on my shoulder.

"What are you two up to?" she asked. "Anything fun? Can I play, too?"

THIRTY-SEVEN

I chewed a strip of meat we'd overcooked earlier in the day and sighed.

We were, in fact, not able to *play* as Ysduil had asked the night before. No sooner had the words left her mouth than the sound of yet more soft footfalls came down the hall as Amelie slinked toward us. It seemed that none of us were meant to get a full night's sleep.

In the end, we'd taken blankets off one of the beds, spread them out on the floor, and fallen asleep in front of the fire. I added wood to it as Amelie snuggled in next to Ysduil like the foxgirl was her safety blanket. I thought maybe I should be irritated because it was my job to sleep close to Ysduil like that, but the bunny girl looked so adorable and warm curled up there, I didn't have it in me to be petty. Ysduil winked at me and I could only shake my head, settling in on the other side of her.

I ended up on one end, with the two beastkin in the middle and Glasha on the other side. It was strange, but it worked. I got to sleep right away and knew nothing until light came in through a window and tickled my face.

After putting everything back in order in the house and eating a quick breakfast, we said goodbye to Melly and headed north.

We chanced upon a buck early in our trip and it was too tempting. Ysduil took it down with a couple of well-placed arrows. I watched Amelie as I helped Glasha dress the carcass, wondering how she would react. As far as I knew, she was a vegetarian. I figured it was pretty much a given for obsil to only eat plants.

The bunny girl wrinkled her nose but didn't show any kind of real disgust for what we were doing, just the normal squeamishness at seeing blood and flesh cut up. When we cooked the meat, it didn't seem to bother her.

We—all of us but Amelie—ate a fair amount of the venison and thoroughly cooked the rest of it so it would travel. It wouldn't last as long as jerky would, but we'd be able to eat it for dinner that night. Ysduil had foraged wild vegetables for Amelie to eat and to supplement the meat for the rest of us.

The travel had been uneventful and there were hours yet until we needed to stop for the night. The urgency we'd had before was gone, and without monsters lurking around every tree, it was more of a leisurely, even lazy, pace.

We'd compromised on the route. Still wary of the roads and being seen by those using them, we were walking a little-used path that was barely a trail. Ysduil said it was used by loggers, hunters, and gatherers who made their living in the forest surrounding it. The chances of someone else using it were less than on a road, but it was faster than tromping through the brush on our own.

Twice so far that day, we'd heard others on the trail, coming toward us. We slipped off to the side and hid in the foliage until the other travelers passed, then returned to the path.

With not much else to do, I spent my time watching the women. My position at the rear of our little formation gave me an excellent vantage point.

Glasha strode boldly in front, the warrior acting as the first line of defense in case we ran into trouble. She spoke little, seeming content to scan the area ahead for danger. Her posture was impressive, and I wondered if she had worked to develop it as she grew or if it was simply a byproduct of her combat training and her outstanding level of fitness.

Ysduil's gait was lighter, bouncier, but still with a graceful glide. Her lithe body passed through the air like an eel would through water, effortless and beautiful. She was expressive as she spoke softly with Amelie, gesturing and moving her head animatedly. I enjoyed the view of her back, slender but with defined and toned muscles. Especially when she shrugged or brought her arms out wide to gesture, my eyes were drawn to the lines etched in her smooth skin, easily visible through the holes in her dress.

But Amelie, she was the one who fascinated me most. It was mainly because she was new and I hadn't really observed her before. True, she was as stunningly gorgeous as the other two women, but it was more than that. On the trip to Riverview, I'd made some assumptions about her personality. She was timid and quiet and did not seem to like me much at all. Actually, it wasn't so much that she didn't like me as she seemed afraid of me.

As I watched her, though, I got other impressions. She spoke with Ysduil, sometimes even with Glasha. She was quiet, but not nearly as shy as I first thought. My view of her had been skewed by how she interacted with me. She smiled when conversing with the foxgirl, even laughed, her ears bouncing cutely as she threw her head back to chortle.

More than that, though, even when not talking with Ysduil, she had a certain flirtiness. It reminded me of what Glasha had said.

It had long fascinated me how girls, even without any specific training, did things so provocative, boys couldn't help but stop and stare. A slight turning of a knee, an angling of a hip, the gentle roll of a shoulder, a very small tilt of the head, even a twitch of a lip or eyebrow. These little cues at times triggered something in an observer and... well, turned them on.

I'd read how a lot of interpersonal actions were based on evolutionary things, trying to get the best mate for procreation and protection and all that jazz. I wasn't sure about it, but it sounded reasonable. I did know that it was fascinating to observe.

The women those girls become unconsciously arranged their bodies to snatch attention and bend others to their will, whether the "others" were men or women. Not in a bad, manipulative way, but in a deliciously appealing way.

Amelie had that skill in spades.

I thought back to the few very short interactions I had with her, trying to remember if she'd done that to me. It was a lost cause. I decided to try to pay more attention in the future. It captivated me, even scared me a little that I might be twisted around the bunny girl's finger like a cheap carnival ring.

She *was* a joy to watch, though. Ysduil oozed sexuality and she could position that fantastic body of hers in ways that could literally make me drool, but with Amelie, her innocent look coupled with provocative movements had a different effect. It made me want her, sure, but it also made me want to protect her.

"Like what you see?" Ysduil said from right next to me.

I whipped my head around. How had I missed seeing her approach me? I ran my eyes over her body.

"I do now, yes."

She swatted my shoulder. "You know what I mean. You were checking out Amelie, weren't you?"

"Honestly, I was trying to *figure* her out. I enjoy watching all three of you, either alone or interacting with each other. I mean, the land we're passing through is beautiful, but it's nothing compared to you three."

"Awww, that's sweet." She gave me a quick kiss on the lips. "Glasha says we'll start looking for a place to camp in the next hour or so. We should be clearing this forested area by then, so we'll have more options. I'm not sure exactly where we are, but we may even be close enough to a village to visit there. We don't have much money—only what Glasha had—so we probably can't stay at an inn, but we might be able to get some supplies and food. There may not be as much to eat traveling the plains."

"Right. That's a good idea. The supplies, not the inn. We probably shouldn't allow ourselves to be seen. Especially me."

She pouted out her bottom lip, but couldn't hold it for more than a few seconds before she laughed. "You're right." The foxgirl leaned in and put her mouth right next to my ear. "I miss you. I thought about you when I was doing my daily duty yesterday. If it weren't for Amelie being skittish after what she's been through, I would have dragged you into the room with me so you could do what I fantasized about."

I turned to meet her lips and gave her a good, long kiss.

"I'd like that, too, but you're right, Amelie's condition is more important. We have lots of things still undone, but we'll do them when we get a chance. I promise."

"Mmmm. I like the thought of that. It had better be soon. Just hearing you say it is making me wet."

She kissed me again, the faint citrus taste lingering on my tongue long after she returned to Amelie to start chatting again.

I made sure none of the women were watching and quickly adjusted myself. Damn, I couldn't wait until I could spend some time with my little priestess.

CHAPTER

THIRTY-EIGHT

After we reached the sparser area Ysduil had talked about, we moved into a place where the ground was flat to rolling hills dotted with rock formations. Close up, each formation was a jumble of boulders ten or fifteen feet high, but no actual cliffs.

In the failing light, we found the perfect spot to camp for the night. It wasn't quite a cave, but several large stone formations leaned together almost like a teepee. A very big teepee. It wouldn't cover us completely if it rained, but it was a lot better than camping out in the open, especially since a fire would probably be visible for miles on the plains.

"I think I know where we are," Ysduil told us after she returned from her daily duty to her goddess. "If I remember correctly, there's a village over the hill there to the east. Maybe we should try to get some supplies? If you will lend us some of your money, Glasha. I can pay you back when we reach my sisters."

"No need to pay me back," the dunim woman said.

"I can't go into a town, obviously," I said. "I kind of

stand out and the Sodality would find out quickly, even if they don't have soldiers there."

"You definitely have to stay here," Ysduil said.

Glasha pointed to the foxgirl. "So do you. Someone might recognize that dress and they'll snap you up in a second."

Ysduil's lower lip protruded. "I...could wear other clothes over the top of my dress, if it will protect us."

"We have no other clothes. Stay here with Adam. I will take Amelie. We're not being hunted by the Sodality."

The priestess raised a finger to start arguing, but then she blinked, registering what Glasha had just said. She put her hand down. "Okay. Fine."

It took all my self-control to keep from smiling. It would take hours to get to the town and back. I'd be here in our campsite, alone with Ysduil. *Alone.* At last. But that was tomorrow. The night still lay ahead of us.

We set a watch schedule and slept in shifts, like we had when traveling through the Dreadlands. There were wild animals about, possibly bandits, but the tension of being attacked as we slept wasn't as great as it was before. Amelie took a turn, with instructions to wake us up if anything scary happened, but Ysduil slept literally at the obsil's feet to make the bunny girl feel better.

The night passed peacefully and in the morning, Ysduil and I accompanied the green woman and the bunny girl to a bordering hill. We said a quick goodbye and they started off toward the village Ysduil said was there. No sooner had the two disappeared over the hill than the foxgirl and I looked at each other and broke into grins.

"What do you think about doing your daily duty a little bit early today?" I asked.

"I am open to that," she said primly, "but to dispense

with my responsibilities early, it would have to last a long time."

"Hmmm. How long, do you think?"

"How long will they be gone?"

I swept my arm under her legs and picked her up. "I like how you think, Yssy. How about we make it last as long as possible?" I carried her back to where we'd set up camp.

I laid the foxgirl down gently on the thin blanket we'd gotten from Glasha's house when we were in the Dreadlands and stood there for a moment, marveling at her. She shook her head and lifted her delicate chin, settling her hair out of her face, then struck a pose that apparently was shared between the two worlds. One hand went to her head, the other she placed on the curve of her hip, and she pursed her lips.

"Those things you promised me," she said. "I call them due now."

She didn't have to tell me twice.

I lay down beside her and kissed her while wriggling one arm underneath so I could settle my hands on either side of her firm ass. Her musky sweet citrus taste pulled my eyelids down. She settled into my arms like she was born to be there, humming her pleasure.

"I haven't been able to explore your body like I want to," I said. "Can I?"

"Mmmm. Yes, but I wanted to try some things I've read about but never done. Things I can only do to a man."

That perked up more than my attention.

"I asked first."

She leaned back and rolled her eyes at me. "You can do something, then I'll do something. You need to be fair. I want to make you feel so good."

"You already are. I accept your proposal. I will do what I can to make you feel good, then you can do the same to me. We'll take turns, like adults. Consenting adults." That last part didn't sound nearly as funny when I spoke it out loud as it did in my head.

"Okay." She laid back and spread her arms. "Explore me."

I immediately went for her slender neck, kissing her and dragging my lips up along her throat. I loved the sound of her breath as I did it, so close to my ears.

I ran my fingers up her taut belly, skipping them over the pieces of cloth. Really, her dress was more holes now than it was cloth, so the sight and feel of her body as she arched her back and threw her arms up over her head to stretch were wondrous.

Long before I focused on her breasts, her nipples were pushing up what little cloth was left covering them. I took them in my lips, then my teeth, and applied pressure through the dress. I was rewarded by sighing breaths and—on my sharp nibble—Ysduil gasping in air.

I moved my hands to lift the bottom of her dress up, fully revealing her toned legs and her enticing pussy. I licked my lips at the sight.

"No hair?" I asked, moving up to kiss her hard on the lips.

She let her tongue wrestle with mine for a moment before pushing me away so she could answer. "I usually shave it completely, but without my razor, I haven't been doing it as often. I borrowed Glasha's knife and shaved last night for you. Do you like it?"

I took her bottom lip in my teeth and sucked on it. "Oh yes. I love it."

She giggled and pushed me away again. "Good, because I like the feel when it's bald and wet. Things slide so smoothly across and between my lips that way."

"I better confirm that."

I reached down and moved my finger across her outer lips. They were already covered with a thin layer of her juices.

She sucked in another breath and her eyes flipped up in their sockets.

"Ooh, I do like that."

I continued to rub her, moving my fingertip in a circle, darting in to fold back her outer lips to lightly touch the wetter, soft skin inside. She wriggled and moaned softly.

I lifted her dress over her head and set it aside, looking down at her body.

"God, you're perfect."

"Mmmmm. This feels perfect. Why are you stopping? Is it my turn?"

I opened my mouth wide and took her right nipple, areola, and a large part of her breast into my mouth. I sucked hard while pushing my finger a little further into her folds.

"Unnh."

I released her breast. "No. I'm not done yet."

I brought my finger up to my face and sniffed it, then licked it. The slightly citrusy smell and the sweet, sharp taste of her juices drove me wild. She whimpered and when I looked at her, she was moving her mouth and licking her lips.

"You want a taste?" I asked.

A wicked grin stole onto her face and her smoky eyes locked onto mine as she nodded. I put my hand back down

—two fingers this time—and got them good and wet rolling them around her lips. Not inside—that was for later.

When I offered her my wet fingers, she snapped them up, sucking them into her mouth with so much force, I almost panicked. I'd seen how sharp her teeth looked.

"Mmmmm. I taste good."

"You do. But I need to taste it at the source."

Before she could answer or respond, I dropped my head down between her legs and bit her softly on the inner thigh.

"Oooh. Goddess. Yes. That feels so good. More. Please, more."

I trailed my tongue up the inside of her leg and across her mound. Her skin was smooth under me and her taste was even stronger than what I had sampled. The *thought* of licking pussy was always enjoyable, but with Ysduil, the taste was actually better than the thought. I wanted more.

"Lick me, Adam. Lick my wet pussy."

I circled her slit a few times, mainly focusing on her outer lips. They were plump and engorged and her juices mixed with my saliva as I gradually worked my way inward, flicking her lips with my tongue to reach the inner folds.

"Uh-uh-uh-uh." She was huffing breaths quickly, spiking my heart rate and driving me to want to take my pants off and ram my hard dick into her.

I licked her like an ice cream cone, greedy for every drop. From the bottom of her slit, all the way up to where I flicked the tip of my tongue to tickle her button, pushing the hood aside. Her body shuddered and hot, wet juices flowed onto my tongue and into my mouth.

I drove my tongue into her, as deep as I could push it.

"Yes-yes-yes-yes..."

She really reacted when I pushed inside, so I stretched my tongue and rammed it into her, moving it around to rub against the walls of her canal. Meanwhile, my finger found her little clit and I carefully stroked it. Up and down first, then side to side, then in circles. By far, the biggest reaction was up and down, her body jumping and her breathing doubling its rate. I filed that knowledge away for later and worked the little button of flesh—softly—with a steady intensity, all while giving her a deep tongue lashing.

It didn't take long.

Her breathing increased. The gyrations of her body got faster.

"Yes, yes. Goddess, yes. Oh, Adam. Oooooohhhh." She let out a moan that actually hurt my ears as she bucked her hips, trying to force every fraction of my tongue further into her.

As she started to tense every muscle in her body, I reached up with my other hand and pulled hard on her nipple.

It was like I'd set off a bomb inside of her. She moaned loudly, the sound trailing into a growl as she grabbed my hair and pulled my face hard into her creamy wet slit. Her body tremored, her back arched, her tight ass clenched, and the only part of her touching the blanket were her feet and the top of her back, near her shoulders.

Then she dropped back down and exhaled a breath she'd been holding for I don't know how long. After that came the panting as she tried to catch up.

I licked clean the gush of juices and moved up to lie next to her. She pulled me into a kiss, licking my mouth inside and outside until my lips tingled. When her breathing came back under control, she sighed.

"Goddess. That was fantastic."

"It was," I agreed, but noticed the frown on her face. "What's the matter, lover?"

"No fair. I didn't get my turn."

I laughed. "It's your turn now. I'm all yours."

THIRTY-NINE

When Glasha and Amelie returned to camp, I was sitting with my back against one of the huge boulders, Ysduil nestled in between my legs and arms, eyes closed. Her tail was off to the side of her body and I stroked my fingers through its strands while my other cupped one of her breasts. Even without access to a brush, the fine hairs were soft and untangled.

The motion made the foxgirl mumble and hum in pleasure. I wished I had another hand so I could rub her ears at the same time.

Glasha snorted when she saw us and shook her head. Amelie took in the scene with wide eyes.

"Well," I said, dropping my hand from Ysduil's chest. "How'd it go?"

"Fine," the dunim said. "It's a small village, but we were able to find a few things. Some vegetables, some dried meat, even some spices."

Ysduil opened one eye. "That's good. Thank you for going and doing that. I wish next time you could stay and relax and I could go, but..."

"It's fine. While we were there, we talked to a few people and listened to others speaking. We learned things."

The foxgirl sat up straighter, both eyes opened now. "Good things or bad things?"

"Not good. There were some Sodality people there, but not in great numbers. Searchers, I think. They don't wear uniforms, but I have seen enough of them visiting our village to know what they were."

"The Searchers are always around, looking for any males that may have slipped between the cracks. They're not a problem, normally. Of course, they would be if they saw Adam. They've also been doing more to look for other Sodality enemies. Like Odona's priestesses."

"That's not all. There are other Sodality troops in the area. They have been going through communities and taking women to conscript them into the army."

"That must be what happened with Sharton's Hollow and Riverview," I said. "Though it doesn't explain why they attacked the people and burned down the village."

"We heard a few stories about people refusing to join the army. The soldiers respond with violence."

"Why are they all of a sudden trying to increase their army?" Ysduil asked.

Glasha frowned and sat down on the ground in front of us, Amelie pausing for a moment before finding a spot on a rock to sit. "I don't know. We heard that the Sodality is asking a lot of questions about Odona's priestesses. I don't know if that's the reason to get more soldiers. Maybe there are people rebelling in other parts of the world."

"We need to get to my sisters. If the Sodality is hunting them this energetically, we will need to find a safer place than where they are. The hideout they're using now relies too much on the area being remote. It won't be hard to find them if that many people are scouring the countryside."

After packing up our things, we headed out again.

"It'll be probably two more days until we get to my sisters," Ysduil said. "I think there may be another village or two on the way. Possibly even a town. We should stop there to get more news about what's going on."

"The same as before," I told her. "Glasha and Amelie can go there for news. We definitely can't be seen, now."

I watched Ysduil carefully as we traveled that day. On the surface, she acted like she always did, chatting with Amelie, Glasha, and even dropping back to talk with me at times. I could see in her eyes, though, and in the little cracks in her smile, that she was concerned about getting to her sisters. I suggested we travel as fast as we could, even when it was dark.

"We can move when it's light out, but I don't think we need to keep going at night," Ysduil said. "We need our rest, and even with the moonlight, it'll be more dangerous to travel when it's dark. Better if we take fewer breaks during the day."

I reluctantly agreed. Regardless, we set up camp late that day, just after nightfall.

The news had soured our moods and all four of us were quiet and contemplative. I went to sleep right away, seeing as I was assigned the middle watch, and was nudged awake a little later by Ysduil, whose watch was ending.

"Anything to report?" I said, stretching.

"I heard some howling and yipping. Hyenas, I think. They're common in the desolate areas in this region. They don't like fire, so they probably won't come close, though."

"Okay. I'll keep an eye out." I kissed her tired face and she curled up on the blanket I'd been sleeping on. She sniffed as she settled in and hummed to herself, mumbling something about "good smell."

I settled in near the fire so I could easily add wood to keep it burning during my watch. With my back to the flame, I scanned the darkness surrounding us. The firelight illuminated some of the rocks and hills closest to us, but beyond those was pitch black. A feeling like a cold finger tracing up the center of my back brought a few shivers. Anything could be out there, watching us.

What was I thinking? I shook my head at myself. I'd gotten so used to being in the Dreadlands, I expected danger to come at me from everywhere. We were in what they called the civilized lands, which meant that there were few, if any, monsters. There was nothing to be afraid of.

Something howled in the darkness. The sound ended with a few yips. No wolf made those last sounds. Another chorus came from another direction, as if in answer. It must have been the hyenas Ysduil had been talking about.

As far as beasts were concerned, I didn't think hyenas were up there with lions or tigers, but then, I'd seen giant insects here. Were hyenas super-sized, too? Even if they weren't, the doglike creatures traveled in packs and were dangerous in their own right.

A slight sound behind me snatched my attention and I wrapped my hand around my sword hilt, my eyes scanning the campsite.

Amelie stood a few feet from me, hugging herself with her blanket wrapped around her. Her amber eyes almost glowed in the light of the campfire. They were huge and shimmering.

"Amelie," I said softly. "Are you all right?"

The bunny girl shivered and shook her head.

"Did the howling of the hyenas wake you?"

She jerked a nod.

"I'm on watch. I'll make sure that if they come close, everyone is awake to fight them. Don't worry. Get some sleep."

She stood there, visibly shivering. I really wasn't sure what to do.

"Do you want to lie down over here by the fire?" I asked. "That way, I can make sure nothing can get to you."

Again, she nodded. She glanced nervously out at the darkness, then tentatively stepped over to where I sat. It was a bit of a shock when she laid her blanket down precisely at my feet and curled up on it.

I shrugged. I guessed that was as good a place as any. Poor thing must be scared to death to even talk with me. Replaying the scene in my mind, I realized she *hadn't* talked to me. Anyway, she interacted with me, which was more than she usually did. That was a good thing, even if it was brought about by fear.

I thought the bunny girl had gone to sleep, but when another chorus of noises sounded around us, she grabbed one of my legs and curled herself around it. I could feel her body trembling.

I reached a hand down and put it on her head. "It's okay. We're here to protect you, Amelie. Try to sleep."

She nodded, bouncing one of her ears off my hand. Ysduil hadn't been kidding. The fur covering her ear was really soft. Like velveteen kind of soft. Without really thinking about it, I stroked the fur with my fingers.

Amelie froze. Even her shivering stopped for a moment. I realized what I'd done and pulled my hand away quickly.

"Sorry. Your ears are very soft."

"You can touch them," she whispered. I could hardly hear her over the crackle of the fire. "If you want."

Wow. She'd said a whole sentence to me. Two, actually. Short ones, sure, but still more than before.

I took her up on her offer and started to stroke her ear again. She settled a little bit, the death grip she had on my leg loosening. A soft sigh escaped her lips.

"Do you like that?" I asked. "Does that make you more comfortable? Less scared?"

She nodded, but also spoke. "Yes."

"Good. I'm glad I can help. Just relax and I'll give you an ear massage." A silly term, but if it would help the scared obsil get some sleep, I was all for it. Besides, I did like the feel of her fur in my hand. I wondered what it would feel like against my cheek.

I stroked Amelie's ears until her body eventually relaxed and she stopped shaking, even when the howls sounded again.

As I continued my task, the bunny girl snuggled up to me, wrapping her arms around both my legs, but not in a deathgrip this time. It felt more like a hug than anything else. She laid her head on my knees and sighed contentedly. I smiled down at her. It was like scratching a pet in just the right place. That sense of calm and enjoyment for both involved.

I heard a shift in her breathing after a few more minutes, but it wasn't to the deep, even breaths of sleep. Instead, Amelie sucked in breaths when I stroked up her ears and let out a sighing sound when I stroked down. A sound like a moan.

Maybe she was enjoying my attention more than I'd thought. To test my theory, I changed up the rhythm, stroking her soft ears in circles. Sure enough, little sounds of pleasure escaped, synchronized with my petting.

I wasn't sure what to do. I know what I wanted to do,

but the bunny girl had just started talking to me. I didn't want to freak her out by kissing her ears or...other parts. For all I knew, she made those sounds when she fell asleep every night. The safe road was probably best, so I continued to do the things that made the most sounds, experimenting with what seemed to affect her most.

Her head was still on my knees, inches away from my rapidly stiffening cock. I did my best to put it out of my mind, but my body wouldn't let me. As her little moans and breathless gasps continued, I kept the rest of my body motionless, closed my eyes, and enjoyed the sensations. I could have sworn energy waves were being emitted from her body and shooting right into mine. Most of them to one particular spot.

Soon, the sounds weren't enough release. Amelie started to squirm, rubbing her chest on my lower legs and wriggling her entire body. I dutifully kept up my ministrations on her silky soft ears, not knowing what else to do.

When I changed my approach a little and lightly rubbed inside her long ears instead of just outside, Amelie gasped and crushed my legs to her ample chest with an iron grip, dragged her breasts across my legs, then stiffened for a long, quiet moment. The tension transferred directly to me and it took everything I had not to pull her head toward my crotch. After a few endless seconds, she relaxed her grip on me again. Soon after, she took her head off my knees, settled into her blanket, and finally began to breathe like she was sleeping.

I sat, looking down at the bunny girl, wondering if what just happened was what I thought had just happened. She had a smile on her pretty face, the first I'd seen so closely since she appeared in front of me scared out of her wits. Whatever it was, it was apparently a good thing.

"Good night," I whispered to her, taking a fold of blanket and covering her with it. I put some wood on the fire and sat back down to finish my watch. The hyenas must have gone somewhere else because the quiet night was only disturbed by the cracking of the fire and the breathing of three sleeping women.

At that moment, I felt more peaceful than I could ever remember being. I'm not sure what that meant for me as far as the future was concerned, but in the moment, it was pretty all right.

CHAPTER

FORTY

When I relinquished my role as watcher to Glasha, I joined Ysduil on my blanket. After a few short hours of sleep, I got up with the others to prepare for another day of travel.

Amelie had slept the rest of the night where she'd fallen asleep at my feet. She didn't say a word about what had happened the night before and though I was very curious, I didn't ask any questions about it. She did, however, say a nearly sub aural good morning to me. Progress.

Ysduil noticed and raised an eyebrow at me.

"She was scared last night and came over to sleep by the fire. I can't say we had a long conversation, but I talked to her and she seems less afraid of me now."

"She wasn't afraid of you so much as she was intimidated by you," the foxgirl said. "The only men she's ever seen have been Sodality soldiers, which destroyed her village. She knows you're not one of them, but still, you're big and strong."

"I get it. I'm trying hard not to seem unapproachable or

anything. I think it's best to leave her alone and let her make up her mind about me over time. She's been through a lot."

Ysduil kissed me. "You're a good man, Adam."

I laughed at that. "This world has set a pretty low bar over the last twenty years."

Once we broke camp, Ysduil told us what she knew of the path ahead.

"There's a town to the northwest of where we'll be. Do you want to go and see if there's anything we need to buy there, Glasha?"

"It's bigger than the village we just went to?"

"Yes. Quite a bit bigger, if I remember correctly."

"I'll go. Amelie?"

The bunny girl nodded.

"Okay, good," Ysduil said. "I think this time Adam and I can keep going, then we can meet on the other side of the village. The mountain range curves around, so the road from the town swings back to the north. We can meet you near where that road meets with the road going north. A mile or so north of the fork, there's an old castle—just ruins, now—and we can meet near there. It's off the road some distance, so we won't have to be exposed. We'll get there before you."

"Good," Glasha said.

Ysduil let the other two know when to leave us and how to find the town, and we continued with our normal routine, paralleling the road but staying out of sight. We were still in a relatively remote area, but it would only take one observer to bring the Sodality down on us.

When Ysduil stopped and set down her weapons, I turned to her. "This is the castle you were talking about?"

"Yes."

The plants had gone wild, covering the entire area, though I did see what might have been part of a road or driveway. What I didn't see was a castle. Bits of stone poked through the plants, but none of them were very high. The remains of what could have been a wall marked out a rough circular area, but I'd seen pictures of ruins buried in the desert that were more pronounced.

"They're very old," she told me. "A lot of the stone blocks were taken away and used for other buildings. I was told it had been a castle. To be honest, I don't really see it, either, but who am I to argue?"

"Okay then." I sat down on a vine-covered chunk of stone. "It's the only thing around here, so it shouldn't be a problem for the girls to find us."

The priestess sat next to me and rubbed her shoulder against mine. "We can keep ourselves occupied while we wait." She ran a finger up my cheek.

It sounded like a great idea, but then my more rational side took over. "We're out in the open here. We also don't know when they'll get back. Glasha and Amelie used the road, so even if it's a little longer trip, they probably traveled faster than us."

"True," she said, her mouth forming a moue. "We don't have to do anything serious. How about you just kiss me and hold me?"

"Now you're talking. I'm sorry I can't do everything I want to do with you. I'm not as...open as you are about sex. By that I mean having sex in the open. And I'd prefer that if someone chances on us, that's not the way we're discovered."

"I understand. I loved what we did the other day and

always want more." She moved to my lap and swished her tail in front of me, tickling my face with the tip.

"Me, too. We'll do more, when we get the chance. We'll make the chance."

The foxgirl wriggled in my lap, sending all kinds of sensations through my body. I leaned in to kiss her and we passed the time waiting for our friends learning more about the little touches and locations that produced pleasure. It was nice, though hanging on the edge of passion like that was exhausting.

We took turns trying out new erogenous zones and ways of stimulating them, then stopping just as it became unbearable. Hot and cold, we cycled like that, bringing each other to the edge of giving in, but stopping before going too far. Frustrating, but also pretty damn hot.

When the other women found us, I was caressing the base of Ysduil's tail and nibbling on her neck. We both had our clothes on, which was actually remarkable after all the time that passed and the things we'd done. Luckily, I heard Glasha's voice before we saw either of the women, and Ysduil jumped up and sat down a foot away from me, a disappointed look on her face.

"Later," I whispered to her and her face brightened a little bit.

"We saw more Sodality troops," Glasha said, getting right to business. "We heard some of the officers talking. They were given orders to focus their efforts on hunting down and killing all the priestesses of Odona they could find."

"Isn't that how it's always been?" I asked.

Ysduil shook her head. "No. We have always been taken when we could be found, and there are the Searchers who are now dedicated to finding my sisters, but to give orders to the entire army to hunt us? That's new."

"That's not all that's new," Glasha said. "A new commander has been assigned to handle the search. Tallyn Kineth, a wustol. She was the commander of the Neallir Fortress on the other side of the Dreadlands."

"A wustol?" Ysduil said. "They're rare in the upper echelon of the Sodality. Wait, did you say she was the commander of the Neallir Fortress?"

"Yes. Apparently, she is upset about an escape and the killing of some of her soldiers."

"Uh-oh," I said. "It sounds like we've got a powerful enemy with a grudge. What is a wustol?"

"A monster race," Ysduil said. "They are tall and lanky, with skin ranging from blue to green. They often have tusks, sometimes large ones, and they're usually skilled in combat."

Huh. The picture that popped into my head was of a troll as they appeared in video games as playable characters. I wondered if that's what wustol were. "Great. Well, that won't change our plans to go find your sisters."

"No, but I wish now we had taken the time to kill the commander when we left."

"I'm still not convinced that would have been a good move. Besides, I'm not sure I could kill someone in cold blood like that. In battle is one thing, but while they're sleeping? I don't think so."

"There is another observation," Glasha said. "I watched the soldiers carefully. They are not as united as it may appear. Some even showed disgust at their orders to sweep the town to find as many conscripts for the army as possible. Especially when one of the officers said they would kill any who even spoke up against the practice. It may only be new soldiers that are unhappy."

I sighed. The news wasn't so good that it made me feel better about what else the dunim told us. "At least it's something. I don't expect they'll help us, but I'd rather there be reluctant soldiers on the other side than those who enjoy doing what they're doing."

"There are those, too."

I noticed Amelie—quiet as always—holding a long leather case or sheath.

"What's that, Amelie?"

The bunny girl pulled two wooden sticks about three feet long out of the leather pouch. I could see now that it had a strap on it so it could be worn over the shoulder or across the chest.

"Are those...fighting sticks?"

"Yes. Glasha said I could get them."

"I did," Glasha confirmed. "She told me how she's afraid all the time and wanted to learn to defend herself. There weren't a lot of blades for sale, but we found these and they were cheap."

"Ooh, that's a great idea," Ysduil said. "May I see them?"

Amelie handed them over and the foxgirl stepped away and started whirling the sticks in some kind of form. She wasn't quite as fluid as she was with her staff, but she definitely knew how to use the weapons.

"I like them. They're light enough to move quickly but they're solid, too. I can teach you how to use them, but practice will be your best friend in learning."

"Yes, yes," Amelie said, receiving the sticks when Ysduil handed them back.

It seemed like a good thing, the obsil learning to fight,

but it also saddened me. From what I'd seen of the species, they were pacifistic. The necessity for her to learn to hurt others would break the innocence I'd seen in them so far.

Then again, there was no telling what Amelie would decide to do as the other two women and I searched out Ysduil's sisters and then decided what our path was after that. If there was one thing that was clear in this world, it was that there would soon be fewer safe places for normal people wanting only to live their lives.

When we made camp later, I gathered firewood as the three women smoothed out some areas for sleeping and set up rocks in a fire ring. The dull buzz of their conversation was unintelligible as I dropped wood off and went off searching for more. I was on my way back to the fire ring with my third armful of wood when Glasha's voice rang out clearly, in a volume that far exceeded anything the three had said since we set up camp.

"What?"

I hurried to the girls to find out what they were discussing.

"Are you crazy?" the dunim said, glowering at Amelie. The obsil wouldn't meet the green woman's eyes.

"No," the bunny girl managed to say.

I dropped my wood and looked over the three. "What's going on? Is everything okay?"

Glasha regarded Amelie and threw her arms up. "Psht."

Ysduil stepped closer to Amelie, but turned her eyes to me. "Amelie just told us that she wants to join the priestesshood. She wants to become a servant of Odona."

"What?" I said, and it wasn't lost on me that it sounded the same as Glasha's exclamation from a handful of seconds ago, if not as loud.

"A lot of obsil become priestesses of Odona," Amelie said.

"Yes," Glasha spat, "and they're now being hunted down and killed as fast as the Sodality can manage it. Do you have a death wish?"

"No. I also don't have any family left. Or anywhere to go."

Ysduil put her arm around the bunny girl. "You have us. Just because we haven't decided what we'll do yet doesn't mean you have to make a decision like that."

Amelie's eyes grew large and shimmered as she looked at the foxgirl. "You don't want me to become a priestess? Like you?"

"Oh, sweetie, it's not that. I would be thrilled for you to become my sister, but Glasha's right. It's a very dangerous time to be one of Odona's servants."

"But...traveling with you puts me in the same danger. Whether or not I become a priestess, the Sodality will try to kill me because I'm with you and Adam. I don't want to go off alone without you. What would I do?"

Ysduil's eyes flicked to me, a sad query within them. I didn't know how to answer that, either.

The foxgirl squeezed Amelie and in a moment, answered. "I don't even know if the Grand Priestess will allow the addition of initiates with how things are."

"We're going to find your sisters. We can ask them when we get there."

"Tell you what, how about we wait to find out. You don't have to make a decision right now."

The bunny girl's mouth turned up into a smile. "I can wait. We're almost there, right? You'll talk to the sisters for me?"

"I'll talk to them," Ysduil said. "I don't know if a high

priestess or the Grand Priestess will be with them, though. We'll have to see."

Amelie hugged the foxgirl. "Thank you. In the meantime, you'll show me how to use my new sticks?"

"Yes. That I can do."

I glanced at Glasha behind the obsil's back. Her face had fallen into a half-frown. It probably matched the expression on my face. I got the terrible feeling that we had scooped up Amelie only to drop her right into the fire.

CHAPTER
FORTY-ONE

For the next two days, we adopted Ysduil's idea to take fewer breaks during the day and stop to camp when the sun went down. During that time, the priestess had started teaching Amelie the basics of the fighting sticks she'd bought.

She also started training her in other things.

"Really?" I asked Ysduil when we had a moment away from the other two women during a rest stop. "You're teaching her about sex now?"

The foxgirl patted my cheek. "It's fine. I'm not inducting her into the priestesshood or anything. Part of my responsibilities as a priestess to Odona is to help others get in touch with their sensual and sexual sides. You didn't complain when I showed Glasha how to give herself pleasure."

"I know, but...Amelie's just a kid."

"She is not. Even on your world—as you've told me—she would be considered an adult."

"Okay, yeah, according to her age. But she's so naïve and innocent. So...pure."

Ysduil treated me to her raucous laugh.

"What? What are you laughing about?"

"You're so silly. She's not as naïve as you think. There's a reason why obsil make good priestesses of Odona. They are naturally very sensual. Haven't you noticed how she moves, how she positions herself?"

"She does seem able to make herself look her best. On my world, we'd call it photogenic, but it's more than that."

Ysduil leaned in and put her mouth to my ear. "She is extremely sexy. Her every move is meant to stir the blood of anyone watching. Male or female. She doesn't even have to work for it. She does it instinctively."

"Uh, okay. Glasha said the same thing. Yes, she is. What's the point you're trying to make, though?"

"Most of what she does is natural, but not all. Do you think a woman like that has gone her whole life without exploring herself? Or others? I haven't asked, but I bet she's been with every woman in her village that's within fifteen or twenty years of her age."

I blinked at the foxgirl.

"Now you see. She is ignorant of some of the basic concepts of the art of pleasure, but she more than makes up for it in her experience and enthusiasm. She has asked me —several times—if I would lie with her. She is no child."

That sent my thoughts spinning, some of them going toward places that were uncomfortable for me, though I didn't know why. "Did you...?"

"No. I failed to allow you to help Glasha to orgasm first. I refuse to enjoy Amelie until you have done so."

I shook my head. I wasn't sure I'd ever get used to this world.

"I've told you, I have no plans to be with her. I'm happy with you, though it would be nice to get more time with you."

"Awww, that's very sweet." She placed a kiss on my lips. Not much more than a brush of her own, but it still got some heat flowing in my chest. "You'll need to do her, though. For both of your sakes."

"I don't think…"

A slender finger across my lips stopped me from finishing. "Trust me, Adam. I know what I'm doing. Don't worry about my training of our beautiful obsil. There will be more than enough other things to worry about with the Sodality out there hunting us."

She turned and glided away from me, swaying more than she normally did. A few steps away, then looked over her shoulder and caught me staring at her ass. She wagged her tail, blew me a kiss and put on her devilish grin, then continued to where the other two women sat.

Ysduil continued to lead us toward the place she said the priestesses would be hiding. It was an old safehold in a remote and largely uninhabited area. Two other villages were close to the path we took, each about a day away from each other. The second was barely over a day away from where she said we would find her sisters.

As we neared where the first village was supposed to be, we stopped on a hill, under cover of a small group of trees.

"What is that?" Amelie asked, pointing off some distance.

I stepped up next to her and looked toward the northeast. Smoke from cookfires drifted up from the smudge on the landscape, though it was too far to see details of any of the structures. The thing the obsil was asking about, though, was what surrounded the village.

In a big lopsided ring around the settlement was a conglomeration of colors and shapes with their own smaller fires adding to the soot rising lazily into the sky.

"Sodality army," Glasha said.

Ysduil held her hands in front of her chest. "Oh no. Do you think they know where my sisters are? They would love to get all those priestesses at once."

"Just how many priestesses are we talking about?" I asked.

"I don't know. I have seen a few dozen at times, but it has been a while since I visited. There may only be a handful left. Still, the Sodality would want to get them."

"We better hurry, then. No stopping at this village, obviously. Come on, let's go. They may have scouts out."

We plunged back into the thicker vegetation near the road and picked our way carefully through until late in the night. We didn't build a fire and only slept for a handful of hours so we could get ahead of the army, assuming they were heading the same way we were. When we reached the second village the next day, my discomfort grew.

"Another army?" Ysduil asked as we looked over the closest village to where the priestesses were hiding.

It almost seemed like we'd walked in circles, and we stood there looking at the same scene as we did the day before. From a distance, the village was only another smudge with more troops around it. There were fewer than the other army, but still a large number of little camps making up the bigger ring around the homes of the villagers.

"Ysduil, can we still get to where your sisters are hiding with the army so close?" I asked.

"Yes. We'll need to be careful because there won't be as much tree cover where we're going. We should still be able to make it through, though."

We found a nice little clearing more than a mile from the road and went to sleep early so we could rise in the middle of the night to continue under the cover of darkness. I volunteered for the second of two watches and had a chance to think about some things while I watched over the sleeping women.

I'd put off going to search for a way home so I could help Ysduil escape the fortress dungeon. Then, I had extended that to accompany her through the Dreadlands to safer lands. One final time, I promised to help the foxgirl get to her sister priestesses. We would be finding them in the next day and, at that point, she should be about as safe as she was ever going to be.

It was time I started thinking about trying to get back to my own world.

Though there was a little spark of excitement at the thought, there was another, more powerful, feeling in me. I was going to miss Ysduil and her cheery personality, Glasha and her stoic steadfastness, even Amelie with her timid but super-cute personality. I wondered what they would do, *how* they would do.

That was not even considering the way Ysduil made me feel. I mean, God, she was a sex priestess. I enjoyed looking at all my companions, not just the foxgirl, but that was probably just me being a guy. How was I supposed to ignore the pure sexual attraction I had for all three?

Ysduil woke up early and came over to sit near me, interrupting my thoughts.

The foxgirl tilted her head and brought it close to me, studying my face. "What're you thinking about with such a serious face?"

"Oh, just what lies ahead for us. You're sure you know how to get to your sisters, and that you can find the way while it's dark?"

She grinned at me. "I know where it's at and I have very good night vision, remember?"

"I remember." I put an arm around her and brought her in close to me. Her warmth against my side felt good, like she belonged there.

"Maybe when we get there we can stop running and we can take some time to relax and spend more time together."

"More time together?" I repeated. "I'm with you every minute of the day. We've spent all our time with each other since we escaped the dungeon."

Her eyes narrowed as she raised her chin, and her lips moved into her wicked grin. "All of that was great, too, but you know what I mean. I want to spend *better* time with you. Time without having to worry about our journey for the day or about anyone else being around that can be insulted or offended."

I kissed her forehead. "That does sound good. But won't there be a lot of priestesses around? We won't have time alone."

"We will." She snuggled in to me. "You'll see."

"I can't wait."

We woke up the other two women later and Ysduil led us through the trees and toward the road. The half-moon would have been enough light to travel on the road, but within the trees, I couldn't see a thing, only a few glimpses of silhouettes in the moonlight filtering through the canopy. Once we broke free and got to the road, though, it wasn't bad. I still occasionally tripped over a rut I didn't see, but there were no big obstructions. I'd hiked in the dark before, in my old life, but I usually had a headlamp if the moon wasn't bright enough.

When we neared the village, we left the road again to go wide around the many fires burning. After traveling through the trees, it almost seemed bright with all the background lighting.

"Are we far enough out?" I asked. "Won't the army have sentries out that might spot us?"

"There's no need," Glasha said. "Who would attack Sodality forces? They may have a few guards within the boundaries of their camp, but they won't have anyone this far out."

I grunted. She made a good point. I hoped she was correct.

After passing the village, far enough to feel safe, Ysduil brought us back to the road. The moon had moved directly overhead and without the trees obscuring its light, we marched along at a quick pace for another three hours before we once again left the hard-packed dirt. To my surprise, we didn't enter a forest, but an area with only scattered trees and bushes spaced out enough that if it were light out, we could probably see for miles.

When the sun cracked the horizon, the dim tableau in front of us became clearer. Not only had the trees thinned, but the ground itself had changed. The dirt and rocks were no longer the familiar brown and grey, but were darker, nearly black. The trees, too, were different. Twisted and misshapen.

"What is this place?" I asked, eyeing a bush nearby that had thorns nearly the size of my little finger.

"It's called the Scar," Ysduil said. "Though some call it by a nickname: the Dragon's Privy."

"That doesn't sound ominous at all. Is it another place like the Dreadlands? Are we going to be attacked by monsters again?"

"No. The Scar is a large area where an ancient battle

happened. It was a magical battle and it was so disastrous, it burned the land and everything on it."

"What's with the plants, though? Did the magic act like radiation, contaminating everything? Does anything that comes in here die or become like those trees, all grotesque and twisted?"

Ysduil laughed. "Of course not. It's just a dead and barren place. There's not much that can be found to eat here and the soil has no value, so it's desolate. There aren't any monsters. Not many large animals, either. It's simply a place that no one goes, so it's perfect to use as a hideout."

"But where do the priestesses hide? Are there caves or something nearby?"

The foxgirl winked at me. "You'll find out soon. We're almost there."

CHAPTER
FORTY-TWO

The sun rose higher and Ysduil angled to the northeast. I shaded my eyes from the glare to look out over a rugged and barren land. It actually reminded me of some of the desert areas in Southern California, with dirt and rocks and scrabbly bushes with sharp angles and points.

What I didn't see was anything resembling a place where a group of priestesses could hide. Then again, I guess that was the point.

"Are you sure you know where we're going?" I asked Ysduil.

She gave me a toothless smile and raised her chin. That wasn't any kind of answer.

The sun started to really get on my nerves. My head ached. This new world didn't have sunglasses that I'd seen. Barbaric place.

We marched steadily ahead. Suddenly, Glasha stopped and put her hand on her sword. I'd learned long ago that when the dunim thought there was a need for weapons, I had better pay attention. My hand slipped to my own sword.

"What is it, Glasha?"

"It's fine," Ysduil said. "Everyone stop here."

Amelie did as instructed and waited between myself and Glasha. The green woman hadn't actually drawn her sword yet, so I waited. But my hand was twitchy as I came to a halt.

"Stop where you are," a woman's voice said. I didn't recognize it, but that didn't mean anything. Essentially every person who had a thought in their head in this world was female. I was tempted to laugh about that—many of the women I knew in my world would agree with the statement. It wasn't time for jokes, though.

"We're already stopped," Ysduil said with more sass than I thought was wise.

"Y-Ysduil?" the voice said. It didn't sound nearly as demanding as it had just a moment before.

"Maressa, is that you?" the foxgirl said.

"Goddess, it is you!" A woman with a figure much the same as Ysduil's suddenly appeared a few feet from the foxgirl, wearing leather armor colored the same greyish-tan as the surroundings and carrying a spear. She stabbed it into the ground and lunged toward the foxgirl, wrapping her arms around Ysduil in a hug, her long dark hair swishing softly.

"We thought you were dead," the woman said.

"I almost was. I was captured and put in the dungeon at the Neallir Fortress, awaiting my escort to Aycrish Summit to be executed."

"Neallir Fortress? How did you get out of there?"

"I had a little help." She turned toward the other two women and me.

Six other women in armor like Maressa's appeared around us. They all had spears, too. Pointing at us.

"They have a *sotin* with them," one of the women said.

Ysduil put her arms out. "No. He's not a *sotin*. These are my friends. Stand down."

I put my hands up, just to be safe. Glasha did the same. Amelie glanced around, then with a little hop threw her own arms into the air.

"I'm not one of the Sodality puppets," I said. "I'm a *khresha*. I don't mean any of you any harm."

"He speaks in sentences without provocation?" Maressa said.

Ysduil stepped up beside me and put her arm around me. "Yes. He's not from this world. They found him in the sunken ruins near the fortress. He helped me escape. His name is Adam Townsend and our friend Glasha, the dunim, helped us to cross the Dreadlands. Amelie is our companion, a victim of the Sodality. They razed her village and either killed or captured everyone there but her. Everyone, this is Maressa Starlingsong, one of my sister priestesses."

A few of the spear women whispered amongst themselves, but Maressa silently inspected us like we were bugs she had caught in her house.

"We'll have to talk to Nysea about this. Are you sure, Ysduil? You vouch for all three of them? Otherwise, we cannot bring them into Haven. Even with your assurance, I may suffer punishment for bringing you in."

"I vouch for them. They have both saved my life many times. They are no friends of the Sodality."

Maressa sighed. "Very well. Surrender your weapons and we will lead you in."

I looked to Glasha, but she didn't hesitate to unbuckle her sword belt and hand the entire thing to one of the women. I shrugged and did the same. Seeing us, Amelie removed the case with her sticks from across her chest and handed them over as well. When Ysduil went to hand her staff over, Maressa chuckled.

"You're fine, Ysduil. We have no call to distrust one of the goddess's servants. Come." She gave Ysduil a genuine smile. "It is truly good to see you. I am glad you're not dead."

"Me too," Ysduil chirped.

As we walked, I tried not to look around too much at the women who had surrounded us. I didn't want to make them nervous and definitely didn't want to make *myself* more nervous.

Ysduil walked ahead of me, side-by-side with Maressa, while Amelie came up behind me and Glasha took the rear. The rest of the warriors surrounded us in escort. As the priestess warrior swept her hair over her ear, I realized that she didn't have fur on hers. Instead, they were slender and pointed. I also didn't see a tail or any other sign she was a beastkin. An elf? She was the first of her kind I'd seen since coming to this world.

She was, of course, beautiful. Her face was narrow, but pleasingly so, with nicely angled features and high cheekbones. She had the same kind of sway in her walk that Ysduil had, half confidence and grace and half pure sexy motion.

All those thoughts shot completely out of my head when I saw where we were going.

The two women in front passed between two other armed women, then disappeared while I was looking at them.

"What the—"

"Come on, Adam," Ysduil's voice called back. "Watch your feet."

I looked down to find a set of steps going down into the ground. Now that I was closer, something that looked like a lid or cover of some kind, perfectly colored and textured to look like the surrounding terrain, lay off to the side.

I glanced back at Amelie and she gave me a nervous wave. I returned it, adding a smile. If I was nervous, the obsil was probably terrified.

While I wondered if the steps were an entrance to a cave, I descended them to find Maressa and Ysduil at the bottom, maybe eight or ten feet from the surface. Beyond them was a hallway, well-lit with lamps and stretching as far as I could see. Openings where the corridor branched were visible, too, shooting off on both sides at uneven intervals.

"Are these...trenches?" I asked.

Ysduil smirked at me. "Yes. Isn't it fantastic? I helped to dig some of them. This has always been a good hideout for the priestesses of Odona."

A handful of women bustled through the corridors. Some were in armor but most wore dresses that Ysduil's probably looked like when it was whole. Something was happening, but if it had anything to do with us arriving, I couldn't tell.

Our little procession marched through what seemed like miles of tunnels. The floor, sides were all hard-packed dirt. The roof, however, looked like strong reinforced wood planks, like a hardwood floor. It would probably stand up to people or horses walking across it, but there would definitely be a sound that would give away what they covered.

Maressa looked at me quizzically when she noticed me inspecting everything. A slow smile curved her lips.

"He's a smart one. He's figured out that our trenches are only for camouflage, not for resisting or hiding from those close."

"*He* figures that if anyone rides or walks on these, *they'll* figure out something is under the wood," I said.

The elf laughed. "My apologies. I am not used to speaking to...men. I've only ever known males that were Sodality slaves."

"That seems to be going around," I said, then took a breath. "I'm sorry. I've always hated when people spoke of me like I wasn't right in front of them. I didn't mean to snap. All of this takes some getting used to. The world doesn't exactly have a high standard to meet for men."

"I will accept your apology if you accept mine."

"Of course. Thank you."

"And I thank you. As for what you have discerned, yes, this place is good for being unseen, but if someone comes into the area searching for us, it's not ideal. That's why we are in the process of evacuating Haven."

"What?" Ysduil said. "Why? Where will we go? What will we do?"

"I think I will leave that to Nysea to tell you. If she decides to do so."

Ysduil growled under her breath, but Maressa only laughed and led on.

The path we took seemed strange to me. If my sense of direction was on, we took a looping approach, going around certain sections and coming back to what would be a much shorter path. I wondered if they were trying to hide something held in those sections.

Soon enough, we reached a large room where more women in white dresses busily moved around, boxing items up. A black-haired woman with bunny ears covered in fur of the same color turned at our approach. Her dress was the same as the other priestesses, but the way she held herself made me think she was in charge, even though I hadn't seen her give orders to any of the others.

With so many of the same dresses around, I couldn't help but to look more closely at the clothing. I'd gotten used to Ysduil's shredded attire and all the glorious skin and curves it revealed. Surprisingly, the dresses the others wore, whole and clean, were just as enticing. My foxgirl had said repeatedly she would get a new one when we reached the sisters. A spike of excitement shot through me at the thought of seeing her in a pristine dress.

I let my eyes roam over the leader. With a classic hour-glass figure, she had a chest that strained the cloth of her dress and legs that were made for stroking. She, like all the priestesses I'd seen, was fit and had tight, toned muscles. Her red lips looked perfect for kissing. Basically, she was yet another gorgeous female. Big surprise.

She tilted her head slightly, then her delicious lips curved into a simper as her eyes moved up and down, looking over every inch of Ysduil. She tsked.

"The dress is not revealing enough? You had to tear holes in it?"

Ysduil laughed and dove at the woman. They clashed, four arms wrapping around two bodies.

"Nysea."

"Ysduil. I am glad that the reports of your capture and death were false."

Ysduil giggled. "The death part was not true, but the capture was true enough. They brought me to Neallir Fortress and sent for escorts to bring me to the Summit for execution. I escaped with the help of my friends, especially Adam. He was to be taken to the capital to be trained."

PHIL AERIX

The bunny woman's head turned to me and she gave me a smoldering look that nearly made me hard right there on the spot. It wasn't just her umber eyes, but the promises they held. It was perfectly evident that she was the priestess of a sex goddess. I didn't understand how someone who looked to barely have cracked into their twenties could be such a big muckety-muck among the priestesses, but maybe age didn't mean much to them.

"Nysea Ott," Ysduil said, "these are my friends Adam, Glasha, and Amelie." She pointed us out as she called off our names. "Nysea is a high priestess, the leader here at Haven."

I raised a hand to her. So as not to have to deal with the misunderstanding about what I was like before, I decided to address my situation right away.

"You're the high priestess?"

She quirked an eyebrow at me. "I am *a h*igh priestess. There are three of us, supporting the Grand Priestess, who is our leader under Odona."

"It's a pleasure to meet you, Nysea. I'm new to this world and to the Sodality and everything else. I guess I'm a *khresha*. I didn't want you to think I was one of those controlled puppets."

The priestess glided over to me. "I know. One of the sisters came before you to tell the story." She ran a finger across my cheek, making a scratching sound over my few days' growth of stubble. "You're a handsome one. We'll have to...talk later. For now, though, we have other issues to deal with."

Ah. The circuitous route had allowed a messenger to go straight to the High Priestess and report before we arrived. Clever.

"What issues?" Ysduil asked.

Nysea pursed her lips, so close to my face I thought she might kiss me, but turned to Ysduil. "The Sodality, of course. They're searching hard for us. Harder than I've ever seen. They're also coming this way. There's no way we can hide from them. We're evacuating."

FORTY-THREE

"Evacuating? What do you mean?" Ysduil grabbed onto Nysea's arm and tugged on it.

"Are you unaware of what the Sodality has been doing?" the bunny priestess asked. "Some of the sisters have been risking their lives to act as spies in the surrounding towns and villages, a few even going into Dunim Dell. They all bring back the same news: something has really stirred up the Sodality and they are committing more troops than we've ever seen to find us and execute all of us. Their orders come all the way from the top, from Imorith Sartyne herself. Every priestess of Odona is to be found and killed. They brought the commander of the Neallir Fortress over here to the east to direct it all. We don't know why they're so angry, but this shelter was never meant to defend against an army.

"You should all go. Except for Ysduil, of course. She will be hunted like the rest of us, but for the other three of you, it would be better if you leave. Being with us will only mean you will be caught up in the Sodality's plans. It could mean your death."

Ysduil dropped the other priestess's arm. She took her bottom lip in her teeth and avoided the other woman's eyes. "I think maybe I know why they're so mad," she said in a voice suitable for a child admitting he stole a cookie he was warned not to eat.

"You do?" Nysea asked. "What is the reason?"

"I think it's me."

"You and me," I said. "Tallyn Kineth is probably mad because you escaped, but I'm betting everyone, including the Paragon, is *really* upset that I escaped. Not to sound arrogant or anything, but there are still lots of priestesses of Odona on the loose. I, on the other hand, am potentially a lot bigger problem. A man, free and able to…uh, help women to reproduce, without the Sodality controlling it? That's something that could take down the whole Sodality. In several years or decades."

"He is right," Glasha said. "His existence is a threat to all the Sodality stands for. They know he and Ysduil were together. They will assume he will work with the priestesses."

I continued. "So you can see that it wouldn't do me any good to leave. But me staying might actually make it worse for all of *you*. If you want me to leave so you won't be even bigger targets, I'll go."

"I'll go with you if you do," Ysduil said.

The high priestess held her hands up. "No. We will not cast you off. If you choose to stay with us, we will respect your decision. I merely don't want our situation to cause more trouble for others." She trained her eyes on Glasha and Amelie.

Amelie cleared her throat daintily and stood up straighter, throwing her shoulders back and her chest out. "Pardon me, Your Holy Priestessness, but I have asked

Ysduil if I could join the priestesshood to become a servant of Odona. If you will allow me, I will stay with the sisters."

Nysea's eyebrows shot up her forehead. "You desire to join us? Even with what I just said, with the danger involved in being one of Odona's chosen?"

"Yes, Your Majesty."

The bunny priestess laughed, her eyes crinkling in the cutest way. "I'm sorry, these things are not a laughing matter, but please, call me Priestess or simply Nysea. I have some authority over the sisters, but I am not the Grand Priestess and I am definitely not royalty."

"Yes...Nysea."

"If you would like to join the priestesshood, Amelie...?

"Lendon," Ysduil and I said at the same time.

"If you would like to join the priestesshood, Amelie Lendon, then you have my blessing. We have many obsil within our ranks. Our kind is especially suited for the task. But you must be sure. It is a dangerous undertaking you consider."

"I'm sure."

"Very well then. We will allow you to begin the initiate process when we are in a safer position. The only thing to be resolved then—"

"I will stay with my friends," Glasha said.

Nysea narrowed her eyes at Glasha like she was using some kind of magic to look inside her. Or through her. "Then I guess it's all settled. You four should get some rest. We will be traveling at night to try to evade those hunting us. We depart an hour after darkness falls. Maressa will show you to a place where you can sleep."

I realized that the elf woman hadn't left after escorting us to Nysea. She stepped up, ready to take us to where we could get some rest.

The high priestess turned to face me squarely. "I would like to speak with you, Adam Townsend. Later, when circumstances allow."

"Let me know when it's convenient," I said. "Thank you for your help."

"Thank you for returning one of our cherished sisters, and for bringing a new one to us. I have a feeling we will be thanking you for other things soon enough. Rest. We will send someone with food and drink before we depart."

Maressa motioned for us to follow and she headed through one of the openings into a different tunnel than the one we came in through.

Glasha walked beside me, with the other two women behind. We'd lost our escort, other than Maressa, which made me feel a bit more comfortable. Behind me, Ysduil hugged Amelie with one arm as they walked.

"You will truly be one of my sisters. I'm so excited."

Amelie gave the foxgirl a shy smile. "I'll do my best to be a good priestess."

"I know you will. I will help you in any way I can."

I turned back to Glasha, who had a smirk on her face, even though she was shaking her head at the other two women.

"I thought you were going to go looking for your way home," she said.

"Yeah. I will. For now, I didn't want to leave Ysduil in the middle of a worse situation than we were in before. Amelie is wrapped up in it now, too. I guess I can stick around until they get to where they're going. Wherever that is."

"You are a good person, Adam," the dunim said.

Not wanting my friends to face danger alone didn't mean I was a good person. It just meant I wasn't an asshole.

Again, I was surprised by the low bar this world had for men. Was the collective memory so short?

It did make me think more on my decision, though. I couldn't keep putting off what I wanted to do. Needed to do. I definitely shouldn't be trying to help other people with their problems. I couldn't even deal with my own. I'd keep an eye on Ysduil and Amelie for a little while longer, then I'd go my own way. Who knew, maybe one of my friends would even go with me. Glasha probably would.

Maressa brought us through areas of the shelter where priestesses in those small, tight white dresses worked to package their belongings up for the evacuation. I saw fewer of the women with battle garb in here, but that made sense since we were in the interior.

"Are the women dressed like you the army for the sisters?" I asked Maressa.

Her musical laugh vibrated my insides. In a good way. "No. All you have seen are priestesses, as am I. When we take guard duty, we wear this armor, both for protection and because it blends in with the surroundings better. Our normal dresses would stand out too much."

"Oh. How many people are here in Haven?"

"There are one hundred seven priestesses...oh, pardon me. With Ysduil and our newest initiate, Amelie, there are one hundred nine dedicated to Odona plus forty-two other women. They are servants, helpers, or simply those who appreciate Odona enough to risk their lives to be with us to aid in many ways. This includes craftswomen."

"A hundred and fifty-one?" Ysduil said. "I've never seen so many in one place before. Are things truly so bad that so many are gathered together in one hiding place?"

Maressa shook her head, a frown stealing onto her beautiful face. "Times are desperate, sister. The best news any of us have received in weeks is your arrival and proof that you are not dead." She reached over to take Ysduil's hand and squeeze it.

Ysduil beamed at the elf priestess. "Thank you, Maressa, but that's not true. Just today, you received news of a new initiate, the presence of a *khresha* alive and well, and the alliance of a fierce warrior dunim who will travel with us for at least a little while."

"Truly. You are correct. Those negative thoughts are unbecoming of one in Odona's service. I bow to your greater wisdom. Ah, here we are."

Maressa led us through a doorway into a fair-sized room with eight pallets scattered throughout. It was one of the few rooms I'd seen in the shelter that had a door.

"I hope this will be sufficient. Most of the quarters have been cleared of everything in preparation for our escape."

"This is perfect," I said. "Thank you. I hope we're not being any trouble needing to sleep while everyone else is working."

The dark-haired elf winked at me. I couldn't decide whether I wanted to examine her long hair, which I noticed wasn't black but a dark purple, or her pale blue eyes with a lighter color that leaked into her sclera, giving her an other worldly glowing quality. I settled on her eyes and only blinked when she spoke again. "It is no trouble. Rest and we will bring food when we awaken you." She glanced at Ysduil and gave a tentative pause. When she finally spoke, her words were broken, like it was something difficult—or embarrassing—for her to say.

"Sister, we will be traveling all night. Have you...fulfilled your sacred duty this day?"

The sly grin on the foxgirl's face pulled at me to kiss her. It was seductive and, even directed at the elf, started blood

PHIL AERIX

rushing through my body at double its normal rate. When she turned to me, I couldn't help but to fall into her orange-red eyes.

She slunk up to me and put her mouth right next to my ear. Electricity shot down to the soles of my feet and back up in less than a second. "Adam," she whispered. "Would it bother you if I did my daily duty with Maressa? I haven't seen her for some time. I would do it with you, but I am unsure if you would do so with Glasha and Amelie here. I know you're shy about such things."

"I...I...yes. I mean, no. That is, it's fine. Thank you for asking." I didn't know what I was trying to say. It surprised me that she even asked. Did that mean we were...something? Were we together?

"You could join us, if you like." Her tongue flicked out and touched my ear, sending the most delicious sensations straight to my nether regions.

I closed my eyes to try to control myself. Three other women were watching us at that very moment and I had to fight with everything I had to keep from grabbing Ysduil and getting started on what she offered right then and there.

When I opened my eyes and looked around, I first saw Amelie's confused stare. Then, Glasha's dazzling blue eyes set in her striking green face met mine. She had a neutral expression. I struggled to pull rational thought through the fog of desire.

They wouldn't mind if I went off with the other two women for a little while. I mean, they knew what Ysduil—what all the priestesses—did every day. I wanted Ysduil so badly right then, even more since the hot-as-hell Maressa would be included in the deal, even if Ysduil hadn't asked the elf yet. My cock was rapidly growing in size and hardness at even the possibility.

Then I saw Glasha's expression drop, for just a second, to...something else? Was that disappointment in her eyes? Damn.

"God, Yssy, I would love to. I mean, really, *really* love to. But I should probably stay here with the girls and get some rest."

"It's fine, lover." Her whispers tickled my ear, making it even harder to keep a rein on what I wanted to do to her right then. "We'll have time later. Thank you for understanding, though. It will be quick and then I'll curl up next to you so I can feel your warmth as we sleep." She kissed my ear. "I'll be back soon."

She turned my head and gave me a hot, hungry kiss, so amazing that I almost changed my mind about joining her and Maressa. I kissed her back, running my hands along her back, drawing her into me, until I finally gathered the strength to pull away. I was proud of myself for not grabbing her perfect ass or for grinding on her.

I turned to Maressa to find her running her tongue across her upper lip. *God, why did I say no?* I was a bit self-conscious of what I was sure could be easily seen even through the thick pants I wore. I nodded to her and chose a pallet to sleep on.

"I'll be back in a little while," Ysduil said to the other two women.

I watched the two as they exited the room. Ysduil in her remnants of a dress and Maressa with her tight armor swayed through the doorway and closed the door, blocking my view and making me wonder what I'd be missing.

Glasha gave me a comforting smile, patted my shoulder, and took the pallet next to the one I was sitting on.

Amelie took the one on the other side of me, settling into it like a cat choosing a comfortable spot to nap. All wiggles and languorous stretches.

I was really going to need to find some time to be alone with Ysduil. Otherwise, I was going to start walking stiffly all the time.

FORTY-FOUR

I t didn't take me long to get to sleep. With all the excitement earlier, my body was ready for rest, so I went out like a light as soon as my head hit the pallet, which was surprisingly comfortable.

My slumber was broken when I heard someone speaking nearby. Warm flesh was nuzzled up against me, bringing a smile to my face. I was getting to really enjoy Ysduil's body pressed into mine when I slept. I rolled halfway over and put my arm around her, pulling her further into me and leaned my head in to give her a kiss.

It was one of those slow, sensuous kisses, our lips meeting softly and smoothly before parting, only to come back together. The barest flick of a tongue across my lips and a gentle probing with my own tongue in response.

Two things set off my internal alarm bells. One was the feel and smell that didn't compute. A crisp, lilac-type smell and faint rose-like taste, along with softer flesh than I was used to holding. My half-asleep brain registered something was...off. The other was the feel of the lips I was kissing. They were also different than I was used to. Fuller.

PHIL AERIX

My eyes snapped open, only to find myself looking into Amelie's beautiful amber eyes wide with shock. It didn't stop her from kissing me even as I was kissing her, but it appeared that I'd woken her up with my actions.

"Oh," I said, pulling away quickly. "I'm so sorry. I thought you were Ysduil."

The bunny girl gave me a shy smile and licked her lips. It was the sexiest fucking thing I'd seen in...well, since I'd gone to sleep. It was hard to keep all the sexy things straight that had been happening to me.

From behind me, a set of arms wrapped around me as familiar furry ears tickled the back of my neck.

"Are you turning your back on me now, lover?" Ysduil's voice said. God, I was sandwiched between the two women. I could only wonder if Glasha was on the same pallet as the three of us. Wouldn't that be something?

"No!" I almost shouted. Then I repeated it more softly. "No. I'm just confused." Amelie had closed her eyes again and wriggled her body against me. It didn't help that I had my typical post-sleep wood going on.

"Good, you're up." It was Maressa's voice. "I've brought some food for you. We'll be leaving soon, so it's time for you to get ready."

"Awww," Ysduil said, but I could feel her shifting to sit up. Glasha—still on her own pallet, by the sound of it, grumbled unintelligibly.

When I extricated myself from Amelie to sit up, I found the elf woman staring at me. Her dark hair was pulled over one pointed ear and her slender face conveyed her amusement with the slightest slant upward on the left side of her mouth.

"We missed you," she said. "Earlier." That was it. She turned and headed back down the hall. When she had turned the corner, her voice echoed toward us. "I'll be back in about ten minutes."

After scooting off the pallet between the sleeping beauties, I crossed the room to find bread, cheese, and bowls of thick stew that smelled fantastic. The women joined me, Glasha first, then my foxgirl, and finally the cute bunny girl. We ate every crumb of food quickly and efficiently and gathered all our belongings for our night-time escape.

Ysduil kept glancing at Amelie and smiling in the way she did that indicated that she had some kind of hidden information. She slinked up to me and gave me a long, passionate kiss just before Maressa came to fetch us.

"We really did miss you earlier," she whispered. "Maressa made me promise I'd have you make it up to us when we get a chance."

God. Damn. It. I can't tell you how hot that simple sentence made me, and so soon after finding myself kissing Amelie. I really needed to talk to Ysduil about that, once we started traveling.

When Maressa led us out of the shelter and into the cool night air, dozens of women were arrayed in front of us, all of them carrying some kind of pack or large item. A few small wagons were scattered about, the kind pulled by hand, not by horses. In fact, I didn't see any animals at all, making me wonder how they'd all gotten here in the first place. I mean, did they all walk?

We ended up being slotted in near the front. Maressa escorted us to Nysea Ott and then took her leave to join those guarding the sides and rear of the assembly.

As we set out, I scanned all the women around me, most in the white priestess dresses. Ysduil had gotten another one to replace the torn one. Though I missed seeing as much of her skin as I was used to, the new dress was elegant and clung just as enticingly as the previous one.

I eyed her up and down, not hiding what I was doing. She watched me, a curious look on her face.

"Damn, you're hot," I told her.

She giggled and turned around a few times for me. "Do you like my new dress?"

"I do. Somehow, even with more of you covered, you still look just as sexy as ever."

She bounced on her toes and threw herself against me to give me a kiss, nearly knocking me off balance. "I can't wait to see Amelie in her new dress. Can you?"

My face grew hot as I glanced over at the bunny girl, happily walking along between us and the high priestess.

"She'll look stunning in it, too," I told Ysduil. "Umm, that reminds me. I've been looking around at the priestesses surrounding us. Besides wondering about why every single one of them is beautiful, I wonder about something else."

"Hmmm?" she hummed at me.

I put my mouth near her cute fuzzy ear because I didn't want to offend anyone. "What's the deal with obsil women? Are they all...do they all...I mean...?"

She laughed and put both hands on my face so she could kiss me. "You're so funny. What you mean is, do all obsil have really big tits?"

I rubbed the back of my neck. "Uh, yeah."

"To answer your question, yes. They tend to all be very big-chested, no matter if they're curvy or very thin. To give you more information, though, I'll tell you this. Not only are they well-endowed, but their chests are also firm. Very firm. Like unnaturally, magically firm. Even when they're older, their breasts stand out straight without support. It's really unfair."

I looked down at the foxgirl's chest. She was not small-chested by any means, though she wasn't what would be considered large, either. I estimate she was a solid C-cup, and though I'd never seen her with a bra on, she definitely didn't need one. Her body was damn near perfect.

"Look who's talking," I told her. "I don't know one woman where I come from that wouldn't kill to have your body."

"Oh, you always say the nicest things to me." She hugged me. With all the physical affection, it was getting hard for me to keep a steady pace as we walked. That wasn't the only thing that was getting hard. "Still, a lot of us girls are jealous of the obsil and their magic tits."

I barked a laugh, making several of the other priestesses around look over at me. I waved and smiled at them.

"Speaking of obsil," I said, "what's the deal with Nysea? Isn't she a bit young to be in charge of this many others?"

"Maybe," Ysduil said. "Not really, though. She is fairly high in the hierarchy. She's been a priestess for a long time."

I scoffed. "How long could she have been a priestess? She's like my age."

"Oh, I see. You believe she is in her early- to mid-twenties?"

"Yeah."

"No. She is thirty-eight years old."

"Shut up."

"Oh," she said, her eyes going wide. "Did I say something wrong? I'm sorry."

"No, no. I didn't mean it like that. It's an expression people in my world use when someone says something unbelievable. It means, 'you've got to be kidding.' Like that."

"I see. Well, unbelievable or not, it is the truth. She is twice Amelie's age. I told you obsil look much younger than they are." She shot a glance at the lead priestess. "She looks very good, no?"

"Damn," I said. "She looks..."

"Hot."

"Exactly. I'm having some real trouble believing that everyone in this world is so damn good-looking. Maybe it's the magic or something."

She grabbed my hand and interlaced her fingers with mine. "I don't know. I have only seen one person from your world, and he is very handsome and sexy. Maybe both worlds are filled with attractive people."

I chuckled. If she only knew. "I don't think so, but it's an interesting concept."

"You know, don't you, that besides being good-looking, you are literally the only man in this world with whom we can carry on an intelligent conversation? Do you know how desirable that makes you? And you can naturally get aroused without the use of stonedraught tea. Every woman traveling with us would gladly have sex with you. In fact, I'll have to keep a close eye out because if you drop your guard, you will be accosted like you were in the dungeon by that guard."

"The ferret girl? That was definitely strange."

"You should have had sex with her before rendering her unconscious. She was very sexy."

I stared at her for a moment, my mouth hanging slightly open. Some of the things that came out of that enticing mouth of hers still shocked me.

"What? I would have had sex with her if she had done

that with me. I still would have knocked her out, but not until after." She half-skipped as we walked, humming happily.

I could only shake my head. One of these days, I was going to wrap my head around this world and these priestesses. Either that, or I was going to wake up from this amazing dream and wish I had taken more advantage of every single second.

FORTY-FIVE

Glasha, who had been walking with Amelie behind us, joined Ysduil and me after a couple of hours. The green woman had been even quieter than usual since we had reached the shelter.

"Hi Glasha, how are you?" I looked past her, but didn't see the bunny girl. "Where's Amelie?"

"She went to talk to a couple of obsil priestesses."

"That's nice," Ysduil said. "It will probably do her good to talk to some other obsil, after what happened to her village. And now we get to talk to you, so it's good for everyone."

Glasha grunted.

"Are you okay, Glasha?" I asked.

"I'm fine. Crowds of people are not on my list of favorite things."

"I totally get it. I don't much like them myself. At least we're in a line and not one big bunch. With it being dark outside, I can pretend that I'm not surrounded by more than a hundred people."

"True."

We chatted for a while, but then something occurred to me.

"Ysduil, do you know where we're going?"

"Yes."

"Where, and how long will it take?"

The foxgirl's eyes darted to Glasha, then back to mine. "Uh, we'll hide when it gets light and then travel tomorrow night. We should reach the town before it becomes light again for a second time."

"That's not bad," I said. "How are we going to keep from being found by the Sodality forces? I mean, even though we're traveling at night, and on a road, if we go someplace to hide, we'll leave a trail the Sodality can follow right to where we're going to hide."

"You'll see. A lot of thought has gone into where Haven is located and what kinds of contingencies might need to be addressed. Don't worry. We're in good hands."

"Cool. So, where are we going? Does this town have a name?"

Again, orange-red eyes flicked to Glasha, then returned to me. "Yes."

I waited for a moment, but no other words came out. "And?"

"It's called...Dunim Dell."

Glasha snorted so loudly, half a dozen people around us suddenly turned their attention on the three of us.

"Dunim Dell?" I repeated. It was kind of a stupid name.

"Yes." She watched Glasha warily. "I'm sorry. I didn't name it. Please don't take offense."

The dunim woman looked behind her, then back. She tilted her head at Ysduil. "Me? You're talking to me?"

"Of course."

"Why would I take offense?"

"Uh...because...the name...I don't know."

I chuckled at the foxgirl's discomfort. "Why is it named that?"

"I guess that a long time ago, there was a settlement of dunim in the area. It's a small, sheltered valley. The story I heard was that when other groups started building towns and villages in the vicinity, the dunim decided they didn't want to live there anymore, so they moved. Some of them went into the Dreadlands. They might even be Glasha's ancestors."

My chuckle boiled into genuine laughter. "So non-dunim people moved in and basically the dunim figured property values were going down so they went to find new homes."

"Property values?" The priestess scratched her ear and darted looks between me and Glasha, tilting her head.

"Never mind. What types of people moved in? What races?"

"I think at least half were human, though there were some beastkin races, too. I don't think there were many—if any—of the monster races." She eyed Glasha again. "Are you sure you're not offended?"

Glasha winked at the foxgirl. "I am not offended. I will be honest, though. That is a stupid name for a town or even for an area. That's like calling a village Human Hovel or some other silly alliterative nonsense."

"Alliterative?" I said.

"It means repeating the same first sound."

"I know what it means. I just didn't expect it to come up in general conversation."

The dunim woman turned her wink on me. "I know words."

I cackled a laugh. "Apparently you do."

After another few minutes, Ysduil seemed to forget her worry that Glasha was offended and we continued to engage in light conversation.

"Ooh, I need to go talk to Nysea," Ysduil said. "I'll be back in a little while." She darted to me and kissed my cheek, then took off at a brisk walk.

I turned to find Glasha shaking her head. "Sometimes I wonder if that one is a child, the way she bounces around so much."

"She's just spirited."

"Evidently."

"So, you never answered me. How are you? I haven't talked to you much since you decided to go with me even though being with this group will put you in danger."

"It worries me not. I do not fear danger."

"I know. I really appreciate you sticking with us. I feel safer with you around."

"Safer." It wasn't a question.

"Of course. You're brave and an awesome warrior. It's more than that, though. I enjoy having you around. I like talking to you. Hell, I like just looking at you."

"Thank you."

I looked around to make sure no one was close enough to hear us. Even though it didn't seem like anyone was, I wasn't quite sure about how well some of the beastkin could hear. I leaned in to whisper. "And I really liked kissing you."

She stared blankly at me for a moment. Then her cheeks darkened enough that I could tell the difference by the light of the moon.

"I..." she said. "I enjoyed that as well."

I gave her my best smile. "I'm glad. No pressure or

anything, but you let me know if you ever want to do that again. I'm all for it."

Her eyes darted around us and, of all things, her hand gripped the hilt of her sword.

"I'm just saying," I said. "Not that I expect to do anything like that when there are other people nearby. Ysduil goes in for that kind of stuff, but I'm more of a private person."

"Me, too."

"I know. It's one of the things I love about you."

"L-l-love."

I put my hands up. "Whoa. Hold on. I said it's something I love about you. I didn't say I love you. Uh, I mean—"

"Awwww, that's sweet," Ysduil said, suddenly appearing. "You love her."

"No. That's not what I—" I started.

"Oh, there is Amelie. I'll see you two later." Glasha all but ran back toward the rear of the line.

"Nice going," I said.

Ysduil winked at me and I had a sinking suspicion that she hadn't mistaken what I said. I wasn't going to even bother trying to discuss it. I'd talk to Glasha later, after I'd made sure there was no one else around.

Ysduil grabbed my arm and snuggled up against me as we walked. "So, tell me about kissing Amelie when we woke up. Pretty hot, right?"

I sighed loudly enough that a few of the priestesses near us laughed.

"You're too much," I told Ysduil.

She kissed the air toward me. "I'm just enough."

I snorted. I couldn't be irritated with the gorgeous beastkin for more than a few seconds.

"That reminds, me, though," she said. "I need to spend

some time with Glasha. Continue teaching her some things. I need to know if she's been practicing what I showed her before...and if she wants to try some new things." Her orange-red eyes got a faraway look in them.

"Are you really going to try to push more sexual things on her?"

"Push? No, of course not. She enjoyed our first lesson. You saw, or at least heard. I am a priestess of Odona. My job is to explain how much pleasure one can gain from physical stimulation. With a partner or all alone."

"Yeah, I guess. It just seems like—"

"I am very careful, Adam. I go as slow as she wants. You know how much I don't want to make others uncomfortable." Her eyes glimmered in the moonlight.

"I know. You're right. You are very considerate. It's just... I don't know. I don't think I would call Glasha shy, but all this sexual stuff, she's not used to it."

Ysduil's mouth formed the familiar mischievous grin. "You really care about her, huh?"

I didn't answer for a moment, not wanting her to misconstrue anything I said. The simple fact was that, yes, I had grown fond of the green woman. I just wasn't sure what it all entailed. I mean, did I lust after her or want to be her friend, or was it a combination of the two?

"I do," I finally said. "She's a good person and she's had a hard enough life. I don't want her to feel uncomfortable. Ever."

"Have you told her that?"

"Maybe. I don't know. I think so?"

"In these things," the foxgirl said, "it's better to be sure. Talk to her about it. Ask her what she thinks about my teaching. If she's uncomfortable in any way, I won't even mention anything sexual to her again. Okay?"

I cocked my head at the priestess. "Yes, okay. You know, you're a fantastic person. Have I told you that?"

"Not nearly enough."

I pulled her to me, nearly causing her to trip. "I'll have to tell you more often then."

She kissed me and ran her fingers through my hair. "Mmmm. You can show me, too. Just like I'll show you and tell you how fabulous you are."

"Deal," I said.

Just before the sky started lightening, I caught up with Glasha again. The priestesses were drawing the line of people longer so we could travel through a maze of crevasses in the stony ground. We could only walk two abreast. Ysduil was kind enough to drop back to chat with Amelie so I could talk with the dunim woman.

"Hi," I said.

"Hello."

"Sorry about earlier. I didn't mean to embarrass you."

"It's fine."

I squeezed in front of her to thread my way through a narrowing section and then stepped to the side after a few steps when it widened so I could walk side-by-side with her.

"I have a question, if that's okay."

"Yes?"

"Umm, the stuff that Ysduil taught you, the night before we kissed, does her teaching you make you uncomfortable?"

"Not as uncomfortable as talking about it with you."

"Sorry."

"It's fine."

"I'm asking because...well, she can get pretty excited about the stuff that Odona teaches her and I'm afraid maybe she's pushing you and that she'll make things awkward."

"No."

"No? No what?"

"It's not uncomfortable. I...like it. I am sorry. I have been raised not speaking of such things."

"I get it," I said. "I do. I don't want to make you talk about it if it's uncomfortable. I just want to make sure that she's not pushing you too hard. That she's being considerate of your feelings."

"She is, just as you are. I do like it. Very much. Just the few things she taught me...they feel soooo good."

"Okay, good. That's the whole reason for it."

"I have practiced," she continued. "When you and the others aren't around. I think I am learning to be more competent."

Oh God. I don't think I was ready for her to confess that. Looking at her, even in the moonlight—especially in the moonlight—and hearing her talking about practicing sexual things she was doing to herself. My pants were already getting tight.

"Just yesterday, I found a spot that I rubbed correctly and my body spasmed in the most pleasurable way. I was afraid you might have heard me, even though I was some distance away, *scouting*."

"Really?"

She looked at the ground.

"Glasha, that's fantastic. It's probably good I didn't hear you because I would have wanted to join you. You know, to see if I could make you do it again, to feel even better."

She glanced up at me like she was checking to see if I was laughing at her. "It does not disappoint you or offend you that I speak about it?"

"What? Hell no." I looked back to see Ysduil and Amelie a fair distance away and to gauge how far the people in front of us were. Then I leaned in to whisper in Glasha's ear. "To be honest with you, it really turns me on. Uh, arouses me. You are so sexy and the thought of you being aroused... so hot."

"Hearing me speak of it, does it make you stiffen?"

I glanced around again, then quickly unbuckled my pants, grabbed her hand, and pulled it toward my crotch. "You tell me."

At first, she started to pull her hand back, but once I spoke, her eyes drilled into mine and allowed me to guide her to the rapidly hardening lump trapped in my clothing. She tentatively touched it and I couldn't help but to suck in a breathful of air. She explored a bit more, tracing the outline of my dick through my underwear.

When she grabbed the cloth between two fingers and pulled it out enough to allow my shaft to straighten, it was her turn to breathe in sharply. I was almost fully hard and the head of my shaft was peeking out under the waistband of my undershorts.

"Well?" I asked.

She stared at the tip of my dick basking in the cold night air. I guessed she had night vision because of her race, because I couldn't have seen such a small piece of skin in the shadow.

"That's...because of me?"

"Completely because of you," I confirmed. "Between what you were talking about, how sexy you are, and you touching me, yeah, it's all you."

Her eyes darted around us and I could see the fire in them, but also the potential for embarrassment. I closed up my pants and continued walking.

"Sorry if that was embarrassing. I figured it would do more than having me tell you about it. Now you know how much you arouse me."

She tapped her lips with her finger for a moment. "Thank you. It makes me feel good that I do not disappoint you by speaking of those things."

"Oh, Glasha, you can talk to me about those kinds of things anytime you want. Just be prepared for me to enjoy them immensely."

"I believe I could accommodate such things." Her lascivious smile made me want to pull her aside and show her accommodation right then and there.

"Good. I'm satisfied that Ysduil isn't pushing her beliefs and *teachings* on you. I'm glad. Not only that she's helping you, but that you're gaining so much pleasure from it."

"I am. I look forward to her giving me further lessons."

"My God, so am I."

CHAPTER

FORTY-SIX

We followed the women in front of us through more of the twisty, rocky area until the way widened out into what amounted to a huge stone pen. Boulders and stony outcroppings surrounded the area and popped up from the ground even within the largely empty area. Already, as Glasha and I entered, Ysduil and Amelie right behind us, a couple of dozen women were breaking off into smaller groups and finding a spot to rest.

Maressa came around a boulder and walked up to us.

"We'll rest here for the day and head out again at night. This place rarely sees visitors and the path we trod to get here won't have left much in the way of trails. This is about as safe a place for us to rest as exists within fifty or so miles."

"If that's the case—" I said.

"No. It's not viable for a long-term hiding place. I said it rarely gets visitors, not that it never gets them. Those on scout duty can take care of any individuals that chance upon us for today, but if people go missing, others will look for them. It's not a place to be trapped in if an army comes calling. There are a few ways out, but they are more difficult than the one we came in through. We'll move on when it gets dark again."

"Oh," I said. "Too bad."

"Just so you know, we sent two of the sisters ahead to Dunim Dell to scout out the area and make sure there's not an army there waiting for us."

"Isn't that dangerous? If someone recognizes them as priestesses, they'll be taken."

"*Living* is dangerous for priestesses of Odona right now, Adam. One of the sisters is an elf and the other is a human. Because most of the people of those two races are part of the Sodality, they are suspected less than other races might be. Neither of them are well known in this part of the world, so they should be safe if they keep their wits about them. Obviously, they are not wearing their priestess garb. There is risk, but not too much, we hope.

"Find a spot that suits you, wherever you want. It won't be too crowded, but the good places will be taken up quickly, so I suggest you move on it. I'll see you all later." She nodded to Ysduil and the foxgirl waved to her.

"Come on," Ysduil said. "Let's find a good place. I've been here before and there are some out of the way spots that will give us a little more privacy than sleeping out in the open with most of the others."

"Lead on," I said.

We were early enough in the caravan that the first place Ysduil checked on was empty. We could still hear others talking and moving about, but because of the way the stone wrinkled, we couldn't see anyone else. The space wasn't large, maybe ten feet by fifteen feet. After a little work on the fairly level ground, the gravel scattered around had been swept into a pile at the edge, leaving plenty of space to lie down without being on top of small rocks.

Ysduil ducked out once we got settled and when she returned a few minutes later, she announced that everyone was taking care of their own meals instead of there being a large communal meal.

"That suits me fine," I told her. "I'd rather relax here in our little cubby hole than to go out and have to mingle with everyone anyway."

With my new endurance, I wasn't that tired despite hiking all night long. But poor Amelie looked exhausted. I doubted she was used to such exertion. Ysduil and Glasha didn't seem to be any worse for wear, but I already knew they were in phenomenal shape from all the traveling, training, and fighting they did. I imagined that even though it was still early in the morning, we'd end up asleep in no time, ready to get up and make it to the next hiding place before the sun came up again the next day.

"Uh," Ysduil said, her hands clasped in front of her and her right knee kicking in to affect a pose that was too adorable. It was the classic sweet, innocent, shy girl image. A personal favorite of mine.

"What is it, Yssy?" I asked.

"Because of the schedule swapping day for night, things other than meals and sleep have also shifted."

I narrowed my eyes at her. "What are you...? Oh. You mean stuff like daily rituals are on another schedule now?"

"Exactly. Some of the sisters do theirs in the morning normally. For that matter, some do their rituals two or three times a day. Most, though, are like me and do it in the evenings. With our travel, though, right now is like evening."

"That means you..."

She looked at the ground. "Yes. Not just me, though. Some sisters are...louder than others."

I barked a laugh. Whether it was because of how shy she was acting or simply because of the strange situation itself, I wasn't sure. "We'll survive it." I glanced at Glasha and Amelie, who were both watching the conversation. "Are you going to go meet Maressa again?"

The foxgirl shrugged and pursed her lips.

I still wasn't comfortable abandoning the other two women, even for a little while, when they had to tolerate that going on all around them. It seemed like a kind of betrayal to me. I would like nothing more than to go off with Ysduil—with or without Maressa—but I didn't want to leave the dunim and obsil women to do it. I wasn't keen on helping Ysduil with her ritual in front of a group of people, either, even if they were doing the same thing. Especially if they were doing the same thing. I hoped she understood.

"I may find a place and take care of my duty myself," she finally said. A cute smile stole onto her face when she saw my relief. I kissed the air in her direction, since the other two women were at my back, just to let her know how much I appreciated what she was doing.

"Thank you," Glasha said. Amelie looked between the green woman and the foxgirl and me. When no one else spoke for a time, the bunny girl settled onto her bedroll and closed her eyes, and that was that.

The dunim removed the armor from the top of her body, leaving her in the tight, cropped shirt and her leather skirt. I wondered why she didn't ditch the skirt, too, but then realized the tiny thong she wore underneath probably revealed too much with others around.

No sooner had Glasha gotten more comfortable than sounds began to echo from the other areas around us. Sounds that were as varied as voices themselves, but all with one thing in common. Grunts, moans, whispered words, all of them clearly indicated that the time of satisfying the daily ritual to Odona had started. Ysduil had headed the opposite way from where most of the noises were coming from. I couldn't hear her, but as she'd said, others were much louder.

I laid out my bedroll close to Glasha's and prepared myself for an auditorily erotic period before I would be able to get any sleep. When I met the dunim's beautiful blue eyes, I saw both helpless resignation and a bit of fiery passion there. I doubted I'd forget this day for quite some time. I metaphorically buckled my seatbelt and got ready for a wild ride.

I wasn't disappointed. I'd thought the noises were loud a moment before, but as Ysduil indicated, some of the priestesses were quite a bit louder than the others. With more than a hundred women, I wouldn't have been surprised if people traveling on the road more than a mile away could have heard them.

All the moans, exclamations, and other sounds that injected images directly into my brain merged into a cacophony that was almost unbearable. It was distracting, slightly annoying, and super erotic all at once.

Glasha, who had settled onto her bedroll on her back, looking up at the sky, turned to her side so we were face to face, a foot or two away. I almost laughed at her expression, switching between confusion, mild irritation, and lust. I could read her clearly. She was feeling exactly the same thing as me.

"You want to talk?" I asked. "It could help distract us from just lying here and listening to all of that."

"Yes. Thank you."

"No problem. What do you want to talk about?"

"I don't know."

I lowered my voice. "Do you want to talk about your lessons with Ysduil? I'd really like to hear more about how you feel about—whoa!" Mid-sentence, something warm and soft pressed up against my back as a slender arm draped over my body. I recognized that arm.

I rolled over, jostling Amelie and breaking contact with her impressive chest for a moment. I found myself face to face with the beautiful bunny girl. I mean literally, our noses were almost touching.

"Hi," I said, resisting my natural reaction to lean back to create some space.

"Hi." I saw her mouth clearly form to say the word, but I barely heard it even though I was close enough to feel the air. For that matter, I could smell her lilac scent, like a rose mixed with vanilla. I had to close my eyes for a second to regain my focus and to cast out of my mind that she was pressed up against me like she was.

"Are...you okay?"

Her eyes shimmered. They were opened more than usual.

"Are you afraid, Amelie?"

She shook her head. Seriously, I was too close to track that kind of movement. I was going to get dizzy. I sat up to open a little space between us.

"What is it then?"

"I...this is strange."

"You've already started training as a priestess of Odona," I said. "You'll probably need to get used to it."

"It'll be fine," Glasha said from my other side. She'd moved in closer to look at the bunny girl over my shoulder as she spoke. My world heated up much more than was physically possible. Glasha's firm, rock hard body pressed me from one side and Amelie's soft and sumptuous figure molded to me on the other. "You're not used to large groups. It will get easier and you will become accustomed to it."

"Really?" Amelie said with a shaking voice.

"Yes. Until then, we are here for you. Would you like to get in between us? Will that make you feel better?"

Amelie nodded and we shuffled around until we were even closer together, with the bunny girl in the middle this time. My arms surrounded her and entangled with Glasha's, and Amelie threaded her legs around mine as if she was trying to keep me from escaping. Yeah, as if.

I ended up with Amelie's face pretty much resting on mine, but could still see the green woman's eyes. They sparkled like she was going to tell me a good joke.

The bunny girl put her arms around me and pulled me in tight, smashing me against her breasts, which were shifting and pressing in very interesting ways in her skimpy dress. She brought her lips up to mine and gave me a kiss, bit down lightly on my lower lip, and then snuggled into my neck. It all happened so fast, I couldn't do anything other than to stare wide-eyed at the top of her head.

Then my eyes met Glasha's.

The dunim woman gave me a sultry smile and moved my hand over a little so it was resting on her breast. She nudged it with her chest and I instantly got hard. Well, hard*er*. With the position I was in, my crotch was basically

PRIESTESS

pressing directly against Amelie's. I hoped she didn't feel my dick springing to life, or didn't recognize what it meant.

I awkwardly stroked Glasha's chest. Awkward because with all of us tangled up like we were, my arm couldn't bend in the direction it needed to in order to do a good job of it. She hummed happily, though, so mission accomplished.

I caressed her breast for a few minutes, lingering over her hardened nipple. She repositioned herself to get more comfortable, making it impossible for me to continue, and I had to satisfy myself with flexing my arm to try to get feeling back since it had fallen asleep.

Amelie had gone to sleep and Glasha was drifting off after kissing in my direction. I figured I was trapped in place, so unless I lost all my self-control and woke up one or both of the women to help me ease my now raging hard-on, the only option for me was to try to sleep as well.

Surprisingly, I managed to do so, and more quickly that I would have thought possible. Though being in a knot with the two women was generally uncomfortable, somehow it was also kind of nice.

When the world shifted, shaking the foundations on which I rested, my eyes snapped open to see what was going on. Not only was I still wrapped up with Amelie and Glasha, but Ysduil had wormed her way into our little cluster and lay partially on me and partially on Amelie, her soft, bushy tail swishing around and tickling my neck.

I moved the furry thing out of my way and, through force of habit, started stroking it.

"Mmmmm," Ysduil said, turning her head to give me a look that instantly made me wish she and I were alone at the moment. "Good morning. Afternoon." She glanced up at the dimly lit sky. "Evening."

355

"Hello, sexy priestess."

I lay there for a few more minutes, afraid to wake the other women up, until Maressa came to rouse us.

"We need to prepare for leaving as soon as it's dark," the elf said, eyeing our sleeping arrangements. "The scouts have come back, and the news isn't good."

CHAPTER
FORTY-SEVEN

Maressa waited as we gathered up our gear and Glasha and I put our armor back on, then she led us to where Nysea and a few of the more senior priestesses were listening to two women in what I guessed passed for normal clothes in this world. They were simple cotton—or other similar kind of fiber—dresses. Though not overtly provocative, they clung pleasantly to the forms of the two, one elf and one human.

The elf had a figure almost exactly like Maressa's, whereas the other woman was fit as well, but curvier. Of course, they were both drop-dead gorgeous. Why wouldn't they be? It was a running theme in this world.

I found my eyes hesitant to leave the human. True, she was a looker, but even more than that, she was the first human I'd seen in this world, other than the older woman, Melly, in Riverview. Supposedly those of my race were plentiful, but my experience hadn't reflected that. Maybe they were all with the Sodality, or maybe they lived in a different part of the world. In any case, I watched her lips as she spoke with Nysea. At least until Ysduil elbowed me in the side.

"What?"

The foxgirl smirked at me. I hadn't been standing there staring at the woman, had I? Heat rushed up my neck, went through my cheeks, and pooled in my ears.

"Ah, good," the High Priestess said. "I wanted to talk to you during our travels tonight, Adam. Would you please accompany me when we start off? Ysduil and your other friends are welcome to join us, of course."

I nodded dumbly. Why did the leader of the group of priestesses want to speak with me? "I...uh, okay."

"Fabulous." She turned to Ysduil. "While you're here, you can listen in on our scouts' report. Continue, Daria. No, in fact, could you repeat what you told us earlier first."

Half of the human woman's mouth lifted in a crooked smile. "Of course, Nysea." She turned toward Ysduil and our little group, but her eyes immediately found me. They were a beautiful shade of light green, complementing her waves of glossy black hair. My mouth started to drop open before I forced it closed. I was glad it was still daylight, even if just so I could see those eyes reflecting the sunlight. "As I said, we went into Dunim Dell dressed like this. We were not challenged in any way or recognized for what we are.

"However, the town itself is surrounded by Sodality forces, much as the last village. What's more, they are utilizing the citizens to help them root out any of Odona's priestesses, offering enticing rewards for any information on us. Most of the people we talked to seemed in favor of aiding the Sodality any way they could. It was more because of the generous rewards than because they agreed with the Sodality, but that makes little difference if we are handed over to the soldiers.

"It goes without saying that our opinion is that we bypass the town and continue on to the next likely location. Though they have been helpful in the past, Dunim Dell holds only capture and death for us now."

I listened to the priestesses discuss the problem for at least fifteen minutes. After they were dismissed so they could change back into their priestess dresses before starting out for the night, Daria glanced at me, raised her chin in acknowledgement, and smiled before turning to leave.

I'd gotten looks and little exchanges like that frequently since we'd reached the sisters. I have to say, I was enjoying it. I'd never been a chick magnet, but here—based solely on my being literally the only man who could think for himself —I was a celebrity. I wasn't planning to exploit it—I was happy with Ysduil and my other two friends—but it was nice to know others were interested.

Once we started toward another town, this one called Axecleft, Nysea began drilling me with questions.

No, actually, it wasn't uncomfortable at all and it didn't feel like she was prying. She did ask questions, but it was plain she was interested in me and my answers simply because she was curious. I didn't get a sense she was trying to find ammunition to manipulate me in any way. It was actually kind of nice to reminisce about the world I'd left. I hadn't been in Tenos long, but sometimes it seemed like a decade or two.

"So in your world, you are not considered very handsome?" she asked, though I'd answered similar questions already.

"Nope, not really. I'm not considered ugly or anything, by most people I've met, but handsome? Nah. I think I'm just average."

She made a show of looking me up and down, her long bunny ears swaying. "Hmmm. Well, in this world, you are very good-looking, even to races other than human."

I laughed. "Thank you, but I'm thinking that has something to do with me being the only man in the world who isn't a mindless puppet."

She smiled at that. "True, that does make you more enticing, but that's not what I speak of. Even compared to before the Sodality, when all men had agency, you would have been accounted as very attractive."

I looked back to the girls. Ysduil was nodding furiously, Amelie's head bobbed in agreement, and Glasha gave me a *I would agree as well if it wouldn't expand your ego* kind of smile. I honestly didn't know what to say to that. Especially since I'd already said thank you.

"But I am not trying to embarrass you, Adam. You are aware, however, that traveling with a group of a hundred and a half women, you are surrounded by those who would like to...sample you?"

"Uh..."

"I know you have been traveling with Ysduil and know something of the priesthood, but let me say that we are a sharing lot. And no one here, except Ysduil herself, has had the pleasure of, well, pleasuring a man, for nearly two decades. We have, from the beginning, been restricted from any privileges with the *sotin*. It is not too much of an exaggeration to say that you can have your pick of any of the women in our group, to do with as you desire. I am included in that collection."

I inadvertently flicked my eyes to her chest and the rest of her body. Unfortunately, though it was a brief scan, she noticed it. Her smile turned almost predatory.

"For the most part, we are considerate, so we will not

pressure you overmuch, but some are more outspoken and aggressive than others. I will leave the subject at me having extensive experience and knowledge in the art of pleasure and I would be more than happy to give you the benefit of my talents."

She ran her tongue over her upper lip and I stumbled a step.

"He-he. Rock on the road," I said.

"I like rock-hard things."

Just when I thought I was going to burst into flame, she changed the subject abruptly. The damn woman was going to give me whiplash.

"This next place we will try to take shelter in is a smaller town. Very nearly a village. If we cannot take refuge near there, I am not sure where we will go. The Sodality is making our lives much harder as it puts more and more of its resources into finding us.

"Several hours ago, we sent two other scouts to investigate Axecleft. We will see what they report when they return."

Despite how awkward the beginning of the conversation was, I actually found myself enjoying the night's journey. Nysea wasn't only fun to look at. She was smart, funny, and her voice was the perfect blend of higher pitched feminine and a lower, huskier voice that some men found irresistible. I'd never been into women with a voice that sounded like they smoked three packs of cigarettes a day, but I did like Nysea's.

After a few hours, when the scouts she'd sent hadn't come back yet, Nysea called a halt for a rest period. The other high-ranking priestesses migrated over and an impromptu meeting started.

With me and the girls standing in the middle, not knowing what to do.

"You can stay and listen," Nysea told us. She must have seen how uncomfortable we were from our fidgeting. "Nothing we will discuss is sensitive information."

The gist of it was that they were unsure if the scouts didn't come back because they were in trouble or if they had simply lost track of time. None of the priestesses indicated that they thought anything was amiss, and they already had a contingency for the situation.

As the other priestesses scattered and went back to wherever they had been in the marching order, Nysea turned back toward us.

"There is a cave that we have used from time to time. We will continue past Axecleft and wait for the scouts there. If it's safe, we'll go back to the town. If our scouts arrive and report that it is unsafe, or if they never return, we can only assume the town is dangerous. At that point, we will need to determine what our next step will be. I can only pray to Odona that our sisters are well."

We reached the cave long before daylight, but as planned, we stopped and set up a camp of sorts in the surprisingly wide and long tunnels that spawned from a narrow opening in a sheltered ravine.

It was no wonder the sisters had used the place before. There were no large animals in it and no sign of people visiting. I was surprised they had found it to begin with.

The girls and I settled in a small cavern that was an offshoot of the main tunnel where most of the others traveling with us made camp. We still had to sit through the sounds of the sisters performing their daily ritual, but because we'd stopped traveling so early, Ysduil had plenty of time to go somewhere and take care of her own pleasure so she could come back and spend the rest of the darkness and into the new day with us.

At what Maressa told us was midday, the scouts returned. For some reason, Nysea called us to her again so we could listen to the report. It seemed strange to me that she was giving us all these privileges, but I didn't argue. Whether it was because of Ysduil's position or friendship with Nysea or if it was because of me being the only man, I didn't know. I did enjoy being unique, but it still seemed surreal that I would be treated like I was so important.

As soon as the scouts started speaking, all that other stuff flew right out of my mind.

CHAPTER

FORTY-EIGHT

The scouts that had gone to Axecleft were not the same women who scouted Dunim Dell. One of them was another human, who I hadn't seen before that moment. The other one, though, I'd glimpsed a few times from when I joined the sisters in the shelter. She was some type of canine beastkin, with a shaggy tail and long, droopy ears. The hair on her head, as well as on her tail and ears, was the color of a chocolate Labrador, her eyes a light brown color, almost a tan. Nysea had called her Aya. She did most of the talking.

"We entered the town without trouble, though there were some Sodality troops camped nearby. We spoke to the contact you gave us and found that the situation was nearly as bad as Dunim Dell.

"Our arrival was in the late afternoon, so the contact allowed us to spend the night at her house. She told us that some of the Sodality officers had been talking to the citizens, asking for volunteers for the army and talking up their work. We stood at the edge of a gathering where a few Sodality personnel gave their pitch to gain support.

"When night fell, Elosa and I decided we would try to take advantage of the discordance within the Sodality troops to throw some confusion into the people in the area. We carried around a pot of paint and a brush and wrote slogans all over the town. Things like *The Sodality way is not the only way*, *The Sodality is using us to attack innocents*, and *If we stand together, the Sodality can't make us do anything.*

"We thought it would do some good, even if just to make people think about what they're doing and what activities they're supporting. Honest, we weren't trying to cause too much trouble with the town. It seemed like some of the soldiers only needed a little push to desert or to start questioning their orders.

"It didn't do that. Not at all." The dog girl dropped her head, her eyes already shimmering.

Nysea waited without pushing Aya to continue. She put a hand on the dog girl's shoulder as a soothing gesture.

After nearly a minute of silence, it was clear that Aya wasn't going to continue. The human priestess, Elosa, took up the story.

"I'll continue from there. We did those things during a couple of hours at night. The next morning, our slumber was broken by loud voices outside. We dressed quickly and went out into the street.

"There must have been a hundred soldiers, a handful of them pushing a line of townspeople to a cleared central area. They explained that dissenters had painted challenges to the Sodality throughout the town and the people they'd captured had voiced their disagreement with Sodality policy, apparently emboldened by our messages.

"As we watched, the soldiers questioned each of the fourteen people they'd gathered. A few of them recanted and were summarily beaten. Those who refused to go back on what they'd said earlier were set aside. After the Sodality questioners had gone through all of them, they lined up those they'd set aside and executed them all in full view of the rest of the townspeople. Nine women of the town are now dead because they acted upon what we wrote and publicly disagreed with the Sodality."

The human priestess looked at Nysea, her eyes slightly glazed like she was in shock from watching the spectacle. Aya still stared at the ground, her tail drooping behind her.

"This is tragic news," Nysea said. "It is not, however, your fault, so I will not have you blaming yourselves. Those people made their own choice. It was the Sodality and its twisted rules that killed them. Though it has come at great cost, this makes it clear that the Sodality will not stop trying to destroy us—and any who disagree with them—until there are no longer any who think freely in the world. I thank you for your service, going to a hostile place and putting yourself in danger.

"It is obvious we will not be stopping at Axecleft. There is one more place we can try to secure shelter, though it is two or three days away. We will continue our march and Odona willing, we will find a place to hide where the Sodality will not find us."

The scouts nodded to the high priestess and disappeared into the darkness of the cave. The rest of us remained silent. I wasn't sure about everyone else, but the news—that the Sodality would beat and execute simple citizens—had stoked a fire within me. Or at least a spark. I almost wished we had a larger force so we could go to Axecleft, attack the army, and kill all of them. That would teach them not to abuse their power over Axecleft's townspeople.

But we were few, and we were not professional soldiers.

It would be far better to find a good hiding place than to cross swords with the most powerful army in the world. Or even a small part of that army.

Nysea informed the other senior priestesses that they would meet together at the end of the night's march to discuss where we would go and what we would do. In the meantime, we would keep marching the same direction we were going.

I gave Ysduil a kiss and, after seeing the sadness in Amelie's face, opened my arms to her. The bunny girl ran into them and I hugged her fiercely. She sniffled into my shoulder, no doubt thinking about her own village that had shared tragic interactions with the Sodality soldiers. Hell, the same soldiers who razed her village might now be in Axecleft.

I soothed the bunny girl, stroking her long, soft ears. I felt a gaze on my back and turned my head to see Glasha watching me. I smiled at her and she nodded. If the news had affected the warrior as much as the rest of us, she didn't show it. She was more accustomed to death and violence, I thought.

When I finally released the bunny girl, she kissed my cheek and fled back to Ysduil, not making eye contact with me. It was going to take me forever to figure the obsil woman out. In the meantime, I hoped I helped her feel better, at least.

Without a word, the column started moving again.

Nysea requested that we stay with her in the front of the column. Maressa was already with us, chatting with Ysduil. I figured she wasn't on guard duty at the moment and she wanted to catch up with her old friend. Either that or she was trying to get dibs on the foxy priestess for the next daily ritual.

After walking for a while, Nysea told the priestesses behind us to back off for a distance to allow us to speak without being heard. Ysduil was still in a conversation with Maressa, but Glasha witnessed Nysea's commands and raised an eyebrow at me. I gave her a little shrug. Whatever the High Priestess wanted to talk about, I was sure we'd find out shortly.

Once the other priestesses gave us some space, Nysea turned to me. "Adam, I wanted to ask you what your plans are."

"Plans? I will accompany you until you have found a safe place to hide. I want to make sure Ysduil isn't in too much danger."

"But what will you do then? After Ysduil is safe with us, where will you go?"

I rubbed the back of my neck. "I need to try to find a way back home. I figure I'll start with those sunken ruins where they found me."

Nysea tapped her lips with a finger. "I see. Would you be open to staying with us for a bit longer?"

"I don't know. I guess so, depending on how long. Why do you want me to stick around?"

Her mouth turned up into a sexy smile. That smile was apparently a standard issue expression for all sex priestesses. Even though I'd seen it plenty on Ysduil, it still had an effect on me and I stared at Nysea's plump lips for several seconds. She watched me as I watched her.

"There are several reasons. The most practical is that I would like you to help us in fighting against the Sodality."

"Fighting against the Sodality?" I repeated, probably more loudly than I should have. Ysduil and Maressa's eyes snapped to me and even Amelie raised her gaze from the ground to me. I continued in a lower voice. "Ahem. Sorry, but fighting the Sodality? Are you crazy? They have the largest army in the world. I don't think anything *I* could do would help you there."

"I disagree. Your unique position as a *khresha* could do wonders for organizing others to fight back. Not just Odona's priestesses. I mean other people, from all walks of life."

"I don't really think—" I stopped mid-sentence as I heard a sound from up ahead and to the left side of us. The noise of a twig breaking. A figure poked out of the foliage, dressed in dark clothes and holding a drawn bow.

It was aimed at Nysea and just as the picture registered, the archer released the arrow.

CHAPTER
FORTY-NINE

S ounds exploded from all around me, though it all seemed distorted. Like we were underwater. Glasha's sword cleared its scabbard, Maressa shouted something, crashes grew from other places in the undergrowth alongside the path, and Nysea released an exclamation that was unintelligible to me. Maybe it was in the obsil language, if they had one.

My body took over and before I knew it, I burst into some kind of superspeed rush. One second I was standing a few feet away from Nysea and the next I was in front of her, my sword already out of the scabbard and chopping at the arrow in mid-flight. Even more surreal, I timed it correctly to destroy the shaft before it could skewer the lead priestess.

When the world flashed back to regular time, I was dizzily facing the archer who had tried to kill Nysea. She smoothly pulled another arrow from her quiver and placed it on the string without breaking eye contact with me. She started to draw back the bow.

I did another rush, a little more consciously this time,

but it petered out when I was still several feet from her. Thankfully, when I stumbled to a stop, I was close enough to slash out with my sword and knock the bow to the side, even though it wasn't enough to do any damage to it. What my strike did do was to keep the arrow from hitting me and —I was pretty sure—Nysea or any of my other friends.

The woman dropped her bow and drew her own sword. Damn. I had been hoping she'd try to use her bow as a staff or something. I'd been trying to practice with the sword, but I wasn't very good yet.

As I prepared for her attack, I glimpsed something off to the side. I flicked my eyes in that direction and found another ambusher with a bow, the drawn arrow trained on me.

A moment of indecision ran through my head. I have to be honest here; I panicked. Instead of trying to take out the first woman or working my way around her to dodge the arrow, I chose the stupidest possible move for the situation: I put my empty hand up to block the arrow. You know, the instinctive defense if someone jumps out of the darkness to scare you?

There would be one word on my tombstone: Pathetic.

I don't know who was more surprised at what happened next. Something invisible flew out from my hand and slammed into the archer. It was powerful enough to spoil her aim and to even knock her backward a little. As far as I could tell, the arrow spun off high into the sky. I hoped it didn't land on any of the sisters.

Both of the women attacking me looked at me in confusion. I was pretty sure I had an identical expression. All the way up until Nysea rammed her knife into the chest of the woman with the sword. The blade made a squelching sound that shook me out of my stupor. The second archer still had her bow as she picked herself up, something she made plain by pulling another arrow out to try to hit me for a second time.

"No," I said, and—inadvertently again—rushed her with my super speed. This time I made it all the way and I rammed my sword through her throat, almost accidentally. The unused arrow dropped from her hand, as did the bow, and she reached up like she could keep the blood in her body with her hands. With a wet, sputtered wheeze, she dropped to the ground, tearing my sword out of my grip as she fell away. It was forced out as she fell, landing next to her.

I stared at the blood along the blade, only a dark shadow in the light of the moon. *Where there are two assassins, there might be more.* I spun, trying to make sense of the jumble of shadows, some of them still in motion. I felt nauseous, almost like my body had split into two parts and now it was trying to pull itself back together.

Four bodies lay on the ground and, even as I watched, Ysduil cracked her staff on another darkly clad figure, dropping her to the ground. Glasha, Amelie, and Maressa were all accounted for, looking uninjured to me, but I couldn't be sure in the dark. As they spoke, their voices echoed strangely in my ears.

"At least one got away," Maressa said. "I saw her as I was fighting. Should we look for her?"

Nysea had her gaze fixed on me, but she shook her head and answered the other priestess. "No. We'll never find her in this darkness. She will no doubt be reporting where we are. Everything has just changed. We were staying out of sight, but now the Sodality will know where we were, and it will be easier to find where we will be."

"Are you sure they're Sodality?" Ysduil asked.

"Who else? No bandit in her right mind would attack the front of a column this large."

I picked up my sword and cleaned the blade on the clothing of the closest body. "That archer was after you. I don't think that was a coincidence. They knew you were in charge."

"Yes," the lead priestess said. "One of the hazards of having some authority. Come, let's report this to the other sisters and then make haste to leave the area as quickly as possible. Are any of the ambushers alive?"

Ysduil kicked the person at her feet. "This one is. She'll have a headache, but I didn't hit her hard enough to kill her."

"Good. Bring her with us. I'll have some of the priestesses carry her. We can interrogate her when she wakes."

"I can carry her for now, until you get others to help," I said. The weird muzzy feeling in my head was starting to dissipate and it was the least I could do. I was sure I was the physically strongest one in the group, and it wasn't just because I was a man. The strange strength and speed I'd felt since I got to this world was useful in a number of ways.

"Thank you," Nysea said. "Once we can find replacements for you, you and I must speak about what you did during the battle."

"Of course." I think there was going to be a disappointed priestess if she wanted me to explain what I'd done. I hadn't even fully accepted the speed rush thing. I had no damn idea *what* had blasted out of my hand, let alone *how*.

There was nothing to do about it for now. I picked up the unconscious ambusher and threw her over my shoulder, then fell in step with the others as we headed out. All except Maressa. She went back farther in the line to inform the other priestesses of what happened and to expect bodies in the pathway.

What a weird night.

After walking silently for a time, I asked a question that had been weighing on me since the ambush.

"All the attackers were women. Why? I thought some of the men were trained for specific jobs, like being soldiers or assassins."

"It's true," Nysea said. "The training is extensive and men are often used for assassination missions, especially ones that do not require them to survive. In this case, we can assume the Sodality decided that the men's inability to think on their feet and make decisions would risk failure. If there is one thing the Sodality knows, it is how to use the tools they have created. Male or female, they have sufficient resources to hunt us down."

A while later, a small group of priestesses arrived to take possession of the unconscious Sodality assassin. The woman didn't look like she would wake anytime soon, so Nysea directed them to move her more toward the center of the group and assign guards to watch her in addition to those who would carry her.

"It's a shame we couldn't bring larger wagons or carts," the high priestess said. "It would make such tasks easier. Alas, though, it is hard to hide the tracks from wheels, even if footprints can be obscured."

I'd already offered to carry the woman until we stopped to rest. She barely weighed anything to my elevated strength. Nysea told me she would rather I be unencumbered in case we were attacked again.

"I wanted to ask you about our battle, Adam," she said conversationally. Like it was no big deal. The intense look in her eyes belied her tone, though. "I can see that your fighting technique is unrefined, but on several occasions, you moved with such speed, it was hard to track where you were."

My face grew warm. I tried not to take it personally that she'd essentially said I couldn't fight worth a shit. I must have made a face, too, because her eyebrows shot up when she saw my expression.

"I'm sorry. I didn't mean to insult you or to accuse you of—"

"No worries," I said. At least it was just a slip of the tongue and not premeditated criticism. "I know I can't fight that well. I've been trying to practice, but where I come from, few people train in combat and of those only a tiny percentage use weapons like the ones available here."

"Still, I did not mean to sound so critical. What I meant was that I can see that you've had little training, yet you are so effective. It wasn't just your speed, though. That thing you did when the archer was trying to target you...what was that?"

I looked the priestess in the eye and gave her an exaggerated shrug. "I have no idea."

"You don't know? How is that possible?"

"That's another thing I don't know. Since I came to this world, I've had more strength and speed than I ever did before. I thought maybe it was because your world is smaller, so gravity is less than my world. That would explain moving faster and being able to lift more weight, but it wouldn't explain other feats of strength.

"Then I thought maybe it was magic, but Ysduil said magic died shortly after the Sodality took charge."

"Hmmm." The High Priestess pulled on one of her long ears as she thought. "It is possible that one of the theories about magic waning is true. It tries to explain the disappearance of magic on an imbalance between the male and female energies. The theory holds that because men cannot think enough to use magic any longer, female magic weakened to equalize with male magic. If that's the case, then as much male magic would be available as all the female magic in use in the entire world. That would mean that if you could master its use, you would be as powerful as all the other mages in the world put together."

"Ysduil mentioned something about that, with the balance between the male and female magic. She wasn't sure about it, though. But even if it's true, how could I have learned to use the magic to begin with?"

"I am not certain why," Nysea said. "It is a pity that Gesin Wenet is not with us."

That was a name I hadn't heard before. "Who?"

"Gesin Wenet is the Grand Priestess of Odona, the leader of our order. As with many of the older sisters, she lived for a fair amount of time before the Sodality took over. She had the use of magic, though her abilities weakened as everyone else's did. I have not heard from her in some time. I believe she might be in hiding. If she were here, she might be able to help you discover how to use your abilities more efficiently."

"That would be nice," I said. "If it's really magic, then the more I could learn about it, the better."

"I witnessed one of the sisters helping a man with his magic when I was first inducted into the priestesshood. I might be able to conduct the ritual to help you come more fully in touch with your magic, if that is what is causing these effects."

"Really? That would be great. If there's even a chance at being able to control these things, especially if I could learn to be more powerful, it would help a great deal."

"I would try, if you like," Nysea said. "However, it is a ritual from Odona, which means that it includes...close contact."

The pause made me suspect what she meant. I looked over to Ysduil, who was walking beside me but had been quiet the entire time. I raised an eyebrow at her.

"I don't know anything about a ritual like that," she said. "You need to understand that for Odona's servants, most things are grounded in physical intimacy. I know you are less used to that than we are."

"Uh," I said. "So, let me get this straight. In order for you to help me to get in touch with my magic, I need to have sex with you?"

"Precisely."

I knew the priestess was older than me, though she didn't look it. Like most of the other women I'd seen, she was smoking hot. Still, Ysduil and I had a nice thing going. I didn't want to ruin that with what may just be a ruse for the bunny woman to get me into bed with her.

I tried to think of how I could stall and try to talk to my foxgirl before I made a decision, but she had other ideas.

"Oooh," Ysduil said. "That's so exciting. I've heard about rituals dealing with magic. I've even heard that the climaxes from such rituals are much stronger than normal. Can I watch?"

My mouth dropped open and I stared at the foxgirl. She shifted her gaze excitedly from me to Nysea and back again, waiting for an answer.

"You...think I should do it?" I asked.

"Of course. Even if it doesn't work, you need to come together with more people. I feel a little bit sad that you've only had me since you came to this world. That's no way for it to be. I've been *trying* to get you to have sex with Glasha and Amelie, but you've been too shy."

Glasha's and Amelie's presence didn't seem to bother Ysduil at all. Just like the thought of me being with other women didn't seem to bother her. I wondered if it would be the same if there were more men than me. Would she want to jump from bed to bed with other men like that? I wasn't quite sure I could handle that. I was also not sure if that made me a huge hypocrite. I mean, she was practically forcing me to have sex with another super-hot woman. It would be rude to reject her ideas, right?

"You have to do it, Adam," the foxgirl said. "Even if you don't let me watch, you have to try. Just imagine if she could help you to assimilate magic more fully. What would you be able to do? Do it for me?"

The pouty look on her face made me want to laugh, but instead, an internal voice was saying *Awww*.

"Okay, fine. We can give it a try. Let me know what you want me to do and we'll see how it goes."

Nysea pursed her lips like she was ready to kiss me right there. "When we stop for the day, we'll figure it out. Between now and then, I will scour my memories for each step I saw performed, maybe ask some of the senior sisters. I'll do my best to make it worth your while, Adam."

I flicked my eyes up and down to check out Nysea's body. I had absolutely no doubt that what she said was true. Even if I didn't get a spark of magic, it was definitely going to be worth it.

CHAPTER

FIFTY

The priestesses scouting ahead of the group found a place for us to hide during the daylight. We reached it just after sunrise. As the new day began, I walked through a heavily forested region toward a ring of small hills. It was strange, traveling all night and then finding myself in a forest that I hadn't even seen as we marched toward it. It was definitely different, moving only in the nighttime.

"There is a small cave in one of the hills," Nysea told me. "We can use that to perform the magic awakening ritual so you won't have to be on display in front of all the other sisters."

"Thank you. I'm not used to being so free in doing things like that in front of people I don't know. Or even people I do know."

Though I didn't really give Ysduil an answer to her request to watch, she accompanied me and Nysea to the cave. Glasha and Amelie set up camp nearby, but not too close to the mouth of the cave. I appreciated them giving us space. The bunny girl peered into the darkness and watched us excitedly as we went forward into it. I half expected her to ask to watch, too, but we were soon swallowed up in the coolness of the stone chamber and I lost sight of her.

It seemed pitch dark at first, but Ysduil and Nysea walked confidently to the back recesses of the chamber. It had a narrow egg shape to it that was probably thirty feet or so deep and half that wide. The floor was relatively level, though it had dust and little bits of rock scattered about.

"I'll go get us some blankets," the High Priestess said. "I'll be back shortly."

I sat down on the floor and leaned my back against the wall. Ysduil sat next to me and leaned into my shoulder. As we sat in silence, my eyes adjusted and I could see as well as I had when we were marching with only the moon and stars for light. The bit of illumination from the morning sun that filtered in was plenty to see by.

"If you want me to leave, I can," the foxgirl said without preamble.

"It's fine. I won't tell you that it's not uncomfortable for me, but I think it's less about you watching than it is being with Nysea. You're sure you're okay with it?"

"Of course. I've explained it to you before. Besides, this is more than just sex. If she can remember the ritual well enough to help awaken magic within you, it will be of immeasurable worth. Part of me wants to witness it for that reason, but a bigger part of me wants to watch you and Nysea. She is very sexy. And very skilled."

"You've...been with her?"

I could feel her smile into my shoulder. "Yes. She is talented and she is fun to be with. It has been some time since I have enjoyed her, but maybe we can find time soon to get together."

The thought of it made some blood rush down to my lower region. Ysduil was hot as hell and so was Nysea. I pictured the two of them together and my body began to kick into pleasure mode.

"Mmmm," she said. "You like the thought of that?"

I don't know how she knew I was getting aroused. She wasn't anywhere near my crotch, even if she did have good night vision. I wondered if my breathing had changed and that's how she knew.

"Your whole body gets warmer when you think naughty thoughts," she told me, like she was reading my mind. "Your temperature just jumped. And your scent changes, gets a little spicier."

I chuckled. "Okay, you caught me. Yes, it's fucking hot thinking about you and her."

She snuggled into my chest. "I'm glad. I would suggest I join you so the three of us could enjoy each other, but the most important thing is the ritual. When we are able, though, I'm sure Nysea would agree to it at a later time."

"Agree to what?" the High Priestess's voice asked as she entered the cave. Those damn bunny ears must hear at least twice as well as mine did.

"I was just telling Adam that you would likely agree to the three of us having sex together at another time, when there was no ritual to be concerned about," Ysduil said unashamedly.

The bunny woman responded without a pause. "Absolutely. If we were not pressed for time, I would suggest we do the ritual *and* the three of us play solely for enjoyment. Unfortunately, I must choose responsibility over pleasure. We will have our time, though, and soon. I promise."

The way her voice changed, especially at the end there, made my dick try to jump in my pants. If it wasn't for being restrained as it was, I wouldn't have been surprised to hear it twang as it flicked upward like a switchblade knife.

Nysea used a small blanket to clear the area in front of me of pebbles and grit. Then she laid the blanket down and placed another on top of it. It might have been my imagination, but her movements accentuated her amazing body even more than normal. Both Ysduil and I sat silently and stared as she shifted and provided us fantastic views of her curves.

The dress she wore was the same as all the priestess dresses. Thin material stretched skintight over her large chest and shapely hips left little to the imagination. Her tail —unlike Ysduil's—stayed under the cloth, barely covered as a fluffy lump. The bump lifted the dress's hem a little bit, allowing me to glimpse her nicely rounded ass, especially when she bent over to lay the blanket down. It was so silent in the cave, I heard Ysduil lick her lips.

I needed to adjust myself or something was going to burst.

A furry ear tickled my face as the foxgirl put her mouth to my ear and whispered. "Let me help you so you are not in pain." She reached down between my legs and gently moved my throbbing cock to allow it to straighten.

"Aaaah. Thank you. That's much better."

She kissed my ear and got up to move a few feet away. As she did, Nysea handed her a blanket and Ysduil leaned in to give her a kiss in thanks. It wasn't just a peck, either, but a deep, hot kiss that had me getting harder every second. Finally, Ysduil put her blanket down and sat on it. In her cross-legged position, I could see the deeper patch of darkness between her legs and imagined her pretty pussy glistening already.

"Adam," Nysea said and I snapped my head toward her.

PRIESTESS

I had lost track of what we were actually there for. What did that say about me? Did it mean I loved Ysduil or that I was an idiot who forgot the buxom bunny woman who was there to sex me into being able to use magic? "Are you ready to begin?"

"I am. What do I need to do?"

"Most of the work will fall to me," she said with a wicked smile. "There are fifteen points that I must stimulate. There is no set sequence as long as I go to each at least once. An important requirement is that you climax before we finish. Without reaching that level of ecstasy, the magic will not take."

"What about you?" I asked. "Do you have to come?"

"No. My pleasure is insignificant, or at least secondary. How I feel and how much I enjoy it has no bearing on the magic. It is all about you."

"That's not really fair. If we're going to do this, I want you to enjoy it."

Her wicked smile turned into a genuinely happy expression. "That is very kind of you. I won't argue against that strategy. I do love to reach orgasm. Be assured, though, that I will enjoy every minute of it, even if I do not climax."

God damn, she was fucking hot. I needed to calm down or as soon as she touched me I was going to ejaculate all over her, but damn. Those too-red lips and her smoky eyes were really doing a number on me. She hadn't even taken off her clothes or touched me yet!

"Are you ready?" she asked.

I nodded eagerly and she stepped up to me. Even only going a few steps, her body swayed so provocatively, my hands raised on their own to reach for her. In the dim light, I saw the bumps of her nipples strain at the fabric of her dress. As if those magnificent breasts weren't enough torture on the poor cloth.

"Do you like my tits?" she asked with a husky voice.

"So much."

"Do you know that obsil nipples are very sensitive? Do you want to feel them?"

I nodded dumbly as she crossed the last step to me and smashed her chest into mine, sliding from side to side. The effect was only ruined a little bit by the clothing between us. But she was one step ahead of me, breaking contact while helping me by taking off my shirt. Then she thrust her chest out and dragged her hard nipples across my naked chest with a soft groan.

She reached a hand out and trailed a finger down my cheek, then leaned forward with her lips pursed and her eyes closed.

I met her lips halfway with my own and sank into the soft warm flesh. Her scent filled my nose—sort of like a washed-out chili pepper with a hint of garlic—and her tongue snaked in to trace over my teeth to find mine. Her hand went back behind my head and pulled me into her as she moaned into my mouth.

CHAPTER
FIFTY-ONE

We explored each other's tongues while I moved a hand down to cup her perfectly formed ass. It was firm and pebbled with goose pimples. I pulled her into me and ground my hard dick against her.

She broke the kiss. "That's one."

I wasn't sure what she was talking about until she trailed her tongue up along my cheek to my left ear. She kissed it, flicked her tongue into it, then nibbled my earlobe softly.

"That's two."

I pulled her into another kiss, and she greeted me with her passionate tongue again before kissing me on the left temple and licking that spot full on like I was one of those big lollipops you get at Disneyland.

"Three."

I got it now. She was going to hit the ritual spots in order, from the top and going down. If each individual motion wasn't sexy enough, the thought of her revealing all the other spots was almost too much to bear.

Nysea repeated her actions on my right ear and temple, continuing to call out the number of spots she'd hit.

"Four."

"Five."

From there, she moved to my neck, one spot on either side.

I savored every little lick, kiss, and nibble as she moved her way through locations that were apparently not only erogenous zones but also magical nexuses. Who knew? When she spent some time circling my nipples with her tongue, sucking hard on them, and even nibbling them softly, I couldn't stand the raging inferno she'd fanned to flame within me. After the ninth spot, I put both of my hands on her head and pulled her up into another kiss.

This one was a lot hotter than before. Desperate, hungry lips and tongues met and engaged so vigorously, I started to get light-headed. I broke the kiss suddenly to take a deeper breath and found her panting as well.

Now was my chance.

Looking deep into her dark eyes, I grazed her hard nipple through the tight, thin cloth with my fingers. Her breath hitched, as I'd been hoping. I brought my other hand up and gave her other nipple the same treatment. Then I tweaked both at the same time.

"Awwwrr," she growled. "I don't want to complain but...augh—" I squeezed a handful of breast hard, breaking her concentration "—but...this isn't about me. I need to stimulate your nexus points to complete the...ah!...ritual."

"I know," I said, pulling her dress down one shoulder and then the other. "I appreciate it, I really do. But I can't stand here passively and let you do all the work. Not when you have a body like this."

"That's fine, but don't forget that...oooh—" I pulled her

dress down to let her tits bounce free. I expected them to droop and even sag the slightest bit without the support of the dress, but they didn't. They stayed exactly where they were, like the pride of a Hollywood plastic surgeon. *Thank God for magic.*

I buried my face in her cleavage and kissed her from the inside out, ending up at her hard, swollen nipple. My tongue traced over the goose pimples on her wide, dark areola and a shudder ran through her body. Turnabout was fair play, so I took her nipple in my mouth and sucked. Her sighs and pants were my reward, and they made me anxious for what we would do next.

I moved a hand down to her upper thigh, aiming for the junction between her legs. She squirmed a little, then put her hand on mine and pushed me away.

"Not yet, Adam," she said breathlessly. "You'll distract me. I want it so badly, but you have to be patient. Please."

I couldn't argue with her, though I wanted to. Patience wasn't something that came easily in situations like this one, but I allowed her to move my hand away as I gave her one last full-mouthed suck on her right breast.

She kissed my abs next and flicked her tongue out to tickle my navel as she loosened the waist of my pants.

"Ten."

No sooner was the word out of her mouth than she had my pants and underwear around my ankles. I kicked them off, leaving me completely naked, with my hard shaft nearly poking the bunny woman in the eye.

I knew there were five more spots left and though I couldn't quite figure them all out, I expected she would eventually get to the promised land. Instead of going right to it, though, she left me standing there and circled around behind me. My excitement didn't wane in the least, but a little shred of doubt and concern popped into my head. What were the last five spots?

The bunny woman kissed the back of my left knee and an unexpected jolt of electricity shot up my leg and into my dick.

"Twelve," she said as she stimulated the opposite knee.

From there, I thought she would come back around to the front of me. Nope. She dragged her tongue up the back of my leg, over my left ass cheek, and plunged it into my crack.

If the behind-the-knee spots sent jolts in a way I wasn't accustomed to, the pressure of her tongue on my asshole was like lightning. My entire body jerked and I sucked in enough air for ten breaths all at once. I may have even let loose a sound or two. I can't really remember. My knees weakened and nearly buckled.

"Mmmm," she said. "Thirteen."

She lingered there for a moment, doing some kind of tongue-twisting thing that caused pre-cum to dribble out of my rock-hard cock. Then she came around to the front.

The beautiful priestess looked up at me from where she was on her knees and flashed her white teeth at me. Then, without warning, she put her whole tongue out and licked my balls like a cat cleaning her kitten.

"That. Feels. So. Damn. Good." I grabbed both her super-soft ears and kneaded them. She moaned when I wrapped my hands around them and licked me again.

"Fourteen. Can you guess the fifteenth location?"

I could, and I waited impatiently for when she was going to give it equal treatment to the other spots.

But she didn't. Instead, she remained still, panting as I stroked her ears. I wasn't sure what she was waiting for, but the suspense was killing me. Again, it was time to take things into my own hands.

I gently pulled her ears up and she got the hint, sliding her body along mine, dragging her firm breasts up my thighs, my abs, and my chest until she was standing again. I roughly pulled her into a hot, wet kiss and moved my hands down to her ass to squash her body to mine.

"Too many clothes," I said, and pulled her dress down over her belly and hips to let it pool at her legs. She kicked her feet out of the clothing and finally stood equally naked before me. The feel of my hard dick on her silky-smooth skin made me ache to put it inside her.

I reached down and stroked her tail. It really did feel like a huge cotton ball and judging by the moans that escaped her lips, it was sensitive like Ysduil's tail was.

"There is more than one way to stimulate nexus points," she said when our kiss ended. "Here's another one."

She squatted a little and grabbed hold of my stiff member. While holding it in place, she flicked her tongue out and licked off the pre-cum on the head. I threw my head back and let myself be swept away in the pleasure.

"Uh. You're so damn sexy," I said to her.

She leaned in and put my dick between her tits.

"Oh my God."

Then she started to move, rubbing those amazing breasts over and around my cock, giving just the right amount of friction, lubricated by the perspiration she'd worked up and more pre-cum that seeped from me.

The sight of myself fucking her lush tits brought me so close, but then she applied pressure from the outside, pushing each of her breasts inward to increase the pressure and the friction. It was almost too much to take, but I didn't want to come without getting her off, too. I clamped down on my willpower, closed my eyes, and enjoyed the ride. But I didn't let myself go. Not yet.

Then she squatted even lower, her breasts pressing in on the less sensitive lower part of my dick. I took a quick breath, but the reprieve only lasted a moment before I felt something hot and wet surrounding the head of my shaft.

"Oh." I'd relaxed my focus and came really close to an orgasm. I locked my will on not coming and, once I had myself back under control, I opened my eyes and looked down to find Nysea with half my cock in her mouth.

It was hard to keep my eyes open. The pleasure seemed to want them to close. She pulled her mouth off with a pop and looked up at me with squinted eyes.

"I want to taste you, Adam. I want to suck your seed from you."

"Ah. No."

Her eyes widened a little, and they were filled with confusion. "No?"

"I want us to come together. I want to come inside you. Is that okay?"

A wicked smile jumped onto her face. "Yes." She licked the head of my dick, squeezed her tits together on it, and stood up, creating the most delicious friction as she did so.

I wanted the priestess right then and as soon as she was standing in front of me, I pushed her and guided her down onto the blanket. The sight of her naked body sent heat through me. There was only one thing to do. I spread her legs and laid down on top of her.

"I want you so badly," I said.

"Take me, Adam. I want you inside of me. I have stimulated all the nexus points. All that remains is for you to reach climax."

The time for words was past. I guided the head into the wet folds of her pussy, letting only a fraction of an inch in to push them aside.

"Yes. Yes. Put it in me. All of it."

I shifted my weight, moving my dick side to side to tickle her lips, then put it in a little more.

"Don't tease me. Fuck me now. Fill me up."

I wanted to tease her some more, but she was writhing beneath me and I was afraid I might lose control. I eased more of my shaft into her hot, wet hole, latched my lips onto her nipple, and sucked hard. She bucked and squirmed beneath me. Her gasps and moans elevated the pressure to release. Panting, I held back.

I wasn't sure how much longer I could hold on, so I slowly began to push in and out of her while alternating running my tongue over her amazing tits and biting down softly on them.

"Oh. Yes, Adam, yes. More. Give me more."

We settled into a rhythm. Slow at first, but the speed increasing. For a sex priestess, she had a very tight pussy. My dick fit perfectly into it. Before long I was ramming it into her harder and harder and she was bucking and meeting me with equal force. I kissed up her chest and neck, finally locking lips with her as the wet, slapping sounds increased into an erotic symphony.

Her kisses got stronger and more aggressive, especially when I moved a hand up to stroke her ear. That was the final straw for her.

"Oh, oh, oh. Yes yes yes yes. Fuck me Adam. Harder. Fill me with your seed now. I'm going to...I'm going to...aaaaaah."

The bunny priestess grabbed a handful of skin on my back at the same time her pussy clamped down on my shaft. Her entire body went rigid, only her shoulders and her lower legs touching the blanket. With her final moan, the pressure exploded out of the end of my dick and I sprayed the entire contents of my balls into her.

As our orgasms slammed into me, lightning and a frigid ocean wave ran through every cell of my body at the same time. It racked me and drained any little energy I had left after my climax. My eyes shot wide open and a flash of light from somewhere almost blinded me.

Then I collapsed onto Nysea and rolled over, still inside her. Our eyes met as we lay on our sides and we kissed one final time.

"I think...it was a success," she panted.

I had to agree.

CHAPTER
FIFTY-TWO

Nysea and I lay there for a few minutes, our skin touching and my member still within her. Eventually it softened and retreated from her slick hole, dribbling fluid after its exit. It was a different experience for me. Before I got to Tenos, after I came, I'd immediately go soft. Here, I could easily have gone again had I been given the chance.

The bunny priestess caressed my face with one hand, a smile on her lips. Her eyes flicked past me and the expression widened. I turned to see what she was looking at and spotted Ysduil, leaning against the wall of the cave, face flushed and dress pulled up to her waist. Her fingers were still wet.

The foxgirl saw me looking and beamed at me. "Thank you for making my daily ritual much easier. I think I could have climaxed without even touching myself, only watching you two."

Nysea chuckled and then snapped her head to direct her eyes down to watch my shaft spring to attention.

"Mmmm," she hummed. "It looks like you're ready again."

"Always," I said, giving her a big cheesy smile. "But it'll have to wait." Another thought crossed my mind and I had to ask. "Uh, Nysea? I asked if I could come inside you and you said yes, but what I meant to ask was if it was safe to do so. Do you have some kind of special sex priestess herbs or something so you won't get pregnant?"

She looked at me like I was simple. "There are such things, but we don't use them. Why would we?"

"Because there's a man around who isn't a puppet?" I ventured.

"Oh, Adam. Don't be silly. Any priestess—in truth most any woman in Tenos—would give anything to become pregnant after twenty years of Sodality control. If any priestess should do so, she will instantly be the favorite child of the entire body of priestesses. You don't understand how precious children are in the world with the way the Sodality runs things."

I could see her point, though it did make me a little nervous. If I was going to get as much action as all signs indicated, there may be several little ones running around before too long. What would happen when I went back to my world? I pulled the brake on that train of thought. This was not the moment.

I tore myself away from the lead priestess, padded over to kiss my favorite foxgirl, then got dressed. I was self-conscious at first, but a little strut crept into my step.... I mean, who wouldn't feel a little jaunty about that kind of attention?

Nysea sighed and pulled her dress on. "You're right, it will have to wait." It took me a moment to realize she was talking about what I'd said earlier, about having sex again.

"There are things to do. The first of those is to gather the senior sisters and decide what we'll do next. Will you two join us?"

"Of course," Ysduil said, pulling her dress down to restore at least some modicum of modesty.

"Good. I'll meet you at the edge of the communal area in ten minutes. It's easy to find. The large area where everyone else is resting." She winked at me, blew me a kiss, and walked out of the cave.

"Goddess," Ysduil said. "That was so exciting watching you two. I can't wait until we can all three play together."

I laughed. "You, me, and Nysea; you, me, and Maressa. You're going to end up booking appointments for us for weeks in advance."

"I will. Don't forget about Glasha and Amelie. We can mix and match. That will provide us for at least another week's worth of *appointments*."

I shook my head at her. "You leave those girls alone. There's no rush. If they want to join in, I'm sure they'll say something."

She dropped her eyes to the ground and her mouth formed a little pout.

I snorted. "Damn, you're good at that. But not good enough. You promised. Don't push them."

Like a switch was flipped, her expression brightened and she giggled. "You're too smart for me."

I put my arms out and she rushed into them. "I'm just smart enough for you. Be nice, okay. I mean it. There's no rush if they are interested. If they aren't, it'll only cause problems to try to get them involved."

"They're interested."

"We have other things to deal with right now. Come on,

let's go find out what Nysea's going to talk to the other sisters about."

I gave her another quick kiss, picked up the blankets, and headed out of the cave to find Nysea's meeting place.

The High Priestess was right: there was only the one big area where it looked like everyone was resting. As always, many eyes followed me as we spotted some of the more senior of the sisters and headed over. I was a novelty, but I didn't let the stares—even the hungry ones—go to my head. I probably could have been butt ugly and they still would want me. I guess I knew now how a rock star felt. I'd seen some pretty fugly rock stars who were always surrounded by hot women. But I was happy with Ysduil. And Glasha and Amelie, too, though I hadn't done much with them.

The point was, I didn't need other women. Even if Ysduil seemed to have made it a personal goal to get me laid by as many as possible.

I spotted Nysea and walked over. She gave me a smile. "A few more minutes to allow the remaining sisters to arrive and we'll get started. There's food if you're hungry."

She stepped aside to reveal a table with fruit, bread, cheese, and dried meat. It wasn't a feast, but after traveling for so long, it seemed like it. I thanked her and selected a few morsels to snack on.

As promised, after the last sister arrived, with apologies for being late, Nysea addressed the group.

"As you've heard, I was attacked last night by what was clearly a Sodality assassination squad. They stayed hidden as the scouts passed, and when I and my group got within range, they tried to kill us. Thankfully, Adam and Ysduil, along with their friends, were there to defend us.

"One of the assassins escaped, which means the

Sodality army now knows where we are. Or at least where we were last night. It won't take long for them to find us. We...have run out of normal hiding places. With our presence clear and our ability to find safety compromised, I am not sure what to do. Never have I heard of a time when the sisters have run out of places to safely avoid enemies.

"I would ask for your opinions and suggestions. I fear it may take a miracle from Odona herself to survive our current dilemma."

One of the sisters raised a slender hand. She was what I thought might be a deer beastkin. A doekin? Some of her hair was greying, but as with all the sisters, she was still beautiful, with a slender, sexy body. Nysea nodded to her.

"What if we headed into the wilds to the northeast? That is an unforgiving land, one where they might not look for us."

"That is an option, though we are getting low on food and there are not many opportunities for foraging that way."

Another sister, a bunny beastkin like Nysea, though with white ears and hair, spoke up next. "Sister, perhaps it is time for us to scatter to the wind. Continuing as a group will make us easily identifiable. If we are alone or in groups of two or three, we could disappear into towns and cities, perhaps biding our time until the Sodality's fervor for hunting us cools. Then we could come back together at a predetermined location."

Nysea's face dropped in disappointment. "It may come to that, sister, but I pray it would be our last resort. Isolated from each other, I believe it would be easier for the Sodality to find us within communities and execute us one by one, much as they have done in the last several years. I am loath to do such a thing. I believe it could spell the end of Odona's priestesshood."

Ysduil spoke up. "It could also cause problems if even a few were captured. The Sodality made it clear that they would subject me to torture before my execution. If they do that, even one sister being caught might reveal where we planned to meet. Not on purpose, of course, but the Sodality uses brutal techniques for extracting information, both mundane and magical. I don't think I could have resisted, which may have led them right to Haven."

"A fair point," Nysea said.

Several other sisters named areas that meant nothing to me. I listened quietly, noting in my mind that each suggestion consisted of a place to hide, temporary holes to wait for the Sodality to lose its enthusiasm. When it seemed that the other sisters ran out of ideas, I finally spoke.

"Pardon me, priestesses, but I'm a little confused. I know I don't have a right to speak in this group, but—"

"You have every right to do so," Nysea said. "Do not underestimate your importance."

"Thank you. Like I was saying, it sounds like we're all thinking the Sodality will lose interest. I don't think I agree. They might, eventually, but it will be a long time. They seem to want me, and because Ysduil and I escaped together, I think they've figured out that if they find you, they find me. They won't give up on that easily. Also, the commander of the fortress has a personal stake in this. She is now in charge of the army searching for us and she's acting like her honor depends on finding and executing all of us.

"That begs the question: are we all set on trying to scrape by, hiding and moving when possible, living on the run for what might be years? Wouldn't it be better to find a place that's defensible, set down roots, and create our own community? If it's some place that is well hidden, then we'll have time to establish ourselves, maybe build walls or something. Maybe by the time they find us, we'll be dug in and possibly even have allies. I find it hard to believe that with all the abuse the Sodality dishes out, there aren't people in the world who would jump at a chance to be independent. I know everyone says the Sodality controls the entire world, but are there borders somewhere, places so remote that they could field an army against us and still not be able to crack our defenses?"

"Create...a community?" Nysea said. She tapped her finger on her lips. "Hmmm."

That sparked an entirely new discussion. I listened to the first few comments, but it sounded like a rehash of the same old things they'd been saying before. My eyes glazed over and to keep from zoning out, I scanned the crowd. A flash of green caught my eye and I locked in on Glasha standing at the edge of the group, Amelie right next to her. The beautiful dunim woman smiled at me and nodded, tapping her temple. Well, at least she approved of what I said.

After probably twenty minutes more, Nysea ended the discussion. "I thank you all for your suggestions. I will ponder them all and would urge you to do likewise. We have little choice at this point but to continue heading north, possibly northwest. Much depends upon how quickly the Sodality finds us and from which direction they come. We will continue to discuss the subject as new information is obtained. Rest now, sisters, for we must prepare to leave as soon as it grows dark. Odona make it so we can continue to slip away from the army that will surely be chasing us."

The sisters dispersed as Glasha and Amelie fought against the stream to join me and Ysduil.

"I like your idea," the dunim woman said. "But you said *we* in many instances. Is your plan to join the sisters and help them to build this community?"

I played back in my head what I'd said and she was right. "Huh. I hadn't even noticed. I probably said that because it always sounds better when you include yourself into any suggestion. As for actually being part of it, I don't know. I can't really go off looking for a way home when Ysduil is still in danger, let alone a whole army of priestesses. Part of the trouble is my fault, after all. I have no desire to try to start a city, but I can't abandon everyone, either."

The green woman smiled. She didn't say anything else, but her approval was evident, which made me happy.

"Are you ladies ready to get some rest? I predict we're going to be marching quickly tonight to try to outrun the Sodality."

FIFTY-THREE

As I settled in to rest with the three women, I felt strangely tired and energetic at the same time. The sensation I'd gotten when I climaxed with Nysea—the glowing, electric, invigorating feeling—was still with me, though muted.

The high priestess had told me that the ritual was to open my body up to being able to use magic. That could definitely be the reason I felt so different. The problem was that she didn't know how to use magic herself and, even if she did, I had no idea if it worked the same with men as with women.

Despite my abundance of energy, I went to sleep right away, losing myself in images that reminded me of kaleidoscopes and Kirlian photography mixed together.

An insistent buzzing in my head woke me up. The sky above was still lit up, a pale blue with white, puffy clouds drifting lazily. Had I just gone to sleep or had some time passed? The vibration in my mind wouldn't let me try to regain my slumber, so I extricated myself from Ysduil and— to my surprise—Glasha, who was curled up with her back pressed to mine. I managed to stand without waking them, noting Amelie on the other side of the dunim woman, face mere inches from Glasha's.

For the most part, people were still sleeping when I crossed the communal area, but a few guards stood watch and I could see Nysea and a few other of the senior sisters at the edge of the area, near the entrance.

"What's going on?" I asked as I stepped up to them.

Nysea gave me a suspicious look. "What do you mean?"

"I don't know. You're not sleeping and there's a buzzing in my head. I don't know what it means, but I think it might be a side effect from...you know, before."

Her eyes darted to the other sisters. She sighed. "Come with me." Then she turned and walked out of the area, back to the path we'd originally taken to get to our current hiding place. She led me to a small hill with only a few trees. When we got to the top, she gestured toward the south, left of the sun hanging low in the sky to our right.

What I saw froze me for an instant. Some distance away was a dark smudge. Flowing from behind and to the side of it was a huge cloud of dust.

"What...?" I said. It didn't really register at first.

"They're coming," Nysea told me. "More quickly than I had feared."

"The Sodality?"

"Do you know of another army in the vicinity that might be coming toward us? Perhaps some heroines coming to our aid?"

I flushed, feeling like an idiot.

She put her hand on my arm. "I'm sorry. That was rude. I am...out of sorts. Looking at what might be the end of all our lives can have that effect."

"I understand. How...how many are there? And how far

away are they? I don't know how to judge those things. I've never been chased by an army before."

Nysea let loose a nervous chuckle. "They're too far to determine how many, though it will be several hundred at least. Perhaps several thousand. As for how far, well, at the rate they are moving, they will be here within three or four hours. Darkness is less than an hour away. At least, twilight is. We should be able to move then without being seen. If it matters."

"We can still outrun them, right?" I asked. "We're a smaller group and we're not wearing heavy armor or anything."

"I doubt we can match their speed. They are professional soldiers. They are efficient at marching. We are simply a group of priestesses who, though we are in fair condition, are not as practiced as they in moving quickly over long distances. They will catch us eventually, unless we can find a place to evade them and hide. Their scouts will be watching for any tracks that lead away from the road now, however. They have our scent."

"Damn. Is there anything I can do?"

"I thank you for your offer, but unless you can destroy an entire army or somehow lift our whole group to fly away to a safe place, I am afraid not. For now, how about you rouse Ysduil and your other women while the senior sisters wake the rest of our company. We must leave as soon as the sun goes down."

I racked my brain to think of anything that might help, but came up empty. "Understood. I'll go wake them now."

I ran back to where the women still lay sleeping and paused just inside the entrance to the cave. The trio were snuggled up against each other, having closed the distance where I had been. They looked about as adorable as new puppies huddled together for warmth.

If fierce warriors could be likened to newborn dogs.

Glasha's eyes flicked open and she turned her head to look at me, her pale blue orbs nearly glowing in the fragment of dim light coming from behind me. Her mouth turned into a smile, but then she raised an eyebrow at me. I waved back, but then remembered the urgency of what I was about.

"I'm afraid it's time to get up," I said, walking closer to the three. "There are...problems. We have to be ready to flee as quickly as possible."

Glasha and Ysduil sat up instantly. It surprised me, honestly. Ysduil did not like rising early, even if that *early* was in the evening. She didn't waffle or complain, though. She took my word as truth and was on her feet after a short pause to push on Amelie's shoulder to rouse the obsil.

In no time, we had the blankets up, our armor on, and our packs hitched on our backs. I filled them in while we moved toward the front of the line where Nysea would be.

We threaded our way back out to the road as the sun was going down. I tried to spot the approaching army, but the land dipped where we were located, so I couldn't see more than a few miles to the south.

A thought occurred to me and I turned to Nysea, whose group led the column onto the road.

"I'm going to stay farther back, near the middle or end of the line," I told her. "I want to see how far away the army is once we climb out of this little depression."

"Very well. I have rear scouts that will report such things, you know."

"I do, but I'd like to see for myself, if you don't mind."

"You can go where you please. You are not in my charge."

I smiled at the priestess. "No, I'm not. Thank you. I'll see you a little later."

As I moved out onto the road and back toward the south a bit so I didn't block any of the others, Glasha strode along beside me.

"Where are you going?" I asked the dunim.

"With you."

"Do you even know where I'm going?"

"To make trouble." It was a statement, not a question.

I laughed and she chuckled in response. "Not really. I want to get a look at the army chasing us. You don't have to go with me."

"I know. I will be marching. Whether in the front or where you are, I will still have to move my legs."

"I guess that's true. Fine. It'll be my pleasure to travel with you." I put a hand out and she slapped it with her own. I was glad I'd taught her about high fives, fist bumps, and giving me five. It was silly, but it made me feel closer to the fierce warrior. And a little less homesick.

"You'll be traveling with more than her," Ysduil said, walking up to us, Amelie on her heels.

"You're both welcome, too, but it won't be interesting or fun. In fact, it'll probably be dustier and stuffier than being in the front."

"Understood," the foxgirl said. She made no move to leave.

The rest of the column headed north more quickly than I thought a large group could move and the four of us brought up the rear. Two women in leather armor stayed put, like they were guarding everyone, until we started walking, then they fell in behind us. I realized they must be the scouts Nysea told me about. I waved at them and smiled and they both nodded amiably.

Darkness came and we finally got to a place on the road where we could look back more than a few miles. What I saw made me feel like a giant fist was squeezing my entire chest.

Winding up the road toward the low spot wiggled a wide and very long line of lights.

"My God," I said, prompting the women to look back at our pursuers.

Ysduil squinted her eyes at the sight for a moment. "If they're organized about how many of them carry lamps and torches, I estimate there are more than two thousand troops coming after us."

"Two thousand?" I repeated.

Ysduil looked to Glasha and the green woman nodded.

"I agree. At least two thousand. Clearly they are not concerned with letting us know they are coming as well, with all that light."

There seemed to be a lot of pinpricks of light, but that many? I had no reason to doubt the women's ability to estimate troops, but I hoped they were wrong. Then again, what did it matter? If there were only a few hundred, we'd still be screwed if they caught us. From what I'd seen of the sisters and their skill in combat, they could probably handle being outnumbered two or three to one, but more than that was insanely unlikely.

"Well," I said, "we have to hope we can move faster and can find a place to lose them. They've probably marched all day, so they won't be continuing all night without rest, right?"

"You're probably right," Ysduil said. "Probably."

One of the scouts—a pretty obsil woman with tawny

fur and hair—took off at a jog, heading up to report to Nysea and the other senior sisters.

I stared at the army that was coming to kill us. "Damn. I sure hope we can move faster than them."

Silence was my only answer as the women and I turned to flee for our lives. As we did, I couldn't help but to think that if I'd had a better presence of mind during the assassin attack, I might have been able to stop the one that got away to report our location to the Sodality. If they caught us and killed us all, it could be my fault for hesitating when I should have been attacking.

I needed to make sure that never happened again.

Ysduil, Glasha, Amelie, and I stayed at the tail end of the column, mainly because I wanted to keep an eye on the army chasing us to see if they got closer or, hopefully, farther behind during the night.

The obsil scout that had gone to the front to report returned. No sooner had she gotten into step with her partner than the other scout nodded and the bunny kin dropped back.

The remaining scout was the human priestess who had gone to Dunim Dell, Daria Menseth. She glanced at me and explained, "She will sweep behind us to see if any advance scouts have gone ahead of the army to get information on us."

The pace we kept to stay with those ahead of us was faster than we'd gone since leaving Haven, but it wasn't hard to keep up. Ysduil and Glasha were in fantastic shape from fighting and training, and my new strength hadn't failed yet. The only one I thought might have a problem was Amelie. One look at the bunny girl disabused me of that idea, though. She strode confidently and easily alongside Ysduil, chattering nonstop in a voice so low I only caught maybe one in every five words.

Amelie was always so timid around me, I'd worried she would have trouble interacting with the sisters. Maybe she only needed to get to know someone and then she opened up. She'd even been talking a little more to me in the last several days.

I was smiling at the thought when the sound of motion from behind us caught my ear. The whisk of clothing and soft footfalls preceded anything I could see, but Ysduil had stopped and was staring into the darkness. In a moment, a figure came into view and I drew my sword without hesitation.

Tamalan Veela, as I found out was the name of the obsil scout who went to look for an advance guard for the army, slid to a stop in front of us. Her left arm was pinned to her side, the broken shaft of an arrow sticking out of her bicep. Blood darkened her armor.

"A group of Sodality scouts is right behind me," she panted. "I took two out with my bow before they got me."

"Why did you engage?" Daria asked while she examined the arrow.

"No choice. I ran right into them. Luckily, I reacted first, shooting as I ran. There are at least seven left. Three bows that I saw, the rest melee weapons."

"Go," her companion said. "Can you make it to the front to get a healer to look at that?"

"No problem. Sorry I can't help more."

"Just go. You've done a great job. Now finish your task and let Nysea know."

The woman rolled her shoulder and winced in pain. "Fine, but what about the Sodality soldiers?"

"We'll help take them down," I said. "Let Nysea know

and send any of the guards back you see on your way up. This time, we're not going to let them escape to report."

She nodded to me and took off at a fast lumber, the women in front of her making an opening and calling up for others to do likewise.

"We should probably go out to meet them," I said. "I don't want them to try to get to the others at the back of the line. Amelie, you can keep going with the others. Actually, Ysduil and Glasha, you can too, if you don't want to fight. You don't have to."

"*You* don't have to," Ysduil said. "This group consists of my sisters and our helpers and servants. I won't let them be hurt."

"If there is battle to be had," Glasha said with a grin, "I will go toward it, not run from it. Zartuka!" I eyed her at the word I thought I'd heard before.

"I want to come, too," Amelie said meekly. "I've been working with Ysduil to be able to use my weapons better. I want to help."

"Fine," I said. "Just be careful. Amelie, please stay back a little bit so you don't have to fight more than one at a time, okay?"

The bunny girl lifted her chin and gave me a confident smile. "Sure."

There was no more time for talk. Along with Daria, we headed toward the faraway lights of the Sodality army. The moon was nearly full, casting cool light on the open road. It would be a different experience for me, fighting in the moonlight, but I didn't feel any more nervous than any other battle I'd been in since I came to Tenos.

That is, I was scared to death, but not any more so than every other time I'd had to fight. I swallowed hard and focused on the darkened landscape ahead of me.

The women and I padded south on the road, separated by a few feet each. Close enough to see each other, but spread out enough so that the Sodality scouts couldn't easily pass by us.

Not that I thought they would try to slip past. They'd want to do as much damage as they could before a defense formed. They might have even turned around once they realized Tamalan made it to where she could get reinforcements.

With Daria, there were five of us, though Amelie probably didn't count as a full combatant yet. Hell, maybe I didn't either. Still, five against seven were not bad odds. As long as we could get close enough to mix it up with them before the archers saw us. In this, the darkness was a boon. We could see well enough to fight—especially those with better than human vision—but even the enhanced vision of the beastkin wouldn't allow archers to see as far as they would during daylight. I hoped.

A sensation pushed at me like the wind had increased a hundredfold, but without impeding my progress. It was almost like a gale was pushing on my mind, but my body didn't get the memo. I'd never felt anything like it before.

I made some kind of noise, probably closest to a grunt of frustration, and the women stopped and looked at me.

"What is it?" Ysduil whispered. "Did you see something?"

"No. I felt something...like I was trying to walk through water."

Ysduil's eyes, almost glowing from the reflected moonlight, widened. Then, she whispered urgently, "Down!"

I blinked at her as the others—even Amelie—did exactly what she said. Their compliance registered and kicked me into motion. Belatedly, I dove at the ground.

An arrowhead glinted as it passed over me, and another to my left slammed into a small tree bordering the road.

"There," Ysduil said, taking off at a full sprint.

For the second time in less than half a minute, the foxgirl had surprised and confused me. One thought made it through my muzzy mind, though: the priestess was running straight toward at least two archers with nothing but a staff in her hands.

I jumped to my feet and followed, pumping my legs as fast as I could. Which was actually pretty damn fast now.

In half a dozen steps, I saw the archers. Ysduil, with her dark vision and her incredible reflexes, dodged another arrow and actually deflected an additional shaft with her staff. It was impressive, but she wasn't going to be able to keep that up. I was gaining on her, but I hadn't properly thought through what I'd do when I caught up.

Ysduil twisted to dodge another arrow and I had to throw myself to the side so it wouldn't hit me. I was within a few steps of her, but I was more concerned about what I saw ahead. A third archer got into position and the trio drew back their bows at the same time, only about a dozen paces away from us. There was no way my foxgirl was going to be able to dodge all the projectiles, not as close as we were to the enemies.

Just before the three Sodality scouts released their arrows, I focused on what I'd experienced in the last battle. If I could only...

Three shafts with razor sharp metal heads on them zipped toward Ysduil, spread in a pattern that guaranteed at least one or two would strike her, no matter what she did.

She bravely tried to avoid them all anyway.

The lithe priestess twisted and ducked while somehow

swinging her staff with the aim of intercepting at least one of the arrows. A half second later, she made a questioning sound, her voice raising at the end, but continued forward to attack the closest archer.

As for me, I ran after her, a big smile on my face. I had pushed on the arrows with my aura or magic or whatever it was, just like I'd done in the previous battle.

But this time, I did it purposely. And purposefully.

I called the power and it answered. Tentatively, tenuously, and not all that powerfully, but it did answer. Enough to scatter the three arrows away from Ysduil. I couldn't have asked for more than that.

Now it was time to kick some ass.

FIFTY-FIVE

My fearless foxgirl jumped the last few feet, bringing her legs up into a perfect flying side kick while swiping her staff to the right side to attack another of the archers. Her lead foot landed square on the face of one of the bow wielders. The other archer she attacked moved fast enough to get her bow up to try to block Ysduil's weapon.

Instead of blocking the staff strike, the bow stave nearly left the archer's grip, bouncing back from the priestess's staff and hitting the Sodality scout in the face. Both archers fell back from the attacks, scattering arrows to the ground as they did.

Before I reached the scouts, Ysduil had landed, spun, and struck the last archer on the arm with her staff. From where I was, half a dozen steps away, I heard a bone in the archer's arm breaking, like the sound of a brittle branch wrapped in a towel snapping.

And then I was there, just as five other women rushed toward me and Ysduil, all with swords. That made eight scouts, instead of the seven Tamalan had counted. I hoped there weren't more hiding in the shadows.

Two of the scouts peeled off to come toward me while two more went for Ysduil. I heard footsteps behind me, and hoped that whoever it was would take care of a few of the attackers. I had enough to deal with, with the two in front of me.

I'd been practicing with the sword, but was far from skilled with the weapon. My increased strength and speed were my greatest weapon. That and magic that I didn't really know how to use. I would have to do what I could and hold on while the others finished off their opponents and then came to help me.

I could do that. Maybe.

The first sword came in at me with an overhand chop. It had been a while since I'd been in a battle and with my recent advances, I thought I'd be able to watch the women attacking me like they were moving in slow motion because of my speed skill.

Not so much.

I frantically raised my sword to block, barely getting the job done, though I moved it quickly enough to get it into position in time. Just as I was feeling proud of myself, the other sword came in horizontally, aiming for my midsection. I jumped backward as fast as I could and the blade scratched across the bottom of my breastplate, scoring the leather.

My eyes darted around, hoping that no one had seen my lackluster performance. Ysduil was still fighting with two of the Sodality scouts, Glasha had picked up the other melee fighter—a woman with two swords—Daria traded sword slashes with two of the archers that had regained their feet, and Amelie seemed to be doing an adequate job in keeping the other archer busy.

Relieved no one was watching me, I lashed out at the woman who had almost cut me with the horizontal swing. I willed my body to surge in speed and cut at the scout three times in rapid succession. Downward vertical strike, diagonal strike, then a less-than-expert change in direction for a looping horizontal strike. The woman's eyes went wide as she frantically blocked the first, barely deflected the second, and wasn't able to get her sword back up in time to mitigate the third blow.

My blade cut deeply into her side and got caught on a rib. Though I was successful in increasing my speed, I didn't focus on the strength of my blows. Still, the wound was serious enough that she dropped her sword and fell to the ground, screaming in pain.

I knew I should have skewered my enemy to the ground, but I couldn't bring myself to do it. It would have been a mercy because there was no doubt she'd be dying soon with the gushing blood pouring out of her, but I froze, trying to make a decision.

Meanwhile, Glasha met her opponent's blade and took the woman down with a savage combination that bashed her guard down and ended with a picture-perfect lunge that rammed her sword through the scout. Before the body had even finished falling, the dunim turned, took a few steps, and cut so deeply into the woman I had injured, she almost cut the woman's head off. Then she was on to attack the Sodality soldier Amelie was fighting.

The rest of the battle was a blur, with Glasha helping the bunny girl finish her enemy, Ysduil taking down one of her opponents with a hard staff strike to the head, and

Glasha moving over to help Daria take down the two women she was fighting.

Ysduil finally defeated the last scout, shattering her knee with a powerful blow of her weapon, then crushing her windpipe with another hard swing.

I still stood there, not knowing what to do when the only ones still upright were me and my friends. I wouldn't meet the eyes of any of the women, embarrassed I'd frozen up.

"It's normal," Glasha said as the others checked the corpses for gear and coins. "You are kind-hearted and killing is serious business. It will get easier."

I stared at the dunim, marveling at the wisdom she conveyed with a few simple words. I appreciated not only her understanding of what I was thinking and feeling, but also her kindness in explaining it to me.

"Thank you," I said.

She gave me a sly smile and a wink. "Don't let your tender heart get you killed."

Another scout came toward us from the rear of the line as we finished up and were heading back to catch up to the trailing group. She was Aya, the dog beastkin scout we'd met the day before. Along with her were five other priestesses dressed in armor.

"Did you already engage with the enemy scouts?" she asked us.

"We did," Daria said. "We defeated them all. Their bodies are a few hundred yards back to the south, on the road."

The new scout's eyes widened and darted to each of us, stopping to linger on me. "Well done. Nysea would like to see you at the front of the column. We'll take over guarding the rear."

I gestured to Ysduil and she took the lead in front of us, with me right behind her, then Amelie, then Glasha. Daria stepped close to Aya and spoke quietly for a minute, then jogged to catch up to us.

"Is everything all right?" I asked her.

"Yes. I wanted to clarify that I was supposed to accompany you and I wanted news on Tamalan."

"Oh, how is she?"

"She delivered her report and then went to the healers. She's doing fine. We have a few sisters that can do small healing magics. Our mundane healers are skilled, too, using their extensive information and herbs to accomplish things that seem like magic. She is walking with the group of healers, though a little stiffly. She refused riding on any of the carts. I knew she would." Her eyes sparkled in a way that made me wonder if the two were close.

"That's fantastic," I said. "I was concerned about her pushing too hard being injured like that."

Daria rolled her eyes as if the thought was purely ridiculous. I chuckled and left it at that.

As we walked, I moved closer to Glasha. "Can I ask you something?"

"Of course," she said without batting an eye. "What is it?"

"That thing you said after the battle…"

"Zartuka?"

"Yeah, that's it. I heard you say it before, after you chased the aanem off. What does it mean?"

Her eyes darted from mine. "It's just something I say. Sometimes. It's an old dunim word. A few words combined, actually. It has no direct translation."

"Can you give me an idea of what it means generally?"

"It…is an exclamation. Sometimes a statement or a

question. Most often, in the way I use it, it means...something like 'fuck yeah!'"

I barked a laugh. "That's awesome. And perfect. Thank you for sharing. I look forward to hearing its further use."

The green woman chuckled, a look of relief washing over her face.

Zartuka. I loved it.

Soon enough, we'd made it to the front of the line of people and found Nysea.

"Oh, good," she said, spotting us. "First, I want a full report. Then I want to brief you all on what we're doing and where we're going."

As we walked at our increased pace, I told Nysea about our fight with the scouts and how we'd made sure to kill them all to delay the army from realizing we'd killed them for as long as possible. Then, it was her turn to give us information.

"The other senior sisters and I have decided the only chance we have is to get through Hollow Wood. Once we get within the thick trees, being a smaller group will be to our advantage. We will break into even smaller groups, which have already been assigned, then we will disappear, only to reunite on the other side of the forest. From there, we will decide the best way to proceed, depending upon whether the army has followed some of us or not.

"We will be at the forest's fringes late tomorrow. The time has passed where we will travel only at night. We will march, taking short breaks of only a few hours to get some sleep and to eat full meals, then we will continue. In this way, we hope to put more distance between us and the army to increase the chance our escape into the forest will be successful."

"So if we can keep ahead of them until late tomorrow, we'll be able to escape into the forest?" I asked.

"We believe so. It is possible that they have some well-trained groups that can hunt down our small parties and inflict injury or completely defeat them, but it's the best chance we have. We need to get to Hollow Wood before the Sodality catches us."

"Wait," I said. "What did you say the name of the place is?"

"Hollow Wood. It is a place where strange and absurd creatures dwell."

I laughed and Nysea stared at me like I had lost my wits. So did Ysduil. And Glasha. Amelie, too.

"Sorry. It sounds a lot like a place I know called Hollywood. It's funny to me. I'll explain it to you sometime."

FIFTY-SIX

O n our way to Hollow Wood, several other skirmish groups were sent ahead to harry us. Between the guards sent to the rear, along with myself and my friends, we eliminated all of them and stole the horses they'd rode in on besides. That went a long way to providing transportation to some of the slower elderly members of the group, or younger ones who had been injured. It was the first time I'd seen the animals in Tenos. I hadn't even been sure they existed here.

The Sodality didn't make sense to me. I could understand them not sending the entire army after us because they were still a fair distance behind us and wouldn't be able to catch us easily on foot without tiring themselves out, but I couldn't understand why they sent the small groups. What was the use? We'd already shown we could take down groups of up to ten harassers without too much trouble. Why not send a few dozen cavalry soldiers to take us out?

"They're keeping pressure on us," Glasha explained.

"Pressing us may make us do something rash. Or distract us from something else."

Ysduil called over a priestess that had been acting as a messenger between the rear group and the leaders in the front. When the woman jogged up to us, the foxgirl spoke with an air of command I hadn't heard before.

"Please go to Nysea and tell her to double the scouts at the front and sides. Inform her that the Sodality continues to send sorties at us and that they might be trying to distract us from something ahead, possibly a trap."

The woman nodded and took off running along the edges of the column. She was soon out of sight.

The foxgirl watched the messenger until she disappeared and turned to find us all staring at her.

"What?"

"I've never heard your voice like that," I said. She dropped her gaze to the ground. "I like it."

Her eyes met mine and she smiled.

We continued to fight off the groups sent against us. Soon, it was apparent that the Sodality army, or at least a portion of it, was moving faster than us, making up space and time. They would eventually catch us.

It seemed that Nysea and the other senior sisters came to the same conclusion. Daria informed us that we were to report to the front of the line, which we did promptly, as soon as our replacements arrived to handle the rear of the column.

"We will not be able to implement the plan we discussed before. The Sodality is too close. The only chance we have is to head through Shadow Pass. It's a narrow area within the forest, to the northwest, that winds between small cliffs and rock formations. If we can make it through before our pursuers, we could hold off the entire army for a time. Or we might be able to collapse a portion of the pass to block the bulk of their forces."

Ysduil shared a concerned look with me and then turned to address Nysea. "But what about the troops behind us? If they're coming as fast as it seems, they'll catch us before we can get to Shadow Pass."

The lead priestess swallowed and her pale face conveyed her disgust at the plan even before she spoke it.

"Sisters have volunteered to stay to the rear and to fight off the Sodality. They are to keep the soldiers from reaching the main body any way they can. If the army pushes hard and it looks like they will reach us, the sisters will stop and make a stand. They all understand what that may mean."

The foxgirl put her hand to her mouth. These were women she'd grown up with, friends and even lovers whom she cared for.

"I'd like to go and stay behind with them, if it comes to that," I said before I'd even formed the thought fully in my head.

"No."

Nysea's one emphatic word didn't register at first. I blinked at her, then narrowed my eyes to focus on her.

"Why?" I asked.

"You and your friends are too valuable to fall in such a way. That is not to say the sisters are not valuable, but what you represent cannot be allowed to die so easily."

"What I represent? We're talking about people—your friends—dying here. Nothing is more valuable than that. And that still doesn't explain why you won't allow the others to join the troops."

"We cannot afford for you to die. That's all I have to say

about it. This column is under my authority. Please respect that and do not sneak back to the rear guard."

Ysduil gasped. "Has Xanali had a vision? Did she see something you're not telling us?"

Nysea shook her head sadly. "I will explain no further. If you trust me, then do as I say. Please stay up here in front with us."

I rationalized that the Sodality army might not even catch us. If it did, I could try to argue, maybe even go against Nysea's wishes, which I didn't really want to do. For the time being, I'd do as she asked. At least until I could get more information. I was definitely not okay with others dying and me being prevented from helping.

Soon enough, though, I saw the wisdom in Nysea's commandment. Within the hour, the forward scouts, who were only a short distance ahead of the group I was in, spotted a number of people ahead of us.

Ysduil and Glasha sprinted to the front, with me following. Sure enough, there were what looked like more than two dozen figures walking toward us in loose ranks. They were still some distance off, but it was easy to see from their shape that they wore armor and carried weapons.

"It looks like we're not going to be bored here up front," I said, and drew my sword.

My three companions, as well as a few of the priestesses, engaged the first group. Then the second, after we had defeated them. Three more groups after that also stood in our way. Each one, we bested, though not without injuries.

"This makes no sense," I said. "Why don't they come as a large group? We've already proven we can beat these smaller groups back." None of the clusters had more than thirty Sodality soldiers in it.

Glasha glared at the fresh corpses on the ground. "Maybe they are testing us. Also, they could be throwing lives away to tire us out. There are still the soldiers behind us. They are gazing far, not simply acting for the present."

"Yeah, but still, I don't get it. There's an even mix now between men and women, but they're still losing a lot of fighters."

One thing I did understand, though, was that as I fought the Sodality troops, I gained valuable experience in using my...whatever it was. Magic, internal energy, mana, whatever you want to call it, I was getting better at moving the energy around in my body and using it for combat. It was mostly supercharging my limbs, but even that made me a lot better fighter.

"There!" Ysduil said. I wasn't even sure if she'd been paying attention to the conversation. She had grown quiet during and after the last few bouts.

I looked where she was pointing. We hadn't quite reached the forest proper yet. The sides of the road were treed, but up farther, the vegetation grew so dense that the road looked to have been carved through it with a giant drill. The day was growing long and the shadows from the trees had dimmed the landscape, but I could pick out what she was indicating.

Ahead of us, engulfing the road going through the forest, was a crowd of people.

Another army.

"Shit!" I said. "Is that what I think it is?"

"Yes," my foxgirl answered. "Maybe they were distracting us all along. Trying to slow us down so the army behind could reach us."

Nysea had approached us after the last skirmish and caught the end of our conversation. She narrowed her eyes at the people ahead. I wasn't sure how good the eyesight of rabbits—let alone rabbit beastkin—were, but the way she studied the scene, I think she saw more than me.

"They are Sodality troops. They've been maneuvering us into a vise all along. Adam, you need to flee. There is too much you can do to help this world to allow them to capture you and control you. The only reason they would be using this tactic is to capture instead of kill us. More specifically, you."

"I'm not leaving you," I said. "I may not be a hero, but I'm not a coward, either. How bad would I be if I left you to be executed and didn't stay to help, or to share your fate. You're not getting rid of me. I'll fight to the end alongside you and your sisters. My friends. Besides, I probably couldn't get away anyway. There's an old saying from a group of warriors on my world called Vikings. 'Stand and fight. If you run, you'll only die tired.'"

Glasha threw her head back and laughed, while Ysduil and Nysea chuckled. Amelie looked at me with confusion. I decided I'd explain it to her before we died. Just because.

"Very well," the High Priestess said. "I'll inform the rest of our people of what stands before us. Most of us will choose to die fighting rather than to be captured and executed. I will give everyone a choice of fleeing into the forest as well, though I doubt any will take it. Even the servants will undoubtedly choose to stay and fall with the rest of us. Unfortunately."

The bunny woman left as my friends and the few priestess guards still left with us turned to stride toward the waiting army.

"It's possible we will be able to defeat them," I said. "Maybe even fast enough that we can still escape the one behind us."

"Stranger things have happened in some of the stories," Ysduil said.

"Too bad most of those stories are loads of bullshit," Glasha added, but did so with a smile.

CHAPTER

FIFTY-SEVEN

The line continued to move forward, though at a slower pace. We couldn't stop completely because of the army behind us, but every step took us closer to where the army in front of us waited.

I stared straight ahead, not really focusing on the army or anything else in particular. I racked my brain to come up with a way to get out of our predicament, but kept coming up empty.

"Is it time for you to use your ninety movies?" Ysduil said. I swung my head to look at her just in time to see her wink.

I forced a chuckle, mainly because she deserved it. She was obviously making a joke, but I couldn't drum up any amused feelings.

I thought of all those movies I'd watched. With my mom, later with my girlfriends. Sooooo many romance movies. The guy found the girl, fell in love through hardship and toil. Just when things looked good, something happened to break them up. Sometimes it was arguments between the two of them, sometimes it was another person coming between them or a misunderstanding, and sometimes...sometimes it was a villain that was responsible.

Through it all, in every movie, they let nothing stand in the way of their being together. The man would face any danger, sacrifice anything, even his life, to ensure the one he loved would be safe and have a good life. With or without him.

You know, maybe my foxgirl had something there. I'd been thinking within the constraints of a reasonable person. A person who expected whatever plans he made to fail. The world was not a kind place to dreamers and planners. That's what I'd learned in my life up until then.

But what if... What if someone put everything out there, did something so unexpected that even fate couldn't hold him back. What if...?

"Ysduil, you are a beautiful, sexy genius. Go and get Nysea. I think I have an idea that will work."

The priestess's furry ears perked up and her eyes widened. No doubt, she hadn't expected that kind of reaction to her joke. She did as I asked, though, and ran to where Nysea had gone.

"Adam," Glasha said, "what are you thinking?"

I was too busy figuring things in my head—calculating —to answer adequately. "I'll tell you when Nysea comes back." The gorgeous dunim tilted her head at me, but didn't press me.

As soon as Nysea came back, a few of the senior priestesses trailing her, I laid out my plan.

"I know you're going to argue," I said, "but don't bother. I'm doing this with or without your consent. The only adequate response is for you to do as I suggest."

"I don't like this already," Ysduil said. "What are you going to do?"

"Hopefully? I'm going to allow you to escape. I'm going to light up a powder keg."

She must have focused on the first few words, listening carefully enough to detect my distinction. She didn't even ask what a powder keg was. "You hope *we* will escape? Not you?"

"Maybe. Here's the deal. We can't win being crushed between two armies. If we slow down too much or stop, the one behind will get us. If we rush forward, we'll run into the one in front. There is a way, though.

"In all these battles, I've become more skilled at the magic or whatever you opened up in me, Nysea. I'm still no superhero or anything, but I am faster, stronger, and tougher than anyone they can field. If I go out to meet the army ahead, I should be able to occupy or at least distract them long enough for you to go past and get to Shadow Pass. Once you're there, you can cause several rockfalls, if it is like you explain it. Once you do that, it's going to take the armies some time to get through en masse. It'll be dark by then and you'll have your chance to escape."

Nysea stared at me, speechless.

Ysduil wasn't as quiet. With her eyes large and misty, she shook her head. "No. No. You're suggesting that you go and fight an entire army by yourself? That's ridiculous. You'll never survive."

I took her hand, brought it to my mouth and kissed it. "That's not really part of the plan, Ysduil. *You* will survive. That's the point. If we do it right, nearly *all of you* will survive. I'm okay with that. If I can buy you enough time, I'm fine with my part."

"I will..." Glasha started, but I cut her off.

"No you won't. Listen. I'm not sure what the deal is with me getting this magic power, but I have to think that it should be used for something. If not this, then what? I have a chance to stretch and use it more fully than I have yet, and by doing so, I can help to make sure most of those with us can escape this trap. If I don't, I'll die along with the rest of you, smashed between two armies. If I'm going to go anyway, I would much rather do it knowing that I may have helped you all survive, at least for the time being.

"I've really enjoyed being with you, especially you three." I nodded to Ysduil, Glasha, and Amelie. "I want you safe. This is the only way I can think of to do that. There's no time to argue, no room to try to split our forces to perform some sort of miraculous strategy. All I know is that I can do things I never dreamed possible, and it is my choice to use that power to give you a chance. Please allow me to give you that?"

"But...but...we just met," Ysduil said. "We've spent hardly any time together. I wanted to—" A harsh sob broke free.

I swept the foxgirl up in a hug and kissed the top of her head. "I know. My sweet foxgirl, my skillful warrior, my love. I know. I wish there was more time to talk about it, but there's not. I'll give you a few minutes to get everyone ready, then I am going to sprint to the army ahead, drawing them to the right edge of the road where the bend is over there. I plan on keeping them occupied enough that I hope they won't notice you until it's too late.

"Nysea, you'll have to have warriors on the side of the group to fend off any that go toward you. I think once they see me, especially if they see me defeating their soldiers, they'll choose me over you. No offense, but they believe they'll be able to find you and get you any time they want. I, though, am what the Sodality leaders want. Like you said, I am unique and can cause lots of problems for them. They may even swarm me to capture me, not kill me. If that's the case, we'll see if this magic you opened up in me can fight their training. If I know you got away safe, I'll do my best to come back to you, I promise."

The lead priestess nodded stiffly, her own eyes liquid. She wanted to argue, but didn't. Like a true leader.

I kissed Ysduil, then turned to Glasha to hug her. The dunim crushed me to her chest with her strong arms and brought her mouth to mine for the most passionate kiss I'd ever received from her. That she did it in front of everyone was not something I took lightly. When I went to give Amelie a hug, she opted for a kiss as well, though it was a soft, sensuous kiss that somehow conveyed more feeling than any we'd shared previously.

I took one last look at my three beautiful companions, turned, and began to stride toward the army.

"Remember, get everyone through as fast as you can. You will be literally running for your lives. As soon as you're within the pass, drop every boulder you can down onto the path. Don't hesitate."

I had to accept Nysea's second nod as agreement and shifted my focus to the road ahead. I started to jog. To the army that would most likely deliver me to whatever gods ruled the land of the dead in this place.

CHAPTER

FIFTY-EIGHT

I slowed to a fast walk as I got closer to the Sodality troops, giving them time to get a good look. I wanted them preoccupied to allow the priestesses and my girls the time to gather and slip around the enemies.

The people up ahead of me hadn't gotten into rank, which I took as a good sign. Many of them were watching me, the majority of them with confused looks on their faces. They had to recognize who—or what—I was. It didn't make any sense for me to deliver myself to them. Hell, it didn't even really make sense to me.

The urge to turn back and take one look at what I was leaving behind nearly overpowered me. I locked my neck and stared straight ahead with chin raised.

Sudden movement in the group told me that the priestesses were on the move. I couldn't let the Sodality troops go to intercept them.

It was time.

I drew my sword and began to jog again. Then to run. By the time I was within fifty feet of the soldiers, I was about as close to a full sprint as I'd come since high school track meets. Suddenly, I was the focus of everyone's attention.

Just as I'd planned.

The rasp of dozens of swords leaving their scabbards reached my ears above the pounding of my feet and my heart. I had to show these enemies that I deserved all the attention so none would try to stop the sisters.

Diving deep within myself, I brought up the vitality that I'd discovered there and pushed it into my muscles. My speed increased and new strength flooded my body. More of the soldiers readied their weapons to receive me, the men with slack, expressionless faces and the women with more emotion. Luckily, none yet had fired off a bow or crossbow. No doubt they'd been told to take me alive so I could be trained.

I would see how long that illusion lasted.

The group of sword wielders directly in front of me were split evenly between women and the automaton men. I didn't like the idea of killing the latter because they weren't controlling their own actions. As for the former, it wasn't long after I'd entered this new world until I realized that if someone came at me with intent to kill, it was either them or me. I hated that they were women, but I was under no illusion that I should stick to some sort of chivalrous code to allow them to kill me at will.

They had tried to kill me, I would kill them. For that matter, if they tried to capture me to kill my free will, I would kill them. I wasn't only fighting for myself, but for everyone I'd come to cherish in this world.

I leaped toward two women with finer armor than most of the others, figuring they were higher rank. My speed was not something they counted on, and they were completely unprepared for how quickly I battered their swords down.

One I elbowed in the face as I landed. With a crack, her nose split and splashed my arm with blood, then she was flat on her back, knocking the man behind her down in the process.

The other woman wasn't quite so lucky.

My sword circled around from slamming into hers and cut diagonally, splitting the leather armor on her chest with the power of my swing. She cried out, her skin splitting even more easily than the leather, and she collided with another woman and a man behind her. All three were knocked off balance.

From there, it was a messy melee. Combatants could hardly swing a sword with so many people around. If anything, I had the advantage in this because literally anyone else nearby was an enemy, so I could lunge, slash, and barrel my way around while my opponents had to be careful not to injure their companions.

It worked fine for a few minutes, truly a long time in battle. If it weren't for the strange increases in strength, speed, and stamina, I would have been panting and gasping. Many of my enemies were.

As I fought, I kept my eye out for groups rushing away to try to stop the sisters. There were a few individuals or even small numbers that did so, but I knew the priestesses could handle that many. For now, I was the succulent rabbit to the foxes surrounding me. The anger and battle fervor in their faces assured me most would stay.

Their positioning worked in my favor and was a liability for them. The trees at the edge of the road hemming us in, and only one of me to attack, it was pure chaos. The soldiers lost all appearance of discipline in the face of my unorthodox attack. At least as far as the ones who could actually think and feel were concerned.

My plan just might work after all. If I could manage to keep from being captured, I would be satisfied with death. As long as the sisters got to where they needed to be.

A hurried glance showed they were almost halfway to the narrow path. Just a bit longer and the Sodality would have to run them down to catch them, instead of running toward them from the side.

A female voice barked out commands and, like magic, my enemies started fighting more intelligently. Instead of being under a general command to stop me and try to capture me, whoever had started shouting orders gave the men more specific direction. The difference was immediate.

That was not good for me. Not at all.

The soldiers stepped into distinct ranks and advanced on me, much of the front line with shields snugged into their shoulders.

I backed up as much as I could, but other soldiers began to flank me to prevent my retreat. They were finally taking advantage of their numbers as soldiers instead of as a mob.

The first line reached me, and I bashed swords away from me as fast as I could. Even with my increased speed and strength, though, I couldn't deflect all the steel. I started to collect cuts and gashes. Small ones, but dangerous still. One or two solid injuries and I was done for. If I weakened, they could capture me easily.

I couldn't allow that. It was victory or death.

I decided it was time to try something I hadn't fully explored yet.

While my body continued to fight mechanically and automatically, I dove down deep inside my mind and searched for the power I knew was there. I found it quickly and pooled it in one location, just underneath my navel. I let it build for a few seconds, all I could afford.

Then I blew it out in all directions as forcefully as I could.

The results were...impressive.

I opened my eyes just as I released the energy. What I saw looked like a movie special effect. But for me, at that moment, it was real. Maybe too real.

An eerily silent explosion threw my opponents away from me like I was a bomb surrounded by matchsticks. Four full ranks all around were picked up and flipped through the air, leaving ten or fifteen feet in a circle around me clear.

I dropped to one knee, breathing hard. I was surprised, shocked, and a little light-headed. Giddy. After a few seconds, I stood and raised the sword still in my hand. I had in no way defeated the army, but I had accomplished something, gained a little bit of breathing room.

Those who dared to meet my eyes held fear in their own. Physically, the attack was probably a five or six on a scale of ten. Psychologically, it was an eleven.

Predictably, the men recovered first. With no free will, intimidation wasn't a great weapon.

"Stop," a female voice cried out. It sounded like the same one that had started giving orders to turn the tide of my fight. A moment later, the officer pushed her way between the ranks and stood fifteen feet from me.

She wore elaborate leather armor and carried two long knives, almost as big as short swords, in one hand. In the other, she held her helmet. Her face was clearly visible.

A face I recognized.

I'd heard Kelena Forsta had joined her commander in the mission to find Ysduil and myself. I knew she was one of the lead guards at the fortress. Until now, though, I hadn't put it all together. She wasn't just some middling guard; she was Tallyn Kineth's second-in-command.

It rankled that so many of the female warriors in this world were so fucking hot. Even in armor, with her enchantingly gorgeous face and her supermodel body, Kelena dragged out thoughts that didn't belong anywhere near a battle. *Damn, I probably should have fucked her when I had the chance.*

With her adorable ferret ears and her tail fluffed up like a bottle brush behind her, she gave me a slow, wicked smile.

"You've led us a merry chase. You're probably thinking right now that you should have cooperated with me. I know you wanted me, just as I wanted you. That opportunity has passed. I have been commanded to take you alive." She glanced at her soldiers around her, then tsked. "But I am second in command of this army and neither the Paragon nor Tallyn Kineth has prohibited me from maiming you. Prepare yourself, *khresha*. This lesson will be painful. And then you will be taken away and trained.

"Don't worry, we will catch up to your paramours. There is no rush. You have been the greatest prize all along. Maybe the Paragon will postpone your training long enough for you to see the execution of that filthy vinem priestess bitch you helped escape."

Her all-too-kissable lips twisted into a sneer and she spat at me, then put her helmet on her head. She cracked her neck and gripped the knives in her hands. Then, without another word, she charged.

CHAPTER
FIFTY-NINE

For a second, I stared at the woman sprinting toward me, not quite believing the situation I was in. When it sank in she was deadly serious, though —ramping up her speed, if anything—I settled back into a defensive stance and held my sword out to prepare for her attack.

This was no theatrical fight or fancy combination meant to dazzle onlookers. When Kelena reached me, she committed to cutting me to shreds. One knife came high, toward my throat, while the other slashed at my midsection.

What the hell had happened to not killing me?

I pivoted away from her, crossing my arms and sweeping my sword into an outward vertical block. With my enhanced speed and strength, I pulled the move off, and two loud clangs—along with the lack of sharp metal slicing into me—told me I was successful.

Something tugged at me internally, though, forcing my body to fall backward into an awkward roll. I came shakily to my feet a pace back from where I was to find Kelena's blades finishing their arcs, the left one slashing horizontally and the one in her right hand cleaving upward.

Exactly where I'd been just before my forced roll.

I found myself panting heavily, and our fight had just started.

The ferret beastkin scoffed, but it seemed to me it was more directed at herself than me. The look in her eyes showed surprise—she hadn't expected me to survive that move. No time to analyze how she could commit so fully and still follow her command not to kill me; I was just happy the troops around her seemed to be engrossed in the fight and didn't take off after the priestesses. Even Kelena hadn't thought to order the troops to go after the sisters. She really did think they could be rounded up at any time.

She came at me again, weaving the knives in graceful combinations. They were almost hypnotic in their smooth movements, but at all times, they covered her to prevent attacks from getting through. I continued to evade them, sometimes parry them. But I felt like I was being herded into a trap.

It wasn't until she'd already thrown a few dozen strikes at me that I lashed out with my sword to counterattack. The first attempt was clumsy, but so fast that the woman aborted her current movement and dove to the side as my blade came straight down at her head in a vertical chop.

I was outmatched. If it weren't for my magical reflexes and speed, she would have already cut several pieces off me. Necessary pieces, as far as I was concerned. She was a hundred times more skilled than me. It was only a matter of time before she injured me seriously. Maybe even killed me, despite her orders.

It was definitely time to cheat.

The next flurry of attacks came quickly. She lunged to

close the gap between herself and me and thrust her left knife toward my belly while hooking her right arm around to stab at me from a diagonal direction. Instead of blocking with my sword, I flexed my mind and new talents.

A ball of force blasted out and struck Kelena in the chest. I couldn't see the power I'd generated, but I did see the effects. In super slow-motion, Kelena's hardened leather breastplate bowed inward like she'd run into a brick wall. Like in those boxing clips where they show a fighter's jaw deform from a punch. The sound of the leather caving in merged with the rush of air being expelled from the beastkin's body and for the briefest of moments, it seemed like everything stopped, reaching a type of equilibrium.

Then time resumed and the woman's torso wrapped around the invisible ball. She left her feet to land on her admittedly fine ass two yards away from me.

I blinked. Regret rushed through me, a long-held aversion to hitting women. Especially beautiful, hot women. Maybe I was a bit chauvinistic. Or maybe I was just stupid.

My body jerked again and I flowed with it, jumping to the side as another blade came out of nowhere and nearly took my head off.

"What the fuck?" I turned to find another armor-clad woman—this one an elf—bringing her blade back to a guard position. So much for fair, one-on-one combat. I guess I couldn't complain much after using magic on Kelena.

In the corner of my vision, the ferret beastkin was already back on her feet, working hard to get air back into her lungs. She wasn't done fighting, though she was a bit the worse for wear.

Another attack came from behind me, but I caught the motion in my peripheral vision and jerked my sword up in time to block a blow from one of the men. After fighting Kelena, his strike was easy to intercept. Though technically, he seemed to be more skilled than me, his speed was pretty lackluster. I battered the strike away and kicked him hard in the chest, sending him skittering back into two other warriors behind him.

Things were getting ugly. Kelena had not commanded the others to stop this time, and they were taking full advantage of it. Three more soldiers, two men and a woman, rushed to engage me and I wasn't sure I'd be able to stop or dodge all three swords. A quick look through the ranks showed that the priestesses were far enough away now that even if the army pursued them, the sisters would probably get into the pass in time.

I'd succeeded in my task. Now I had to figure out if I could escape without actually being killed, or maybe surrender, hoping I could escape later. Funny how the threat of defeat changed what one would consider. At least a hundred armed people surrounded me, probably more.

One look at Kelena, though, told me it might be too late for that option. She stomped toward me, even as her underlings were trying to cut me to ribbons, and the look in her eyes promised exactly the opposite of mercy. Shit.

I blasted out one of those force walls toward the three closest attackers and panicked when it came out so weak, it barely deflected one of the men. The other two continued with their strikes as if nothing had happened.

My eyes wide and frantic, I swung my sword out as quickly and as hard as I could. It wasn't a smooth, calculated strike. Hell, it wasn't even an acceptably performed sweep to make them keep their distance. It was one hundred percent Babe Ruth swinging for the fences and hoping to hell it allowed me to live for another few seconds.

Apparently my magic couldn't be used over and over again in succession. Good to know. It was something that would have been better to know before I started my foolish gambit.

Kelena had almost reached me and two other warriors joined the fray to my left. It was hard to even register how many people were close and what they were doing, but I got the sense of weapons coming at me from all different directions. It all turned into a blur. My panic threatened to freeze me solid, and without anything but my slightly higher speed and strength, there was no way I was going to survive the dogpile that was about to occur. I spared a thought for my girls and drew a deep breath.

It was time to go big or go home. So to speak.

My best bet was to focus on Kelena's attack. She was by far the most skilled of the Sodality attackers, if I could keep her expert strikes from landing, I might be able to get away with some non-lethal attacks from the others. My vision zoomed in on the beautiful villainess and I prayed my enhanced abilities would be sufficient to allow me to survive.

As the ferret girl grew close, her eyes widened, and her mouth opened to say something. Loud clashes from beside and behind me drowned out anything she might have said.

Then the most beautiful sound I'd ever heard rang out clearly in the stunned silence.

"We'll take care of these, Adam. Concentrate on her."

It was Ysduil's voice, accompanied by a grunt of affirmation that I recognized all too well. My girls had come to help me, despite my orders to flee.

In the fraction of a second before Kelena's blades got close enough to cut me, conflict flared in my middle. I was happy to hear my girls so close, but I also despaired that they had just traded their lives for mine. The Sodality soldiers were under orders to capture me, but there was nothing to prevent them from killing Ysduil and Glasha. Had my inability to fight well just killed them?

I shoved that thought down deep within myself. There was exactly one thing I needed to think about at the moment.

I needed to beat Kelena.

The woman's dual blades came down at me, surprise and rage on her face. I sidestepped and positioned my sword to deflect the knives, knowing full well she would change directions and come in with another attack immediately.

A man reacted to my repositioning and began a slash with his sword to cut into my unguarded side. Before I could react to him, though, a flash of silver took his arm off at the elbow and his weapon spun off to clatter against another soldier. The green hand holding the sword that had caused the damage moved onto the next aggressor.

I could have kissed Glasha right there in the middle of battle for saving my life yet again.

Kelena whirled and cut at me with both knives like she wasn't required to obey the laws of physics. I grunted as I slashed out at her blades and pivoted to put a Sodality woman between me and the attack. Kelena was able to avoid cutting her fellow soldier, but her form broke and the smooth motions she'd been aiming at me faltered.

The battle was too chaotic with so many people crushed together. I kicked a man who was facing my girls—of whom I'd only seen flashes up until now—and sent him careening into three other soldiers. I used the distraction to shuffle-step into a clearer space, maybe six or so feet wide.

It was the best I was going to be able to get, so I brought

my sword up and watched Kelena as she pushed another of her soldiers out of the way and charged me again.

I'd survived so far solely by being slightly faster than the ferret beastkin, but I couldn't rely on simple speed and luck forever. I had to do something to counteract her greater skill. As she came at me again and again, I managed to keep her knives mostly away from me. She laid down a few minor cuts—one on my arm, one on my leg, and one that could have been fatal on my side if I'd been a hair slower—but as she did so, I noticed something. Something important.

It was time I took advantage of it.

I glanced at my girls. Ysduil was a demon with her staff, whirling it and striking out so quickly I could hardly see the weapon. Glasha and her brute strength that was still somehow amazingly graceful, battered any near her and took limbs and life left and right. Both had evidence they hadn't avoided all damage, lines of red made fuzzy by the blood dripping from them.

I took a breath. What I intended to do would either make it possible for us to escape, or it would doom all three of us. I hoped I didn't fuck it up.

Kelena launched a furious attack consisting of no fewer than five separate phases. Her long knives flashed and blurred as she struck out from all different angles, moving so quickly it taxed even my new abilities to track them.

My longer sword swept out and foiled the first two attacks, angling it to upset the trajectory of both her blades. One of them circled around and lashed out to lick my cheek, laying down a thin line of fire on my skin. I resisted the urge to jerk backward away from her and rotated my sword just enough to catch her other knife as it came around to punch a hole in my head where she expected me to be.

I slashed horizontally and foiled her follow-up attacks, and then pivoted to my right side to evade the last two attacks completely. A miniscule pause followed as Kelena wound up to launch another flurry.

It was the moment I'd been waiting for.

I was jostled from behind and almost turned to defend myself—but I trusted Ysduil and Glasha to watch over me. Instead, I implemented my shoddy plan.

I batted Kelena's knives to the side and threw my body at hers. My shoulder rammed the lower part of her breast-plate and forced her back, slightly off balance.

Without pausing, I harnessed every drop of speed I had within my body and cut at her like my—and my two girls'—lives depended on it.

SIXTY

J ust because I'd decided on a course of action didn't mean I was in any less danger of being cut to pieces by Kelena. I forced my face to remain neutral, and though my heart was beating even faster than the exertion merited, I focused on my breathing so the woman couldn't see how much I was panicking.

This was my one shot to win.

I used every bit of my increased strength, speed, and endurance to cut at the Sodality officer like a maniac. I relied on simple, straight-forward attacks. No twirls, no fancy redirections, not even any feints. I swung my sword at her head and other vital areas over and over again, bashing at her as quickly and powerfully as I could.

But Kelena was a true warrior, and much to my chagrin she had not focused her training solely on offensive techniques. With a mix of clever parries, evasive maneuvers, and a few outright blocks, she kept my sword from striking her.

I couldn't say the same thing about her knives. Despite my greater speed, she still managed to slip in a few counterattacks, slicing more of my skin than had already been damaged. I hardly reacted to the new injuries, my mind laser-focused on one idea.

Beat the woman down with sheer persistence.

I stopped thinking so much as following my imperative. I needed to keep the pressure on her until she made a mistake, broke, or fled the battlefield.

I tried not to think about the other thing that could happen: she could maintain her defense until I left myself open enough for her to kill me.

After what had to be several minutes of nonstop fighting, something I'd never have been able to do in my old life, I finally saw a chink in the woman's figurative armor. In response to a diagonal downward attack, she parried later than normal, barely evading my blade. What's more, she didn't take the opportunity to lash out at me in response like she normally did.

Kelena Forsta was getting tired. It was about damn time. I was well on the way to fatigue myself.

I poured on the juice, repeatedly slamming my sword down at her head in simple attacks, changing the angle slightly so I wasn't too predictable. I gave it everything I had, but promised myself I wouldn't overcommit to allow her the opening I didn't doubt she'd take advantage of immediately. For all I knew, she was faking her sluggish reactions.

My sword blurred from attack to attack, moving up and down and in and out like a piston. Relentless and powerful.

Finally, on a simple horizontal slash that I'd performed dozens of times in the fight, Kelena flubbed a parry. Her knife turned at too sharp an angle and instead of my sword skipping away, it pounded hard into her weapon. With my strength and her fatigue, her entire arm rebounded away and she almost lost her grip on the hilt.

I flipped my hands and crossed my arms so my left, controlling hand, was underneath and jerked back to send the blade in a tight arc to head toward the beastkin from her right side. But instead of committing, I pulled my arms back in to reposition my sword as it moved, then shifted my left foot forward half a step. That motion, combined with a lunge that began in my legs and engaged my whole body, allowed me my first real win of the fight.

Kelena's eyes widened as she tried to move out of the way, but she'd already twisted her body to lend strength to allow her to block the strike that had only been a feint after all. My sword point entered her body just under her breasts, skipped off her sternum, and punched through the cartilage holding her ribs in place. With a wet sucking sound, my blade rammed through her body and exited through the center of her back.

Kelena's mouth opened in a sickly gasp, and though she tried to bring her knives up to finish me as well, she'd lost her strength. I shouldered her right arm aside—getting another cut for my effort—and twisted the sword, my eyes locked on hers. A quick pivot with my right foot and a shifting of my hips cut deep toward her center and essentially bisected everything in her chest cavity.

When I pulled my blade out and stepped back, Kelena dropped to the ground.

I slumped for a moment as relief, fatigue, and immense sadness flowed through me. Should I finish her off to save her any pain she was feeling? Was there something else I needed to do?

"Adam!"

Ysduil's voice shocked me out of my stupor. Here I was,

mourning an enemy, freezing in the middle of a battle, while my girls were fighting for their lives. Theirs *and* mine. I didn't deserve them.

I performed a quick salute with my sword toward the ferret woman, feeling a bit silly for it, and turned to see what the situation was with the rest of the army.

I really wish I hadn't.

Glasha and Ysduil were fighting like dervishes, doing their best to keep from being overwhelmed. Bodies littered the ground and both women were splashed with red. How much of the blood was theirs? We needed to get the hell out of there.

I charged two men and a woman who were going at Ysduil along with several others. A powerful horizontal slash cut into two of them as I body slammed the third, throwing her into other soldiers.

The enemies were at least three or four deep around the women, but in some places the soldiers were a lot denser. If there was any chance to leave, it would have to be by attacking the thinner ranks.

"Get ready!" I swung my sword wildly to keep from being engulfed with bodies. I desperately hoped I could do what I was planning. If I couldn't, we were in big trouble. Like getting cut into pieces kind of trouble.

Taking a deep breath to prepare myself, I ran toward the thinner ranks, slashing ahead of me as I did so. Some of the soldiers were skilled enough to evade my charge. One or two even lashed out as I passed, though most of the damage was mitigated by what was left of my leather armor. The important thing, though, was that by sheer momentum and extreme thuggery, I broke a hole in the surrounding soldiers that was a little wider than a body.

"Come on," I yelled. "Now."

The women, to their credit, had already been maneuvering themselves to follow me, so with a few well-placed attacks, they were able to make a run for it. Glasha was limping, but hopefully she wasn't too injured to run fast. We were definitely going to have to run fast.

I blocked a few attacks that seemed glacially slow after my fight with Kelena, and let the women pass by me. Ysduil looked at me questioningly and I answered her with a word.

"Pass."

I cut down another man who tried to impede my two girls and they both put their heads down and sprinted for all they were worth.

This was going to be the tricky part. With us in the open, we would be fair game for archers and cross bowyers. I couldn't let them kill us from afar like that.

Dredging up the last of my reserves, I went into myself and started the energy within me swirling. If there hadn't been enough time for my power to regenerate—or if it didn't work like that at all—this was going to be the shortest escape attempt in history.

I flexed the powers I still didn't really understand and was relieved when something responded. I put my hands toward the troops trying to surround me and mentally heaved with everything I had.

A wall of power exploded out all around in front of me and flattened the mob trying to kill us. Sodality soldiers were thrown for dozens of feet, causing collisions and injuries from flying bodies and weapons. More importantly, with everyone knocked onto their asses, the archers couldn't target us until they were able to disentangle themselves. Maybe we'd have time to escape and maybe not.

At this point, I had to take what I could get. I tore off

after the women, my legs burning with fatigue and I didn't know how many cuts, sluggish in building momentum. I refused to look back, but poured all my willpower into running. Ysduil and Glasha were a few dozen yards ahead of me and my goal was to catch up to them so all three of us could enter the pass together.

As I finally started to move faster, closing the distance, a thought jumped into my head. What if the sisters had already collapsed the pass to protect their escape? Like I'd told them to.

Shit.

As per its name, the Shadow Pass revealed itself as a dark smudge ahead of us. There was too little light for me to see yet if it had been blocked up with rocks, as was the plan.

A clacking sound just behind me tore my thoughts away from what was ahead. As I looked over my shoulder, a projectile punched into the ground to my left about ten feet from me. Among the army we'd left behind, at least some of the ranged soldiers were up on their feet and doing their best to poke us full of holes.

Splitting my attention between the archers and crossbow wielders trying to kill us and the path ahead of me so I didn't take a nasty tumble, my initial panic calmed a little. I was already a hundred yards or so away from where the soldiers stood and it was obvious that the crossbows, at least, didn't have the range to be a danger. Sure, the odd bolt came close, but most fell short and all were wildly inaccurate.

The arrows posed more of a threat, being able to make the range, but I wasn't too worried. It would take a hell of an archer to hit a target from that range and as we got farther from them. There were also overhead tree branches to contend with. The forest became denser at it got closer to the pass, with foliage encroaching on the path as it narrowed from the wider road.

As if to confirm what I was thinking, a crack and a thump above me and off to the right demonstrated an arrow skipping off one branch and anchoring itself in another.

The women looked back to see what was going on and I gestured for them to keep going.

"Don't worry about it," I panted. "Get into the pass and hope it's not blocked."

They did as I said and within another minute, there were no longer the reports of arrows seeking us out. The archers had finally given up.

When we reached the pass proper, I let out a relieved breath. The rolling terrain became earthen walls, which then transformed into a chaotic mixture of dirt and stone. The sides of the passage rose up to thirty feet and more. I finally could pick out people scattered about at several different levels on the walls.

Ysduil waved at them and her greeting was returned.

"We're the last," she shouted to them.

I'd finally caught up to the two women and we slowed our desperate sprint to a jog. As we passed by the priestesses up on their perches, one clear voice rang out.

"Ready, sisters. Group one, release your payloads now."

The clatter and crash of the precarious stones I'd spotted high up on the walls drew my head around, afraid we were about to be crushed by a landslide. It was only a trick of acoustics, though. The tons of dirt and stone were dozens of yards behind us.

The same voice shouted cues in between waves of deafening crashes as more and more material fell into the pass.

A huge dust cloud spread out to envelop my entire world and I decided it was a good time to stop gaping and focus on moving faster.

When the sounds had receded and the dust had settled, I inspected the results of the sisters' efforts. The once-viable path was clogged with rocks and dirt piled up at least twenty feet—probably more. It wasn't quite impassable, at least for individuals. But there was no way an army was getting through there.

I turned to find Nysea walking toward me with a huge smile.

"That worked out better than I could have hoped."

"Yeah," I responded, more than a little breathless. "Who would have known? Thank you for not dropping all those rocks before we could get through, though you probably should have."

The high priestess winked at me. "I would never block the only escape for Ysduil."

CHAPTER
SIXTY-ONE

Nysea led Ysduil, Glasha, and me further into the pass to an area where it widened out. Much of the tension in my muscles bled away as I looked out over the large clearing. A great group of people were before me. It lightened my heart to see what looked like the entire assembly that I'd been traveling with for the last week.

I knew some had fallen, mostly the brave priestesses who acted as a rear guard to keep the army behind us from sandwiching us against the army in the forest.

"How many?" I asked. "How many did we lose?"

Nysea's lip curled in disgust. "Fourteen. A small number for the odds against us, but still too many. Their bravery saved the rest of us. As did yours."

I couldn't think of anything to say to that. No words from my mouth would make it less a tragedy. Luckily, no response was necessary.

"We have escaped, for the moment," Nysea pointed out. "We have few choices, none of them good. Come over here, please."

Ysduil latched onto to my side, wedging herself under my left arm. I put my arm around her and squeezed her, kissing to top of her head near her ear. I wriggled my nose as the soft fur on her ear tickled me.

Glasha, standing tall next to me, had the expression I'd expect of her: the look of a warrior who had lost companions to an enemy. She was stern and fierce and beautiful. My hand found hers and our fingers entwined. Our eyes met and I recognized that I didn't need to say anything at all. She understood my support and I hers. Her lips curved into a sad smile.

"Zartuka," she said softly.

As I followed the high priestess, someone ahead of us moved and I caught sight of two long straw-colored ears. Amelie's beautiful face showed part of itself before noticing my gaze. Then she ducked back behind two armored priestesses.

"Amelie?" I said, and watched her blushing face appear again. Her eyes were sad and downcast, as if she'd done something wrong and I'd just caught her. Her ears even drooped a little bit. I gave her my best smile and opened my arms, one hand still in Glasha's.

Her eyes flicked up to mine, confusion in them. I gestured with my free hand and Ysduil, still wrapped around me, gave her a similar gesture. She swallowed hard enough that I could see her throat move, hopped out from behind the sisters, and ran at me to bury her face in my chest.

"Hi there, beautiful bunny girl," I whispered and put both my arms around her and kissed one of her ears. "I'm glad you're okay."

She snuggled into my chest with a contented sigh and

mumbled, "Me too." The vibration of her voice on my skin tickled and I let out a laughing breath.

It was a little awkward following Nysea—who didn't look annoyed at all, but rather like she was searching for any available space to join us—with me and my three girls shuffling along as a bundle of arms and torsos tangled together, but we made do. We'd only gone maybe a hundred yards, up a small mound at the edge of where the pass ended.

Nysea gestured outward to where I thought might be the northeast. My mouth dropped open. I'd seen pictures and movies of my world's great deserts, even a National Geographic special or two. Those Earth deserts had nothing on the endless miles of sand and stone in front of us.

"Behold the Surtoran Waste," Nysea said.

I scanned the area which came right up to the badlands we were in. From my vantage point, I would have never known that there was a dense forest behind us or lush areas surrounding that. There was no way that desert was natural, not the way it abruptly changed within the space of a few miles into Hollow Wood.

"We can skirt the edges of the waste to the northeast and head toward more civilized parts of the world, including Aycrish Summit, the Sodality capital. We could also skirt it to the west, balancing on the line between the waste and the Dreadlands, eventually getting to safer lands beyond."

"What's north?" I asked.

"The waste."

"I can see that, but I mean, what's north of the waste?"

"There is conjecture, but I know of no factual information about it. If anyone has ever crossed the waste and survived, they have never returned to tell anyone. It stretches from one massive mountain range on its eastern border to another on its western border. Beyond that are oceans on both sides, with whirlpools, sea monsters and jagged rocks where no ship has ever accomplished a crossing."

"So we basically have only two ways to go if we want to survive," I said.

"Yes. If we stay too close to the edges, the army will simply follow us and destroy us. If we go too far into the waste, we will perish as there is little game and no water that we know of."

"We didn't really gain much by coming through the pass, then, did we?"

Nysea's umber eyes drilled into me. "We survived for a little while longer. If we can escape death for another hour or day or week, then there may be time for Odona to bless us with another opportunity. When the choice is between immediate death and a postponement of it, the wise person chooses to go on. Even if a choice can only buy a little more time."

I sighed. "You're right." I scrutinized the landscape, catching something I hadn't noticed before. Sure, it looked like an endless sand dune, but there was a band of what looked like more solid terrain at the edges, rock interspersed with the sand. I wasn't sure how easy traveling on sand was. The only experience I'd had that I might compare it to was hiking on sand hills near the beaches in Southern California. Which kind of sucked. I definitely didn't want to trudge dozens or hundreds of miles through sand like that.

If we could move on more solid ground though...

"How long is it going to take them to get through the pass to come after us?" I asked.

"For the army to travel freely, it will probably be many

days, even weeks," Nysea said. "The bigger danger is scouts that come through one at a time to see where we go and then report back to the main force."

I tapped my temple with my finger. "Is there any way to lay down a false trail, trick them into thinking we go one way while we go another? Maybe watch for scouts and take them out before they can see anything or report back?"

"I don't know about a false trail, but we certainly have scouts who can lie in wait for their scouts. What are you thinking?"

I ran my eyes along the more solid ground. "It would be stupid to go toward the capital, which might make it the most surprising way to go. Going out into the desert sounds like certain death. I was thinking the only option we have is to head back toward the Dreadlands, but to make them think we either went east or that we went straight into the desert, trying to beat the odds to survive that way. If they believe we went any way but west, they probably wouldn't follow us. Not right away. They'd probably post troops to watch for us to come out again."

"And?"

"And if we could get to the Dreadlands, we might be able to get lost within it. Ysduil, Glasha, and I came through the Dreadlands once. Maybe we could do it again. Or, maybe we could stay there."

Nysea's eyes panned to the west. "Stay there?"

"Yeah. Can you think of another place where we might be able to get lost and set up a new home where we can be safe?"

"Maybe about a thousand places. The Dreadlands aren't safe."

I eyed Glasha. "People live there. Glasha lived there."

Nysea shook her head. "All the more reason for us not to

go there. Not because of Glasha's tribe, specifically, but because there are lots of tribes of the monster races who already live there. Plus, there are the wild monsters that we know nothing about. We would be killed quickly."

"We would if we have to deal with the Sodality army chasing us all over the world. How long can we keep from getting swallowed up? They're afraid to go into the Dreadlands."

"With an army, they won't be afraid to do so for long," she pointed out.

"Maybe, if they were sure we were in there. If we can confuse them, buy some time by making them think we're braving the desert, by the time they realize we've gone into the Dreadlands, they'll have to throw every soldier in the world at us to find us and root us out. Do you think they'll take all their soldiers from other places just to come after us?"

"They might."

"If they do, then those places of unrest will explode and there may be a full-scale rebellion. While they chase us, the world may rid itself of the Sodality for good. As for us, well, we'll have bought a little more time for ourselves." My sly smile brought my point home, if Nysea's chuckle told me anything.

"I think it's a good idea," Ysduil said. "Dangerous, but we're way past playing it safe."

Glasha grunted. "Though there may be problems with local tribes, most of the Dreadlands is not inhabited by people. The wild monsters will be the biggest danger. Food is more plentiful than in that sandy place." She pointed out toward the desert.

Nysea's shoulders slumped. I'd worn her down. "We will discuss it with the senior priestesses. Whatever we do, we will have to do it soon. I have scouts watching for Sodality soldiers in the pass, but we do not have long to decide."

She sent priestesses around to gather the other senior sisters. Ysduil, Glasha, Amelie, and I talked while some of the sisters worked on our injuries. Whatever our choice, it wasn't going to be pleasant. We'd need every ounce of strength we possessed, all the luck in the world, and maybe the blessings of as many gods or goddesses we could wrangle.

Here I thought the hard part was going to be escaping into Shadow Pass.

CHAPTER
SIXTY-TWO

Twenty minutes later, I was in the middle of a handful of senior priestesses nodding their heads at my brief explanation of the idea for us to go forward.

"One thing I haven't figured out," I said, "is how we can keep the Sodality from tracking where we went, or how to convince them we went a different way."

Nysea, who seemed a little more on board with what I proposed than she was earlier, glanced around the group. "There are no good ways to eliminate the trail from a hundred thirty-five people. I think the chances are good that we won't be able to escape their notice for any length of time. This is simply the choice that gives us the most time to try to figure something else out."

That didn't make me feel great about my idea.

"What if we used the dunes to our advantage?" Ysduil asked.

"In what way?" one of the senior sisters asked.

The foxgirl said, "I've heard that the sands in the waste shift so often that tracks are erased within a few hours of when they're left. If we head out toward the north, then swing around to the west for several miles, by the time we get back to land where we'll leave a persistent trail, our tracks through the sand will be gone."

"Same with false trails," Glasha said. "Have a group make a path east at the edge and then go into the sand and come back."

Looking at the edges of the waste, where it met the rough, stony terrain that formed a wall between the sand and the forest, I thought the girls were onto something. If a group of people stomped around at the fringes, where it was mostly stone and dirt, the plan just might work.

"Right," Ysduil said. "With the composition of the edges, not a lot of footprints will take, but that can work to our advantage. If only a few footprints between the stone show up, it'll be more convincing than hundreds of prints. If their trackers have to work to find a path, it'll seem more realistic. Meanwhile, we'll be miles away in the other direction, having gone through the sand."

The more we discussed it, the happier everyone was with the plan. We immediately started the bulk of the assembly north, through the sands, while smaller groups prepared to lay down tracks for the Sodality to follow.

"It is crucial that no Sodality soldiers make it far enough through the pass to see any of us," Nysea said. "I have a dozen of our best archers posted where they can spot any individuals who may come through to scout out where we are. They will stay on guard for the rest of the day. When darkness falls, they will skirt the edge of the waste and meet the rest of the contingent. They are skilled scouts and will not leave any trace of their passing."

I headed off with the last group, going north into the sands for a time, then turning west when several large dunes shielded us from sight of the pass entrance, just in case one Sodality scout did make it through. Marching along the ridge of some of the lower dunes was not a leisurely stroll, but it wasn't as horrible as I had thought it would be, either. Some of that could have been my stronger constitution. Still, I was happy when we had gone all the way around and back toward the southwest where we made it to more solid ground.

From there, it was a long, many-day slog until we reached the imposing wall of trees and other vegetation that was the Dreadlands.

Glasha warned us that she knew virtually nothing about the northern part of the monster-infested land, but I was glad to have her along in any case. She might not know the specifics of this new territory, but having lived in the more southwestern part of the Dreadlands, her knowledge and experience were invaluable.

The pace of the column slowed to almost a standstill once we entered the lush land that we hoped would become our home. With Glasha, Ysduil, Amelie, and myself at the front, along with a few of the best remaining scouts, we carved a path south and west.

With such a large number of people, relatively speaking, we were probably not attacked as often as a smaller party would be, but there were still injuries, and a few deaths. The daily camps as we traveled were little more than blankets thrown onto the ground, surrounded by priestesses guarding it. Any tents left to us were used by the older sisters or for those who were injured or infirm.

Each evening, when we stopped and organized ourselves into the most protected configuration we could, Nysea and the senior sisters met together and discussed the plans for the next day. They kindly allowed me and my girls to be part of the conversation, though I still wasn't exactly sure why they extended that privilege to us.

On the fifth day from when we had left the pass, we finally found something promising. One of the scouts—who only ranged ahead a minimal distance for safety reasons in the unknown land—reported she had stumbled upon an opening to a cave.

Glasha and I accompanied Daria to explore the cave. While it turned out to be a small, shallow cavern, barely going back twenty feet from the entrance, we located another, less conspicuous tunnel nearby. By the time we returned to the group, which had made a temporary camp to wait for us, we had found several promising caverns, one of which had a huge chamber near the entrance and several tunnels continuing on into the stony ground.

It looked like we'd found ourselves a home, even if just a temporary one.

Our little scouting party didn't go too far into the tunnel systems we found, though. After scoping out an area about half a mile in diameter outside, we headed back to report to Nysea.

"Thank Odona," the head priestess said when we told her what we'd found. "Is there an area big enough outside for us to camp while we explore the tunnels to make sure they're not infested with monsters?"

Daria looked toward me, for some reason. It was almost like she was asking my permission to answer the question. I didn't really get why, but I gestured for her to go ahead and speak. She'd do a much better job of it than I would.

"While we lead everyone toward the large cavern, a few search parties can do a more thorough job of checking out the tunnels attached to it. It seems that the system is too large for us to map it all out quickly, but if we can make sure there is a clear perimeter for some distance and we post guards, everyone can camp in the large chamber. I believe it would be better than camping outside, even if we cleared an area. We will not be out in the elements and we will not be as visible, in case Sodality trackers were able to follow us."

"We haven't seen any evidence that they were able to do so, but your reasoning is sound, as always," Nysea said. "Adam, Ysduil, and Glasha, if you would be willing to lead a small group each to search as Daria said, or to be the one to lead the bulk of our group, we should be able to sleep without fear of rain tonight."

"I'll do whatever you need," I told her. "It's not very far."

In the end, I stayed with Nysea and helped to organize everyone and then lead them—at a leisurely pace—to the largest cavern. Meanwhile, the girls helped Daria by taking three other sisters each and exploring the tunnels to make sure we weren't walking into danger.

Before Glasha left with her squad, I pulled her aside.

"What do you think about the caves?" I asked.

"I think they will be adequate shelter until we can decide what to do."

"Yeah, me too. But, what do you think about them being empty like they are?" We'd found one shallow cave that looked as if something had lived in it, with some fur, bones, and other evidence of some kind of predator. "Wouldn't you think there would be more animals taking up residence in a convenient cave? For that matter, what happened to the one that used to live in that one den we found?"

"I...don't know. If caves are plentiful, perhaps there are better choices than what we have seen. With the one that had evidence of something living there, it may have been killed or moved on. There is no telling."

"I guess," I said. "Doesn't it seem odd, though, that we haven't seen more monsters than we have? Up until now, it's just been those dog creatures and some of the giant insects. I know we're still near the edge of the Dreadlands, but isn't it too quiet?"

"That thought does bother me. I do not know this part of the Dreadlands, but yes, there seems to be a lack of monsters, much like when we crossed the central area after I first met you. I don't know what it means."

"That's fine. I know you don't have all the answers. I just wanted to find out what you thought. It's not so much I have a bad feeling about the place, but I keep expecting the other shoe to drop."

The beautiful dunim's brows furrowed. "Have you lost one of your boots?"

I snorted at that. "It's an expression. I meant, it feels like some danger is lurking, lying in wait for us, and I feel like it's going to catch up to us soon."

"Ah. Yes. I, too, am on edge."

"No 'It worries me not?'" I asked, winking at her. "Okay, good. We'll watch each other's backs. Be careful exploring the caves."

She gave me a sly smile and looked past me to the women preparing for me to lead them. Then she held up a hand with her palm forward so I could give her a high five. "Zartuka. Be careful being surrounded by women devoted to the sex goddess."

SIXTY-THREE

We got everyone settled in the large chamber we'd found, just as planned. The exploration groups found nothing dangerous to us in the surrounding tunnels—at least to the distance we'd searched—and a guard rotation was set up to make sure we weren't surprised by anything from farther outside our perimeter. Nysea and the senior sisters discussed the longer-term plans of exploring our connecting tunnels completely, but for now, we had a safe place to rest. There would be time enough for planning in a few days. Now was the time to recuperate from our long exodus from the Shadow Pass to our current location.

Nysea set aside a smaller cavern off the main one for me and my girls to share. Similar chambers were assigned to the priestesses with seniority. When I argued that we didn't need—or deserve—a separate room, Nysea made a sound like she'd been punctured and was leaking air.

"You do deserve your own separate place," she told me. "You and your companions have done so much for us. You are also one of a kind, someone very important to this world and to all of us. Finally, you are the only male among us. Among nearly a hundred priestesses of Odona in addition to our companions or helpers. What do you think will happen if you are accessible in the middle of a large cavern? Do you think you will ever sleep, with women doing their best to find a way into your bed?"

Ysduil barked a laugh at that, while Glasha and Amelie smiled at the implication. I couldn't really argue with her logic, so I accepted our new place as gracefully—and gratefully—as I could.

The first night, after hiking to the closest stream to wash, I found myself in what would be my room for the foreseeable future. I sat down near the wall, where bedrolls and a rare animal skin had been spread out, and sighed. It was the first time I'd been alone for a long time. Since I was in the dungeon cell right after I found myself in this new world.

It had been quite an adventure these last few weeks. I shook my head at that. A few weeks. It seemed like a lifetime ago when I went to explore that cave with Colin and Greg. I wondered how my friends were. Had they gotten out of the cave safely?

A small scuffing noise drew my attention to the opening of the little chamber. A silhouette moved in front of the lamp that had been placed out in the tunnel going to the large communal chamber. I recognized it immediately. The shapely form of my favorite foxgirl, fluffy tail dancing behind her.

"Hi, gorgeous," I said, watching the smile on her face grow larger as she swayed toward me.

I watched Ysduil's rocking body with all of its sensuous motion. I'd thought I'd be sad when she traded that torn-up dress for a new, whole dress.

How wrong I was.

Turns out that the priestesses of Odona knew a thing or two about looking super fucking hot. Her mint condition dress, while revealing less actual skin, cranked up the intensity of all the many sexy curves and lines of the foxgirl's body. With every swish of the hips and graceful movement of her arms, the skintight dress, if anything, magnified the body beneath it.

"I've missed having alone time with you," she purred, stopping right in front of me. With the angle—me looking up and her still standing—I was so close to getting a free show, my crotch tingled like I'd bitten into a lamp cord.

"Me, too. I have to hand it to all you priestesses, you kept up with your daily rituals, even though we've been running for our lives for days. It'll be nice to be able to slow down and take your time with it now."

"Mmm. That's what I was just thinking."

There wasn't really the opportunity to take our time, but we used what we had well. In a blink, I had that white dress off Ysduil and she had my body stripped of clothing as well. Our spontaneous lovemaking was hot and animalistic...and pretty quick.

Both satisfied, Ysduil and I put our clothes back on and laid on the furs and blankets blissfully for a time. It was the first real rest I'd gotten since we found the sisters and started our crazy escape from a region that was no longer safe for anyone having anything to do with the priestesses of Odona. Or had anything to do with me.

After less than an hour of dozing, I felt guilty about lazing around, though. There was still plenty of work to do to make the rest of the refugees more comfortable. I sighed and sat up.

"We should probably see what we can do to help Nysea."

"Awww," Ysduil said, tugging at my arm to pull me down to cuddle some more. "We deserve a break."

I leaned in and kissed the sexy foxgirl. "We do, but so does everyone else. As hard as the escape and travel was for us, it was worse for most of the rest of the group. I'm going to see if Nysea needs anything. We can *rest* some more later." I grabbed a handful of her firm breast as I said it. A giggle erupted from her gorgeous face.

It was slow going, but I forced myself to sit up. I was just levering myself onto my feet when footsteps form the entrance of the room grabbed my attention.

"Oh, good," Amelie said. "I've been looking for..." In the dim light, I watched her wriggle her nose. It was the cutest thing I'd ever seen, just like the way a bunny did it. Her nostrils flared as she sniffed. "What's that sm—" She stopped mid-sentence and her eyes went wide as her mouth formed an adorable little O. Then her eyes narrowed as she scrutinized the foxgirl and me one at a time.

Finally, she shook her head. "I've been looking for you. Nysea wants you to come and listen to news we just got."

"News?" I said.

"A long-range scout caught up with us and has news that Nysea thinks is important. Are you coming or should I tell her you're busy?" She raised her eyebrows as she finished.

"We'll come...I mean, we'll go with you," I said. My face got a little warm, but I didn't think the light was good enough for the girls to see it. Or so I told myself.

We walked together into the chamber Nysea had set aside for meetings and official activities, finding Glasha nearby. Besides the high priestess, three of the senior sisters were also present.

As we walked up, Nysea spotted us. "Wonderful. Thank you, Amelie. You can stay with your friends, if you want." She turned to me. "A scout that has been on a long-range assignment happened to meet up with one of our rear scouts and was able to locate the main group. She has some news you might be interested in."

A slender woman in the greens and browns of a scout stepped forward to introduce herself, but then a flash of white dress and auburn hair and fur slammed into her.

"Oh!" Ysduil said into the woman's shoulder as she tried her best to squeeze the life out of her. "DD! I haven't seen you in months."

The scout's arms went around Ysduil's body and she laughed, a little breathlessly. "Ysduil, sweetie. I thought the Sodality had caught you." I noticed as she tilted her head that she had gracefully pointed ears. An elf.

"It did, but...I'll tell you all about it." She glanced at Nysea's face, engaged in a long-suffering expression that was nearly an eye roll. "Later."

The women held their hug for a few more seconds and then separated. Both straightened and adopted identical postures that looked an awful lot like a military attention stance.

"Ahem," Nysea said. "Yes. This is Delmia Dewsheen, priestess of Odona and one of our most talented scouts. She's been on assignment near the city Mistlight. She has important news, but one piece in particular I thought you should hear. Delmia?"

The elf scout nodded toward Nysea. "While I was gathering information on several of the cities near the capital city, I heard whisperings and rumors that, at first, I thought were tales made up by people who were simply bored with their everyday lives. As time went on and I heard more, I actively started seeking out further information. In the end, I was satisfied that there was at least some truth in the information I gathered.

"Evina Isameine, princess of the Isameine dynasty and —as far as we know—last member of the Isameine family, is alive."

Ysduil and several other priestesses present, and Glasha and Amelie along with them, gasped or whispered words I didn't quite catch.

"Uh, I'm sorry," I said. "I don't really know what that means."

Ysduil grabbed my hand. "Don't you see, Adam, Evina is a princess from the family that ruled Tenos for centuries. When the Sodality orchestrated their coup, they slaughtered every member of that family. Or tried to. There have always been rumors that someone in the family might have escaped, but nothing worth getting excited about. But if she *is* alive, that changes everything.

"Technically, she is the legitimate ruler, not the Sodality. If she tries to gather people to her, she could very well build an army large enough to take back the throne."

Ysduil was obviously excited, as were the others. Even Glasha, who didn't usually care much for politics and how the rest of the world lived outside her own tribe, looked toward me with eyes flashing with enthusiasm.

"That's...great," I said. "I guess. Do you think she'll do that?"

"It has been twenty years," Nysea said. "My thought is that the princess is scared to come out in the open. It wouldn't be safe. If followers were gathered first, though, maybe she could be convinced..."

I narrowed my eyes at the head priestess. "Are you suggesting starting a rebellion?"

The obsil priestess gave me a wide smile. "Of course I am."

"But you've just finally found a place that you may be able to build a community, where you might be safe."

"Exactly. What better place to use as a base of operations?"

I had a bad feeling about this. I'd stuck around to make sure Ysduil—and others, to a lesser extent—were safe from the Sodality for the time being. I was only now starting to think about how I could find my way back to my own world, and Nysea was trying to draw me into some big resistance movement?

The priestess's long, silky bunny ears leaned toward me and she put a hopeful, beatific face on. "Will you help us?"

I sighed, but nodded.

"But Adam, you had planned on going home," Ysduil said, her expression a war of hope versus sorrow.

"Yeah. I still plan on finding out how to do that. Later, though. For now, I think we have a spark to ignite."

CHAPTER
SIXTY-FOUR

The next day passed in surveying the immediate area and planning out our rudimentary campsite. With the girls helping various sisters, I found myself alone in our little section of the cave.

Almost a repeat of the day before, Ysduil slinked into the room, her body swaying enticingly as she stepped silently closer to me.

With each step, she shimmied and pulled her dress up farther on her hips. There wasn't really all that far to go and still have her unmentionables covered. Her expression turned wicked as she watched my eyes lock onto the dark spot right in front of my face. She knew I didn't have dark vision like hers or I'd be able to read her lips from my vantage point.

I was about to beg her not to tease me, but she'd already started kneeling down so our faces were at the same level. I pulled her toward me and smashed my lips into hers, kissing her hungrily, almost violently. She responded with similar fervor, darting her tongue into my mouth as if she hadn't rubbed mine for months.

It felt like it had been that long.

"Hi," I said, licking my lips and catching a hint of her taste on them.

"Hi."

"We didn't have much time yesterday."

"No. I think we have more today."

"Wanna use every bit of it?"

She ran her tongue across her top lip and her teeth. "Yes, please."

My hands glided over her tight muscles, savoring her silk-smooth skin and I kissed her again.

She moaned into my mouth, wriggling like she was trying to burrow into me. Adam junior sprang to attention, if only to remind me it was still there and not getting any action. I reached down to adjust myself, but Ysduil grabbed my wrist.

She broke our kiss long enough to say, "Uh-uhn. Let me." Then her lips smothered mine again as I felt her hand go unerringly to my pants. I couldn't see a damn thing with her blocking what little light came into the room, but she didn't have a problem finding my significantly larger needle as it strove to get lost in her haystack.

Her tangy citrus scent washed over me, tickling my tongue with her taste. I sometimes dreamed of the smell of her, catching a whiff when she wasn't even around. It was enough to swirl my sex energies all by itself.

A small sound, barely louder than when Ysduil had shown up at the entrance to the small chamber, reached my ears. My body stiffened and went on alert. Ysduil, as much a veteran of the dangers we'd faced in the last few weeks as me, broke contact and spun toward the noise.

The larger-than-life silhouette of a muscular—and very

pleasing—figure stood there, the unmistakable topknot erupting from her head.

"Glasha," I said, willing my heart to slow down, at least from the panic.

"I...I am sorry," the dunim said. "I'll leave. I..."

"You will not," Ysduil said firmly.

Glasha's shadowy form froze instantly at Ysduil's tone. I'd only heard her commanding voice once before. The sound of it caused my member to jump and harden even more.

"Come here, Glasha," Ysduil said. "There's no reason for you to leave. This is your room as well. Please, come here."

Glasha looked back toward where she had come from, but walked slowly toward us as she was instructed.

I watched the dunim as closely as I had with Ysduil. Though Glasha was larger and far more muscular than the foxgirl, she had her own grace and, even in silhouette, she was sexy as hell in anything she did. Even walking hesitantly toward us.

Ysduil nonchalantly rubbed her hip again my rock-hard dick and that maddeningly arousing growl thing she did welled up in her throat. It took everything I had to keep from moaning in pleasure. Between the two women, I was just about ready to explode, and I hadn't even really touched either one yet.

Glasha stopped in almost the same place Ysduil had stood just a minute or two before, looking down at us. Ysduil put her hands on my shoulders and moved me over to the side to sit on the makeshift bed. From my new vantage, I could see better in the light from the hall.

Ysduil reached up and took Glasha's hand and brought it to her mouth, then kissed it.

"Glasha, you don't really want to go, now, do you?"

"I..."

"Come down here so I don't have to crane my neck to look at you."

The foxgirl pulled the dunim's arm and the green woman went to her knees in front of us.

"You've been such a heroic companion," Ysduil said in what I liked to think of as her *sexy voice*. Not that her normal voice wasn't sexy, but this one, with just an edge of longing and a slightly lower pitch, sent jolts through my body whenever I heard it. "You have been fighting to protect us and have barely taken time to rest, let alone relax." Ysduil slowly wrapped her arms around Glasha and squeezed her hard enough I could hear the air coming out of the dunim's mouth. "Mmmm. We haven't even been able to work on our...little project with everything that's been going on."

The green woman breathed a whimper, so faint I wasn't even sure I heard it.

"It's about time to continue our work, don't you think?" Ysduil asked.

Glasha's piercing blue eyes caught the light and shone in the darkness as she glanced at me. My eyes were adjusted enough that I could see both women clearly now. Glasha nodded her head.

Ysduil broke the hug and moved her face to meet up with Glasha's. The next second, their heads tilted and their lips touched. The kiss went deeper, hungrier, and two sets of arms wrapped around bodies that weren't theirs as first Ysduil, then Glasha, hummed and moaned into each other's mouths.

In the broken light, their tongues danced and wrestled more and more frenetically. Honestly, I was frozen like an obsil in a spotlight. Despite the ache in my pants, I kept as silent as I could and tried to control my breathing before they remembered I was there.

"Uhhhn," Ysduil said when they parted. She licked her lips in a way that made my dick jump. "I miss our practice."

Glasha looked down like she was embarrassed, but then seemed to realize she was staring right at Ysduil's chest. It wasn't lost on the foxgirl and she threw her shoulders back and thrust her firm and perfectly rounded tits into the space between them. She reached up and ran her fingers through Glasha's hair where it came out of the topknot and splayed out. Their eyes met for a moment and Ysduil turned her gaze on the dunim's armored chest.

"Oh, that won't do at all." The fox girl started loosening the straps holding the breastplate in place. "You can't possibly relax and enjoy yourself with all that hard leather covering you."

Glasha's look of horror almost made me laugh, but I restrained myself. If I fucked this up and got kicked out so I couldn't see what happened next, I'd never forgive myself.

Soon enough, Glasha's breastplate was on the ground, and her leather skirt followed. She was left in what could barely be called a g-string and her tight, barely-there top that looked to be losing the battle to hold the green woman's larger but no less perfect tits in place.

"Much better," Ysduil purred. She ran a finger up Glasha's trembling abs to circle one mound thrusting proudly up under the tight cloth covering her chest. "Goddess, you have an amazing body."

"I...uh...thank you. You, too."

Ysduil gave a little shimmy and her chest moved in the most delicious way. "Don't you think she's sexy, Adam?"

I froze. I'd thought they forgot I was there. I had to answer, and quick, or I'd call too much attention to myself.

"It's not even an exaggeration that I am sitting in front of two of the most beautiful and excruciatingly sexy women I have seen in my life." I wasn't proud of how I panted when I said it, but give a guy a break. I'd never seen anything so arousing in my entire life.

"I'm not..." Glasha started, but Ysduil put a slender finger over her lips.

"You will not say that you are not stunning. I've heard it before—from you—and it's not true."

The look on the dunim's face nearly broke my heart. I took one of her hands and put it to my chest. "Glasha, please believe us. You say you're unattractive to other dunim. I don't know anything about that. All I can tell you is that you are so fucking hot, even in my dreams about you I can hardly keep from reaching orgasm. You are genuinely so gorgeous that you could have any man you wanted in my world. I'm thinking just about any woman, too."

"It's true," Ysduil said. "Have you not seen how the sisters look at you? Several have asked me if they thought you would be open to being with them. Many of them dream of you, too. As do I."

Glasha shook her head, but I stroked her cheek with my other hand, stopping her. This woman was a goddess in her own right—just being near her, I...

Without thinking too much about it, I leaned in and kissed her. We'd done it before, but this time she gave herself over to it completely and sank into me. I continued to stroke her face and to run my finger up her pointed ear, caressing the tip. She softened more.

As we kissed, her breathing rate increased, which made my heart rate jump, too. When we broke the kiss, I found the reason. Ysduil was playing with Glasha's nipples over the tiny undershirt she had on. As soon as we parted, the foxgirl pulled the cloth strip up and over Glasha's head and latched her lips on a green nipple that looked hard enough to cut glass.

Not to be outdone, I paid homage to her other breast, licking and sucking my way up and around to end with twirling my tongue around her other nipple. If there was one thing we'd learned in the last few weeks, it was team-work, and Ysduil and I would do our best to remove any doubts from the sexy green woman's mind.

SIXTY-FIVE

"Do you like that, Glasha?" Ysduil asked as she fingered the dunim's hard nub of a nipple.

"Uh-huhn."

"Do you want more?"

"Uh-huhn."

"That's my girl." Ysduil gracefully pulled her dress over her head, then leaned in to rub her own nipple on Glasha's while she kissed the green woman's ear. The dunim's body shuddered, as did her breath.

As I continued to service Glasha's other breast, I felt Ysduil's soft hand grab mine and pull it down. Toward Glasha's tiny little panties. I let her guide me down, to a spot where I felt heat pouring out. The foxgirl left Glasha's ear long enough for her to kiss me, then whisper into my own ear. "Why don't you take that off so you can enjoy what's underneath."

My hips involuntarily thrust forward, grazing Glasha's outer thigh as a moan of frustration escaped my lips. "That is a great idea. What about you, my gorgeous, sexy green warrior? Does that sound good to you?"

"Uhn. Yes."

The way the word came out, more of an exhalation than real speech, turned me on even more. I flicked my tongue out to lick her nipple, then closed my mouth around it to give it a good hard suck while my hands pulled the delicate threads of her thong down her toned thighs. Glasha bucked, a keening sound emitting from her clenched teeth. Even the muscles in her thighs and butt tightened to be rock hard, like she was straining to control herself.

Once I got the panties completely off, I looked down at what I'd uncovered. The light from the hallway shone perfectly on it like it was a spotlight and I froze.

It had to be the most beautiful pussy I'd ever seen. Her full and supple lips glistened with moisture, and the slick skin was completely bald. Her particular scent—earthy with a hint of aged honey and leather—mixed with another, tangy and slightly metallic, wafted up from between her legs. I licked my lips, not able to tear my eyes away from the sight.

"Isn't it delicious," Ysduil purred. "Adam? Why do you look surprised?"

"I didn't know she shaved," I said dumbly.

"She doesn't, lover. Dunim don't have any hair on their bodies but eyebrows and on their head. She's naturally clean down there."

God. She was like that *all the time*?

The throbbing in my loins finally snapped me out of it and I drew a finger down the smooth, soft skin surrounding her slit. Glasha wiggled her ass and writhed at my touch, letting out a grunting exhalation.

I couldn't resist. Bringing my wet finger to my mouth, I licked it. The taste was just as I thought it would be: her scent magnified with a sharper bit of metallic tang.

"I want some, too," Ysduil said, just before she latched her lips onto Glasha's neck. I watched as she bit down and the green woman's body jerked again, her hips thrusting up toward me.

I rubbed two fingers along her lips, until my digits were dripping with her juice. Then I brought them up to Ysduil, who took my fingers and sucked on them. Hard.

"Mmmm," the foxgirl said, licking her lips. "I think you should show her how soft your tongue is. I'll help her get into a more comfortable position."

She moved around Glasha, wrapping her arms around to fondle her breasts while leaning her slowly down so she was lying flat. As she did, I watched Glasha's impressive ab muscles twitch and then relax once she was prone. I only took a moment to enjoy the show, though.

I had more important work to do.

From the moment I touched my lips to her inner thigh, the green woman's already fast and deep breaths increased in intensity. I left the talking to Ysduil as she leaned over and kissed Glasha hungrily upside down while her hands roamed over the dunim's chest.

"Huh-huh-huh." Glasha's breathing and lack of speech somehow made me want her all the more. I licked her from the bottom of her hot, wet slit to the top and relished the change in the cadence of her breaths. If anything, her juices were even better than I had tasted on my finger, fresh from the source.

I took her lips into my mouth and sucked gently on them, moving up and down, flicking my tongue into her folds. Her moans were muffled by Ysduil's mouth, which somehow made it even sexier.

"Do you want more, Glasha?" Ysduil said. "More of what Adam is doing and...more of me?"

A sound like a whimper came from Glasha and it took a second for her to breathlessly say, "Yes."

Ysduil gave her another quick kiss, then got up on her knees and straddled Glasha's face. I ran my finger up to the green little button at the top of her slit and put a slight pressure on it while I watched both women. The warrior's amazing body rocked.

"Ooh. That must have felt so good." Ysduil's voice cut right through my clothes and wrapped my dick in vibrations that threatened to make me come. And I still had my pants on.

Another second, and Ysduil's pussy—also bald, I might add, though not naturally—met Glasha's mouth and the dunim's tongue lashed out to lick the foxgirl's nectar.

"Uhhhnnn," Glasha moaned.

"Aaaaaah, yes," Ysduil said.

"Goddammit," I whispered.

As Ysduil rocked on top of Glasha's face, she and I both reached up and our hands met on top of the warrior's heaving chest. One hand entwined with Ysduil's while the other worried the nipple of the left green breast. With the two women synchronizing their moans, I bent down to resume my sampling of Glasha's dripping pussy.

The time for foreplay was done and I thrust my tongue deep inside her folds, flicking it out and trying to reach as deeply into her as I could. That caused a chain reaction with Glasha bucking, going at Ysduil's luscious slit with more fervor, and the foxgirl bouncing to increase her own pleasure.

I pulled my hand away from Ysduil's, but she didn't seem to mind. Instead, it shot toward her own pussy, rubbing herself as Glasha licked her. My hand went to Glasha's clit as I started rubbing her nub in soft circles. She writhed on my tongue, faster as I applied more pressure with my finger.

Their jerking bodies and panting moans told me they were getting close. I doubled down, moving my finger faster and harder while curling my tongue up inside Glasha. My other hand savaged her poor, hard nipple.

I could hardly contain myself as every muscle in Glasha's body started to strain, her legs becoming rock hard around my head and her abs transforming into a chunk of chiseled marble. My cock throbbed so hard it felt like it was going to explode. At the same time, Ysduil moaned in a manner I was familiar with.

"Uh-uh-uh-uhhhn."

With a massive heave, Glasha's back and fabulous ass left the floor as her entire body tensed. Hot, tangy liquid flooded past my tongue and into my mouth, then over my chin.

"Huuuuuuuh."

The next second, Ysduil's body tensed. I watched her firm tits bounce as she slammed her pussy down hard on Glasha's mouth and clawed a handful of the dunim's breast so hard it probably left a bruise.

I froze on my hands and knees, afraid to even move for fear the friction from my pants would make me cream myself. My breathing was a little harder than normal, but nothing compared to the girls'.

"Goddess, Glasha, that was fantastic," Ysduil panted. "Did you like that?"

Glasha sucked breath as Ysduil swung off her face. "Uhhhn. Yes. Yes."

I stayed motionless, enjoying the sound of the women breathing and the sight of their heaving breasts. Then, Ysduil gave a little gasp.

"Adam. I'm so sorry. We are so inconsiderate. I got caught up in our play and we left you all alone."

"No," I said, though my pulsing cock argued with me. "I'm glad I could help you two get that much pleasure."

"No, no, no," the foxgirl said. "That won't do. Come on, Glasha. We're not finished yet."

Ysduil literally tackled me, knocking me over so I was lying on my back on the furs. Without a word, she unbuckled my pants, pulled them off, then tore off my underwear. My titanium hard cock bounced free and shot out straight like a hunting dog pointing out a rabbit.

"Mmmm."

God, I loved it when Ysduil made that sound.

I noticed Glasha's breathing had quieted, but when I looked at her, I realized that wasn't quite true. She had *stopped* breathing, and sat up staring at my dick.

"Glasha," Ysduil said in a sing-songy voice. "It's time for you to get acquainted with one of the most magical things in the world. You need to do exactly what I say. Trust me, you'll thank me later."

A few seconds later, I laid on my back watching Glasha's beautiful pussy dropping toward my face. She straddled me and bent over so her breasts bounced on my abs, her hands already grasping at my rock-solid member.

"That's right," Ysduil said. "Now, rub it around as you go up and down. Kiss it, flick it with your tongue before you put it in your mouth. You'll know when; he'll start to leak fluid."

As if that hadn't already started minutes ago.

Goddamn. As if it wasn't hot enough that the super-sexy green woman was on top of me, spread open and ready to take me in her mouth, Ysduil was calling the plays blow-by-blow. Even as she said it, I could feel more pre-cum spilling from my dick.

I grabbed Glasha's firm ass hard, pulling her bald pussy to my face so I could lick and suck her lips. Meanwhile, she put her mouth over the head of my cock and sucked with such perfect pressure that I almost came right then.

I could hear Ysduil licking her lips. There was another sound, too, one I finally recognized. The slushing sound of a finger being thrust in and out of a wet pussy. Too much more and I was going to lose control. Though I was in heaven at the moment, there was something I had been wanting to do.

"I'm sorry, ladies," I said. "But I'm going to have to change your plans."

I put my hands on Glasha's firm waist and all but bench-pressed her up off me. Then I guided her to straddle me more conventionally, her thighs resting on mine.

"Are you ready for this, Glasha?" I asked. Her eyes were still a little glazed as she continued to rub my dick—which she hadn't let go of—and nodded.

Ysduil growled in her throat. "Ooooh, that's a great idea." She scooched closer to Glasha and started to kiss her and fiddle with one of her ears. "Here, honey, let me help you get in position."

The foxgirl had Glasha get up onto her knees, then move over me so she could guide my member into her sweet spot.

"This might hurt a little," Ysduil told her, but Glasha had already lowered herself down so my head was at that moment spreading her folds.

"Uhhhn."

"That's it," Ysduli encouraged. "Go slow. Feel every inch." She stopped abruptly as she darted in and latched her lips onto Glasha's nipple and sucked hard while she fingered herself.

I had to close my eyes for a moment, the feeling and the whole experience too much. Glasha lowered herself incrementally to settle in while Ysduil worked both of them up into a frenzy.

The two women kissed and groped each other as the green woman impaled herself further on my pole. As Ysduil touched and caressed, Glasha moved more frenetically, grunting and groaning as her body was pleasured from several different angles. I pulled her down to kiss her, then shifted to suck on her breasts, bouncing freely near my face. Ysduil joined me and took a break occasionally to kiss me, too.

Glasha, warrior that she was, didn't react when a sudden obstruction snapped away, which had to be painful for her. Even that turned me on and she finally started bouncing on top of me to increase friction, her moans coming more and more often.

Ysduil was having a good time, but I knew she could do better. I grabbed her around the waist and dragged her over to me. She let out a little yelp of surprise, until I planted her exquisite pussy on top of my face and started lapping at her swollen folds with abandon.

"Oh, yes. Yes, Adam. Glasha, kiss me. Let me rub my nipples on yours. Aaaaaaah."

It was like a switch had been flipped. Ysduil bounced on my face, moaning and gasping while she and Glasha made out and tried to rub their nipples off on one another. Glasha bounced and thrusted until I bottomed out inside her. Her thrusting became more and more urgent as her pants— muffled by Ysduil's mouth—were firing so quickly I thought she might pass out.

PHIL AERIX

It was becoming too much. Ysduil's sweet, citrusy juices covered my cheeks. The way the women devoured each other, small hands pulling at bouncing tits, and the feel of the hot, tight massage inside Glasha, I knew I was about to explode.

"Fuck her, Adam," Ysduil panted. "Spray your seed inside her. Make her come like she's never done before. Fuck her hard."

I felt the effect Ysduil's words had on the green woman. She increased her pace and clenched the muscles inside her so tightly it brought me to the edge of pain. Ysduil, too, rocked faster, moaning as she bit at Glasha's neck and chest.

The foxgirl came first, her sweet nectar gushing onto my face. Her strained groan set Glasha off and the woman's body turned to solid steel again. The last, hard clench of her pussy sent me over the edge and cum exploded out of me, into the deepest recesses of her tunnel.

Two, three, four separate surges racked me as my body pumped out every bit of tension and energy.

The three of us collapsed into a pile, our muscles turned to jelly. I was too tired to even wipe Ysduil's remaining juices off my face. I sighed, snuggled between the women that had rolled off me, and smiled.

That was what I called a great homecoming.

PARTING WORDS

Thank you for reading Priestess: Aycrishi Sodality Book 1! I hope you enjoyed it. If so, **could you take a moment to leave a review**? Especially seeing that this is my first book, it would mean the world to me if you could help spread the word about my stories. There's no better way than recommendations from someone who has read the book. Building a base of readers will allow me to continue to write, not only in this series, but in several more I'm eager to start.

Also, if you want to get a similar standalone story for free, I've written Elf Queen just for you. You can pick it up by going to my website (https://philaerix.com/) and clicking on the button next to the cover.

Finally, if you want to find more harem stories, or just hang out with those who appreciate them, check out the Harem Lit and Harem Gamelit groups on Facebook!

Want to always know when the next book comes out...and get another full-length novel for free?

Join my newsletter to get the news on what's coming next and you'll also get Elf Queen for free.

Go to philaerix.com and click on the cover to join!

ΛBOUT THE ΛUTHOR

I'm Phil Aerix and I write fantastical stories with some heat.

I like tales about regular guys who through some twist of fate meet beautiful, sexy women of all kinds who may need some help, a little attention, or someone to go into battle beside. Elves, faeries, beastkin, monster girls, I love them all, and I love writing about them.

You can catch up with me via e-mail at Phil@philaerix.com or on Facebook (https://www.facebook.com/PhilAerixAuthor). I love getting questions or just chatting about the genre. I hope to see you around the block. Or in some harem-centric world, whichever is easiest and the most fun.

https://philaerix.com/
Phil@philaerix.com